"DO YOU [...] YOU WANTED FROM ME THEN?"

She nodded.

"Ask me, Jaime!" he said huskily, raising both hands and threading them into her black tresses. "My bonnie Jaime! Ask me now."

Their eyes connected, and a lightning bolt of desire filled the space between them.

"Kiss me, Malcolm."

His lips claimed her in a kiss that shook her with passion. She had waited so long. Clutching at his hair and returning his kiss, she thrilled in the joy of his embrace.

"My bonnie, bonnie Jaime," he whispered, drawing back slightly and then taking her with him as he lay back on the bed. "How did I ever let you go?"

"I thought I'd lost you forever. How can this be?" she whispered.

"You've grown so womanly," he growled. "Worthy of a better man than I."

"Kiss me, Malcolm," she whispered against his lips. "Kiss this woman."

The Intended

May McGoldrick

A TOPAZ BOOK

TOPAZ
Published by the Penguin Group
Penguin Putnam Inc., 375 Hudson Street,
New York, New York 10014, U.S.A.
Penguin Books Ltd, 27 Wrights Lane,
London W8 5TZ, England
Penguin Books Australia Ltd, Ringwood,
Victoria, Australia
Penguin Books Canada Ltd, 10 Alcorn Avenue,
Toronto, Ontario, Canada M4V 3B2
Penguin Books (N.Z.) Ltd, 182-190 Wairau Road,
Auckland 10, New Zealand

Penguin Books Ltd, Registered Offices:
Harmondsworth, Middlesex, England

First published by Topaz, an imprint of Dutton Signet,
a member of Penguin Putnam Inc.

First Printing, March, 1998
10 9 8 7 6 5 4 3

 REGISTERED TRADEMARK—MARCA REGISTRADA

Printed in the United States of America

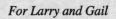

For Larry and Gail

CHAPTER 1

The Isle of Skye, Scotland

April 1539

As brilliant as they were, the jewels of the wedding gown could not match the sparkle of the bride's eyes.

Servants bustled about the room amid unpacked trunks, but Jaime Macpherson remained—silent and still—beside her bed, unable to lift her gaze from the magnificent white gown. Unable to shake from her mind the glorious dream. She had waited a lifetime for him and now the waiting was at an end. Finally, she was back where she belonged. Finally, they were to wed.

The tap on the open door and then the barely subdued voice of her maid, Caddy, brought Jaime back to the tasks at hand—and to the chaos that surrounded her.

"You'll miss your wedding if we don't hurry, m'lady," the elder woman said breathlessly, her red face proof of the speed exerted in bringing her mistress the news.

"Can it be today?" Jaime tried to contain her excitement. "We've only just arrived. How did Malcolm know that we would get here in time? How . . ."

Caddy waved a hand in agitation to get her young mistress's attention. "There is no time, m'lady. Lord Malcolm has already gone off to the Priory . . . Everyone has!"

Jaime felt her stomach jump in excitement as she watched Caddy take charge of the room. The time had come. Malcolm had been true to his promise and was taking her as a wife. She reached down, took the gown into her arms, and whirled excitedly about the room, but then she came to a sudden stop. "How am I to get there? With everyone there . . ."

"You are the bride. They saw our ship coming," the older woman scolded as she started ordering the other servants about. "The steward told me the wedding is set for vespers. There will be an escort of Lord Malcolm's men leaving Dunvegan in a short time, so we must make haste. Their job *is* to take you to your intended. We must hurry, m'lady."

"Aye, we must," Jaime whispered excitedly.

Malcolm MacLeod, the laird of the clan MacLeod and lord of the Isle of Skye and the Hebrides, glanced in the direction of the newly opened door. Stepping away from the group of men gathered in the large hall, he motioned his messenger to approach.

"Her ship has docked, m'lord!" the young man announced.

"Did you meet with Mistress Jaime?" Malcolm asked, impatience evident in his tone. "Did you give her the news?"

The man shifted uncomfortably from one foot to the other. "Aye, m'lord. I mean, nay, m'lord . . . not face to face. But I did see your steward, David, speaking with Mistress Jaime's woman. He was telling her, m'lord . . . and . . . and . . ."

Malcolm's gaze took in the messenger's embarrassed face and averted eyes. This was too much to put on the young man, he had to admit. He should have gone back himself, but with all that still needed to be resolved here—there just hadn't been enough time.

"Very well. I'll see to it . . ." Malcolm stopped as the Mac-Donald clan chief's approach drew his attention back to the matters at hand.

"I am so excited, Caddy," she said. "I feel giddy."

"Well, I'm certainly happy to hear that, mistress," the maid replied tartly. "But if you swoon before we get you into this dress . . ."

At the sound of someone crying out, they both turned in

time to see pearls scattering everywhere on the rush-covered floor. The serving girl was looking on in horror as the white beads bounced and rolled into every shadowy corner and crevice. The young lass's gaze snapped up to Jaime's face as she folded to her knees and burst into tears. "I am so sorry, mistress. The string . . ."

Jaime came to her feet at once and moved across the chamber to the woman sobbing on the floor. "The string was too old, lass. I could have done that myself."

"But . . . m'lady . . ."

"Think no more of it," Jaime whispered reassuringly. "Let's gather up these beads together, why don't we?"

The young servant looked up gratefully with the tears still on her cheeks.

"Then you can help weave these flowers into my hair. I think they will be much more becoming with my dress than those pearls, don't you?"

From the confines of the small cemetery where Malcolm had only moments ago knelt at his mother's grave, the warrior chief emerged and faced the joyous tidings of the gathered throng. The sounds of bagpipes filled the air, and the villagers and the gathered clansfolk, dressed in their finest clothes, crowded in the Priory yard.

The young laird looked around proudly at the happiness that surrounded him. This was surely as it was meant to be, he thought, walking toward the chapel.

A hush fell over the crowd, and the pipers ceased their tunes as the bride and the escorting warriors entered the gates of the Priory. Everyone stared approvingly as the young woman was helped from her magnificent bay horse by an armed knight before the steps of the chapel.

Then, as they started for the open door, she staggered at the top step. The crowd surged around her.

"Mistress, are you well?" the knight asked, concern evident in his voice.

"Aye," the bride whispered. "It is just the excitement. Take me in."

Blades of golden light from the small slits of windows cut brightly through swirling clouds of incense. At the altar of the Priory chapel, in the sight of a congregation filled with islanders and family, the bride and groom exchanged expectant glances, and listened to the ancient priest who stood at the altar with his back to them.

They made a magnificent pair. She, young and beautiful, her pale skin glowing—the light gleaming off the golden threads that were woven with the white flowers into her dark hair. In her hands, gilded branches of rosemary—symbols of love and fidelity—were intertwined with prayer beads, while her white gown shimmered in the golden shafts of light.

And he, too, radiated the magnificence of the moment. A ribbon of gold bound his long brown hair at the nape of his neck, and the ornate broach that designated his position as chief of the powerful MacLeod clan held in place the tartan that crossed the flawless white of his silk shirt. As he turned slightly to look at his bride, the dark plaid of his kilts moved over sinewy thighs and high, soft boots. Seeing her blush slightly at his glance, Malcolm smiled what he hoped was a reassuring smile and turned back to the priest.

Behind them, the gathered throng stirred restlessly in the little chapel, waiting in anticipation for the exchange of vows. The people of Skye were well represented, with members of both MacLeod and MacDonald clans, all decked out in their most colorful finery, constituting most of the assembled crowd. But the Macpherson clan also stood out prominently among the group in the chapel. Alec Macpherson, former laird of these lands, stood beside Malcolm and looked on with a fatherly affection at the young man he and his wife Fiona had raised as their own.

The priest's voice rose and fell in the measured cadences of the mixed Latin and Gaelic. From behind the grate of iron bands to the right of the altar, the sound of women's voices—

the nuns of the Priory—could be heard responding to the prayers.

The priest raised up his hands in offering, and then turned and preceded his acolytes down from the altar. It was time, and the young laird turned to face his bride. Her black eyes shone with excitement. They were misty, reflecting her joy in their imminent union. Malcolm took her hands in his.

The priest paused for a moment, and the congregation seemed to hold its breath. The chapel's silence was profound, so silent in fact that Malcolm's eye was drawn upward at the crackling hiss of a candle on the far wall. The incense curled upward in a lazy spiral, and the young laird's mind raced at the thought of the step he was taking. An important step, and one he knew was long overdue. Nay, he thought. For every purpose, there is a season. He looked back into the beautiful face of his bride.

The candle on the far wall flickered again, and Malcolm became aware of a sound at the entrance to the chapel. Turning his head, he could see the great oak door had swung partially open, but he could not see who was entering—only that the folk by the door were backing away with looks that changed rapidly from mere surprise to shock.

And then he saw a young woman step uncertainly into the chapel, her wedding gown glittering in the light of the thousand lit candles. Like everyone else, the young laird stood, immobile, stunned by the sight of the beautiful woman whose face now grew bloodless, nearly matching the whiteness of her elegant garment.

She couldn't stop her body from quaking. Clasping her hands tightly at her waist, Jaime rested her weary frame against the door. Her legs now seemed to function of their own accord, for she couldn't manage to make them either hold her weight or propel her back out the door. Every eye in the hall had turned, and she felt them burning into her. Painfully, she swallowed her tears, fighting back the anguish that threatened to burst her heart into a million pieces. Once again her eyes followed the open path from where she stood to the altar, where he stood hand in hand with another.

"I hate you, Malcolm MacLeod," she whispered. "To the day I die, I will."

Finding her legs at last, Jaime yanked at the door and lurched out of the chapel.

CHAPTER 2

The Palace at Kenninghall, Norfolk, England

June 1540

The sound of shouting and the clattering of horses' hooves on the stone paving of the yard drew Jaime's attention from the young children's faces to the window. Remnants of the passing shower still clung to the diamond-shaped panes, and the late-afternoon sun sparkled in the multitude of droplets like so many little gems. Jaime listened for a moment to the tumultuous welcome that the duke of Norfolk's household was giving the returning warriors. Through the boisterous racket, the young woman heard the voice of Thomas Howard, the old duke himself, booming out a welcome to his second son. She smiled, and turned her attention back to the waiting faces of her pupils. Tonight's feast would give her plenty of opportunity to convey her best wishes to Lord Edward Howard on his latest triumph.

Straightening the music sheet before her and picking up her lute, Jaime nodded to the assortment of girls and boys, and watched the young singers as they turned their eyes to the book of madrigals that they were sharing. Jaime raised her eyebrows at the three older boys in the back who were casting longing looks at the windows. She couldn't really blame them for their restlessness, with the excitement outside. But they were almost finished here. She turned to the four girls standing beside her with their instruments. They watched her, their eyes round and attentive.

"Make this last one perfect, now," she said. Looking back at the singers, she smiled at a little redheaded sprite in the front of the group. "Little Kate, this time I'd like you to try to raise your pitch just a wee bit higher. Could you do that for me?"

The tiny girl bobbed her carrot-topped head and tugged shyly at a faded ribbon that she wore at the waist of her dress. Her singsong voice was barely a whisper when she spoke. "I will try, mistress."

Jaime gazed at the little girl's pink cheeks as the child glanced nervously to her right and left. Kate was, at the moment, the youngest of the nine children belonging to Evan, the duke's falconer, and she was surrounded by two girls who were each a head and a shoulder taller than she was. But Jaime knew for certain that in that small body lay hidden the pure notes of a child soprano. She'd heard hints of it on a number of occasions already.

Turning to the rest of the children, Jaime raised a finger, and on the cue they all began their version of "I Will Give You Joy." The trilled notes of the pipes and the deeper tones of the lutes played in perfect harmony, and Jaime prompted her chorus encouraging them as they sang. The three older girls were magnificent, but Jaime's eyes watched Kate's trembling lips as she barely mumbled the words. With a raised hand, Jaime silenced the group. Reaching forward, she gently drew the small child to her.

"I did try, mistress," Kate said nervously. "This is as loud as I can be."

Jaime placed a hand around the little girl's shoulder and nodded in understanding. After a moment, though, she looked up into the bright green eyes. "Your mama told me how much you liked the pink ribbon I gave you yesterday."

Kate nodded her head up and down with glee. "Indeed I do, mistress. I put it next to my bed last night. I am saving it for Midsummer's Eve."

Jaime nodded with understanding before continuing. "I want you to imagine this, Kate. You get home from our lessons here, and your ribbon is missing." The look of horror on the little girl's face told Jaime she had captured the child's full attention. "So you run outside and into the mews, and you see your brother Johnny has tied the ribbon around one of the falcons' feet. Now, a hunting party is preparing to leave and your brother is taking the falcon with him. Don't forget, all your brothers and sisters are there, the grooms are milling about, and 'tis really quite noisy in the mews. He is leaving now, and there is no way you can catch up to him before he goes. Call to him, Kate! Go ahead, call out to him and let him know you want your ribbon back."

The little girl's shriek brought everyone's hands to their ears. Then, after a moment of complete silence, a burst of childish laughter by the entire group followed the shock of her cry. Jaime's eyes were smiling as she cradled Kate's giggling face with her hand. "I knew you had it in you."

With a gentle pat on the cheek, Jaime nodded Kate back to her place.

Once more through the piece—with a tremendous difference in the little girl's contribution—and Jaime decided to dismiss the children for the day. No sooner had she uttered the words, though, before the door of the music room burst open and in flew an energetic figure, her blond hair fluttering behind her.

Standing to the side and holding the door open for the escaping onslaught of children, Mary Howard smiled as the last ones filed out.

"That little red-haired imp in the front of the pack almost knocked me down," she said to Jaime. "She was certainly in a rush!"

"I believe she has a ribbon to rescue." Jaime smiled after the departing children and began to sort the loose sheets of music before her. She stood and moved toward a table by the window with Mary on her heels.

"Leave your music, silly. Can't you hear the excitement? Lord Edward has returned!"

Jaime glanced over her shoulder into the bright face of her cousin. With a twinkle in her eye, Jaime carefully stacked the sheets, and laid the bound book of music upon them. "Oh,

Mary, must we make a spectacle of ourselves every time an eligible man rides into the courtyard?"

"Pooh, Jaime! Pooh! You know that Lord Edward is interested only in you. And now he's home from a grand sea battle with the enemy!"

Jaime shook her head at her vivacious cousin. Though the duke's household seemed to be filled with Howard nephews and nieces, as well as with the children of other noble families, Jaime had never ceased to be amazed that from the first day of her arrival from Hever Castle—following the death of Thomas Boleyn, her grandfather—her cousin Mary had attached herself to her with an almost childlike affection. And indeed, though they were both cousins to the duke's sons, Mary had never shown anything but delight in the fact that Edward Howard had taken such an evident liking to Jaime.

Mary, quite a prize herself, prided herself on her knowledge of every noble family and every eligible man in England. So after seeing her cousin Edward's infatuation with Jaime, Mary had been quick to remind Jaime that even as second son, Lord Edward was a Howard and had wonderful prospects as a husband. He was, after all, handsome, wealthy, and the ideal embodiment of knightly behavior. Jaime—Mary argued—had to wed someday, so why not open her heart to someone so worthy, one who sought her heart so resolutely.

Jaime had not disagreed with her cousin's position. Marrying Edward would certainly be an excellent match. One that would settle—once and for all—the question of her desire to live outside of Scotland. Jaime knew that Elizabeth and Ambrose Macpherson, her parents, would grant their approval—albeit grudgingly—to the match. After what she had faced at the Priory on the Isle of Skye little more than a year ago, after the embarrassment from which she had felt compelled to run, Jaime knew that her parents would agree to whatever she wished. She knew they understood her desire to begin her life anew, even though it meant a life far from the rugged Highlands of Scotland.

Jaime took a deep breath and gazed vacantly at the portrait above the fireplace. Holbein had painted it just that winter.

Edward and his older brother Henry mounted on great hunters before the palace, their dogs and servants around them. Very well, it was settled. That was how it must be, she thought. Edward wanted her. That was obvious to Jaime and everyone else. She knew he was just waiting for some sign from her— something that would tell him that she was ready to accept all he was ready to give. But that was the difficult part, she thought with a sigh. He wanted her to open her heart and take him in. This she hadn't been quite able to do . . . yet.

Jaime looked at the orderly pile of music sheets on her desk. Music. She realized, looking at the neat inked lines on the top sheet that she would have been perfectly happy busying her-self with music for the rest of her life. She had no need for love. She felt no desire for passion in her life. She longed for no husband.

Jaime wished Edward were not so persistent.

Mary's voice broke into her thoughts. "The messenger said the ship had been laden with *treasure,* coz." She took hold of Jaime's elbow and turned her around, surveying her dress. "What treasure do you think he has plucked from the French *this time* to bring his sweet Jaime?"

"Stop it, Mary! You really do talk so foolishly, sometimes."

"But it is true. On his last excursion out onto the German Sea, when he came upon that Spanish galleon, you were given the most prized gem of all he brought back. That medallion with the giant ruby . . ."

"I didn't ask for it. Mary. I don't even like it. I have no need for treasures nor for precious gifts. You know I haven't worn it even once."

Mary let out a deep sigh. "Oh, to have such choices. Ah, well. Perhaps his gift will be more suited to your taste, this time." The young woman paused. "Now that I think of it, I am certain you'll accept and cherish this one. After all, the ship Lord Edward has taken was French and, knowing you and your inclination to their styles, you'll probably treasure what-ever it is he gives you."

Jaime shook her head indifferently. "Nay, my love, no matter how charming the token might be, I will accept nothing stolen off a French ship. You know that it is impossible for me to think of them as the enemy."

"Play Lady Disdain to Lord Edward's attentions if you like, Jaime Macpherson," Mary said, frowning and shaking her head in disapproval. "But you'd best refrain from such talk of the French. It's bad enough that you're half Scottish, but talk like that is treasonous, I'm quite sure. The French are our enemy, now, and that you *must* accept."

Jaime knew that it would be fruitless to argue with her cousin. Mary—as dear as she was—had been raised in the duke of Norfolk's household from childhood and would never understand anything beyond the walls of her narrow world. And Jaime—at least for now—was only a guest, and it was hardly appropriate that she should raise havoc in the household simply because her view of the world was a bit broader.

"Very well, my patriotic cousin." Jaime said resignedly, sensing Mary's anxiety. "I promise I will limit myself to less dangerous topics. And, therefore, armed with my promise, you may feel comfortable leading me on to our cousin Edward, the conquering hero—as I know you must."

An hour later, Mary was still pulling her cousin along. Dressed in their finest gowns of summer silk, trimmed in velvet and gold, the two young women made their way into the Great Hall of the palace, and into the crowd already gathered for the celebratory feast.

Aside from the king's palace at Hampton Court, there was no other palace in England that could rival Kenninghall, the home of the duke of Norfolk, in size or in magnificence. Designed in the shape of a great H with its open wings extending to the north and south, the palace was, by its very design, a tribute to the Howard family that called it home and used it as the center of their vast holdings in East Anglia. The night that Jaime had arrived from Hever Castle in Kent, she had entered this very hall only to find two dwarves from a traveling show mounted on ponies and charging toward each other from either end of the huge room in a mock joust. Tonight, however, the festivities focused on Edward and his successful return, and garlands of flowers—strung gracefully from one long window to the next—decked the walls of the hall.

Disengaging herself from her cousin, Jaime moved to one side and stood in the shadow of a huge tentlike marionette stage that had been erected for the evening's festivities. There, half hidden from the boisterous throng, Jaime's eyes traveled over the room. It was difficult not to be impressed by the magnificence of the place, even after almost a year. In an exaggerated way, its opulence reminded her of the houses that her parents kept in various cities across the continent.

Her parents . . . she thought of them with a swelling heart. She could still see them in her mind's eye, Elizabeth's sad tears and Ambrose's fierce embrace when she had told them of her desire to escape Scotland. But as difficult as it had been for them to let their only daughter go, as painful as her departure had been from those she loved, all had agreed that it was the best thing for her to do, under the circumstances.

Jaime stared vacantly at the crowded hall, her mind traveling back in time to the events that had led her to the small chapel at the Priory on the Isle of Skye.

Nay, she thought, her face darkening. Why must she—for the thousandth time—recall in anguish how she fell in love with Malcolm MacLeod the first moment she had ever laid eyes on him that summer at Benmore Castle, so long ago.

She still remembered it as if it were only yesterday. There had been so many new things she had faced that summer. First, her brother Michael had been born soon after their arrival at the Macphersons' ancestral stronghold on the north bank of river Spey. Suddenly she had been surrounded with family—cousins, grandparents, people she had never known. And then she had met Malcolm. Jaime had been only a child of four and he a man of sixteen. She had not been able to call him cousin, since he had been the ward of her uncle Alec Macpherson and not a true relation by blood. But she had all the same taken to his kindness—to his courage—to the compassion he showed to all he loved. And she so desperately had worked hard to be included in that love.

It had all started there, Jaime thought with embarrassment. A silly, childish love. And the pursuit that had begun then had ended with the bitter taste of reality fourteen years later when he had taken another woman as his wife.

Jaime wrapped her arms around her middle to soothe the still lurking misery she felt at her memories. To think how foolish she'd been, how idealistic and innocent—until that day. She had grown up knowing him, seeing him, cherishing the moments that she could be beside him. For her, during all those years, he had been the Sun and she the Moon, crossing the sky in pursuit of her love. She shivered at the thought.

She had thought he loved her. All the while that he was off at St. Andrew's and with Erasmus, being educated. All the while that he was fighting on the borders, and in with the French. All the while that he was working so hard to bring peace to his own people in the Western Isles. She had thought he'd been waiting for her during the three years that she was sent to France. Before she'd left, he'd always been loving—he never balked at spending time with her. But now she understood clearly that he had never treated her with any passion. Nay, she had been only, at best, a friend—that wee lass who always tagged along after him.

Jaime brought her hands to her face to try and soothe her burning cheeks. She still remembered how desperately she had wished for him to kiss her before she'd left on that ship for France. She'd been fifteen—a woman, she had thought— but he clearly had not thought so. He only placed a gentle kiss on her brow and wished her well.

Three years in France and she had grown, she had changed, she had become educated. But, all the while that she had been reciting her poems, she had only seen Malcolm in them. When she had played her music, she had felt only Malcolm in her heart. She had mastered her studies, and she had done it all only with the thought of returning to Skye as his woman. As his wife.

And during those years they had written each other many letters. She was certain that their relationship had changed, matured—that he was growing fonder of her with each missive. It hadn't been her imagination, that she knew. His words had been caring; he'd written her long accounts of his life. He *had* led her to believe that he cared. He had.

But then, it all had happened so quickly. She had been ready to leave for Scotland when the letters arrived. The one from her parents telling her that Malcolm had decided to wed. And the one from Malcolm telling her of the continual feuding on his land, of his decision to wed, of his desire to bring about stability in his lands by producing an heir.

Even now, Jaime burned with the wish that the ground would open and swallow her whole for the mistake she had made.

The news had been enough to set her off blindly. She had asked no questions but had set out to plan her own wedding. Her wedding!

Feeling the tears starting to sting her eyes, Jaime looked about the room, unable to endure any more thoughts of that dreadful day.

But her parents had been wonderful throughout the ordeal. After the spectacle she'd made of herself, Elizabeth and Ambrose had excused themselves, taking Jaime back to Stirling as quickly as they could. And there she had remained in seclusion, until word from her ailing grandfather had come to her. She knew she needed to get away. As long as she stayed in Scotland, she would be forced to see him, forced to face his bride. She simply could not live there any longer, miserable, watching another bask in the glow of happiness that she'd always thought was intended for her. She needed to leave Scotland and never come back.

And she had left Scotland, arriving in time to see her grandfather die, in time to see Hever Castle reclaimed by the king's officers. And when her great uncle, the duke of Norfolk had sent for her, she had gone with a grateful heart. Now she had no need for . . .

Stop, stop, stop, she commanded silently. Shaking off the darkness of her thoughts, Jaime forced herself to turn her full attention back to the people who now filled her life. From where she stood she could see Mary talking excitedly with Lady Frances, the beautiful wife of the absent earl of Surrey. The young woman caught Jaime's look and smiled across the room. Odd, Jaime thought, still no sign of Edward.

"If I were to tell you that I've brought you ropes of pearls longer than the garlands that deck these walls, would you be impressed?"

Hiding her smile, Jaime shook her head. He was standing closely behind her. She could feel his tunic brush against the back of her dress.

"If I were to tell you that I've brought you sapphires as large and as black as your eyes, would you be impressed then?"

Edward's soft breath now tickled her ear. For an instant she felt his lips brush against her neck. She took a quick step forward and turned to face him. He stood before her—fresh and bold and smiling.

"You are a bold, naughty creature, Edward Howard," she scolded, bringing a laugh to his lips.

"I am a lonely, forsaken, and rejected suitor, Jaime Macpherson." He reached out and took hold of both of her hands. His eyes roamed meaningfully over the low neckline of her dress, over the curves of her high round breasts, and she blushed under his shameless inspection. "But you are a fine sight for a returning warrior."

"I would assume, Lord Edward," she said, recovering her wit, "that after spending so many days at sea, even the sight of a mangy cur would be a pleasurable sight."

"Ah . . . your modesty." He let go of her hands and slid his hands slowly up the bare skin of her arms beneath the long loose sleeves. She drew back and, smiling, he grasped her hands again. "So many nights I dreamed of this—of coming back and seeing your shining face—of feeling the silkiness of your skin beneath my lips . . ."

"Clearly I erred just now, Lord Edward," she broke in, trying unsuccessfully to pull her hands from his grasp. "I believe *you* are the cur!"

"Aye," he responded, bringing her hands to his lips. "But I am no common cur. I am a noble dog, a hound trained for the hunt, for battle." Edward looked into her eyes. "Won't you even pet this loyal and stouthearted beast who pants here at your heel?"

"You are a foolish puppy, Edward."

"So true, my sweet." His voice dropped to a whisper. "But one whose blood smokes in his veins for the chase . . . for you."

Jaime tore her gaze away from him and looked about the hall in hope of some relief. Crowds of people were still pouring in, but everyone seemed occupied with other matters. To her dismay, the tent served to shield them, and Edward seized the advantage of her looking away to grab her by the waist and pull her inside the canvas of the tent. Her eyes snapped back to him, her hands trying to keep his powerful body from crushing her to him.

"Edward, don't," she whispered. "There are so many here."

"Then come with me to my chamber."

She blushed crimson. "We've never before—"

"It's time, Jaime," he said hoarsely. One hand moved higher, his fingers following the curve of her waist. She felt his hand lift the weight of her breast, the friction from his thumb raising the nipple through the silk of her dress. "I am tired of waiting—tired of these virginal games. I want you for my own, and you know it. I've courted you enough, and I am not one to wait until our marriage night to take what is mine."

"Edward," she snapped, digging her fingers angrily into his wrist in an attempt to loosen his grip. "This is no way to talk to me. I am your cousin, not some harbor wench for you to drag off to your bed whenever you come to port."

The young man stared into her bloodless face. A regal coldness had hardened her features. He released her, and she took a step back, putting some distance between them and taking hold of the canvas wall.

"What has happened to you?" she asked shortly. "You have never behaved this way before!" The faint blush on his tanned and chiseled face did not go unnoticed by her.

"I am a man, Jaime. A knight. A warrior." He drew himself up to his full height. "I am no monk."

"And this is how a knight of your king treats a woman?"

She watched as a smile broke across his lips. He reached for her, but this time she was prepared and quickly slapped away his darting hand. He laughed in response.

"You *are* an innocent, Jamie Macpherson. But trust me—

that is soon to change." He took a step toward her, and as she turned to escape, he caught her wrist and drew her fiercely to him. His voice was a ragged whisper. "I always get what I want. During this trip I took the time to think, and I've decided that I've left things in your hands too long."

"Don't, Edward," she whispered as he used one arm to mold her body to his. She didn't care for the glazed look that was darkening his gray eyes.

"Aye, I've decided that it's time to teach you a few things about pleasure." Jaime felt her spine involuntarily stiffen and her blood run cold as Edward's mouth descended to capture hers.

"Please," she gasped, turning her face abruptly, avoiding his lips. His teeth took hold of her earlobe and moved greedily to her neck. She felt herself sickening as one hand moved up to squeeze her breast through her dress. She tried to push away at him, but he was too strong. Frantically, she looked around for help—she even considered crying out.

"Please stop, Edward. Please," she begged softly. "Not now—not here."

She knew only a moment passed, but it seemed like eternity before he straightened up. Then, with a look of longing, he eased his grip on her body. She felt an overwhelming need to pull away, to run, but he wouldn't let her go entirely. Holding on to her hand, he hooked it into his elbow and pushed open the canvas wall for her to pass.

"You will sit beside me at dinner, my reluctant little raven. Then perhaps we can pick up where we left off. Tonight, after all these meddling interlopers have gone their way."

But Jaime just looked away, avoiding his gaze.

The dinner, sumptuous as it was, held little joy for her. Seated quietly beside the guest of honor, Jaime listened to the conversations going on around her, partaking only when necessary.

Few were interested in the progress of her music students. The family and the retainers of the duke of Norfolk had considered her thinking far too radical at first, and Jaime was certain that more than a few still thought her that way. Being well-trained in music herself, she had taken great pleasure in setting up music classes for the children when, upon arriving, she'd found the music master had recently and—for mysterious reasons—abruptly departed.

Jaime's problem from the start had been that she had chosen to accept her pupils not on the merit of their lineage but their desire to learn music. So when it was discovered that she'd had a washerwoman's son sitting beside a nobleman's daughter, a small furor had erupted—only to subside when the duke himself surprisingly declared that he could see no harm in the innocent mingling of voices in song.

Now nearly a year had passed, and Jaime felt that she was at least winning the battle. While it was true that not everyone was attending the lessons that could have, it was also true that many were. The dishonor of sitting beside someone the world esteemed as less worthy for an hour a day was a concept totally lost on a young child, but unfortunately many parents continued to be horrified at the prospect. Nonetheless, the lessons had survived, and the young musicians were improving.

Later on, as trays of cakes and other sweets were being cleared, Jaime found herself at the center of the discussion between Edward and the duke. She had tried to ignore the young knight's flirtatious behavior during most of the meal, but now the conversation seemed to have taken on a more serious note.

"Aye, Your Grace," the young warrior was saying. "Tomorrow I will steal this maiden away to the castle in Norwich."

"Not an altogether pleasant place for a young woman, Edward."

Jaime's eyes looked questioningly into Edward's face. She had heard grim tales of the Norwich Castle. Less than half a day's ride from the palace, it was—by all accounts—a place of death and horrors too terrible to behold. And it was the place where Edward kept all of his captives taken in battle.

"Will you go there with me, Mistress Jaime?" he asked casually.

She didn't know how to refuse his request. But after what

had occurred earlier—with so many present in the hall—she could hardly feel safe alone with him. Nay, not even for the briefest of moments. "The lessons . . . I have the children's lessons . . ."

"The devil take me," Edward interjected, "but I'm quite certain those brats can survive a day without you."

"Edward, this is certainly no way to impress a young and gentle woman!" The duke could easily see Jaime's hesitation. "There is nothing about a handful of prisoners you've captured at sea that would be in the least bit pleasing. On the other hand, the size of some of the gems you captured might interest her a bit more . . ."

"Father." Edward's determined voice quieted the older man's speech. "Mistress Jaime has never had the opportunity to see Norwich, the center of our family's power and wealth, and I believe it is important to see if the English half of the blood that flows in my lovely cousin's veins warms to the sight of one of England's greatest cities. As indeed it should."

The two men just stared at each other, a silent message passing between them. Then, as if understanding his son's meaning, Norfolk nodded in agreement.

"As indeed it should, my boy."

"Well, m'lady?" Edward asked again, directing his attention back to her. His gray eyes flashed his challenge. "Will you accompany me and my officers to Norwich on the morrow? We can leave at daybreak and shall return no later than sunset."

Every eye at the head table was upon her. She understood the test she was to go through. The ship he'd just captured was French and there were, from what the duke said, prisoners that had been taken to Norwich Castle. And now Edward wanted to sound the depths of her loyalty. Mary had told her that it was treason to think of the French as friend rather than a foe, and now Jaime was about to be tested. But what option did she have? She had, long ago, set her mind that she would live in England, and now she had to prove her intentions. She must make her break with the past. Make her future with Edward a reality. Edward's methods were rough, but he left her little choice. He wants to be sure of me, she thought, and that is his right.

"I'll go," she answered Edward at last. "I'll go to Norwich with you."

CHAPTER 3

The Norwich road, a wide and well-traveled thoroughfare, provided an easy ride from the duke's palace at Kenninghall, and Jaime reined in her sprightly, dappled mare at the crest of the rolling hill that led down toward the city walls. As the others rode on, she shaded her eyes against the late-morning sun and surveyed the bustling city of cloth makers and merchants, the beautiful spires of the cathedral, and the sinister, gray form of Norwich Castle—an ominous presence on its hill—sullenly guarding everything below. Though the fortress belonged to the duke of Norfolk, it had been used for nothing other than a prison for longer than anyone remembered. Involuntarily, Jaime shuddered at the grimness of the sight.

Edward pulled up and started to trot his hunter back toward the crest of the hill, but as he approached, Jaime spurred her little mare past him, leaving him in a cloud of dust as he wheeled and chased her back to the rest of the party. She simply couldn't bring herself to be alone with him—not now, not after what had happened in the Hall. Last night, immediately following the dinner and while the festivities were still in high glee, she had escaped to her bedchamber and barred her door, admitting only Mary when she returned from the Great Hall. As her cousin put on her shift, Jaime had been tempted to talk to her about the events that had transpired, but a sense of complicity—of guilt, almost—kept her from discussing the matter.

And this morning, Jaime had done her best not to allow him a moment alone with her. She knew the questions he would ask—questions to which she had no answers. Jaime knew inside that she was partly responsible for Edward's attentions. And somehow, perhaps through her actions or her words, he had come to assume she was ready for a more intimate encounter. He was wrong, but she didn't know how to tell him without destroying all that might lie in store for them.

The castle was no less forbidding up close, and as they passed through the thick walls and the huge gates, Jaime suddenly found herself faced with an appalling number of men, women, and children who seemed to be living in the courtyard. A dozen soldiers roughly cleared the way for them, and Edward led the group up the wooden steps of the keep.

Jaime held back. It was the faces. She couldn't tear her eyes away from the thin, drawn faces of the children who gawked at her fine dress. Their sad, round eyes bore through the small openings between the row of soldiers—their starved expressions piercing her heart. She wrenched her attention away as she heard Edward retracing his steps, his eyes locked on her. She thought she glimpsed a spark of annoyance in his gray eyes before he glanced at those in the yard.

"Who are those unfortunates?" she whispered as he took her arm.

"Mostly the king's enemies," he said quietly. "Though some of them are county criminals."

Leading them up the winding torchlit stone stairwell, Edward came to a stop at the next landing. Ducking under the low round arch of the doorway, he stepped into a very large room—into what had at one time been the Great Hall of the castle.

Jaime looked at the hundred or so men huddled in groups or lying in the filthy straw that covered the wood floor. The stench of the place struck her, sickening her, but she clenched her teeth and moved into the hall.

"Perhaps this was a mistake to bring you here," he said mockingly. "To expose such a delicate flower to the unpleasantness of the real world."

Jaime shot him a hard look and stepped past him. Through

the sharp odor of men and their waste, the smell of burned porridge reached her senses. At one end of the hall, a loud and greasy-looking man was ladling mush out of an iron cauldron onto thick crusts of what Jaime was sure must be week-old bread. And as she watched, a boy nearby poured water out of a huge skin bag into a stone horse trough. A steady line of filthy, ragged men made their way past, every now and then one of them casting a furtive glance their way. She turned to Edward.

"Why do you keep all these prisoners?" she asked, her voice hushed.

"Well, we serve the king." He peered through the murky light. "Some of these men may have trespassed against my father in some way, but most are foreigners, and interrogating them takes time."

"And once you've questioned them, you keep them here . . . forever?"

"Nay! That would hardly be worth our while now, would it?" Edward's face was grim, his eyes the color of flint. "Few survive their sessions with Reed, the jailer. He is a brutal but necessary man. Using those in his employ, he has become my eyes and ears all along the coast. He knows all, and what he doesn't know . . . he extracts."

Jaime cast her eyes about her, but all she could see was the sordid suffering that surrounded them. "This is a foul place, Edward," she whispered raggedly.

"Aye, Jaime. There is a foul side to the most glorious business. And war is no exception." He took her by the arm. "But it is important for one to see the refuse to fully appreciate the splendor."

"Show me what you brought me here to see," she whispered under her breath.

With a nod, Edward looked into the center of the hall. Following his eyes, Jaime saw a group of five or six men half sitting and lying down. They had to be the ones, Jaime thought. His prisoners. Her challenge.

"M'lord!" A burly, round-faced man carrying a stout club approached them, and Edward turned irritably toward him.

"What is it, Reed?" he snapped.

"Well, m'lord, this 'ere Spaniard in yon corner may be done

fer. I thought—since ye happened by this morning, ye'd like to talk to 'im. All of the sudden, seeing his end 'afore 'im, 'e appears to 'ave a bushel full to pass on. Some of it ye might just find to yer liking, m'lord."

"Very well." Edward turned to Jaime and glanced over his shoulder at the officers who had ridden in with them. Taking her by the hand, he said, "Wait for me right here. This should only take a moment."

Jaime watched him follow the jailer into a dark corner and down a few steps where they pushed aside a ragged piece of cloth that did little to conceal the murky, torchlit antechamber beyond. As they passed into the small room, she could see a man hunched against a wall. Dark patches spotted the wall above the man. She wondered if it was the Spaniard's blood. If not his, she thought, then whose? Looking back at the group Edward had indicated before, she paused. Two of them, standing in conversation over another, were wearing clothes of the French nobility. She threw a glance at Edward, and then at his officers.

This was, indeed, why he had brought her here. Aye, he meant to test her loyalty, but perhaps he also wanted to see if she might be able to identify these men, perhaps to give him a sense of their true worth? The thought of him bringing her into such a sordid business repulsed her all the more. But, she argued inwardly, how else could he be assured that her years of study in France or the Scottish blood that he thought ran in her veins would not divide her loyalties.

The crack of a whip tore through the air, followed by the shrill scream of a man. Her hands instinctively rose to her mouth to stop her own shocked cry. She turned toward the antechamber. Edward was bent over the cringing heap that she knew to be the Spaniard. She shut her eyes tightly as Edward stepped back, giving Reed room to strike again at the dying man. She backed away in an unconscious attempt to put more distance between herself and the horrifying sight.

Jaime stumbled slightly as she tripped over the outstretched foot of a prisoner sitting nearby. The man's vacant eyes looked up at her, but they didn't seem to comprehend what he was seeing. And then he began to cough—it was a painful, consumptive fit—and Jaime found herself edging away in the direction of the French prisoners.

More cries emanated from the corner room and again the crack of the whip—again and again the lash fell. She looked about—the officers, the coughing man at her feet—she could see Edward speaking to someone just inside the antechamber. But no one seemed to hear the man's cries. Everyone but Jaime herself seemed deaf to the sounds of the torture. The coughing man vomited a sizable amount of blood. She took another step back while trying to swallow the bile in her throat. These men were dying before her eyes.

As she continued to move off, she heard a few words of French and realized she was almost on top of the new prisoners. *Northerner . . . late . . .* With an anxious look at Edward, still in the corner room, she slowly approached them, but they backed away in silence as she neared them.

There was a man lying in the straw before her. With a start Jaime bent over him—he was an elderly man wearing the red and gray tartan of the MacGregor's. A Scot, she thought. Edward had never mentioned that he had taken Scots in his victory. A bloody cloth covered the man's eyes, and his face and beard were caked with dried blood. Before she even knelt, she knew that the man was dead. She placed her hand on the man's cold, stiff fingers and said a silent prayer for his soul. Then she stood up and tried to step back.

But she couldn't. The hem of her skirt was caught, and she couldn't move anywhere. She looked down in shock, thinking wildly that the dead MacGregor had come back to life, but instead she saw another large and bloody hand holding her gown. In spite of the flash of panic, she couldn't call out for help. These men had suffered enough. She would not bring more misery into their wretched lives. She would handle this.

Following the outstretched arm, she turned slowly to the side and saw the man who lay propped up on a bundle of rags in the straw. The man's face was turned, his tangled hair bloody and matted, and blood soaked his traveling cloak, as well. Her eyes immediately took in the fine boots that covered the man's long legs to his knees. He had to be another one of the French nobles captured by Edward. She looked furtively about her, making sure she was bringing no attention to herself, nor to this dying prisoner. Edward still occupied himself with the Spaniard, and his officers stood a few paces away, involved in an increasingly animated argument. One of the officers, though, returned Jaime's glance. She just gave him an indifferent nod and pretended that she was preoccupied with the study of the hall's structure. The man's attention returned to his friends. Jaime tugged at her skirt again, but the man's grip on her skirt's hem was strong.

The flat of a sword blade slapping on flesh and a cry of pain jolted Jaime as she caught a glimpse of one of Edward's officers using it on a prisoner's hand that had reached out to touch his boots. Turning away, she squatted at once and took a hold of her skirt, trying to wrench it free from the man's hand. He wouldn't release her. With both of her hands now at work, she touched his hand—but with the speed of lightning, the prisoner's fingers clamped onto her wrist.

She summoned all her courage and swallowed her urge to scream. Panic raced through her as the prisoner raised his face, pulling her closer to him. Beneath the tangle of hair, she saw his jaw move.

"Jaime!" the man whispered.

Her blood froze at the sound. She didn't have to see his face to recognize the man. She had heard his voice call out to her a thousand times in her dreams. Malcolm.

As he weakly shook back the mass of hair, a tumult of thoughts and emotions surged through her. How could it be that he—of all people—should be here?

"Jaime," he whispered her name again. "I thought it a dream, but 'tis you!"

In an instant, shock gave way to confusion and hate as an icy shiver ran down her back. Here he was, the man whom she had loved—the man who had rejected her so callously. She gazed on him, bloody and pale. She heard a cry and glanced quickly in the direction of the antechamber.

"Draw no attention to us," Malcolm ordered, bringing her attention back to him.

"You're wounded," she whispered, trying to keep her voice flat and calm. "I'll have someone look at your injuries." She took a sharp breath as the pressure of his hand nearly snapped the bones of her wrist.

"Nay," he commanded. The pressure eased on her wrist. "Say nothing. You don't know me."

"You could die."

"Then let me die," he whispered hoarsely. "I'll gladly take death before giving these blackguards any knowledge of who I am."

As surely as she was kneeling there, she felt the tearing in her chest as she looked on him. A flood of molten liquid poured into her heart, and a pain engulfed her, smothering her attempt to speak.

"Jaime, I won't let them ransom me. I won't let them steal my honor. Go, lass. Just walk away and forget you saw me. But . . . later . . . let my kin know what happened to me. If you ever cared for me, do this. 'Tis little I am asking of you."

Jaime pulled her hand slowly out of his grip, and he let her go. She stared into his dark eyes. They were pleading with her, so unlike the eyes of the Malcolm she remembered. She stood up slowly and took a step back. Edward's voice stopped her, swinging her around.

"I see you've found the bagatelle I've brought home."

"Your treasures, you mean?" she asked, matter-of-factly.

Edward's eyebrows shot up in interest. Jaime pointed at Malcolm, her eyes defiantly matching the wounded Highlander's glare as Edward's arm encircled her waist.

"That one! The one dressed in French attire. He is Malcolm MacLeod, the chief of the powerful MacLeod clan. Aside from the Earl of Argyll, he has the greatest fortune in the Western Isles."

Jaime turned her gaze back to Edward's face. His eyes sparkled, even in the murky light of the prison.

"That one man—alive—" she continued, "will bring you a king's ransom."

CHAPTER 4

"**B**ETRAYER!" Malcolm gasped with a vehemence that came from his soul. "Vile, treacherous whore!"

Havoc broke loose around her as the Highlander forced himself to his feet with surprising quickness and lunged at her. Jaime stood her ground, prepared to take his fury full on.

"Damn you to hell!" Malcolm screamed hoarsely, his fingers reaching for her throat as Reed's club connected squarely with the side of his head. The Highlander dropped to his knees, and as the burly jailer lifted his weapon to strike the falling prisoner again, Edward stepped forward, sending Malcolm sprawling with a vicious kick.

Jaime looked on—her silent screams ripping at her insides— but her exterior showed nothing but cold indifference.

"You . . . deceiver . . . foul, demon witch!" He tried to raise himself up to his knees. Jaime saw Reed's hand go up, ready to crush Malcolm's skull with the weighted club.

"Hold, Reed. I want him alive." The jailer shot a surprised look at Edward, but without a word lowered his weapon.

Malcolm raised himself to one knee. Jaime could see the toll that the action took. He moved as if his body were made of lead. His head wobbled slightly, fresh blood soaking into the dark crimson stains of his torn shirt. Jaime clenched her hands at her sides; Malcolm's eyes cleared somewhat and fixed with fury upon her face. She could not tear her eyes away from his gaze.

"Trusted you . . . fool that I . . . you've made us all . . ." His breath was short; a spasm of pain contorted his face. "You . . . whore . . . dirty, English whore . . ." He threw himself at her again. But Reed's club knew no restraint this time, and the blow landed with a sickening thud behind the ear. Malcolm crumpled like a dry leaf before a flame.

Jaime's gasp was smothered by Edward's roar as he shoved his jailer to the side. "You idiot. What good is he dead?"

Jaime's whole body shook as she knelt before the bloody body huddled at her feet. She placed her fingers on the gashes to his head, where more blood was seeping through his skull. She tried to stop the bleeding, with her hands at first. That failing, she raised the hem of her skirt and tore a piece from her underskirt, pressing the white linen against the two places. She didn't dare look up. The tears in her eyes—the grief that was tearing at her—were something she couldn't hide.

"Is he dead?"

Jaime felt Edward's hand on her shoulder. Without looking up, she moved her hand to Malcolm's throat, where she could feel a pulse, weak and irregular.

"Not yet," she answered under her breath. "But he is bleeding, and 'tis only a matter of time before you lose him. Unless . . . unless we bring him a physician."

Jaime turned her head as Edward's boots left her side. He drew one of his officers away and spoke under his breath with him. Though she couldn't hear their whispers, the officer nodded and strode off in the direction that they'd entered. Tearing another section from her skirts, she replaced the blood-soaked linen at his head with a new one. She pulled him slightly, rolling him onto his side, and drew the cloak away from his chest and back. There was a huge, jagged gash on his back and a smaller one in his chest right above his heart. A sword had run him through from the back. Jaime gasped, a knot of fear rising sharply in her throat. It was a miracle that he had survived the blow. How the blade had ever missed his heart, his lung . . .

Edward's boots appeared again at her side.

"He's bleeding from his chest, as well," she said.

"We are taking him back with us," he announced. "I'd

wager a crown he wouldn't survive the night in the hands of Reed, here."

Jaime stood up at once. There was no time to be lost. They had to take him now. As she turned to Edward, the Englishman's hand reached out and roughly took hold of her upper arm. She looked up into his gray eyes.

"I am proud of you, my little raven," he announced. "You have done me a service this day . . . a great service."

CHAPTER 5

Turning his back on the two men in the room, the lean, well-dressed courtier glanced out the diamond-paned window, only to catch sight of the raven-haired Jaime Macpherson hurrying through the garden in the direction of the stables. How odd, he thought, watching as the young woman's eyes darted nervously over her shoulder every few steps. So unlike her, he thought.

"The devil take me, Surrey, but you're weak and you're bookish. And if I didn't know better, I'd swear you hadn't a drop of Howard blood in you!"

Henry Howard, the earl of Surrey, tore his gaze away from the window and stared at his brother with a bored expression. "Swear what you like, Edward. Though I think, little brother, you should stop swallowing these French ships whole when you capture them. The wind in their sails is affecting your head quite adversely, I'm afraid."

Surrey was a slightly built man, not as tall or muscular as his younger brother, but he carried a quiet confidence in his face, a hint of carelessness in his attitude, that told of a man quite at ease with himself.

Edward glared back. "Once again, Harry, rather than congratulating me for my latest victory, you insist on being critical of my successes."

The earl of Surrey's nonchalant shrug, as he turned away, only served to fuel his brother's anger.

The duke of Norfolk fought back a grin as the fierce

exchange of words began again. He watched Edward's warlike posture, and took in Surrey's careless response—the leisurely grace in taking his time to walk back across the middle of the room and then to lean comfortably against the carved oak panel that surrounded the fireplace in the study.

Norfolk paused, considering the tremendous difference between his two sons. Harry, though proven in bravery and courtly behavior, had not found the soldier's life particularly appealing. Instead, his eldest son had found a curious delight in poetry, of all things. It was bad enough when he began translating Virgil's *Aeneid* for his friends, the duke thought, but this Petrarch fellow and his love poems were truly beyond the limits of decency.

Edward, on the other hand, reminded the duke so much of himself. Proud, ambitious, short tempered—Edward was a man of action. Like the duke himself, who as a young man had led the attack in the wondrous rout of the Scots at Flodden Field, Edward was now straining at the bit to prove himself, to take his ships and invade France itself. All his younger son needed was a bit of patience—the ability to consider all of the alternatives—and Edward would become a fine leader, Norfolk thought. A very fine leader.

The argument between the two men went on and Norfolk realized he'd perhaps let it continue too long. He'd watched his sons fight this way since they were lads—Surrey holding the edge until their arguing escalated into violence. But he didn't want them drawing swords on each other right now.

"Harry. Edward. That's quite enough." Norfolk's face was stern and he rapped his gnarled knuckles peevishly on the table beside his chair. "We need to hear all of what happened at court, not this foolishness about whether Edward has sunk one too many ships at sea."

Both men turned their attentions back to their father at once.

"My apologies, Your Grace," Surrey replied, smiling and bowing with a flamboyant show of courtesy. His face changed a bit, then, darkening with seriousness. "But to get to the point, Father, the king's displeasure with me has become more consistent, of late. You know that I have been too vocal in my objection to his attentions toward Catherine."

"What *difference* does it make if he should take a fancy to Catherine?" Edward interjected irritably. "Everyone knows the king's marriage to that ugly toad, Anne of Cleves, is about to be annulled, and then . . ."

"The difference, Edward," Surrey said quietly, turning to his brother, "is that since our cousin, Anne Boleyn, met her rather untimely end, the family's fortunes have suffered tremendously. If our cousin Catherine . . . if *any* female in the Howard family were to cause the king any further disappointment, it would probably mean the end of Father's influence at court. And that might just mean no more ships for you to play sailor in."

"Play . . . ?" Edward said angrily, taking a step across the room.

"Stay where you are, Edward," Norfolk commanded, pausing for a moment as his younger son struggled to regain control of his temper, finally throwing himself into one of the carved, upholstered chairs.

Pretty Catherine Howard certainly did present problems, it was true. Norfolk considered his niece for a moment. For more than two months now, the king's interest in her had continued to grow. She was certainly a lusty wench, Norfolk thought, smiling to himself. So full of life and yet so ambitious, she was. No wonder she caught the king's eye. But just before she'd gone off to court last fall, Norfolk had needed to step in himself and put an end to her antics with the damned music master. Aye, he thought, she could be a real problem if she didn't settle down.

Norfolk rapped his knuckles softly on the wood. But Catherine's a bright girl, the duke argued silently, and she *would* settle down. Of that he was certain. And marrying a king such as Henry Tudor . . . well, she knew what had happened to her haughty cousin, Anne. Aye, she would fall into line quickly enough. Just the honor of Henry taking her as a wife rather than as a mere mistress . . .

"Harry." Norfolk turned to face his older son. "Catherine will make as suitable a match for the king as any woman in England."

"Aye, Father. I hope you are correct." Surrey crossed his

arms over his chest and stroked the sharp line of his jaw. "But she is so much younger than he—in body and in spirit. And her youth and vigor will certainly prey on his mind . . . well, in no time."

"And I suppose," Edward said with sarcasm, "you were fool enough to tell him."

Surrey faced his brother with a wry smile. "Aye. And his face went as black as the day Thomas More defied him."

"You know," Norfolk said darkly, "that you play with fire when you trifle with the king's pleasures."

"Aye, Father. But I thought . . ." Surrey cast a glance about the room. "We all know how wild Catherine can be. She won't even last as long as Anne. Just think, as virtuous as we all knew Anne Boleyn to be, once she displeased him, nothing could stop Henry from sending her to the block. Even you, Father . . ."

"That's enough, Harry."

Surrey paused, staring for a moment at the old man before continuing. "Well, it matters little what is past, I suppose. But the short of it is that once the king's color returned to his face, he sent me on my way."

"Well, lad," the duke said wryly, "you didn't have such a long ride home, now, did you?"

"Nay, Father. Nor will your ride be long, either."

"Eh?" the duke asked, shooting his son a questioning look. "What's that?"

"The king sends word that he wants both you *and* my illustrious younger brother to attend him immediately."

"Why didn't you . . . By His Wounds, I just left him a month ago!"

Norfolk considered for a moment. His relationship with King Henry had as many ups and downs as a well bucket. This summons was surely to finalize the marital arrangements concerning Catherine. And perhaps the king simply wanted to reward Edward for his excellent service, but it was always difficult to know whether Henry Tudor intended to reward or punish. One thing he'd learned over the years, though, the quickest way to bring Henry's wrath down on one's head was to keep His Majesty waiting.

The duke looked from one son to the other. Edward's ruggedly handsome face was now shining with satisfaction at the news that the king had called for him.

"Well, Edward," Norfolk said with a heave of his chest. "Before you burst with pride, don't you need to do something about that Scot your men have trundled down from Norwich?"

Edward's face clouded for a moment. "Aye, Father," he responded, moving toward the window and gazing out in the direction of the stables. "Perhaps I should take him to the king, as a token . . ."

"Never!" Norfolk cautioned. "You have already given Henry a new French warship to add to his fleet. This man and the prize he'll bring us is yours to keep."

"What have your got, Edward? The Black Douglas?" Surrey asked, moving next to his brother and peering out over his shoulder.

"Nay, Surrey. But I've caught the laird of the MacLeod clan, and I have him in one of the stable cells."

"The laird of the MacLeods?" Surrey paused. "Well, if you'd like, Edward, I should have time to torture him for you while you are with the king at Nonsuch Palace."

The duke broke in with a short laugh. "Seriously, Surrey, your brother has made a fine capture. But the man is wounded, that's why he is here."

"So, he might not live?"

"It depends," Norfolk answered, "on our treatment."

"Well, I believe that we've enough experience killing Scots in this family that one more should be no challenge." Surrey smiled, but his humor was lost on the old warrior.

"The Howard family has gained the position it holds because of that experience," Norfolk interrupted gruffly. His glare softened a bit, then, and he glanced at his younger son. "Surrey will be able to look after things here, Edward. Your Scot will be in good hands."

Surrey gazed for a moment at his father, then shrugged and turned to his brother. "Certainly, little brother. We'll nurse your prisoner back to health."

Edward smiled.

"Aye, Surrey. Do that for me, won't you?"

"That we will," Surrey said quietly as his brother moved away from the window. "But the cost may be high, brother."

The earl turned his gaze in the direction of the stable yards. "Very high," he whispered.

CHAPTER 6

Malcolm's head jerked to the side as the smell of rotting meat invaded his senses. The world inside his head began to spin, and his stomach heaved as the fibers of his brain twisted under the pressure. There were noises—the sounds of wind and drums, pounding—jumbled in his head. He tried to open his eyes, but even that tiny movement brought on more pain, rushing through him with a sensation of bones straining, cracking, exploding inside. Indeed, Malcolm could feel his bones melting within a gelatinous casing of battered flesh.

A momentary fear . . . nay, terror . . . pushed into the fogged consciousness of his brain. The Highlander suddenly found himself afraid to breathe. He feared, for a moment, even the rise and fall of his chest. Surely in filling his lungs—if he *could* fill his lungs—his chest would burst, pierced by the thousand daggers that even now must be protruding from his perforated carcass. And then there was his burning throat—parched, tight. So dry that he thought it could never again open to the cool elixir of life.

Malcolm MacLeod prepared to give up his spirit.

"My dear, this is no place for a lady of His Grace's household. Why don't you go and call for one of the serving maids to come and give me a hand with the lad."

Jaime shook her head, putting down beside Malcolm's head the potion she had been stirring for the Welsh physician. "I brought him here, Master Graves. Now I have to see to it that he lives."

"It might be that his fate lies beyond the scope of our abilities, my dear. Surely beyond my skill. He has lost too much blood already, and what we have left to do . . ."

". . . Won't get done if all we do is simply stand and talk now, will it?" Jaime cut in decisively, pausing to gently raise Malcolm's head and very carefully lowering it onto her lap. "Tell me what we must do next, and let's just get on with it."

The aging physician stretched a rheumatic shoulder, wiped his hands on a clean rag, and scratched one of the tufts of red hair that adorned either side of his bald head. He studied the young woman sitting at his patient's battered head. Even with her elegant gray cloak already stained with the Scot's blood, Mistress Jaime Macpherson was totally out of place in the filthy cell that the duke kept for prisoners in the stable buildings. She'd stayed beside him since shortly after the prisoner had arrived from Norwich Castle, but they still had a long way to go with this one. Graves knew there would be a great deal more blood on that cloak before he was finished stitching the Scot back together.

He'd tried to send her away immediately; he didn't need a hysterical woman swooning at his feet. But she'd held her own in the early going. She was a far cry from the rest of them. He glanced down at her firm but gentle hands as she coaxed the Scots lips open a bit, tipping the liquid preparation down his throat. Aye, she has her wits about her, Graves thought. I should always have such competent help.

"Make him drink it all, if you can," the physician ordered, watching the throat constrict in an effort to swallow. "His fever will surely kill him without more fluids in him, and this is the only liquid he's taken at all."

Jaime nodded to the man as she trickled more liquid past Malcolm's cracked lips. All the anger she'd felt in the past toward the Highlander amounted to nothing now. Nothing compared to the reality of his suffering. It was almost too much for her to bear. Malcolm MacLeod may have caused her humiliation and hurt, but even in her wildest moments of fury and grief, she could never have wished this misery upon him.

Her heart ached in her chest. Looking down at Malcolm's bruised face, swollen to the point of being nearly unrecognizable, she wondered briefly if he knew who was making him drink this. At the core of her soul, she wished he had the strength to lash out at her for what she'd done, for bringing him here. She wished he would go after her the way he had at Norwich Castle. She would bear his wrath any time in lieu of this life-draining stupor, this battered daze, this shroud of oblivion.

A gurgle erupted in his throat, and the liquid she had been feeding him bubbled out. He was rejecting her even in his unconscious state.

"He'll not make it," Graves said under his breath, watching the Scot's suddenly labored breathing. "Look at his chest, his scalp. He is bleeding again . . . more than before. Much, much more. Look, this gash on the shoulder has begun to open again." The surgeon's hands hesitated for only a moment, and then commenced to sew the wound on Malcolm's shoulder with quick, sure movements.

Malcolm thought the pain would drive him mad. But when his anguish was at its height, he drew back, realizing he had within his grasp the power to walk away from it all. So he did. Rising like a cloud, he moved away. At the sound of the voices, Malcolm turned—the words were murmured, indistinct, but the voices familiar somehow, as if they were a part of him. The Highlander was only mildly startled to see himself lying in a heap of straw, the dirty gold strands stained with his blood. Two heads bent over the motionless frame. Their voices wafted back to him, their words unintelligible, and he drifted weightlessly away from them. He had no pain now.

Somewhere far behind him a door opened, and as he turned, he felt himself slowly drawn toward it. Malcolm watched. Through the door he could see the bright light of a sun in a cloudless sky. He blinked his eyes and tasted the warmth. He could feel the presence of someone, something. It was so close. Within his grasp. A world beyond the door. A peace that pulled him onward.

"Damn you, Malcolm MacLeod. You will not die."

Jaime thought of all who loved this man—of all the hearts

that would be broken to hear of his death—and the thought weighed like a stone on her soul. Fiona and Alec, losing the son they'd raised as their own. His wife . . . what was her name? And . . . oh, by the Holy Virgin, what if there was a bairn? So much Jaime didn't know. Leaving Scotland, severing the lines. She'd never so much as allowed the mention of his name. But, now, fate bringing him here, to take his last breath at her feet. She couldn't let it happen. She couldn't.

"Do you hear me, you pigheaded beast? This is not the place for you to die. I won't let you cause me more pain!" Jaime cursed him again under her breath and pressed a wad of clean bandages against the wound on the side of his head. The blood was everywhere and a panic tore through her soul.

As he neared the crossing point, Malcolm felt the troubles of his life drop from his body like so many plates of armor. Like a snake shedding skin. He was so close now! Eternity! The sky opening up before him. The freedom of flight. Air, sweeter than any he'd ever tasted, filled his lungs! He continued to move toward the light. Toward its promise.

Jaime, tears coursing down her cheeks, watched in horror as his ragged breathing faltered, then came to a rasping stop. She lost all sense. Leaping up, she moved the physician aside and punched at Malcolm's chest.

"Nay, blackguard." She was hammering on his chest, cursing the Highlander. "Nay, Malcolm. You cannot . . ."

Malcolm was nearly through the door. He could see wisps of silk fluttering, waving. He saw his own arms reach out for the flowing silk, felt his heart open to the soft whispers that beckoned him. Almost through . . .

Then, he felt arms encircle him from behind. A hand, strong and sure, pressed against his chest, holding him back. A woman's voice. Why, she was shouting, cursing at him. The bloody wench was calling him names! He could hear her distinctly. She was degrading his honor—his very manhood.

The presence through the door called softly to him, but he could not understand the words. He struggled to shut out the voice behind—to move on.

But she wouldn't let go. The strength, the anguish behind

her angry cries pulled at him. The voice beyond the door called him once again. What is it? Wait, he cried out.

The physician looked on, aghast as she continued to curse the Highlander's carcass. Graves heard language he hadn't thought possible in a young woman of breeding. Language he hadn't heard since he was a young man on the Scottish campaigns.

And after all, the man was dead.

Jaime, tiring, leaned heavily on Malcolm's chest. She was not aware of the sobs wracking her body. She only knew that his spirit was slipping beyond her grasp. And she knew no way to bring him back.

Please, Holy Mother, she screamed silently. Please don't let this man go from here.

The voice beyond the door whispered again. Bloody hell, Malcolm thought. He couldn't hear a thing. He turned back toward the wench, anger pervading his spirit. If she would only quit her ruckus. Suddenly, he could see her clearly. Jaime, her hands on his heart, her black hair down around her face, her lips moving. A pain shot through his chest, his head pounded. Malcolm again felt his bones disintegrating. The agony was back.

Nay, he screamed, turning back to the door. He glimpsed the final flash of light, but the door had closed. Gone, he realized through the pain.

By God, the wench had won.

CHAPTER 7

"Is he dead?" Mary Howard's whisper broke the momentary silence that had fallen inside the cell. Peeking into the open door, she froze at the site of the blood and the bloody wreck of the Scot's body.

The physician cast an admonishing glance at the blanched face of the newcomer, and Jaime's startled expression quickly changed to bewilderment at the appearance of her cousin.

"Did you come down here for a dance, Mistress Mary?" the physician asked, his voice dripping with sarcasm. Turning to Jaime, his gruffness returned as he barked, "Take her out of here at once, Mistress Jaime. The poor lad is barely hanging on as it is. We don't need the entire household tramping through for a peek at his miserable carcass."

"But ... but we're not finished with him," Jaime argued. She had no desire to go just yet. "You need help with his dressings. I should try to clean the blood from his wounds."

"I've done this for over thirty years," Graves grumbled under his breath. "I can manage the rest just fine. As for the cleaning, I'll do what I can and have one of the stable hands sleep in here. We don't want any of the barn vermin getting at him during the night."

The physician smiled wryly as Mary Howard paled again, looking as if she were about to be ill. He looked back at Jaime. Uncertainty showing on her face, she stood looking at him from her place beside the prisoner.

The lass had certainly been a great help, far better than his own hapless, shirker of an assistant. But the truth of it was that the physician needed a bit of time alone to regain his wits. What he'd just witnessed had frightened him. Something had passed between this woman and the wounded man, and he was struggling, even now, to square it in his mind. He could have sworn . . . no. There was no doubt. The Scot had died. He'd stopped breathing.

He was dead.

And then—Graves dared not think of it as magic—Jaime had brought him back to life. Back to life and back to a conscious state. The physician's hackles rose again at the thought of the awakening. The Highlander's chest had convulsed, his fists clenched and then opened, only to tighten into fists once more. And then the lad had opened his eyes, clear and alert and . . . disbelieving. The Scot had just stared at her, anger quickly taking over, wrath eclipsing any other expression on his battered features. He'd silently drunk the entire potion then, never taking his eyes from her face. Then, cursing her by name, his swollen eyelids had drooped, and he'd fallen into a deep slumber.

Over a year ago, when Jaime Macpherson had first arrived, the word had gone about that she was niece to Anne Boleyn. He himself could see the family resemblance between her and the dead queen. In the back of his mind, now, resemblances of another type were pushing forward with an unpleasantness that Graves was trying to ignore. Aye, he'd heard the stories that Queen Anne was a witch—a sorceress of some kind who had cast a spell on the king. That is, until he'd had her beheaded. They'd said she could communicate with spirits. There was even talk that her ghost had been seen in the Tower of London and other places, as well.

But Graves had never believed such talk. He'd seen her before the king fell in love with her, and he'd seen her as queen. She hadn't been an easy lass to like, in his opinion. Proud and vain. But hardly a witch, so far as he could see. Just talk begun by her enemies, by those who wanted her dead. And of course, he thought, 'tis even easier to slander your enemies once they are dead.

But now . . . His eyes looked searchingly into Jaime's

face. Witnessing what had occurred here, what the lass had done . . . and she a niece to the dead queen! Graves pondered a moment. Nay, it couldn't be, he decided, shaking his head. By Jesu, he was even starting to think like these damned English.

"I'll come back," Jaime vowed, touching the physician on the arm as she moved toward her swaying cousin.

Before she even reached the door, Jaime could see the glazed look of horror that was fixed on her cousin's face. The sight was hardly one that Mary was accustomed to. The filthy cell, the blackening blood, the battered and half-naked body of the injured Malcolm.

"Is he dead?" Mary whispered again, leaning heavily on the door frame. Her face was a white mask.

Jaime realized that her cousin had not heard a word that had been uttered by Graves. Not needing another patient at the moment, Jaime took Mary by the arm and led her into the enclosed yard and out of the physician's earshot. Standing in the late-afternoon sun, Jaime squeezed Mary's hand. It took only a few moments for the younger woman to regain most of her composure.

Then, looking at Jaime with eyes wide, Mary started with dismay. "Oh my, Jaime. The blood . . . your . . . your cloak! Your hair! Your face!" The young woman, again too upset to talk, flapped her arms like a bird in distress. "Jaime, Edward . . . and . . . oh, my! Look at you!"

Jaime took Mary's hands in hers. "Take a deep breath," she ordered softly. "You have news of Edward?"

Mary nodded and took not one but a few short breaths.

Jaime waited impatiently for the other woman to regain her composure. A stable boy passed by, carrying two buckets of grain and gawking openly at the two. Horses could be heard, stamping and snorting impatiently to be fed. A cart of feed—pulled by an oxen being led by a tall, stick of a man—creaked into the enclosure from some other part of the series of granaries, smithies, and stables that comprised the stable area. Suddenly, Mary's attention was captured by the activities going on around them, as if it were a world she was seeing for the first time.

"That's enough breathing for today," Jaime said, interrupting her cousin's study. "What of Edward?"

Jaime knew that although Mary had lived on this estate for most of her life, the past few moments constituted the longest period of time she ever spent in the stables. When they hunted, the grooms brought the horses to the house. Jaime cleared her throat to get the other woman's attention.

Sheepishly, Mary turned back to her cousin. "Oh," she exclaimed. "I have news."

"Aye?"

"Lord Surrey has returned from court this afternoon."

"I wondered. There was a great commotion a little while ago when the horses were brought down."

"Aye, well there's more. Something has happened. Effie, my wardrobe maid, who has a . . . well, who is friendly with Surrey's second groom . . . a coarse young man whom I can never see amounting to . . ."

"Please, Mary!" Jaime cut in, her impatience bubbling to the surface. "What has happened?"

Mary scowled at her cousin. "Well, the duke and Edward have been summoned to Nonsuch Palace. That's what has happened!"

Jaime's heart leapt with excitement. With Edward waiting on the king, she would be able to spend the time needed to nurse Malcolm back to health—without involving Edward at all. Jaime's hand squeezed Mary's arm. "And have they gone?"

"Nay, how could they," Mary responded, "when Edward is searching high and low for you?"

"What? You mean he's looking for me now?"

"Aye," Mary said, prying her cousin's fingers from her arm. "And if I have bruises from your rough handling of me, Jaime Macpherson . . ."

Jaime looked about her nervously. "Do you know where he is now, Mary?"

"Probably coming this way, I'd wager—were wagering a ladylike pursuit. I heard him questioning your maid, but Caddy feigned total ignorance—a marvelous performance—

and vaguely mumbled something about flowers and trees. And then I saw him going off toward the orchards . . ."

"Come with me, Mary," Jaime said, pulling her cousin by the hand.

"What on earth . . . ?"

Jaime had been very careful about coming to Malcolm this morning. Other than Mary, and Caddy, her maid, no one in the house knew of her whereabouts. She trusted Master Graves, the physician, but something inside her head told her that letting Edward know she was here would be a terrible mistake.

"Hurry, Mary! We must meet him somewhere else . . . away from here!"

Mary glanced back, and then nodded slowly as her cousin's concern dawned on her.

"Ah! The Scot," she said. They hadn't gone three steps, though, before Mary yanked Jaime to a halt. "But you can't go to Edward like that."

Quickly, she unfastened Jaime's bloody cloak and removed it, carefully rolling it up and even more carefully holding it away from her own skirts. Placing it on a nearby cart, she turned and tried to smooth her cousin's hair. Disappointed with the effort, Mary turned Jaime around, pulled the long black hair over her shoulder, and began to braid it rapidly.

"You've spent the entire day down here, coz. Your cloak is stained with his blood. Your eyes are puffed up from crying. Why are you so worried about this man?"

Jaime felt her face redden as she lifted her hands to her eyes. She was glad Mary was behind her. "I was the cause of the beating he received at Norwich Castle," she replied, hedging her answer. She hoped desperately Edward would not notice her condition.

"There! Now you look at least somewhat presentable." Mary cast a critical eye over her cousin. "Smooth your skirts. And . . ."

Jaime grabbed the other woman by the hand. "Come on, Mary. We must be away from here." Jaime led her cousin out of the stable enclosure and onto the tree-lined drive that led back toward the huge, rambling manor house. The gardens lay behind the high hedges to the left, the orchards to the right of the ornately designed flower beds. Acting on impulse, she pulled her cousin down the lane to the left. The lane leading to the mews. Jaime loved to hunt, and she spent a great deal of time with the falcons that the duke kept. His two peregrines, gifts of the king himself, were among the finest in England. In a moment the wall enclosing the mews came into view.

Evan, the duke's falconer, was watching his eldest son chop three freshly killed rabbits for the hawks when the two women passed through the gate into the small yard in front of the mews. He glanced up, smiling his crooked smile as he recognized Jaime. The two hooded peregrines, black and strong, sat perched on crossed stakes driven into the ground beside the falconer.

"How is your wife, Evan?" Jaime asked pleasantly.

Evan bowed slightly and doffed his cap to Mary. "A mite uncomfortable, mistress, as ye might expect, but due any day, she tells me. Oh, she asked me to thank ye for sending in the meals from the kitchens this past week. 'Tis heavy work, her moving about, and your kindness has been a godsend, to be sure."

"No thanks are needed," Jaime whispered as she stepped over to one of the birds and began petting her magnificent feathers.

"Well, we thank ye all the same." The falconer nodded toward the peregrines. "Ye missed a fine day of hunting today. His Grace stayed in, but some of the young gentles made a jolly time of it."

"I'm sure Lord Edward must have enjoyed the hunt!"

"Nay, mistress," Evan said, shaking his head. "His Lordship has not been down all day."

Jaime hid her relief, gesturing toward the rabbit. "The fruit of your labors, Evan?"

"Aye, mistress," Evan said gravely. "Just a few of the little beasties that we knocked down today. The birds we took went direct to the kitchens. We've still a couple of hours of sunlight. Would ye care to take one of these ladies out, mistress?"

Jaime shook her head, whereupon the falconer picked up several pieces of the meat to feed to the falcons. "Nay, Evan. Not today, but I thank you. Working about in the garden has wearied me dreadfully. Perhaps tomorrow," she said with a smile, taking the wide-eyed Mary by the elbow and steering her back out the gate.

"What are you up to, Jaime Macpherson?" Mary breathed, trying to keep up with her cousin's quick pace. The gate to the garden lay directly before them. A pair of grooms sprinted down the lane in the direction of the stables, crossing the women's path. The young men were clearly in a hurry.

"Mary, don't leave my side." Jaime stopped with her hand on the gate and looked into her cousin's face. "No matter what Edward says, you mustn't leave me alone with him. Promise me."

"What's wrong? You've never been afraid of being left along with him before!" Seeing the quick turning away of Jaime's eyes and the hands that hurriedly yanked open the gate, Mary reached out and caught her cousin's arm. "Jaime?"

Coloring, Jaime turned slightly and shook her head. Then, looking directly into her cousin's eyes, she asked, "Please, Mary. Don't leave my side."

The blonde-haired beauty paused, and then nodded hesitantly. Jaime turned and moved through the gate, but Mary held back a moment, staring after her cousin's retreating figure, before following her into the gardens.

Once safely within the carefully manicured space, Jaime slowed down, leading Mary into the center of a close-cropped, knotlike design of herbs. Shielding her eyes with her hand against the rays of the descending sun, she scanned the far side of the enclosure for any sign of Edward. By a path leading to the orchards, where a half-dozen gardeners were working, she saw one of them straighten up as a giant of a man came into view. The others stood quickly, bowing deferentially, and Jaime's gaze focused on the figure. She watched as Edward said something to the gardener.

Taking Mary by the arm, Jaime moved quickly to a circular, grass-covered bench and sat her cousin on it, putting them in the full view of the gardener. In less than a moment, the man's eyes turned in their direction, and Jaime saw the gardener's finger point toward them. Whirling around, Jaime pretended to be unaware of Edward's presence, staring instead at the carefully clipped design that surrounded them. So far so good, she thought with relief.

"Don't look at him, Mary," she commanded. A pair of swallows flitted across the garden in front of them, and Jaime forced herself to watch them for a moment until they disappeared up and over the ivy-covered way at the far end of the enclosure.

Mary's voice, like that of a stern tutor, broke into the silence. "Jaime, don't ask me to lie to him about your whereabouts this afternoon! I don't like to lie. I can't lie. By Saint Agnes, he is coming this way!" Her voice registered her alarm. "Perhaps it would be better if I should go . . ."

Jaime plunked herself down beside her cousin and took hold of Mary's hand with a forceful grip. Edward must be getting fairly close to them. "Just sit here beside me," she said quietly but firmly. "You won't have to say anything at all."

"But, Jaime, what happens if he asks me something?" the younger woman asked under her breath. "What should I say?"

"Just follow my lead. Think of this as a game, for heaven's sake." Jaime paused and looked into Mary's troubled face. "Mary, I'm just not prepared to be alone with him right now. But neither you nor I have done anything wrong. So please get that guilty expression off your face."

"I'll try," Mary responded, nodding resignedly. "But I just don't understand what's come over you."

Jaime looked away. How could Mary understand? Jaime herself couldn't understand, and frankly, that irked her somewhat. True, she was not married to Edward. They were not even betrothed . . . yet. But she was acting as if she'd been completely disloyal in spending the day at the stables nursing Malcolm. After all, she argued with herself, she was doing Edward a great service in trying to keep his prisoner alive. That was certainly true. Then why had she panicked at the thought of Edward finding her there. Why was she planning to deceive Edward now?

The thought flashed through her mind that Edward was changing. He was still—with the exception of his passionate outburst last night—as courteous as ever toward her. But his changing moods—mercurial enough to keep many servants in a state of constant terror—were becoming more evident to Jaime, and the side of him she saw at Norwich Castle frightened her a bit. As much as she despised Malcolm MacLeod for what he had done, she could not risk having Edward snuff out his life on a whim. And when she considered Edward's passionate feelings for her, she decided that the risk was far too high.

Mary lifted a hand and waved to Edward. Jaime turned to greet him as well, forcing her lips into a smile as he approached them. His strides were long and impatient, but his face was partly obscured by the lengthening shadows. She tried to keep her hands still in her lap.

"By the devil, Jaime! I have been looking . . ."

"So fierce, Edward," she admonished him cheerily, springing to her feet as he came up to them. His face was flushed beneath his velvet tam with the plume of peregrine feathers, and he was wearing a finely worked velvet doublet that matched his russet-colored hose. Jaime noted the high riding boots. Edward was clearly dressed for his journey to the king's court at Nonsuch Palace. "Well, you certainly missed the most glorious afternoon of hunting. Oh, I wish so much that you had been there. The falcons are magnificent and the catch . . ." As he took hold of her hands, she paused and turned a blushing cheek to him when he bent down to kiss her. "You see our cousin Mary here . . ."

"Hunting? I saw you at the house little more than an hour ago, Mary," Edward said, looking skeptically at the younger woman.

When her cousin went brilliantly crimson to the very roots of her hair, Jaime cut in immediately. "Mary didn't go hunting today. But we thought a quiet walk in the gardens would help dispel her headache. And 'tis working, is it not, my sweet?" Jaime detached herself from Edward and glided to her cousin's side, squeezing her hand as Mary nodded and smiled weakly. "In fact, we've just come up from the mews. 'Tis such a fine day to be outdoors, and I was certain the sight of His Grace's beautiful peregrines as well as the fresh air might do her some good."

Edward's face quickly changed as he dismissed the subject

from his mind, and Jaime noted the excitement that flashed across his face. He peered into her upturned face for a moment and then pulled his hat from his head, running his fingers through his hair as he began to pace back and forth before them.

"Mary, leave us," he ordered, halting abruptly and turning to them.

Jaime jumped as her cousin sprang up like a startled pheasant. Tugging hard at Mary's hand, she drew her roughly back onto the bench.

"Edward, she's not well enough to go up to the house on her own," Jaime scolded, looking defiantly into his annoyed expression. He towered over her. "So please stop ordering her around."

His face cleared as he visibly struggled to keep Jaime's rebelliousness from spoiling his intentions.

"But . . . well, I have some news that I would like to share with you, *alone*."

"So you *have* been summoned to the king," Jaime said, springing to her feet excitedly, to the amazement of both Edward and Mary.

"You already know?" He asked puzzled, a smile beginning to work across his face.

"But how could we not know?" she said, clapping her hands. "Everyone knew that, in no time at all, news of your capture would be well received at court." She touched him affectionately on the arm. "Truly, I *am* happy for you, Edward. You are so brave—such a hero. This was too long in coming. But then, it had to happen sooner or later that the king would recognize your successes."

Edward chuckled, pleased with her response. "You talk as if I am about to be made a member of the king's Privy Council."

"Why not? You deserve all good things, Edward." She folded her hands before her and looked up into his face cheerfully. "When do you leave?"

"When His Grace is ready." Edward glanced uncomfortably at Mary's inhibiting presence. Then he reached down and took Jaime by the elbow, pulling her away. "I want to talk to you . . . alone."

"We can speak here, Edward."

The knight looked around, focusing on an arbor of climbing roses not far away. "Nay, Jaime. There in the arbor!"

She dug her feet in the dirt and shook her head. "We cannot, Edward," she whispered back, looking cautiously over her shoulder at Mary. "Why, Mary just told me that your brother's wife, the Countess Frances, spoke to her specifically—and just this morning—about the impropriety of the two of us."

"Who the devil is Frances to meddle in our affairs?" Edward exploded, turning on Mary, who began to stand and then sat again, staring into her lap in embarrassment.

Jaime raised a hand and placed it against his lips. Raising herself on her toes, she whispered confidentially. "She is only looking after my reputation, dear cousin. You wouldn't want wagging tongues to blacken my name in your absence now, would you?"

His strong hands gripped her shoulders hard, and he nearly lifted her off her feet as he pulled her into his embrace. "I've been wanting to do this all day," he said, bringing her face close to his.

"Mary is watching," she managed to get out before his mouth slanted over hers, crushing her lips with his kiss. She planted her hands against his chest and tried to push herself away. Jaime felt her face burn as his lips devoured hers. She could feel his fingers, like iron, digging into the flesh of her arms. Suddenly, he broke off the kiss, and pressed his lips close to her ear.

"This will be our final parting, Jaime. I know you want me, and I believe you are as impatient as I. So think all you want, and plan as you will. When I return from the king's court, we *will* be sending word to your parents. We *will* announce our betrothal."

Jaime simply stared at him as he drew back to look into her eyes. He eased his grip on her shoulders.

"Once the agreement is reached with your family," he vowed, "we can marry the next day or the next year, so far as I am concerned." His large hands framed her face, his thumb running over her full lower lip.

"Once the papers are drawn," he repeated. "You are mine to keep."

She lowered her eyes and stared at the stitching of his doublet. He wanted her the same way he wanted a prize at sea. He would win her—take her—the same way he would take a treasure ship from the New World. By force and strength. That was Edward's way.

"Be good, Jaime," he said softly, as his hands dropped to his sides. "Dream of me."

She looked up, suddenly caught off guard by the tenderness she saw in his gray eyes and heard in his voice. Her heart pounded at the gentleness in his tone, and her head whirled in confusion. How could he be so different from one moment to the next? The two sides of this man tore at her, and her face reflected her bewilderment as he bowed and, without another word, started back for the house.

CHAPTER 8

Malcolm fell. As if from the sky, he dropped like a stone. He could see the heather below, rushing up at him, each purple flower so clear, so distinct. The onrushing air tore at his face, his hair, peeling back his lips, forcing his eyes open. Fear possessed him, but try as he might, he could not close his eyes. He moved his hands to cover his face, but spread his arms with shock, realizing the skin from his fingers to his elbow was ablaze with crimson flame. Malcolm continued to fall. The heather-covered earth opened to receive him.

The Highlander jerked into consciousness with a start. The ground beneath him smelled not of heather, but of old, befouled straw. A noise—the sound of men speaking—could be heard from a distance not far off. The pounding in his ears made the words unintelligible, but the accent was clear. English. Closing in. They were now getting closer to where he lay. Malcolm tried to roll to his side, to rise to his feet. His body would not respond. He set his teeth, willing himself up. Nothing. Move, damn you, he cursed, trying to reach the short sword strapped at his side. His broken body defied him still. He couldn't lift his head, his arm—not even the weight of a finger. The voices were now upon him. Malcolm lay still, doomed, helpless, waiting for the final death stroke to fall. Let it come, he thought.

But the stroke never fell.

His face was hot—burning—and yet his chest and arms were as cold as the grave. He had no legs, so far as he could tell, but he could feel the droplets of sweat scorching a trail down his temples, across his neck. A tightness in his throat—a dryness that threatened to crack open his gullet—consumed him.

He tried to remember where he was. A swirl of pictures, sounds, whirled past his eyes with dizzying speed. A ship. A French ship! And a wolfish attack by the English ships. They were outnumbered, outgunned. And then there had been a searing heat plunging through his ribs, piercing the flesh. The point of the blade coming through his chest. The flash of white. The world out of focus giving way to the aching, yellow light and the wriggling red worm that squirmed across his eyes. And then the rush of wind, the blackness, and then nothing. That's what he remembered.

A spot cleared far back in Malcolm's brain. The vision of his master, the venerable Erasmus, in his study. The bustling streets of Freiburg in Breisgau, shut out by the walls of the university, by the crackle of the fire in the small hearth. He had spent many days at the master's side. Come, Malcolm Scotus, the master used to say, the corners of his shrewd gray eyes crinkling with only the hint of a smile. Let us argue once again the *De Devisione Naturae,* but this time, my boy, we argue in Greek.

But Erasmus was dead now. And that had been the reason he'd given to those who asked about his presence aboard that ship. He'd simply said that he was going to Rotterdam to pick up a small legacy the great scholar had left him a few years earlier as a part of his will. He'd never had time to go before now. He still didn't have time. But a sense of nostalgia, Malcolm had told one fellow traveler, for the peace he had once felt as a student, had drawn him on this trip.

So in the role of a wayfarer rather than laird and warrior chief, he had boarded the French ship. So little had he suspected an attack. Or suspected finding her so soon. Suddenly, Malcolm's head cleared of everything but Jaime.

It hadn't been a dream. She had been there, at the prison. He remembered clearly the cold stone and the stinking air and the gruesome feel of drifting in and out of consciousness. And then, as refreshing as droplets of rain could be against the burning walls of hell, he'd heard the rustle of skirts of a woman and had looked up to see her face. In truth, he had come on this journey in search of peace—in search of her—and here she was, appearing before his eyes like some angel emerging from the mist. His spirit had soared with joy at seeing her, when now he knew he should have turned his face and welcomed death. The anger once again boiled within him.

Traitorous, double-crossing Jaime. He clenched his jaws together as that painful realization stabbed at his heart anew.

There was a yawn and the stirring of straw an arm's length or so from where he lay as the voices—their tone so soft, so unwarlike—could be heard just outside a door. Beyond the voices, the Highlander could make out the morning sounds of horses and the men who worked with them. A kick to the shoulder from whoever was with him made Malcolm groan involuntarily, though the sound seemed to come from outside of himself.

"Filthy Scot," a young man muttered. "If it warn't fer ye, that Welsh boneleech wouldna . . ." The door creaked and a rush of fresh air swept in.

"Ah, Master Graves. Ye finally come down . . ." The young man grumbled, more than a hint of resentment in his tone. "I'll be getting to my duties, if ye two masters are done wi . . ."

"You'll wait."

Malcolm kept his eyes shut. He hardly breathed as a cool hand felt his brow.

"Did he do anything during the night? Did he come awake? Did he fret with his wounds?" With a click of his tongue, the man removed his hand from Malcolm's face and began probing at various points of his aching frame.

"He's been a-lying there like a stone, sir. If it warn't fer once in a while a-groaning as he did . . . I'd a-thought him done fer."

"The man is burning up with fever. During the night, did you give him any of the medicine I left?"

"Nay, sir . . . it . . . it seemed a bit of a waste."

"A *waste!*" Graves exploded. "You, a stable hand, decided . . . By the Virgin, man! If you had a sick stallion in your care, wouldn't you do right by the creature?"

There was a pause, and then the stable man answered,

clearly surprised and hostile at the physician's remarks. "He's a filthy Scot, Master Graves! He ain't no horse. I don't know what fer . . ."

"What for?" the older man's voice shot back at the man. "I'll tell you what for! So we could build up his strength. So he can cut your throat . . . or at least cut off your ears . . . while you sleep. Little use they are to a fool who doesn't listen or do as he's told!"

Malcolm listened to the uncomfortable shifting of straw in the back corner of his cell. Though he wouldn't open his eyes, he could envision the withering look that the stable hand was now enduring.

"Are ye done with me now?" the man grumbled at last under his breath. "If ye are, I'll be on my way."

Malcolm moaned as the physician prodded hard at one of the gashes. He felt the man's hands gentle at once. "Nay, you'll have to stay and give Davie here and the carter a hand moving the Scot."

"Taking him back to Norwich?" Malcolm didn't miss the note of satisfaction in the young man's voice.

"Nay, to my surgery in the manor house."

"To the house, Master Grave?" the hostler asked, dumbfounded. "A *Scot* under His Grace's own roof?"

"Aye, man. What of it?" Malcolm kept his eyes closed but relished the sensation of the cool liquid that had been lifted to his cracked lips.

"But . . . but . . ." he sputtered. "How can it be that he . . . ? A filthy Scot? Why, *I've* ne'er even been allowed . . ."

"You?" The physician's words were pointed. "You are a servant who has a tongue far too long and head far too big for his own good."

"But, sir," the man groveled, "I . . . I ne'er thought . . ."

"Quit your jabbering, man! Ah, the cart is here." The physician's hands withdrew from their examination of Malcolm's wounds, and the Highlander could hear Graves move toward the door. "Damn . . . I didn't want that thing . . ." The older man's steps grew fainter as he walked out into the stable yard.

As he went, the physician continued to mutter under his

breath, but his words were obliterated by the whispering of the hostler and the man called Davie.

"Lord Surrey's the one who said fine to Mistress Jaime's asking," Davie said quietly, "after His Grace and Lord Edward left last night. 'Tis because of her that we're a-taking him back to the house."

"The Mistress and Lord Surrey? But Mistress Jaime belongs to Lord Edward!" The hostler gave a low chuckle under his breath. "Just yesterday in the garden—I was up helping myself to a few words with Tess, the master gardener's girl—I seen Lord Edward a-mauling the mistress. Like a baited bear, he was. His hands and mouth was all over her—and I don't think she was minding it much. I was getting a might randy just a-watching them from afar. Hell, I don't think she cares a jot for no filthy Scot to be messing with no . . ."

"Ye *are* a fool, Jo," Davie put in. "This 'filthy Scot,' as ye call him, is the property of Lord Edward now—thanks to Mistress Jaime. She was the one as pointed him out to the master. An' if he dies, I heard old Graves say, Lord Edward stands to lose a pretty sum of gold. So even if he ain't worth so much as a dog to us, he has value to the masters. So if ye was a bit sharper, Jo, ye'd best . . ."

The sound of the physician returning to the cell silenced the two men. And Malcolm continued to lie still, wondering if in being taken to the house he would have access to "Mistress" Jaime.

With all his soul, he couldn't wait for the opportunity of putting his hands around the wench's throat.

CHAPTER 9

Peering through the diamond-shaped panes of the upper gallery window, Jaime winced each time she saw Malcolm's body shift in the approaching cart. She could see the physician upbraiding the carter each time his human cargo jounced, but from the vacant expression on the driver's face, Master Graves's words hardly seemed to be penetrating the thick-necked man's bald head.

"Go slower," she said quietly, unaware of the auburn-haired woman coming up behind her. "There's a hole ahead. Go to the right of the lane. Don't you see it? Go to the ... Oh! By the Virgin, are you trying to kill him?"

"Aren't they doing a satisfactory job of it, Jaime?" the countess of Surrey asked, looking out the window as the cart lurched out of view beneath them.

Jaime blushed crimson, embarrassed at having forgotten the presence of the earl of Surrey's wife in the gallery. It took her a moment to find her voice. "I believe Master Graves has done all he can for ... for the prisoner."

"You know the man, I take it?"

"He ... He's a great laird in the western Highlands. Many know him."

"And he'll fetch a great ransom for Edward, I understand."

"Aye ... if we can restore his health. He's been horribly wounded, and he took a severe beating in the castle at Norwich."

"So I understand." Frances's eyes sparkled mischievously

as she took Jaime's hand. "But how on earth did you manage to convince Lord Surrey to allow the Scot into the manor house?"

Jaime flushed at the question. She had gone to the earl, knowing of his kindness but with little hope. Nursing Malcolm back to health in the stable cell seemed an impossible task. Master Graves had said as much himself. Malcolm had a fever. And the physician could hardly be expected to watch over him carefully there. And the idea of her going to the stables every day was sure to create a ruckus. So Jaime had to ask. The one question she would never had dared to put to Edward, she felt quite differently posing to the earl of Surrey.

"It took no effort at all, Frances," Jaime said softly, speaking truthfully. "Your husband knows the man. When I told him the prisoner's name, his face lit up immediately. It seems that Malcolm MacLeod visited his old teacher Erasmus at a time when Lord Surrey was under the old scholar's tutelage."

Frances shook her head with a smile. "Leave it to Surrey to have a bond of friendship tying him to one whom Edward considers a foe."

Jaime looked up and studied the soft features of the countess's face. The affection for her husband glowed like embers in her eyes. Frances caught Jaime's gaze and returned a smile.

"Surrey tells me that we will soon be sisters," Frances said casually, glancing out the window. Without waiting for an answer, she turned and slipped her arm through Jaime's, leading her away and down the hall. "I suppose you already know that it is hard for Edward to restrain himself once he's set his mind on what he wants."

Jaime played with the folds of her skirt as the two women made their way down the hall. "I have seen more variations of Edward's moods these past few days than I have seen in the past year." She paused not knowing how much she could reveal about her recent discomfort. With Mary, it was difficult to discuss Edward's ardent advances, since she was an innocent—like Jaime herself. Mary had only a romantic vision of life around her. When Edward had forcibly kissed Jaime in the garden only yesterday—right before her very eyes—Mary had thought it a romantic gesture, one she'd become dreamy-eyed about when they'd gotten back to the bedchamber they shared. She hadn't even paused to think of Jaime's reaction to the moment.

But here, with Frances, Jaime weighed the risk of unburdening herself. The countess, though only four years her senior, was an experienced woman in matters of the heart. She was a woman happily married to an adoring husband. And she understood the difference between lust and love. There were times that Jaime sorely missed her own family. Right now, she especially wished she had her mother here to talk to.

"Is something bothering you, Jaime?" Frances probed. "Because if Edward's moodiness gives you pause at all, then you should talk about it—before all this marriage talk goes much further."

"There is so much that is being assumed by Edward and by the family." Jaime caught the other woman's concerned gaze and quickly placed a hand on hers. "Please don't take my words incorrectly, Frances. There is very little in this world that I would cherish more than becoming a sister to you. This family has done so much for me this past year. And my affection for Edward . . . well, I respect him and have been honored by the attention he has bestowed on me since my grandfather died." She searched for the words to explain Edward's latest behavior—and her response to it. "But lately—and especially since this latest conquest—I find myself . . . well, fearing him. I am discovering things about him that I hadn't seen before. But if only there were some way . . . You see, I never know . . ."

"And you wish Edward were a bit more predictable," Frances put quietly.

"Aye!" Jaime looked down, suddenly ashamed and unsure of herself. "Frances, I am so uncertain of this match! The world seems to know my future, but, to be honest, neither I nor my family have given any consent to such a union. Again, I know I should be honored by Edward's attentions, but he is . . . he is so . . ."

Jaime stopped, suddenly concerned that the discomfort she felt from discussing this topic would far exceed the benefit she might gain from it. This was Edward's family, the Howard household, after all, and she still merely a guest. And an ungrateful guest, at that. She glanced up at her friend's pretty, composed face as Frances began to speak.

"When I was sixteen, my father and Surrey's father sat down together and arranged our marriage." Frances held Jaime's hand as they walked, but her eyes took on a faraway look. "Surrey had seen me at court, and of course, I had seen him, as well. He was—as he is today—dashing and courtly, handsome and yet . . . there was something more. I suppose it was the poet in him that won my heart."

Jaime pursed her lips, wondering why Frances was taking their discussion in this direction as she asked, "And you got to know him well at court?"

"Nay!" Frances smiled. "I was too shy! A mere slip of a girl. We hardly exchanged a word. But he approached his father anyway, asking him to broach the topic with my family. That was the beginning. As you can imagine, they were all delighted with the match."

"As you certainly must have been."

"I? My dear, I was terrified. You see, what you perceive in Edward, I, too, could see in Surrey. I thought him moody and . . . well, rough. I feared what marriage to a man like that would bring." She looked into Jaime's eyes. "But unlike you, I had no choice in the matter. No consent to bestow or to withhold. I simply obeyed my parents' wishes. I don't know if I would have married him if I had been given the choice."

"But you have such a wonderful marriage, Frances."

"Aye, Jaime. But that's the point, isn't it? We women never truly know our future in marriage until our fates are sealed."

Jaime considered the depth of her friend's words as they descended the circular stone steps to the palace's ground level. Was Frances telling her that she should close her eyes and assume that Edward would become the wonderful husband that Surrey became? Or was she just simply telling her the futility of such worries? Either way, Jaime would have to accept Edward for what he was . . . and pray for good fortune. Sometimes Jaime felt she was a bit too practical for such religion.

"Well, we are here," Frances said, raising her finely arched brows and inclining her head in the direction of the corridor that led to Master Graves's surgery. "I believe this is where you were headed, my dear friend, before I took to boring you with my silly tales."

"I? Headed to the surgery?"

Knowing from Frances's look that it was foolish to try to deceive her, Jaime turned and looked down the hall. There were so many prying eyes and wagging tongues in the palace. She hesitated, trying to decide on the wisdom of going openly to Malcolm—and the safety of caring for him there. With Edward gone for at least a fortnight, she knew that he offered no immediate threat to Malcolm's life. But what about the others? she wondered. Undoubtedly, there would be gossip. She tried to consider what would come of her actions once Edward returned to Kenninghall.

"Go, Jaime," Frances whispered encouragingly. "There has been no arrangement made for you to marry him, yet. Do what your heart and your head tell you is the right thing. And if any problems arise from your care, tell Edward that I insisted on you caring for his prize."

With a quick nod to her friend, Jaime scurried away down the corridor, her thoughts now only on Malcolm and on the rough handling he had endured on his journey here. She wondered if he still burned with fever.

CHAPTER 10

It was easy to pretend to be asleep.

After the painful and exhausting trip up from the stable yards, the tough part was staying awake. Though Malcolm had gotten more information then he'd ever thought imaginable, just lying still and pretending unconsciousness, he now found himself constantly dozing and fought off sleep with every ounce of strength he had.

He now knew, at least, that he was in East Anglia, at Kenninghall—the residence of Thomas Howard, duke of Norfolk. And though he was being kept prisoner, he'd been moved out of the foul stable cell at the command of Henry Howard, the earl of Surrey. Biting the inside of his swollen cheek to ward off a wave of weariness, Malcolm thought back on Harry Surrey, the young man he'd found studying with his own master, Erasmus, a few years back. Malcolm remembered him clearly, a sharp-eyed and open-minded lad. Friendly even, the Highlander recalled, in spite of being the offspring of the pig who had betrayed a parlayed truce and attacked the Scottish king at Flodden Field.

Malcolm knew though, that he was the prisoner of Edward, Henry's younger brother, the duke of Norfolk's second son. And he knew, as well, which side of the family Edward took after; stabbing the Highlander in the back. Edward was a coward who had not even had the courage to face him. As a result, the man's face was none too clear in Malcolm's memory. He'd been far too angry with Jaime in the castle at

Norwich to even notice the man at her side. But Malcolm understood it now—this Edward was the man to whom Jaime had betrayed him. Indeed, to please Edward Howard, she had not hesitated an instant in breaking faith—now he knew why. She had fled the loving arms of her family to become a public spectacle—a mistress to a loathsome English coward.

He could hear the rustle of skirts by his bed. At least, he thought the sound was near. The rustling soon gave way to a soft buzzing that the Highlander quickly realized was whispering. The words were indistinct—smatterings of sentences were all he could make out. It sounded like directions of some sort. Aye, that was it—the physician was giving directions. A soft voice responded, a soft voice with only the faintest lilt of Scottish tongue.

Damn her, he thought. He had conjured her like a specter in his mind, only to have her leap from his imagination into physical shape. He tried to clench his swollen fingers into a fist—testing his strength as he imagined an assault upon her.

Jaime couldn't tear her gaze away from his pallid face. The physician continued on with his instructions, and she listened. Malcolm's fever was dangerously high, but the physician believed their patient still had a good chance of pulling through. She committed to memory everything Master Graves told her. The older man hadn't the luxury of being able to remain beside Malcolm. He'd been called to Cambridge for a few days, and he'd have to take his good-for-nothing assistant with him. And as far as getting any help from the others in the household—well, Graves was less than happy with the attention Malcolm had received the night before in the stables.

So the physician left Malcolm in her care, and in spite of what anyone thought of the appropriateness of her presence in the surgery, Jaime would remain where she was needed.

Once the physician had left her alone, Jaime moved quickly, bringing a bowl of cool water to Malcolm's bedside. His skin had taken on a gray, clammy look to it and, in spite of his shivering, beads of sweat were standing out on his face before disappearing into the brown locks of hair. She looked at his parched, cracked lips. Reaching down, she tried to lift his head with one hand, but his muscles were rigid, and she knew she could not do it alone. Looking about for another way, she spotted a number of folded cloths on a small stool by the door. Balancing the bowl carefully beside him on the bed, she turned to move across the room.

The crash of the bowl to the floor behind her spun her around in alarm. Malcolm lay as he had before, his arm in the same position at his side. She bent down to pick up the wooden bowl, all the while scolding herself harshly for her ineptness. This time she fetched the folded cloths before filling the bowl again with fresh water from a jar on the far side of the room. Moving back to the bedside, Jaime placed the bowl carefully on the other side of her injured patient. She leaned over Malcolm, trying to push the linens under his battered head. If she could only raise him a bit, then she might be able to pour the liquid in small portions down his throat without choking him to death.

This time she saw it. His injured hand jerked and struck the bowl, sending it flying off the bed. As the bowl went crashing to the floor, Jaime's eyes traveled quickly from Malcolm's fingers, bloated and useless on the edge of the bed, back to his face. He appeared, beneath his bruised exterior, to be unconscious. She moved her hand and placed in on his brow. He was burning up with fever. If she could only get him to drink something, she could then use the damp cloths to sponge off his body, cooling him in the process.

Straightening up from the side of the bed, she moved around and fetched the bowl again. Wordlessly, she crossed the room to fill the bowl with fresh water, reminding herself that it was completely natural for Malcolm to have fits when he was burning with fever.

This time she tried to be smarter. Jaime dragged a three-legged chair to the bedside and went back for the pitcher, the bowl, and a spoon, placing them all on the seat. Turning back to her patient, she swore under her breath; his head had slipped off the makeshift pillow. She reached with both hands and tried to elevate him again, but his head seemed to be growing heavier by the moment. Finally, having working herself into a glow, Jaime succeeded in raising his head, and sat by his side on the bed.

With one hand holding his head steady, Jaime reached for the bowl and the spoon and placed them both on her lap. Taking a spoonful of water, she brought it carefully—and vainly—to his lips. Her patient wouldn't budge. She could not coax, cajole, or force his sealed lips open.

"Open up, Malcolm," she encouraged in a sweet voice, stroking his cheek gently. "Open your mouth, my battered, overgrown marmoset."

Giving up with the spoon, Jaime dipped her fingers into the bowl and traced his parched lips with her moistened fingers. But a sharp sense of the intimacy in this act swept through her, making her withdraw her hand at once. Suddenly uncomfortable with their closeness, Jaime sat bolt upright. The light woolen blanket had slipped down in her efforts to raise him, exposing his raw, bruised body to the waist. Cursing herself for her foolishness, she had to force herself not to think about his nakedness—not to remember the dreams she had once harbored of being his. Desperately, Jaime tried not to think of how magnificent he was, even in his battered condition. What she had thought of him and had imagined before she had been sent to France was quite different from the thoughts she now harbored.

Jaime tilted her head back and closed her eyes. The past was gone, and she tried to put aside the hurt and the lost dreams. He belonged to another woman now—their marriage would not be undone. He would never be hers.

She opened her eyes, letting her gaze sweep over his body again. The most important thing of all, she reminded herself, was that he needed her care if he was to survive. Setting her mind and her will and her strength to winning that battle, she turned her attention again to making him drink from the bowl.

CHAPTER 11

The dewy scent of roses wafted into the chamber on the morning breeze.

In the first lightening grayness of dawn, Malcolm's eyes focused on the blanketed figure huddled on a chair beside his bed. One pale, white arm extended from the woolen cocoon, and her upturned palm rested lightly against his knee. Wincing as he shifted his leg carefully, Malcolm watched through slitted eyes as Jaime stirred, without waking, and drew her hand back into the folds of her wrap.

Though he quickly pushed the thought from his mind, he realized that she had grown into a woman of tremendous beauty. He had always known she would. Her black hair, loose and in a state of disarray, lay in soft waves upon her shoulders. Her high forehead, the sculpted nose, the pronounced cheekbones and the full, sensuous lips all worked together to create, even in repose, the picture of a Madonna. They were the same features of the vibrant, young lass he'd known years before, but they now had a womanliness that was impossible to ignore. He hadn't seen her like this—at least not since she had grown. With the exception of her strange appearance at his wedding—an appearance that had only lasted moments—he hadn't set eyes on her since she'd been quite young. He still remembered the day when she was to leave for France. She had come to him, managing somehow to find him alone and asking him shyly to kiss her farewell. He recalled how he had leaned down and had placed an affectionate kiss on her brow. But the look of disappointment on her face had been so clear, the hurt so obvious, that he had told her the next time they met, she'd be of a marriageable age. Of an age for proper kissing, he had teased. Remembering now how that little announcement had done very little to pacify the lass, Malcolm's eyes drifted uncontrollably to Jaime's lips. She had grown, indeed.

I must be daft, he thought to himself, flexing his left shoulder gingerly. Some time during the night, he must have rolled onto his right side, and he gazed intently on her as she shifted slightly. She had undoubtedly spent the night in that position, the Highlander decided. He felt no fever, and his mind was clear for the first time in days. The light blanket that covered his naked body hardly moved as he slowly moved his foot from beneath it. The fresh air felt good on his skin. She must have been quite worried to stay the night in that chair. Another thought struck him. Or lonely perhaps, he corrected. He'd heard the talk—her lover was going to be away for awhile. Perhaps she just couldn't sleep without the weight of the repugnant English body upon her.

The sound of a cock crowing far off elicited a low moan from her, and she stirred slightly. Malcolm sent her flying backward—chair, blanket, and all—with a quick thrust of his foot.

The sensation of falling that one feels when dreaming is rarely accompanied by the real meeting of flesh and a floor's paving stones, but Jaime's head struck the floor with a thud and a flurry of blankets and clothes.

It took her a moment to clear the material from her face. Sprawled out on the floor, she flinched with pain as she looked up at the ceiling and lifted herself onto her elbows. It was morning, she realized with a start. And this was the second night she had fallen asleep in this chamber. Cursing under her breath, she rubbed the tender spot on the back of her head. Jaime threw the blanket to one side and raised herself to a sitting position. Looking crossly at the chair, she decided she must have leaned too far back in her sleep and toppled it by accident. Jaime struggled to her feet and thought of Mary and the tongue-lashing her cousin was sure to be giving her when she got back to their bedchamber. Mary had been quite angry with her yesterday morning—but now, two nights in the row! Jaime sighed and rolled her eyes, her conversation with Mary running through her head as she set the chair upright.

"Are you hurt?"

"Just a bang in the back of my head." She probed the spot with her fingers. " 'Tis tender to the touch. But it should go away in no time."

"Too bad!" Malcolm announced.

As if jarred from sleep, Jaime's head snapped around and her eyes rounded as they fixed on Malcolm. "You are awake," she whispered.

"Aye. I'm sorry to say that I am." He rolled gingerly onto his back and put a hand up to his aching head, but then dropped it at once, realizing that the two of them were holding their heads in mirror images of each other.

She pulled herself to her feet and moved quickly to his side. His eyes were clear and he looked far better than he had the night before. Even the swelling in his face appeared to be subsiding. But still, the paleness of his skin—where it wasn't ghastly shades of purple and yellowish green from the beatings and the sea battle—and the dark lines beneath his eyes all bespoke his pain. She tried to place a hand on his brow, but he pushed it away roughly, before she could check his fever.

"Get away from me, wench, before I wrap my fingers around your throat."

"Try, if you can," Jaime challenged, pushing his hand away and planting her palm firmly on his brow. "Aye, no fever. But quite weak."

Drawing the blanket down, she looked carefully at his wounds, gave a satisfied nod, then covered his chest again. He hadn't bled from the chest wound in almost a full day, and only a small gash by his hip was oozing at all. Moving away from him, she started to fetch what she needed to clean the wound once more.

"Where are all your beloved English masters?" Malcolm asked, letting his eyes appraise her retreating figure. Then, as she turned, his gaze roamed the room. "Don't tell me that these dolts are stupid enough to leave me here without a guard?"

Jaime came back to the side of the bed and placed her supplies next to him. "You've been too weak to so much as lift a finger," she answered. "You don't think they fear your escaping?"

The sight of all her implements flying to the floor brought Jaime's eyes darting back to his.

"You insufferable, ill-tempered, Highland pig." She bent down and started to gather the remnants. "And to think that last night . . ."

Malcolm lifted the blanket off his body and tried to lower his legs over the other side of the bed. But even the struggle of pushing himself up, weak as the effort was, the Highlander found to be too much. And as his strength drained out of him, a thousand pains cut sharply through his shoulder and chest. A wave of nausea and dizziness swept over him, and his head threatened to burst as he teetered for an instant on the flashing yellow edge of unconsciousness.

"Nay, you bullheaded fool," Jaime cried, jumping to her feet and drawing him back down. "You've caused me too much trouble as it is. I don't need your carcass sprawled on the floor, now do I?"

"I don't need any help," Malcolm growled as he let her lower him back down on the sheets. "Least of all, yours."

Jaime's one arm encircled his shoulders, his face lay against her cheek, his lips almost touching the soft wool of her dress. The smell of lavender touched his senses. The softness of her skin brushed against his battered temple. Abruptly, Malcolm jerked his head away and turned his face from her.

"Behave yourself, Malcolm," she said sternly, ignoring his ill-humor as she lay his head back on the bed. "There is no purpose served in you getting out of this bed before your wounds are healed. You are far too weak and a long way from being ready."

"Don't talk to me as if I am your bairn, you foul back-stabbing wench," he snapped, his eyes flashing as he wrapped his fingers as tightly as he could around her wrist. "Do you think I don't understand this game? You want me to live for your dirty, English lover. You and I both know that my corpse won't bring him much of a prize."

"Think that as you will, you savage boor," she retorted, easily wrenching her hand free. If he wanted to think her a wench, so be it. "But you *will* get better while you are under my care—no matter what you think my motives might be."

"Your motives require no deep thinking to figure, lass. They are as clear as the path to hell."

"Only in your disgusting mind," Jaime snapped. "Only a blind man—nay, only you—would spurn what I've done for you. I should have let you rot in that prison. I should have closed my eyes and turned away . . . and pictured you dead. Aye. Dead. As I have pictured you every day since I saw you last."

Malcolm raised his head to answer, but she shoved him back down roughly, making him gasp in pain and clutch at the wound in his chest. She averted her eyes from his face as she held him down, trying to keep out the memory of Malcolm's wedding day, trying to hold back the flood of hurt he'd caused her. His sharp words had drawn blood from wounds that she'd hoped were healed, wounds she now knew had barely scabbed over.

Damn this man, she thought. She was here to help bring him back to health, not to allow him to wreck her and leave her in misery. Taking in a deep breath, Jaime checked her temper and turned her attention back to his wounds.

"Now look at what you've done, you stubborn ape," Jaime whispered, watching a thin, broken line of blood begin to soak through the dressing on his chest. He opened his mouth to respond, she clasped a hand gently over it. "I'll gag you if I must, Malcolm MacLeod. And, believe me, silence would be by far preferable to any more of your discontented carping."

She raised her hand ever so slowly from his lips and looked into his dark and sullen eyes. Quite to her surprise the Highlander remained silent, his eyes taking in her every move as she backed away from the bed. Vaguely unsettled by his stare, Jaime averted her eyes.

"I have to change these dressings," she said quickly.

"Where is the physician?" Malcolm asked shortly. "The Welshman who sewed me up?"

"He left for Cambridge three days ago," Jaime answered as she started to spread the clean dressings beside him. "Master Graves takes the uncommon view that a wound loosely bandaged heals faster."

Malcolm grunted at the idea, and tried to turn slightly away from her.

"I'd be grateful if you wouldn't fight me with this."

"Doesn't the man have an apprentice?" he responded, allowing her to untie the strip that circled his broad chest.

Jaime brightened a bit. Malcolm seemed to have submitted to her unspoken request for truce. "He has a man Davie, but he had to accompany Graves."

"Three days he's been gone?" Malcolm's head sank back wearily. "Have I slept away three full days?"

"Slept? Ha! Unconscious, you were!" Jaime answered, pulling the bloodied linen away from his skin. Keeping her eyes on her job, she tried to ignore the weight of his stare on her. "And as helpless with fever as a bairn."

"Have you been here all the while?"

The slight note of gentleness in his voice made Jaime raise her head and look into his eyes. As if caught, he quickly turned his face away with a darkening frown. A silence filled the space between them, but Jaime knew it would be short-lived. She could almost see his mind churning in a search for words to insult her.

"Do you think I haven't better things to be doing?" she lied, breaking the peace. "I've only looked in once or twice."

"Then why do I recall no one else tending me? Why were you sleeping in that chair just now?"

Jaime colored, muttering weakly, "I already said you've been out of your head with fever." She could feel Malcolm's gaze upon her for a long moment.

" 'Tis surprising, lass, how poor a liar you are."

"I think your fever must be coming on again."

"But why are you so desperate," he said, ignoring her words, "to present me, whole, to your lover upon his return?

Why go so far to keep me alive? It seems to me, you're too damned eager to please him."

She continued with her task, dabbing gently at his wound. In spite of the beads of blood seeping through, Malcolm seemed to be healing well. Far too well.

"There are other ways of pleasing him, you know, ways much more appealing to a man who has been away from a woman." Malcolm's fingers moved and softly caressed her exposed forearm. The immediate shiver that traveled up the skin of her arm didn't go unnoticed by him. "But I suppose by now you must be an expert."

Her hand jabbed hard into his wound, harder than she'd intended. Seeing Malcolm grimace with pain, Jaime backed away slightly.

"Wench!" he swore as the wave subsided.

Jaime only gave him a sweet smile and returned to the dressings. Like a summer storm gathering power, his dark mood charged the air in the room, and Jaime waited for the next onslaught. But, meanwhile, she worked with quick hands and hoped her maid Caddy would arrive soon. That was the way it had been the day before. Upon awakening, Mary had sent Caddy after her truant cousin. And Jaime, in turn, had sweet-talked the slight, middle-aged woman into staying with Malcolm until she herself could again return to the surgery.

Jaime thought back over the past few days. The first night after Graves had left for Cambridge, she had been determined to stay away from the surgery. But that had turned out to be mere foolishness, since she'd spent most of the night going back and forth between her bedchamber and Malcolm's sickbed. She was certain she'd brought more attention to herself than if she'd simply stayed beside him. But she hadn't intended to remain here either of the two previous nights.

"If you'll promise to just lie on your back, I won't retie that strip for now," she said, finishing up the dressing on his chest.

Malcolm grunted and she eyed the bloody wrap just above his hip. She feared that the wound might be festering, and she glanced up at his face. Seeing the wry look he wore, a blush crept into her cheeks. It would be quite uncomfortable changing that dressing while his watchful eyes smirked at her every move. She jumped when he spoke.

"I am certain there is nothing beneath these covers that you haven't seen before, is there?"

"Of course not!" she answered tartly, blushing even more fiercely than before.

A gentle knock at the door brought her quickly to her feet. Giving a soft command to enter, Jaime watched as her maid quietly pushed the door open and limped into the room. Caddy looked hesitantly at the conscious prisoner and then at her mistress. Handing the unused dressings over to the maid, Jaime turned back to Malcolm. He had a look of surprise on his face. "I'll leave you in Caddy's care, for now. But I expect you to treat her with respect. Do you hear?"

A smile of amusement wrinkled the corners of Malcolm's eyes. "Are you telling me that these foolhardy English dogs think me so weak that they will entrust me to this wee woman? On her own?"

"Trusting?" She scoffed in a hushed voice. "Hardly. There are more than enough men outside guarding these doors. And I'm quite certain that any one of them would be more than pleased to finish the job their master started aboard that French ship."

Jaime pulled the sheet up to Malcolm's chin, tucking him as if he were a bairn. "Stay right here for the wee time it'll take to regain your strength. You'll have ample time to show us your foolhardiness once you've healed."

CHAPTER 12

As the velvet of the dress pulled off her shoulder, her orb-like breasts sprang free of the low neckline, and the knight fastened his lips to first one nipple, and then the other.

Her moans were deep-throated, resonant with desire, as she pulled at his hair with long, white fingers.

"Take me," she commanded, yanking his head back and looking at him with eyes clouded with lust. "Take me now."

"You're a fool," he growled, pushing himself to his feet, his hands never leaving off of fondling her breasts. The knight looked down at her moist lips, swollen from his rough kisses. He knew he could not resist. "You heard the horns as well as I. The hunting party will . . ."

"Then stop talking," she ordered huskily, leaning forward and pulling at the laces that held his codpiece in place. "I've waited too long . . ."

His manhood, thick and hard, emerged from its confines, and a tremble raced visibly through her as she took it in her hands, stroking its length. The sound of horns again came through the open window, this time they were only an arrow-shot from the palace.

Catherine stood, a daredevil look flashing into her eyes. "Come, my buck," she enticed, pulling off her starched linen cap and tossing back her hair.

He dug his hands roughly into her waist and turned her around, forcing her face and her exposed breasts down onto the billowing mattress. Taking fistfuls of material in his hands, he pulled the dress up, exposing her ivory legs and heart-shaped buttocks. With a laugh, she tried to squirm around and face him, but he wouldn't let her. With one strong hand he pushed her forward onto the high, curtained bed, and with the other he tore away her linen underclothes. Then he stepped between her legs.

Catherine was ready for him, wet. She was always ready, it seemed. Parting the folds of her womanhood with the tip of his shaft, he felt the flush in his face and instantly gave way to the primal animal urge that blocked out all thought, obliterated all reason, all judgment. He drove into her with a single powerful thrust, exulting in the gasping cry that emitted from her lips.

Holding himself perfectly still, the knight clenched his jaw, waiting as she began to writhe beneath him, her hips undulating as she sheathed him. He reached forward with both hands, taking her golden brown hair in both hands and pulling her head back and turning it until he could see her heavy-lidded eyes, her mouth partially open, the tip of her tongue visible between her full lips.

With excruciating slowness, he slid backward, pausing for only a moment before driving again into her. Again he withdrew and again he plunged, his quickening pace matched by the writhing motions of her hips. Faster and faster he thrust, her cries growing in volume and pitch. But he could no longer hear her. Aware only of the pulsing rhythm in his head and the blinding desire to bury himself deeply within her, the knight rode her—holding her hair like a mane and thrusting again and again—until, with a mighty shudder, his body arched and he released his seed into her.

In a few moments, the knight—still breathing heavily from his exertion—began to extricate himself. As he stood up, he immediately laced his codpiece, and gazed down at the voluptuous beauty, who rolled lazily onto her back. One of Catherine's hands lay on her chest and as he watched, her fingers sensuously tracing the curves of her exposed breast. Her mouth was set in a half smile that conveyed a hint of mockery. He'd seen that look many times before and felt his lips curl into a similar look. The sound of horses and shouting could be heard outside the palace gate, and the knight nodded his head at the window.

"You'd best make yourself presentable for the king, my sweet slut."

"Don't you find me presentable now, my buck?" she asked alluringly, her finger circling her erect nipple.

"Aye, for me, you are. But I don't know that the old boar's heart will hold out, if you don't take some care." The knight turned and headed for the door.

"I know how to manage him," Catherine called softly, rising slightly as he pulled open the thick oak door. He paused to cast one last look back at her. Her face was wearing the same mocking smile. "But, Edward, do try to ride ahead of the party a bit earlier tomorrow."

"You are being unfaithful and you know it."

Jaime rolled her eyes and gestured helplessly with her hands as she paced the room. "Unfaithful to whom, Mary?"

"You know who as well as I, Jaime Macpherson. To Edward."

Jaime made an elaborate show of choking back her laughter, trying to make her cousin's words seem ridiculous. But Mary simply stood with her hands on her hips and frowned.

Jaime decided that Mary was not about to be laughed off. "Then perhaps you would be kind enough to tell me what I have done that could possibly be construed as *unfaithful*?"

"Very well! Where have you spent the past two nights? I'll tell you. You've spent them—*two full nights*—in that man's room. And that was only after wearing a path to the surgery every hour the first night Edward was gone. Just how do you think Edward would feel—how do you expect anyone in the family to feel—when his beloved, his *intended,* will happily spend the night in another man's room, but resolutely avoids spending so much as a moment alone in his company? Have you thought of Edward's feelings, Jaime? He is a sweet, loving man—heartsick at having to leave you—and yet you . . . you . . ."

Jaime pressed her hands to her temples and gazed in wide-eyed disbelief at the younger woman's expression of righteous anger on her cousin's behalf. If it wasn't bad enough that she'd had nothing better than a hard chair for a bed these past three nights, that she'd barely been able to close her eyes for more than a few moments—now, to come back to her room and be subjected to *this*! She shook her aching head incredulously. "Mary, I find it terribly difficult to believe you feel this way. You aren't serious, are you?" Seeing no change in her cousin's demeanor, Jaime approached her. "Please tell me this is all in jest."

"Nay, Jaime. I am totally in earnest in my feelings on this!" she answered. "What you have been doing is extremely inappropriate—considering Edward's intentions regarding you. And since I am the only one who has been witness to behavior entirely unbefitting your situation, I see no alternative . . ."

"You see no alternative to what, Mary?" Jaime asked, a note of challenge creeping into her tone. "Do you intend to run to Edward and inform him of my . . . inappropriate behavior?"

Mary's eyes flickered away for a moment. "You don't understand the Howards, Jaime. In this family, well, such misdeeds . . ."

Jaime's fists tightened at her sides as her anger welled up in her chest. "Misdeeds? You call caring for a dying man a 'misdeed'? You consider helping another 'inappropriate'? Is having a heart and showing compassion wrong in this family? Mary Howard, if you believe this, you are the most close-minded, ill-begotten, young woman I have ever known!"

"Nay, Jaime . . ."

"To think for over a year now I've considered you a confidante, a friend . . . a sister!" Jaime stepped back. "How could I have been so blind? If you truly feel this way, Mary, then I want to see your face no longer. Go and tell him, cousin. Go and proclaim all of these faults you see in me. Because if Edward Howard feels the same as you . . ."

Mary came quickly forward and reached entreatingly for Jaime's hands. "Jaime, I . . . I never meant my words to come out so cruel. But . . ."

Jaime turned her back on the miserable woman. Her head pounded with pain. Her eyes welled with tears. "There is no more to say, Mary."

"Jaime, I . . . I would never betray your trust. I . . . simply thought . . . well, you just get these crazy notions sometimes. You don't think about your future." Mary wiped her tears from her own cheeks and laid a hand on her cousin's shoulder, coaxing Jaime to face her. "I just thought that if I were stronger, then I could make you see some sense. Make you think about what might come out of your . . . coldness to Edward."

"My future with Edward—my manner of treating him now—is my concern, Mary, not yours! I will not allow you or anyone else in this family to force me into his arms." Jaime rubbed her temples. "Despite what you think, I believe I am a good woman. And one who will not act against either her will or her good judgment."

"I know you are a good woman, Jaime," Mary conceded guiltily. "Please forgive my foolishness just now."

There was no point in holding back. Jaime had seen Mary's bouts of righteousness before and understood them for what they were. They were short-lived, harmless, and soon forgotten. But somehow this time, it had hurt. Jaime pushed away the thought that perhaps she had struck too close to home. But there was no point in holding a grudge. She allowed herself to be turned around, and the two cousins embraced. "I don't ever want to talk about this again, Mary. Do you understand?"

Mary took a deep breath and nodded.

Jaime drew back and looked into her eyes. "Your anger with me was because of the care I have shown to the Scot and not so much for my treatment of Edward. Isn't that true?"

Mary nodded.

"I know that this noble family is all you have experienced. But the appropriateness of compassion is not dictated by the rank of the person in need. 'Tis true I've spent many hours at that surgery, but I will never believe that caring for another human being is a betrayal of Edward. If one of the duke's falcons were wounded, if one of the dogs in the kennels were ill . . ."

"I am so confused by all this, Jaime." Mary turned and walked to the middle of the room. "In this past year I've learned to love you as a sister. Even before Catherine left for court, you were so special to me. But I fear the way you now break every rule . . ."

"Which 'rule' tells us that we must neglect our Christian duty to care for those in need, Mary? Is this what the good duke asks of his household?"

"Nay, of course not. 'Tis just that you have become so defiant of established ways. And the Howard family is a very traditional family."

"And, of course, the duke and these traditions are always right!" Jaime said facetiously.

Mary nodded vigorously. "Aye, His Grace's ways are always right because he only wants the best for those under his care. And we should be grateful for his generosity."

"Oh, Mary!" Jaime responded, spurning the thought of such blind faith.

Mary's cheeks flushed with anger. "Look at all the family has done for Catherine. She is no older than we are, and yet, because of the duke, she is now in a position to marry the king himself!"

Jaime looked away and said nothing. Though she would hold her tongue on that particular point, Catherine's position was one Jaime hardly considered enviable.

"And look at me," Mary continued, drawing Jaime's attention back to herself. "As a member of this household, I have enjoyed an upbringing that few women in England can boast of. I have been educated and cared for, and I have an excellent prospect of finding a match in the highest ranks of society. His Grace has shown me more affection than one might hope to find in any family of the Howards' stature."

Jaime bit back the overwhelming urge to take Mary to task over the areas of her education that were so sadly lacking: languages, rhetoric, history, logic. "Honestly, Mary, your loyalty is commendable. And I, too, am grateful . . ."

"As you . . ." Mary hesitated before continuing. "Well, you indeed should be grateful, Jaime. After all, His Grace invited you here and has treated you as one of his own family, knowing . . . well, we both know that you were not a true cousin. Everyone knows that your grandmother was a mistress of Thomas Boleyn's. You are not a descendant of his only wife, His Grace's sister. You have to appreciate what His Grace has done for you. We all call you cousin, though you haven't a drop of Howard blood in you."

"Mary, you cannot understand . . ."

Mary continued on. "And, in spite of your French and Scottish blood . . ."

French and Scottish blood. As her cousin proceeded to talk, Jaime's mind dwelled on those words. Though she had always cherished the public knowledge that she was the daughter of Elizabeth Boleyn and Ambrose Macpherson, Jaime knew that in truth they were not her true parents. She still remembered her true mother, Mary Boleyn, Elizabeth's sister. It had been after her mother's death that Elizabeth, and later Ambrose, had proclaimed to the world that Jaime was their own daughter. But this was a story she didn't care to divulge to the Howard family.

How long, she thought, how long she had lived now under this roof. How easily she'd allowed herself to be blinded to all that went against her beliefs, against her upbringing. The Howards saw her as a rebel, in some ways, but Jaime knew that her rebellion had been just a facade. She had allowed herself to be taken in. She had sought to lose herself in the whirl of Kenninghall's palace life.

But in her heart, Jaime could still feel the sharp wind of the Scottish Highlands, and she could not ignore the forces that had shaped her. Because of all that had occurred in these past few days, Jaime knew that she could no longer let these people run her life to earth like some helpless prey. She was grateful; that much was true. But what price must she surrender to repay the duke's kindness? Jaime could not surrender herself, out of guilt or a false sense of gratitude, to anything or anyone.

Mary paced the room, continuing her lecture unabated, ignoring Jaime as she moved to a small wooden box beside her bed. She ran her fingers over the beautifully inlaid lid, and then opened the box decisively. Reaching inside the neckline of her gown, she drew out a long chain and gazed at the ornate ring dangling from it.

Jaime held the great emerald ring for an instant in her palm.

She knew from Elizabeth that it was a token that had once belonged to her true father. To her it was a link with her own history. But she knew she needed to decide the course of her life with a clear conscience and with open eyes. No link to a past long forgotten would cloud her mind. She had no desire to find the man who had fathered her so long ago.

Without a word, Jaime deposited the ring in the box, shutting the lid with a resounding clap.

CHAPTER 13

The light from the chamber's one window was growing dim, and with the growing darkness, a damp breeze began to make its presence felt. Malcolm, bored and frustrated with the forced inactivity of his convalescence, threw back the blanket covering his chest. He glared defiantly at his keeper, more than half hoping the sight of his bared wounds would bring some curse, some verbal response from his imperturbable keeper's lips. But the resigned sigh from the old woman only served to evoke a pang of guilt in him. He watched in silence as Caddy wearily placed her sewing aside and stood up, rubbing a stiff or sore lower back with a gnarled and bony hand. Wordlessly, she shuffled to his side and covered his chest again with the blanket.

Surly and hostile, Malcolm looked away from her, too proud to admit that his anger had nothing to do with her nor with her treatment of him. She had stayed beside him all day—ever since Jaime had deserted him this morning. He would have thought she'd have checked on them at least once during the day. Not that she'd worry about him, of course, but how about this poor old crone? How did Jaime know that he hadn't strangled the dear old creature during the day? By the Rood, Malcolm could have broken her in two and succeeded in escaping.

Escape! Well, there was something laughable, he thought bitterly. The extent of his movements today had consisted of a short and exhausting lurch around the bedchamber, his blanket clutched about his shoulders, and the old woman eyeing him almost encouragingly from the door. That little jaunt had consumed most of his strength, a fact that grieved him dearly. Well, perhaps tomorrow he would be stronger. He was surprised they hadn't put him in chains already. It wouldn't be long—that he knew. He needed to find a way out.

Malcolm looked in the direction of the window again with a heave of his chest. Another day like this and the boredom would surely kill him. This Caddy woman had not so much as uttered a word all day. He knew she could talk, though—he'd heard her conversing with her mistress this morning. But since Jaime had left, no matter what Malcolm asked, the woman had simply stared at him blankly before turning back to her sewing. So much for getting information out of her.

He ran a hand over the rough texture of his unshaven face and rubbed his eyes. He pulled slightly at the linen bandage that encircled his head. He must look like the devil himself, Malcolm thought. If only he could close his eyes and sleep, he would dream all these people to hell. But even that simple desire seemed to be beyond his reach.

The sound of the door swinging quietly open brought a pleased smile to Malcolm's haggard face. It was the she-devil herself coming in. But at least it was company.

Jaime had hoped he might be sleeping. But now, staring at the roguish gleam in his eyes, at a face alert and—for some reason—amused, she knew she'd wasted a wish.

"It took you long enough to show yourself, though I suppose that's understandable."

Jaime ignored him and turned to Caddy. Spending a few moments talking to the older woman, she continued to ignore Malcolm's comments as she tried to listen to Caddy's obviously valid complaints.

She complained of him talking ceaselessly.

He complained of her being no more than a mute.

She grumbled of him being far too bold for a man in his condition.

He muttered under his breath and called her a broken-down nag.

Mustering all her patience, Jaime shot Malcolm a withering

look and ushered Caddy to the door, asking the woman to bring the man the dinner she'd had the kitchen prepare. But Caddy turned at the doorway and absolutely refused to set foot in his room again—for today, anyway—and warned that she'd only come back as far as his door and leave the dish there.

In a way, Jaime was quite proud of her serving woman's behavior. She knew Caddy still held a grudge against the man for the debacle of a year ago. Caddy was nothing if not loyal. But Jaime was also grateful that Malcolm did not know anything about her servant's familiarity with their past, for if— out of sheer perverseness—he had dared to open the topic, Jaime might have renewed bloodshed to deal with as a result.

Caddy left the room with a huffy toss of the head and a reminder that she was done with him for the day.

That was perfectly acceptable to Jaime. Looking around at him, she decided he certainly appeared improved enough that no attendant would be warranted during the night. In fact, she herself was impatient to settle him in and escape this chamber. The sleepless nights and the stress of her quarrel with Mary had taken its toll on her today. She couldn't wait to get back to her room and crawl into bed.

But no sooner had Caddy left the room when Malcolm began his verbal assault.

"So, and where might a young lady such as yourself have spent such a day as this?" His voice dripped with irony. "Counting the gold, no doubt, that you and your lover are going to split selling me back to my people . . . or were you simply continuing to play the whore?" His sarcastic smile broadened upon seeing Jaime's eyes dart to his face. But she was quick to regain her composure, even as he continued. "I have to tell you, lying here all day with nothing to do is not as useless as it seems. Aye, indeed. I've heard the talk, in spite of this deaf-mute you've put in here to torment me. And I've heard what they say. Is it truly required that you should make a public spectacle of yourself, pleasing him in the garden before a crowd of servants?"

Jaime knew there was no point in arguing with him. He was baiting her, and she was not about to participate in his game. So, biting her tongue and trying to ignore his taunts, she busied herself preparing to change the dressings on his head. That had been one area Caddy had not attempted. She'd probably been afraid to get too close to his sharp tongue. Frankly, Jaime couldn't blame her.

"Aye, and look at you. You shame yourself."

She glanced at him over her shoulder.

"Look at the clothes you wear. English. Where's your modesty, woman?"

She glanced down at her attire. She was wearing a summer dress of yellow linen, with a square neckline that barely exposed the flesh on top of her breasts. This was probably one of the more modest fashions worn by any woman in the household.

"There's nothing wrong with my clothes."

"Nay, not for an English whore."

Jaime glared at him from where she stood.

"Well, if that's what you've become, there's little to be done about it."

She shook her head and tucked everything she needed under her arms, vowing to herself that she'd not be reduced to his level. That was what he was after. A reaction. An unpleasant reaction.

Malcolm continued as if her silence were a confirmation of what he'd said. 'Aye, 'tis a pitiable condition, but there you are. What's done is done. Well, then, what are we going to do tonight, wench? You might as well sleep here as on that chair."

Jaime moved ner supplies next to his bed and placed them all on the nearby chair, all the while avoiding his eyes. She could feel her face burning, but she held her temper and concentrated on her pile of dressings. She was now angry enough that she knew even one look in his direction, and she would burst like a bubble.

Malcolm pulled the blanket aside—exposing a sinewy thigh and hip—and patted a spot next to him on the bed. "Aye, dearest. You can sleep here. But I have to warn you that even in this weakened condition, I can still outmatch any English lover, never mind that yellow-livered pustule of a man you've taken up with."

"That will do, Malcolm," she replied curtly, unfolding the strips of linen on the edge of his bed.

"You think so, lass?" He brushed his knuckles roughly against the back of her hand, and Jaime withdrew it as if she'd been stung. "We haven't even started yet!"

This time her control snapped. "Stop it, Malcolm!" she nearly shouted.

"I won't," he growled, grabbing her fiercely by the wrist. "I am no fool. You came to this room of your own free will. And not for any reason of nursing me to health, was it? Your lust drives you to me. You want to compare me to that carrion of a lover, now don't you?"

Jaime stared in silence.

"I know he is away, dearest. So, now that you are not bound by any need to appear decent, you come here to relieve your lust and sharpen your skills—in bed. In my bed!" His hand tugged harshly at her wrist, making her lose her balance and lean heavily on the bed. "Well, here we are, my sweet. I am more than willing. Let's begin. Now, lass, while the evening is young!"

She struggled against his grip using her other hand to keep from falling into his lap. A feeling of helplessness—desperation even—swept coldly through her. She turned her gaze and looked into his embittered face.

"You've gone mad, Malcolm."

"Then it is you who have driven me to it."

"Let go of my wrist."

"I will. When we are finished!"

"Malcolm, listen to yourself." Hurt crept into her voice. She could not keep it out. "It is I, Jaime. It is Jaime you are treating like a whore. Jaime, the woman you've known all your life."

"Don't waste your breath. You are not that woman." He laughed, his tone scornful. "But in case you have forgotten, dearest. The woman I knew would never have delivered me to these devils. She would never have betrayed my trust. The Jaime I knew was gentle and kind. She was passionate and giving. She was a woman raised with love. She was loyal . . ."

"The woman you knew was a fool!" Jaime straightened her

arm to give herself more distance. "Nothing more than a dreaming simpleton. She was a child, blinded with lies. She believed in love and promises. But that child grew up and opened her eyes to the painful truths about what happens to those who blindly keep faith!"

"Seeing the change in her, I wish she had truly gone blind."

"Why?" she shot at him. "So she might lock herself away forever, to mourn her treacherous love?"

"She was too young to know the meaning of the word." Malcolm turned his eyes away for a moment, letting go of her wrist. "How could she mourn the loss of something she'd never known?"

"Never known?" Jaime's voice crackled with rage. She straightened up, but made no attempt to walk away. "But that's where your mistake lies, knave. She had more affection and love in her, even as a child, than you could possibly know. But she . . . she was misled by false words and impossible dreams."

He began to respond, then paused, a troubled look momentarily crossing his face as he seemed to ponder her charge. "False words by whom, Jaime? We had always been friends. What false words? What have I ever said that you could construe as a promise of any kind?"

Jaime turned her back on him.

"You cannot walk away," he barked. "I am tired of having to fight false accusations. Tired of this cloud that hangs over me. This cloud that smacks of wrongdoing when I don't know how I could have done wrong."

"I have never openly accused you of anything."

"It would be much easier if you did," he answered sharply. "The puzzle would be much simpler to solve if I were at least given the pieces." He reached out and, this time, more gently took a hold of her wrist, causing her to turn and face him. "Jaime, since I last laid eyes on you, the Macphersons—with the exception of Fiona and Alec—have never treated me the same. Your parents, most of all, seem distant. If I have committed some great injustice, then 'tis one that I am neither prosecuted for nor pardoned. There is a mist that surrounds me, and though I walk on, there are things that I cannot see. How did I mislead you? Tell me now if . . ."

"You never misled me, but do not blame me for your misfortunes." Jaime wrenched her wrist free. She already knew that he spoke the truth. He had never asked her to marry him. In her mind, though, he was still guilty of allowing her to hope. But she wouldn't reveal that to him.

Taking a deep breath, she reached down to undo the wrapping around his head. She would finish her tasks here quickly and flee this room. Her hands trembled slightly, but she forced herself to concentrate.

"But I do blame you," he said finally, his voice severe. "All that I suffer finds its origin in you."

"You give me more credit than I deserve."

"I don't believe I do."

"Think what you will," she replied quietly. "It is a coward's way, to be sure."

Malcolm stared straight ahead for a long moment as she unwound the outer linen wrapping.

"It all began at that cursed wedding, didn't it?" he said grimly. Turning his head, he looked up into her shocked expression. "When you burst into that chapel at Newabbey wearing that dress. It was a wedding dress, wasn't it? I wanted to think it was just a childish prank. But is wasn't, was it?"

She peeled off the bloodstained linens, and gazed with unseeing eyes at the wounds beneath his matted hair.

"Was it?" he asked with some impatience.

Needing time to compose herself, she moved to a table across the chamber and carried back a wooden bowl of water.

"WAS IT?" he shouted, glaring at her angrily.

"What is past, is past!" she answered sharply. "You are a married man now, and a baser knave than I thought if you cannot leave off tormenting me so. Why should you go on pondering an incident dead and buried?"

She soaked the dressings and began to wash away the dried blood in his hair, feigning a calmness that they both knew was a lie. His eyes followed the movement of her hand, a frown on his flushed brow telling of his agitation. She couldn't hold her tongue, but perhaps by pretending to be indifferent, she might more easily ignore his question.

"I never had a chance to compliment you on your choice. She is indeed a beautiful woman." Jaime's attention was drawn to the sharp movement of his head as he turned his face from her. She pressed her lips together tightly. How he must miss her, she thought. "I never even asked you her name, but if you don't care to talk about her . . ."

Her words trailed off, and the ensuing silence hung heavily in the room. Then his eyes turned upward, and he stared into her face. "Flora," he said quietly. "Her name was Flora."

Her name was Flora, she repeated silently, his words echoing in a hollow place deep within her. Her name *was* Flora. The word reverberated in soft and velvet tones. It clung to the walls of her heart.

"*Was?*" she croaked.

He turned his face toward the window.

"She died only a month after we wed."

He fell silent as an overwhelming sense of guilt, of grief for him, settled in her heart. Suddenly, she wanted to reach out to him and soothe his inner pain. But she held back, knowing that he would toss any gesture back in her face. Then, as she gazed at his grim profile, emotion drained out of his face, and his expression became calm, thoughtful.

Malcolm turned back to her. "She was very young."

Jaime lowered her eyes and stared at her hands, ashamed now of all the times she'd thought of the two of them in anger.

"Have you no interest in how she died?"

She shook her head.

"Do you not wish to hear every detail?"

"Nay, Malcolm."

"Or of the pain she suffered?"

She shook her head again, her eyes misting. "Please don't."

Malcolm gazed on her, his watchful eyes searching her face as if he was seeing her for the first time.

"I should leave you to your rest," she said quietly, suddenly uncomfortable. "Your head wounds no longer need to be covered. I'll have Caddy . , .."

Before she could finish her sentence, his hand again took hold of her wrist. "Stay."

The simple word made her heart leap. Even in the fading light, she could see that his eyes held nothing of the anger she'd seen there before. She nodded slowly, and remained where she stood. His eyes turned away, but they were clear as he began a story in the growing gloom. A story to fill the emptiness of the night.

"It is jarring to think that I knew so little of my wife when she was alive, and yet learned so much about her after she died." He unconsciously let go of her wrist. "Though I knew nothing of it until after our marriage, Flora had been a sickly child since birth. But being the only bairn of Duncan, leader of the MacDonald clan, Flora had always been carefully protected, her sickness kept secret from all who lived on the island. I do not know whose idea it was first, but when she grew old enough to wed, everything seemed to point to a marriage between the two of us, a marriage that would unite the MacDonalds and the MacLeods. Such a union was favored in the councils of both clans. Everything seemed perfect. Both Duncan and I knew it would save the lives of many victims of our senseless clan feuding. The union would improve the lot of all who lived under my rule."

Jaime sat down quietly on the edge of his bed.

"Flora and I met only once before our wedding, in a meeting arranged and overseen by members of both of the clans' councils. I should have guessed it then. She was so pale and so very, very thin. Even at the prospect of the upcoming wedding, she sat silent, hardly responsive at all to the excitement. I was prepared to pass it off as shyness, but Duncan— afraid, I suppose, of me backing out of the contract—was quick to say that Flora had the most delicate of nerves."

"You mean you never talked to her alone until after you wed?"

"Not even after. Alone, that is!" he said with a short laugh. "The MacDonalds always made sure there were a great many present whenever we met. And then on that awful day, halfway through the wedding feast, she took to her sickbed. Not a good omen for a long marriage, I'm afraid, and it threw quite a cloud over the wedding feast. I'm surprised you didn't hear of it. I believe you were still in Skye. She died in that same bed scarcely a month later. Her father later told me that she had consented to the marriage with the hope of being able to bear a child. She had known that an offspring of ours could bring a lasting peace to the islanders of Skye and Lewis. I suppose she hoped to be remembered for something more than a killing sickness and short life."

And here she had been, Jaime thought grimly, sitting in France, entertaining the fancy of becoming his wife. How selfish of her to think only of her own happiness. How loyal he'd been in looking after his people and their welfare. He turned his dark gaze upon her. But he'd never told her, Jaime thought, looking back at him. He'd never made her understand his motives for marrying another. But then, why should he? In the long months that had followed, she'd sorted out the events that had led to her misunderstanding. The letters prior to the wedding had all been misinterpreted by her because of her childish hopes. He had never intended to marry her, but in her adolescent infatuation, she had let herself think so. Into every letter she had injected her own desires and intentions, including that last letter from Elizabeth and Ambrose. Everyone had assumed Jaime knew of Malcolm's upcoming wedding to Flora MacDonald. Their excitement about meeting her on the Isle of Skye had been for no other reason than in seeing her again. Oh, what a fool she'd been. But fool or no, she had suffered a misery that had deadened something inside her.

"I never knew Flora in the way a husband knows his wife. We never had a chance to develop any real affection; we certainly never learned to love each other as a wedded couple should. But I respected her, and I admired her courage. She faced her fate with the fortitude of a warrior." He stroked his fingers along the line of his jaw, momentarily lost to some thought. "I suppose 'twas all for the best that the end came as quickly as it did." His dark eyes fixed on hers. "Now you know it all."

"I am sorry, Malcolm."

He shrugged his shoulders and looked away. After a moment, though, he turned and faced her. "I answered your question, but you've ignored mine."

"Your question?" she repeated vaguely, feigning ignorance.

"Aye, in coming to Skye. That dress."

" 'Tis not important." It was Jaime's turn to shrug her shoulders. She had no desire to answer his question. After hearing all she had about Flora and his marriage, Jaime would die before admitting to him what had been foolish, childish hopes. "But tell me, Malcolm. What happens now?"

"Here? You tell me. I am the prisoner."

"Nay, I mean at the Skye," she corrected. "Between the MacLeods and MacDonalds."

"What else? They are back to their old bickering once again."

"But why?" Jaime asked sharply. "That is how they honor the woman's memory?"

Malcolm's eyebrows cocked with surprise. "Jaime, dearest, they hardly even took note of her passing. The fishermen still fight over the best spots to fish. The crofters still raise holy hell every time a sheep gets filched. Every time some bonnie MacDonald lass gets whistled at by a MacLeod lad, I have to send in warriors to separate them."

"Isn't there anything you and Duncan can do? To make them live together peaceably?"

"Aye, we break a few heads when we need to, and we reason with them when they'll listen." Malcolm lifted one knee and absently leaned it against Jaime's back. "Duncan's a decent enough man. There is no feud between us. But the rest . . . they are islanders. They've distrusted, even hated, one another for a thousand years. It'll take more than the wishes of a dying woman to heal those wounds. The two clans need to be bound by blood. They are—every one of them—as thick-headed as any Highlander, and the menfolk will steal a sheep and kill one another with as much joy as bedding a woman." His gaze rested on her mischievously. "But now that you mention it, Duncan and I *did* talk of a plan. Of one that in time might bear fruit."

She brightened at once. "Tell me."

"Well, Duncan MacDonald has taken a bonnie new wife these six months, and when I left for Rotterdam, the old bull was—by all accounts—busily working on producing a new heir."

Jaime blushed at the image, but then the ramifications of Malcolm's announcement set in. "And? I suppose he expects you to marry this new offspring?"

A smile tugged at the corner of Malcolm's mouth. "Well, I thank you, lass. That's a high compliment from you thinking I'll be . . . well, *up* to it so late in life."

She flushed crimson. "What I . . . what I meant was . . ." Jaime cleared her throat, trying to sound unperturbed. But with his leg resting comfortably against her, it was just too unsettling for her to sit any longer beside him on the bed. She thought it much wiser to stand.

A firm hand descended on her arm, though, forcing her to remain where she was. "Aye? You were saying?"

Jaime stared down into her lap. The veins in his broad, tanned hand looked like strong cords running into thick, powerful fingers. Her face burning, Jaime forced out her words. "Many men . . . many marry younger women . . . later in life."

"Ah! You're assuming, of course, that Duncan's record with this wife will turn out better than the rest."

"The rest?" Startled, she looked up at him. "Have there been many?"

"I believe the man's buried at least five wives—and the Lord knows how many mistresses the old bull has had."

She stared at him wide-eyed. Wives? Mistresses? This was certainly far different from the way the Macphersons behave. Her uncle Alec was laird—he'd even ruled the Isles of Skye and Lewis while Malcolm was a young lad—but she was certain he'd always been devoted to one woman, Fiona. Aye, devoted. At least, she was fairly certain.

"Duncan had only one child out of all those women," Malcolm continued. "So the chances of him having another heir is a wee bit remote. But he is not giving up, by the Rood, no matter how hard he might have to try. And so, lass, who am I to discourage him? Though Duncan's uglier than an old dog, this new one is quite bonnie and young. Who am I to hinder him!"

"Then, if your plan is not to wait and to marry . . . his next infant heir . . ."

"Assuming it is a girl . . ."

"Aye. If you're not going to wait, then how do you expect to bind the two clans?"

"Well, lass, I've been thinking about coming up with an heir of my own," he said, his face growing sober.

"Oh?"

"Aye. That way, if Duncan and his new wife ever produce a bairn . . . well, then that'll be something for our children to work out between them."

"Of course!" she replied lightly. "That sounds simple enough."

"I am glad you think so, Jaime." His fingers locked like a vise on her arm, and there was a gleam in his eye. "Then you're ready to have my bairn?"

CHAPTER 14

"Amidsummer wedding, perhaps?" the duke of Norfolk suggested, eyeing Robert Radcliffe, earl of Essex and new Lord Great Chamberlain, across the table.

"That's too soon," Essex responded, looking noncommittally at a parchment in his hand. "Though we expect to receive word any day now regarding the negotiations with the queen's family, it is unreasonable to expect the king to officially annul his marriage to Anne of Cleves until the end of July."

"A fall wedding, then," the duke growled irritably.

"Nay, Norfolk. Much too late for King's liking."

Catherine Howard picked up her cup of wine and glared petulantly at the two men huddled at one end of the table. Her uncle and the Lord Chamberlain were two of the dullest old men alive—she was convinced of it. Staring at the Lord Chamberlain's bald head, she decided he would probably collapse into a pile of dust if someone were to shake him. She looked at the servants and clerks standing in two small groups by the door and wondered which one of them would be man enough to do it. With a quiet sigh, she glanced back at the two noblemen discussing her wedding—every detail of the blasted thing.

Catherine was bored. She couldn't recall ever being quite so bored. She had been standing in this room for over half an hour listening to their drivel. Why, she thought angrily, couldn't they just finish this? And why did she need to be here, anyway?

Sighing audibly this time, she turned her back on the two men, and her gaze came to rest on Edward, sitting at the far end of the long table. Her eyes boldly devoured all of him. His handsome face wore an expression of boredom, as well, and his eyes flashed only momentarily in her direction. She could tell he was forcing himself to look past her; even his look of boredom had vanished. But she knew he wouldn't be able to keep his eyes off her for long.

Making Edward crazy with desire had always been a favorite sport for Catherine, and one in which she was quite adept. Throwing a casual glance over her shoulder at the two older men, Catherine sauntered slowly down the room, holding the cool cup against her cheek with one hand and letting her other hand trail over the backs of the carved wood chairs. Her eyes focused on Edward's face—on his gray eyes, his full lips. Gazing at that mouth, she could even now feel his lips and tongue tugging at her nipples. Oh, how he had made her cry out in ecstasy, his long, thick shaft nestled deep within her.

Feeling fresh desire stir deep in her belly, Catherine continued to make her way toward him. Edward had pushed his chair back from the table, and he sat with his legs spread before him, one hand resting on the polished wood surface. By his hand on the table sat a pitcher of wine. Catherine's chest heaved slightly as she considered what would happen if the two of them were alone right now. She would move directly in front of him and raise her skirts. As always, he would be far too impatient to let her undress. She would climb onto his lap, straddling him. It would be a simple business to free his manhood of its codpiece. She could feel the heat of his breath on her skin as his strong hands pulled down her dress. His teeth and tongue, rough on her nipple. His arousal, pulsing and hard, probing at her moist folds and driving deep between her legs. Catherine paused, shuddering involuntarily with the exhilaration of the vision.

Letting out a long breath, she moved even closer. The two gruff voices droned on behind her. Catherine thrilled at the sight of Edward's eyes, now focused on her every step, rising only to linger over at her swaying hips, rising again and halting on her breasts as she laid the cup against her skin there. She felt the wetness between her legs and the tightness in her middle that cried out for the man's touch.

Catherine stopped beside him and, with a casual wave, dismissed an approaching servant, picking up the pitcher of wine herself. Her skirts brushed seductively against the knee of one of his high boots.

"Did you have an enjoyable morning, cousin?" she asked sweetly, filling her cup to the top.

"Most . . . entertaining!" he growled softly.

"The hunt went well?"

"The game here is . . . so abundant!" His eyes lingered meaningfully on her breasts before glancing away toward the servants. They were too far away to hear anything.

"Ah, but so little time for the truly pleasurable pursuits!"

"Aye, cousin." His gaze turned slowly and bore into her eyes. "And it would appear the time for those pleasures is growing even shorter."

"You could take me right here, if that would be more to your liking." Catherine's eyes roamed the room. Her leg rubbed suggestively at his knee.

A wry smile crossed Edward's face. "I think that might just upset the negotiations going on at the other end."

"But it would certainly add some excitement."

Edward stared at her. "Excitement? Aye. And danger, too."

"I thought you lived for danger, cousin." Catherine brought the cup to her lips and let her pink tongue lick seductively at the edge. His eyes never left her mouth. "I am quite certain you'd find the rewards worthy of the risk."

"I am certain, as well."

"Then perhaps, tonight . . ."

"Catherine, Edward!"

Her uncle's voice cut through their talk like Lenten sleet. Shutting her eyes, she tried to control her sudden anger, her annoyance at his meddling. As Edward stood, she opened them, turning with the look of a demure and obedient niece. "Do you require something of me, uncle?"

Norfolk pushed his chair sharply away from the table, and the Lord Great Chamberlain followed suit.

"Have the documents sent up, Essex, if you would," Norfolk said to the other man, a note of satisfaction obvious in his tone.

The Lord Chamberlain nodded and bowed to Catherine. "Your servant, mistress."

"It's settled," the duke of Norfolk said, rubbing his hands as Essex and his entourage exited the chamber. "Assuming the negotiations are concluded in Flanders regarding the queen's future, you're to wed at the end of July. And apparently it makes no difference to the king whether it takes place here, at Kenninghall, or on the royal barge in the Thames!"

Catherine nodded. "Thank you, Your Grace."

"Edward," the duke said, rolling up the parchment on the table. "I believe it would be highly politic of you to marry Jaime after the king and Catherine marry."

"Whatever you think best, Father," Edward replied indifferently.

"Besides," Norfolk continued, "we still need to work out the details of her grandfather's estates. And I don't know that the bloody Macphersons are about to give up the lands in Kent without a bit of arm twisting."

"Very well," Edward agreed, glancing up at Catherine's face. Her skin was livid with rage. Her eyes were daggers of fury.

"Come along, Catherine, Edward." The duke started for the door without a backward glance. "We've a great deal to do."

"We shall follow along momentarily," the knight said, trying to keep his voice even as his father passed out of the room.

"You are to marry?" she hissed under her breath as soon as the door closed behind the departing duke.

He nodded, "Aye, why not?"

"To Jaime? A half-blooded Scot?"

"To our cousin," he answered quietly.

"She is no cousin of mine. She's a self-serving prig. She is a Scot . . . barely more than an animal! She knows nothing of propriety. She mixes servants and masters, for God's sake!"

Edward looked away, trying to distance himself from her anger.

"She is a faster worker than I thought." Catherine slammed her cup on the table. "Tell me, how is she in bed?"

He ignored her question. "We should be going."

"She must be foul ... otherwise you would have come bragging to me!" She sniggered viciously. "It must be her money."

His face blackened, and his eyes were narrow slits of steel, but Catherine was too angry to notice. She and Edward were lovers long before she had left for court. He had taken her first when she was just fourteen. And he had come to her bed every day since he'd arrived here. She didn't care a jot whom he married. But to hear from the old duke, and not from him, that he was to wed that half-Scot, half-French hussy! Coward, she thought.

"Well, *dear* cousin, I never thought this day would come."

"Marriage between us was never a possibili ..." Edward began.

"Marriage? Hah!" Her mirthless laugh had the cutting edge of a blade. "Nay, I mean the day when you would bend to being dependent on your wife. To ask her father, a beast of a Scot, for a spending allowance. To have *them* provide you with a home." A nasty smile appeared on her face. "Tell me, does she already carry your balls in her money purse?"

"Catherine," he growled threateningly.

"Perhaps you'd prefer to be living in Scotland. It is no secret at court that once the old duke dies, your brother Surrey will be cutting you off without a farthing."

She watched Edward's hands curl into fists at his side—his jaw clenched, the muscles on the side of his face twitching nervously. Well, she thought with satisfaction, she had struck close to home.

"The second son," she continued, her tone thick with feigned pity. "Poor Edward, the boy needs to marry a rich girl to survive. Ah, desperate Edward, selling his pride and placing his neck under his enemy's foot, just so they will pay his keep."

She leaned forward and hooked her fingers into his belt. Her whisper was barely audible when she spoke to him. "On second thought, I could take care of you, cousin. Do not forget,

I am to become your queen. And you must gratify me as I please. Aye, please me *well,* Edward, and I perhaps will give you enough to keep you out of the Scot's clutches."

Without another word, Catherine spun on her heel and started for the door, never seeing the gaze, cold and ruthless, that he turned upon her.

CHAPTER 15

Jaime tried to leap from the bed, but Malcolm's firm grip on her arm held her in place.

"Have you gone mad?" she cried.

"I don't believe so. Do I look mad?"

She shook her head in disbelief. "But you . . . you are a widower . . ."

"You think widowers swear off women when their wives die?"

"But what of your grief? Your loss? You cannot just . . . just think of such things . . . such a short time after her death!"

"By the Rood, Jaime, 'tis been over a year since Flora died. Under the most tragic of circumstances, a man could not be expected . . ." As he paused, Malcolm's face was calm and his gaze direct. "I never even bedded Flora. In the eyes of the law, I suppose we were never truly married. We never consummated our . . ."

"Please," she said exasperatedly. "You don't have to tell me the details. But I think 'tis quite insensitive of you to harbor such thoughts."

He lifted himself off his pillow and pulled her closer to his chest. "Still my wee, contentious creature," he whispered softly, inhaling her sweet scent. He had already marked the womanly curves of her body beneath the dresses, the gentle flair of her hips, the full swell of her breasts. "Still quibbling, still quarreling for no reason than to partake of a good brawl."

She tried to free herself, but her effort was halfhearted, at best. "No reason?" she challenged, glaring as fiercely as she could at him. "Here you are asking me to give birth to a love child, and you call that no reason?"

"You've no reason to be scared."

"I am not scared!"

"Very well then!" he nodded. "I should tell you I plan to do my share."

"Your share?"

"Aye." Malcolm nodded with a mischievous smile. "I've mended enough to make love to you." She felt his fingers play ever so slightly over her arm. "I'm certain I'm man enough to bring you pleasure—perhaps you will even call out my name. But you'll not be asking for more, right off, for I'll satisfy you, lass. Trust me, you'll enjoy it immensely."

She felt herself blushing to the roots of her hair. It took her a moment to catch her breath. Could this be happening? She stared as Malcolm shifted his weight and laid his hand on her leg. A bolt of lightning exploded in Jaime's brain.

"You are a rogue, a knave, and a scoundrel, Malcolm MacLeod!" she shouted, again squirming in an unsuccessful attempt to get off of the bed. "And if you think you can scare me—or intimidate me with such ill-mannered, churlish prattle, then you have . . ."

"I've always thought you liked bairns."

"I *do* like bairns! I love children!" She swung around and glowered at him. "So long as they are not offspring of yours, you disgusting, thoughtless, sheep stealing . . ."

"You'll be perfect for the job," he interrupted. "You are intelligent and healthy. You've a good build."

"I am not a horse, Malcolm."

"I know, my sweet. If I were looking to produce a colt to be my heir, I would never come to you, lass. As a filly, you were quick enough over short ground, but for a long run . . ." His voice trailed off doubtfully.

"I ran you down every time, Malcolm MacLeod, and you know it. And that was over *any* distance."

"That was because I let you," he answered playfully.

"Let me?" she asked incredulously. "You used to hide like a snake in the grass."

"Aye. And I've always known you'd be as tasty as some of those field rats that kept me company while I waited for you to catch up."

It took a moment for his words to sink in before she began to giggle. "Quite a compliment!" she managed to get out.

He waved his hand in the air. "Only the best for you, lass!"

"I never guessed that a MacLeod could be so refined in his wooing." Jaime looked away from his grinning face and stared straight ahead, trying to wipe the smile from her face. The truth was, she hadn't felt this happy in years. Simply to be able to sit with him, to talk with him. Her smile disappeared without a trace as she recalled that this moment could not last. The reality of their situation lurked right outside this closed door. Her tone was more restrained when she next spoke. "Where were we?" she asked.

"I believe, lass, you were getting ready to accept my offer."

She frowned at him, but he laughed and wrapped one arm tightly around her waist, pulling her even closer to him. Tight against him, she could feel his warmth. Feel her own excitement rising, pulsing through her blood. There was something very familiar about being close to him. Something magical, like a remembered dream. Like the smell of the oat field after the harvest, or the indefinable smell of snow in the air. She realized he was peering intently at her face.

"So then," she asked, "you're no longer angry with me?"

"Nay, Jaime." He shook his head. "But I believe you are still angry with me."

She hesitated a moment to answer. He poked her in the side, making her laugh.

"Answer me, you vixen."

"I cannot remain angry with you any longer, Malcolm. Not for today, anyway."

One large hand covered two smaller ones flitting nervously in her lap. Her shining eyes, her cascading waves of black satin hair, her sculpted lips; Malcolm was falling for a woman he'd known all his life, but never known. Then her words sank in, jolting him into a new awareness. As if stepping through layers of a fog, he saw her clearly. All the teasing now pushed aside, all the past torments forgotten, his own anger long gone—he now saw Jaime.

His Jaime. That's how she'd always referred to herself before. He knew now that he'd always taken her for granted. Jaime was his, and that was a fact. It was all quite clear now. What right had he to place blame on her for the events of these days past. If anyone should shoulder the blame, it must be Malcolm MacLeod, and no other. In his heart, he'd known from the start that Jaime hadn't betrayed him to these people—she was trying to save his life. And all that, even after the pain he'd caused her on his wedding day.

That was why she would forgive him only for today. All the angry words, all the names—they were nothing compared to the disappointment she must have endured entering the church and seeing him with another.

She didn't have to answer him, he knew the truth. That had been no prank. She had worn that dress for the purpose of marrying him on the Isle of Skye that day. She had always thought of them as two bodies having one soul—intended for each other. And, in truth, he'd never really tried to shake the belief. He had let her go on, dreaming that he, too, had shared that faith. Perhaps he, too, really *had* known it, tucking the belief away in some dark recess of his mind. And he'd just spent his life waiting for her.

But when she had gone to France, and he'd faced the problems of the clans in Skye, fate had taken a hand. Marriage to Flora—for the good of his people—was the appropriate course. He was certain it would bring peace to the Isle of Skye and the Hebrides. But he'd been wrong.

Malcolm reached up and let a strand of her soft hair slide over his fingers. Jaime had come back into his life a woman. A beautiful woman.

Their eyes met. Jaime knew something was happening to her—to them. Her life's love of him, shackled and locked away for the past year, was breaking its bonds, escaping the barred cell deep within her. She let her eyes explore his masculine face. His growth of beard. His sensual, unsmiling mouth.

His voice was soft. "Remember when you were leaving for France—and you came looking for me across the hills?"

She felt the burning redness creep into her face, and let out a deep sigh. "Oh, please don't remind me of my wretched behavior. I have reminded myself of it too many times in recent days and . . ."

Malcolm ran a gentle hand across her lips to silence her concern.

"Do you remember, Jaime, how the heather spread up to the crests of the hills and down to the very banks of the River Spey?"

She nodded slowly and lowered her eyes to her lap. "I had no thoughts of the heather that day, Malcolm."

His fingers gently took hold of her chin and lifted it until their eyes met again. "I know, lass. You wanted something from me that I couldn't give."

She felt herself being swept away in the swirling depths of his dark eyes. She was once again that young lass, desperately hoping to be kissed by this man. Her very existence depended on that one touch of his lips to hers.

"I remember that day all too well," she whispered finally.

If he felt any pain, his face never showed it as his strong hands turned her on the bed until they were lying face to face. A delicious shudder shot through her as he raised his hand and touched her face. Her skin tingled, the rushing blood in her head matching the pounding in her chest. As he ran the tips of his fingers over her skin, she leaned her face into his touch. He traced the arch of her brow, the length of her nose—he ran his thumb over her parted lips. Each place, in turn, was left scorched by his touch.

"Do you remember what you wanted from me then?"

She nodded.

"Ask me, Jaime!" he said huskily, raising both hands and threading them into her black tresses. "My bonnie Jaime! Ask me now."

Their eyes connected and a lightning bolt of desire filled the space between them.

"Kiss me, Malcolm."

His lips claimed hers in a kiss that shook her with passion.

He wrapped her in his arms. Like a drought-stricken flower feeling the first droplets of rain, she reached, she tasted, she straightened, and opened her petals for more. She had waited so long. Clutching at his hair and returning his kiss, she thrilled in the joy of his embrace.

"My bonnie, bonnie Jaime," he whispered, drawing back slightly and then taking her with him as he lay back on the bed. "How did I ever let you go?"

She pulled herself to his side, carefully avoiding his wounds. "I thought I'd lost you forever. How could this be?" she whispered, bringing her face close and brushing her lips against his. "This can only be a dream."

"This is no dream." He turned his body to face her. They lay side by side. Facing each other. Drinking from each other's lips. Lost in the abundance of feelings that were pouring from their souls.

Jaime had never been held the way Malcolm was holding her now. Her fingers combed caressingly through his long, brown hair. She traced the soft ridges of his ear, the line of his whiskered jaw. His eyes were focused on hers, and she could see tenderness as well as desire in them.

His hand smoothed the material of her dress—now stroking her back, now her side, now touching the curve of her hip, the rounded flair of her buttock. Jaime drew in her breath as his hand moved slowly upward, fondling the side of her breast as their lips continued their passionate feast.

"You've grown so bonnie ... so womanly," he growled. "Worthy of a better man than I."

"Kiss me, Malcolm," she whispered against his lips. "Kiss this woman."

The Highlander's blood, already roaring in his head, surged at the huskiness in her voice. Desire seemed to take on a life of its own, and pushed him to the edge of his control. He rolled toward her, crushing her to him.

"I want you, Jaime. I want you badly." His mouth descended in a kiss, demanding and hard.

His mouth was hot, possessive, carnal. Jaime's eyes widened as Malcolm's tongue darted across her full, moist lips, searching for entry and finding access. Before she could fight his invasion, a raw passion exploded within her. Her restraint disappeared in an instant. His thrusting tongue rubbed boldly against hers, daring her to follow.

It was madness and Malcolm knew it, but he couldn't stop. She pressed against him, arching her back as he moved from her mouth and trailed his lips downward over her chin and over the skin of her throat. By the Rood, he wanted her. And he would take her, here, in this bed. Her fingers were stroking his bare back with their tips. It didn't matter that someone else had taken her before him. It hadn't been her fault. She had thought him lost to her then. He'd been responsible for that, himself.

Softly, his fingers caressed her ivory skin from her throat down to the round fullness of her breasts. He could feel the warmth of her body, the firm flesh, the trembling shudders that his touch brought on. A moan of pleasure deep in her throat filled him with certainty.

Now! This moment! This is the time that matters most, he cried silently. And what happens from this moment on! And this point hence, Malcolm vowed, she would be his. Forever into eternity, she'd belong to him.

He drew down the neckline of her dress until her breasts sprang free. His lips locked on the nipple rising erect at the center of the rose-colored aureole. He heard her gasp and felt her bloom beneath him. Her hands tugged at his hair, pressing his face even tighter to her breast. Then, as he continued to suckle, moving from one nipple to the other, he felt her knee rise instinctively and take possession of his thigh.

The rush of heat scorching through her body lit Jaime's senses with explosive energy. Her mind whirled with confusion at these newfound sensations, while her body screamed for more. She arched her back as his tongue laved her breasts, and she lost the ability to breathe as his hand pulled her skirt up over her legs. She gasped with shock and pleasure as his strong fingers stroked the skin of her legs above her hose. When his hand found the juncture of her thighs, Jaime found herself reveling in the waves of white heat that shot through her and threatened to obliterate all reason.

As he lifted his head from her breasts and looked deeply

into her eyes, she slid her hand downward over the powerful sinews of his buttock and his hip. Jaime could feel his throbbing arousal, thick and hot, pressing against her thigh. She didn't care if he thought of her as wanton. This moment, this passion—created by the touch of their bodies—was ever so different from the aversion she felt at Edward's treatment of her. Nay, she thought through the fiery mist within her, everything with Malcolm seemed so right. So perfect.

Fighting for control, the Highlander gazed down at the beauty in his arms, knowing that he would certainly die if he did not take Jaime now. More than anything else, he wanted to bury himself deep within her, bring her to heights of unimaginable pleasure, and pour his seed into her. His eyes took in her swollen lips, her heaving breasts, reddened in spots from his rough, unshaven face. He hooked his thumb inside her undergarment.

"Tell me to stop if you like, Jaime," he said raggedly, using the last of his strength. "Tell me if you want to stop this now, for I won't be waiting much longer."

His body was rigid, every muscle tensed and hard as steel. His lips hung only a breath away from hers. But his eyes never left her, sweeping over her features, continuing their soft caress of her face. Jaime paused for only the briefest of instants and then lifted her mouth to his.

He growled deep in his chest as he tore away the cloth.

"Have you seen your mistress?" Mary asked sharply, having come up quietly from behind.

Startled, Caddy whirled, causing the tray she was carrying to bang hard against the frame of the oak door. Food and drink showered down the wall and scattered a good distance across the corridor floor. One of the two soldiers standing nearby began to chuckle but choked it back, perceiving the fierce looks the two women shot at him.

"Oh, look at what I've done!" Caddy muttered to herself, squatting and beginning to pick up some pieces of a broken, stoneware pitcher.

"Caddy," Mary repeated, putting a wooden bowl onto the tray.

"Now I'll have to go back to Cook for more food." The older woman's face tightened in a troubled frown. "Oh, the tongue in that man's head."

"Caddy!"

Caddy straightened her back and looked up into the young woman's serious face.

"Aye, mistress?"

"Where is Mistress Jaime?"

"Where, mistress?" Caddy looked about confusedly. A dark splotch of small beer marked the closed door.

Mary followed her gaze. "Is she in there with the Scot?" Mary inquired impatiently.

"Is she not, mistress?" Alarm lit up Caddy's face. She glanced accusingly at the guards. "I left her there, Mistress Mary."

"Is she in there alone with the man?" Mary stood, towering over the kneeling woman. She shook her blond head slightly and eyed the men guarding the hall. As she did, two more soldiers appeared, coming down the hallway.

"What harm is there in it, mistress?" Caddy asked, again perplexed. "Though he's recovered the use of his tongue quick enough, the man's hardly able to lift a limb off 'n his bed. Mistress Jaime sent me to the kitchen. Aye, that was no more than it took me to go there and back. She was dressing the wounds about his head. She's only been alone in there . . . well, nary a moment or two, mistress."

Mary reached for the latch and, without knocking, pushed open the door.

Caddy looked up in time to see the young woman's face go as pale as a corpse. Mary clapped a bloodless hand to her mouth, stifling a cry of shock.

CHAPTER 16

The hideous creatures—once old men, once human—clawed at her body. They had her—trapped, hemmed in, helpless.

Unable to drag herself away, she stared through the tattered rags they wore at the ulcerous sores in their decaying flesh. Here and there, bones—dry and chalklike—poked through shriveled, leathery skin. Like a circle of starving animals, they stared down at her through black, eyeless sockets. Gray, bony hands clutched at her, tearing at the dress she wore, at what suddenly occurred to her had once been a wedding gown.

Her hands and feet were held in viselike grips by fleshless hands. In the distance she heard the sound of bells tolling, far off, as if in another world. She wanted to cry out, but a cold, rank-smelling hand clapped over her mouth. Suddenly, at her feet the circle opened, and she saw him. More horrible than Death himself, the monstrous cadaver stood, aroused and ready between her legs.

Catherine sat bolt upright, awakened by her own troubled vision. A candle flickered on the table by her bed, and a dark figure loomed over her. Terrified, she drew in her breath, but a huge hand stifled her scream. She looked up into Edward's gray eyes and saw the familiar lust in them, keen and predatory.

"Damp already?" he whispered, shoving her roughly back onto the bed. With one finger, he traced the beads of sweat from her brow down to the side of her face, to her throat and into the opening of her shift above her heaving breasts.

She twisted her mouth into a wry smile. "I gave up hope of your coming."

"So you started without me?" he asked, sweeping with one swift movement the covers from her bed.

Catherine gasped with surprise as he roughly yanked at the bottom of her shift and sank two fingers into the folds between her legs. But it took her only a moment to adjust, and she purred with delight as he began to stroke her womanhood.

His tone was harsh, but she hardly noticed. "Or were you dreaming of me, dear cousin? You are already wet. That is certain."

"Oh, Edward," she breathed, delighting in the sensations his touch was causing her. "This . . . this horrible dream. There were old men . . . standing . . . ready to take me. I am so . . . mmm . . . glad you've come."

"I haven't come yet, my dear." He quickly withdrew his fingers from between her legs and, grasping her by her wrists, jerked her upright on the side of the bed.

Catherine, her mouth set in a pout at his abruptness, looked up at him, tall and handsome, standing before her with his legs spread. His face was dark and shadowy—his attitude masterful.

"Well, aren't we feeling manly tonight!" Her hands reached for his doublet, but as she did, Edward took hold of both of her wrists and roughly pushed them lower.

"Undo it," he commanded, referring to the pronounced bulge in his hose.

"This is a lovely task for your future queen," Catherine replied, smiling and pulling at the ties holding his codpiece. "Though after what I've been through tonight . . . after that horrid dream. I still shudder to think of . . ."

She stopped as the codpiece fell open, and Edward's manhood came free. Humming appreciatively, she began to massage it, stroking it with both hands. She shivered with anticipation as it came to life—hard and long and pulsing in her hands.

"I told the servants not to wake me in the morning," she continued in a whisper, looking upward at him. His face was averted. "We have all night for this."

"Nay, hussy. We don't," Edward said abruptly, turning his gray eyes on her and roughly shoving her backward on the bed. As he reached down and took fistfuls of her chemise in his two hands, he could see a flash of fear in her eye. But that lasted only a moment, quickly replaced by a moan of pleasure as he ripped the garment down the middle. Her large, white breasts spilled out before his eyes.

"You animal!" she said breathlessly, kneeling up on the bed and bringing one breast to his mouth. "I like this."

He suckled at the large, hard nipple for a moment, eliciting a moan from her. But then he bit her hard, squeezing her other breast as he did. She cried out softly in pain, but did not draw back.

"Well! Is this the new Edward? So rough, so masterful! I could grow accustomed to this, Edward." Digging her fingers in his hair, she pulled his face away from one breast and crushed it against the other. He bit her hard again. Catherine took hold of his hair with both hands and leaned back, drawing his head down her belly. More than anything else now, she wanted him to kiss her . . . there, between her legs. But before she could pull him any further down, he pulled back and twisted her wrists, causing her to release him with a sharp cry. Now it was he who grabbed fistfuls of her hair in two hands.

"It is your turn, my dear." He whispered his words against her lips, but he did not kiss her now.

Catherine arched her back like a cat, but she let him lower her to her hands and knees on the bed, until her mouth was at his erect member. His hands never let go of her hair.

"And you be gentle, cousin," he said threateningly, as she opened her mouth and took him in.

Edward looked straight ahead into the darkness of the room as his fingers dug more deeply into Catherine's hair—guiding her head back and forth along the length of his arousal. Suddenly, he thought of Jaime. Of how tight she would be when he sank the head of his shaft into her. He should have done it already. But then, it would be worth the wait. He hadn't had a virgin for a long while. It was always better when they were untouched. They were tight like a glove. Like Catherine's mouth felt right now.

He felt himself on the edge. Full and ready. He looked down as Catherine struggled to pull back, still on her hands and knees on the bed, the whites of her eyes showing as she looked up at him. Her legs were spread wide apart behind her. Her perfect, heart-shaped buttocks were poised in the air. He knew what she wanted. She wanted to entice him to hold back, to save himself for *her* lusty desires, but he only smiled grimly and shook her by the hair, forcing her to continue pleasuring him with her mouth. The scrape of her teeth against his skin brought on a flash of his temper. One hand gripped the back of her neck, and he squeezed sharply.

"Gentle, dear cousin. Gentle! You wouldn't want me to hurt you, would you?"

She shook her head slightly in answer, so he eased his hold and reached down with one hand, squeezing her breasts and running his palm roughly over her nipples. Edward continued to grip her hair and guide her head, and the pressure was now nearly unbearable. Much better, he thought grimly, as Catherine's mouth moved more urgently against his shaft.

His release was explosive, and he continued to use her for his pleasure, making sure she didn't withdraw her mouth until he was finished.

Finally stepping back from the bed, he turned away, pulling his codpiece up and tying it in place.

Catherine wiped her face on her torn shift and lay back in the bed. Her legs were wide apart, her body crying out for his touch. "Very well, cousin. And now we shall see what you can do to . . ."

Edward turned back toward her, his expression derisive, nearly triumphant. He said nothing.

"You are not leaving?" she said, alarmed and angry.

He ran his fingers quickly through his hair. Ignoring her, he smoothed his doublet with both hands, pulled it down sharply at the waist. With meticulous care, he adjusted his belt and arranged the dagger that hung from it.

"You have pleased me well, Catherine. Continue in this

fashion, and I may—at some future time—renew my acts of charity toward you."

"Your charity?" she laughed, ridicule ringing in her voice.

Edward turned on his heel and started for the door. Catherine bolted from the bed.

"Edward, you can't go yet!" She ran after him, taking hold of his shoulder as he reached the door. He turned slowly to face her. "We . . . we have only begun," she said, trying desperately to sound alluring.

"You saw me finish," he said coldly.

"But what of . . . what of *my* pleasure?"

"You are a whore, Catherine," he replied derisively. "Call in some of your guards. Perhaps all of them."

She raised her hand to slap his face, but his hard flat palm struck her cheek first. Catherine spun away, falling to her knees.

"Bastard," she hissed, tasting the blood from her lip. Without trying to rise, she watched him again pull his doublet down tightly. "Perhaps this is the way your Scottish wench has taught you to treat her, but with me . . ."

"Nay, dearest coz. I would never treat my sweet Jaime as I would you. I desire her with so much passion . . . she is such a prize . . . that I would never waste my seed as I do when I am with you! Not when I can pour it into her tight womb and listen to her cry in pure ecstasy!"

Catherine rose silently as his eyes took on a nasty gleam.

"You see, she is mine, Catherine, and she waits for my cock to nestle between her legs. So unlike you, who consider your foul sheath an open market, and then dream of old men to soothe your lust."

Struck dumb, Catherine stared and watched as he turned and strode from her chamber.

CHAPTER 17

One wrong move, Mary decided, her mouth hanging open, and the Scot was clearly a dead man.

Jaime stood, her fingers wrapped around the knife that she jabbed directly at his throat. Bare-chested, the Highlander sat at the edge of his bed, his eyes ablaze with fury. Distracted by the movement at the door, his gaze flickered in her direction before fixing again on Jaime's face. Then, as Mary stared, the Scot's face tightened in an obvious spasm of pain, and his hand clutched at the wound in his chest. Expending tremendous energy in an effort to keep himself upright, the man faced the knife once again.

"Put the dagger down, you murderous wench."

"Not until you agree." Jaime lifted her wrist and pointed the weapon straight at Malcolm's face. "And you give me your word on it."

"Hell will freeze solid before I agree to anything *you* say!"

"Very well, you ignorant beast. Your death is your own making, then."

Mary's scream jerked Jaime's head around. With speed surprising for one as badly injured as he was, Malcolm struck out at the dagger in Jaime's hand, sending it flying across the room and clattering into the corner. Then, as if the exertion drained his last bit of strength, the Highlander sagged onto the bed. Mary watched as Jaime stepped back a bit and turned sharply toward the door, her fists planted firmly on her hips.

"What . . . what are you looking at?" Jaime nearly shouted,

her glare directed just past Mary's shoulder. "Get out until you're needed!"

Shocked at the vehemence of her cousin's words, Mary took a quick step back, only to bump into the first of the four soldiers crowding the chamber doorway. The men, abashed and apologetic like so many naughty children, quickly mumbled unintelligible responses as they backed out into the corridor again.

"Jaime!" Mary said, breathless and bewildered at the sight. "You . . . you were about to kill the man!"

"Step in and close the door, Mary. We have no need to put on a spectacle for everyone in the palace." Jaime spoke impatiently, but turned with a secret sigh of relief, and glowered outwardly at the motionless Malcolm sprawled across the bed. Beads of sweat covered his brow, and she herself felt a bit unsteady after the dramatic spectacle they *had* indeed performed for the onlookers. She knew the last thing either of them could afford was to be caught in each other's arms. Their detection had been a near thing, but she and Malcolm had been alerted by Mary's voice in the corridor and the crash of objects against the door. All in all, Jaime thought, the two of them had managed it fairly well.

But now, looking Malcolm over as Mary closed the door, Jaime realized the danger was still far from over. His manhood, erect and hard at the outset of their subterfuge, still rose prominently beneath the thin blanket. Startled at the sight, Jaime picked up a second blanket and threw it over his groin section. From behind her came the sound of the door latch clicking shut.

"Jaime, what happened?" Mary asked, coming to her side. "Are you all right?"

"Aye, coz. I am very well, all things considered."

Mary took hold of Jaime's elbow as she glanced fearfully at the Highlander. He was lying back, apparently exhausted by the incident. "What did he do to rile you so?"

With a frown, Jaime patted her cousin on the hand and detached herself, avoiding even a glance at Malcolm's face as she moved around the bottom of the bed. "He is a stubborn, filthy, ungrateful, pigheaded . . ."

Her description was cut off by a sudden and well-aimed kick that the Highlander landed on her buttocks. Jaime recovered, whirling and glaring at the injured man.

"I'm going to kill you!"

"Come away, Jaime. For safety's sake," Mary cried as she rushed down to her cousin's side. Jaime's face was flushed with color, her hair in disarray, her skirts rumpled. She looked as if she'd been attacked. Mary put a hand around her shoulder. "He didn't . . . he didn't do anything . . ."

Jaime looked into Mary's eyes and then glanced over her shoulder at Malcolm's motionless frame. His eyes were fixed on the ceiling as if he were in a stupor. He could be an actor in one of the Norwich guild plays, she thought, hiding her amusement.

"You mean, did he attack me? Just look at him, Mary. Though he might muster up a moment of strength, 'tis all just bluff. The man is too weak to lift himself from that bed." Leading Mary by the hand toward the window, Jaime seated herself on a bench, drawing her cousin down beside her. "Nay, he didn't do . . . well, he couldn't do what you think."

A sound something akin to a growl could be heard from the seemingly unconscious Scot.

"Something provoked you, Jaime."

"Aye, that is true. He has! He has been trying my patience for days, now!" Jaime looked away, warming herself to the discussion. "And the pigheaded brute is doing everything he can to make more work for us. He was nothing but trouble this morning with Caddy, and then he has continued his ill-tempered, ill-bred behavior with me. Nothing is good enough for him. He turns over the dishes—breaks the bowls—topples the chairs. And on top of it all, he refuses to let us dress his wounds properly. He is an insulting, arrogant, boorish ape of a man." Jaime puffed out her cheeks before letting out a breath. Setting her lips in a grim line, she planted her elbows on her knees and propped her chin in her hands.

Mary laid a hand on her cousin's shoulder and tried to soothe her obvious frustration.

"So I decided. Just before you came in." Jaime lifted her head and glared in the direction of the bed. "I decided to kill him! And I would have, too, if you hadn't come in when you did."

"Jaime," Mary gasped. "You just can't kill the man."

"I can. The blackguard doesn't care to live anyway—why else would he make life so miserable for the very women who are trying to bring him back to health?"

Malcolm stirred and rolled slightly in the bed, triggering a groan as he put pressure on his wounds. Both women looked with concern in Malcolm's direction, but the stream of blasphemy and foul sexual reference that followed served to redden Mary's fair skin from her hair to the neckline of her dress. Jaime seized the moment to get up and walk quickly to the edge of the room where the knife had fallen. Banging the handle emphatically on the bench, she placed the weapon beside her as she resumed her place beside her cousin.

"He is like a mewling, whining infant, Mary. He never stops. He is never content! Always wanting something." Jaime ran her hands down her skirts, smoothing them.

The Highlander lay on his side, his eyes fixed on them, but he did not even raise his head to speak. "You are a ghastly, unnatural whore, woman. Away! Get out of here. And take your fishface of a friend with you. The sound of the two of you is harsh and grating. You vex me to no end. Away, why don't you?"

"Fishface?!" Mary repeated indignantly.

"You see, Mary! You see how he is. If not a mercy, death by this dagger would at least put an end to such wickedness!"

Never taking her eyes off of him, Mary lowered her voice to a bare whisper. "As despicable as he is, Jaime, you must remember he is still Edward's prize. He'll be angry—disappointed—to find out that you've killed his prisoner." Mary turned and faced Jaime. "The Scot *is* foul tempered, and he certainly has no taste when it comes to a woman's looks, but to kill him for no more reason than the fact that the man is just disagreeable . . ."

"I have seen Norwich Castle, Mary. Edward kills for less reason than that."

"Jaime!" Mary scolded in hushed tones. "What is wrong with you? Edward does what must be done at Norwich Castle.

But nonetheless, you do him wrong to speak as you do. He is your betrothed."

"He is *not* my betrothed, Mary!" Jaime whispered back in anger.

"Not yet, cousin. But you know what is intended."

Jaime could see Malcolm straining to hear their exchange. There was still a great deal that she needed to explain to him about Edward. But they would need time alone to do that. And there was no point in continuing this argument with Mary now.

Following the direction of Jaime's gaze, Mary placed a hand on her arm. "You have taken too much on yourself. In caring for him. In spending so much time here in this room."

"But there has been no other way, coz. With Graves off to Cambridge and every servant in the palace hostile to him for being a Scot, who has there been to care for him?"

"Jaime," Mary said, ignoring the question, "since our earlier talk, I've been giving this a great deal of thought. This is all for him, isn't it? To please Edward? You might not want to admit it openly, but I see it now. You are going through a great deal of trouble to make this man well for Edward. To surprise him with his prisoner's recovery. After all, it was you who gave this man to Edward as a gift, and you know that he is worth a great deal more if he is mended!"

"Mary, I . . ." Jaime turned to Mary with a look of denial.

"Oh, you may shake your head, but your actions speak much louder, you know. Come now and admit it. Am I not speaking the truth?"

Jaime pursed her lips and stared at her cousin. "Very well, Mary! Have it your way, but what is the point of all this."

"Because we need to work this through." Patting her cousin on the hand, Mary looked about the room and then looked back into Jaime's face. "Let's see, you do look tired!"

"Tired?! She looks like hell!" Malcolm contributed from where he lay, now able to hear the two of them. "Take her out of here, Fishface. Make her go." As if suddenly taken with a sharp pain, he twisted his body and lay back panting.

"Serves him right!" Mary started to whisper again against

Jaime's ear. "But isn't there anybody else we could involve in taking care of this . . . this madman?"

Malcolm heard every word and spoke through gritted teeth. "Aye, but try to find someone bonnie if you would, Mistress Carp, with a goodly sized bosom and at least *some* wee talent for healing a poor soul."

"I'll send for Reed, the jailer," Jaime answered. "He should be bonnie enough for your tastes. Though his bosom may be a bit too large even for a base, brutish lecher such as yourself."

"You are a hard, unfeeling wench! A poor excuse for a woman, to be sure."

Jaime glanced into her cousin's shocked face before quickly looking away. The last thing she wanted was to laugh out loud at Mary's expression. Staring instead at Malcolm, she continued in a calm voice. "I've been using Caddy as much as possible, Mary."

"Aye, another beauty. Old Dame Stickleback. Silent as the dead, and the manner of a . . ."

"I wouldn't speak of anyone else's manners, if I were you," Jaime snapped before turning back to Mary. "But other than Caddy . . . well, I just don't trust anyone else. Who knows what might happen!"

"Perhaps he should be chained," Mary whispered. "You don't think he would hurt himself?"

Jaime shook her head vehemently. "Nay. That would only make matters worse. He is still quite weak. Though a gag might improve him somewhat."

"Cousin, does he truly need an attendant at all times?"

"From the flapping of his tongue you wouldn't think so, but . . ." Jaime fell silent, pondering an answer to that. As bad as he looked, it was difficult to think of Malcolm as weak or ill, at all. She could still feel his body pressed against hers . . . Jaime shook her head quickly and looked away to hide the blush that she knew was coloring her cheeks. "Nay, Mary. He no longer needs to be attended at all times."

"So perhaps he *won't* need someone—in the night, I mean," Mary put in. "With the number of soldiers posted about, I am certain if he raises a fuss, they could handle an emergency."

"Aye. That's so."

"And perhaps I could help," Mary continued. "Perhaps between Caddy and me . . ."

"Nay, cousin," Jaime interrupted quickly. "You've already had more than a sample of his abusive, slandering tongue. I cannot do that to you. Heaven only knows what corruptible filth will come out of his mouth." Jaime almost smiled openly as Mary threw a disgusted glance in Malcolm's direction. The Highlander did *look* like a ruffian, to say the least, unshaven and battered as he was. But as she gazed at him, Jaime realized that she'd hardly noticed any of that herself. Even now, conscious of his condition, she thought he looked quite handsome. With an effort, she turned her gaze back to Mary, trying not to lose her train of thought. "Nay, Mary, your help won't be necessary. This is something *I* want to do for . . . Edward."

"Then, Jaime, you cannot allow yourself to give way to your feelings . . . to your anger."

Jaime smiled abashedly at the scene Mary had nearly walked in on. "As you say, coz."

The two sat silently for a moment, each given to their own thoughts, before Mary spoke again.

"Jaime, when I came in, you were trying to force him to give you his word about something."

Jaime racked her brain. They'd hardly had time to think before Mary had pushed open the door. "I want him to stop fighting with us."

Malcolm's growling voice had the fine, soft feel of crushed stone when he spoke. "You're a pair of damned corbies, you are, screeching and cawing till my head is about to split. Now, I'm telling you both to clear out of here. I'll not be needing or wanting either of you, so away . . . the two of you." The Highlander's eyes were just slits in his battered face. "I am tired of your bitching. Tired of your rough handling of my bruised body. Tired of *you*! I'm through fighting with you."

The two women watched as he closed his eyes and rolled onto his back. Mary turned and looked at Jaime questioningly. "Did he just surrender?" she whispered.

"I believe he did, at that."

"And that was it? You were ready to kill him if he wouldn't stop fighting?"

"Aye, for that and to hush his filthy mouth!"

"But still!"

Jaime shrugged her shoulders. "I got my way, did I not?"

CHAPTER 18

As long as he had a breath in his body, she would strive to make him suffer.

Preparing to leave the king's study, Catherine Howard paused as the door swung open to reveal a dark robed figure beyond. Face to face with the earl of Essex, the new Lord Great Chamberlain, Catherine smiled pleasantly, working hard to hide the anger that had been coming over her in waves for the entire morning. His respectful greeting, couched in the most courteous of terms, reflected his awareness that she would soon be his queen, but his deep bow filled her with a satisfaction that only lessened to a degree the humiliation that Edward had heaped upon her. Catherine answered the man's courtesy with a friendly nod of the head and a curtsy, and then continued past him into the corridor.

There was too much on her mind and too much to be done.

Edward was an arrogant, insufferable, damnable pig, she swore under her breath. He was jealous of her; Catherine was certain of it. He had not even a fragment, a shred of the power she held—and he knew it. But he would pay for his behavior toward her. He would pay dearly.

Moments ago, Catherine had spoken confidentially to the king. She knew how to play her part. Coyly, playing the role of the dutiful and devoted intended, she had planted in Henry's mind seeds of suspicion regarding Edward that would quickly sprout and bear bitter fruit. Whisper and innuendo about dishonest dealings after successful conquests were a sensitive subject for the king. But, even though a Howard herself, she had seen it as her responsibility to relay to His Majesty the talk she'd heard of her cousin Edward's . . . well, lack of forthrightness with regard to the loot taken in the course of his privateering along the coasts of Europe.

Catherine knew that an open accusation might mean Edward's beheading. But after his treatment of her last night, she didn't care. He could take his chances. He had belittled her, shamed her, used her. To think that for so long, he'd been the only man she'd truly fancied. He had been the standard she'd used to compare other men. The arrogant, ruthless pig, she murmured under her breath. Short of raping her, he'd taken everything she'd been willing to give, and then had tossed her away. Used her and discarded her like a rag. Like a worthless rag. Nay, she fumed inwardly, no one would do this to Catherine Howard and get away with it. No one.

With her blood hot and roaring in her brain, the king's intended turned a corner and stormed toward her uncle's chambers. Henry would act eventually, but not quickly enough for her liking. In response to her words, the king had sent for the Lord Great Chamberlain, mentioning to her that, to start with, he would cancel Edward's next royal commission in favor of some other. While inquiries were being made, he could very well throw him in the Tower, but Henry had come to believe over the years that keeping an ambitious lad like Edward Howard waiting and ignorant rendered nearly as much satisfaction.

That was what the king had told her, but Catherine knew the truth. Future queen or no, her word alone was not good enough to put Edward Howard's neck on the block.

So now Catherine would attack him from a different angle. Taking away his glory, threatening his life, was not enough. Edward could very possibly weather the storm clouds that she had positioned around his head. She knew he was not one who would easily accept defeat. But there were other ways that she could bring about his destruction. See what use his pride would be when *she* was finished with him.

Edward Howard would know—without a doubt—how

dangerous she could be, once wounded. Indeed, he would learn just how vicious his lecherous act had made her.

Vengeance! Retaliation! Catherine found herself getting excited at the thought. But to accomplish her plans she would have to return to Kenninghall—alone and at once. The king had—albeit reluctantly—given her permission to go. But since she was being married to His Majesty in little more than a month, it was understandable that she would wish to go and begin her preparations for the wedding.

But now she had to convince her uncle. She would go to Kenninghall with only her own attendants. She didn't want to raise his suspicions, but Edward must remain here. For her own purposes, she couldn't afford to be watched.

She came to a stop before the duke's chambers. Running a hand over her skirts, she composed herself and checked her attire.

There was a great deal to be done. It might, she thought again, give her as much pleasure getting at him through Jaime Macpherson as any other way. It was a vile and lovely thought, going after the Scottish prig. After all, who knew—perhaps Edward Howard had a soft spot in his heart for her, at that. He'd said as much himself last night, if he was to be believed. But just the chance possibility of finding a vulnerable spot in the man would be worth the effort of destroying Jaime. Aye, short of cutting off his balls, this would give Catherine the greatest pleasure.

Catherine put a serene smile on her face and told the duke of Norfolk's attendant to announce her.

The physician studied the sealed letter in his hand before looking up into the young woman's face. "But, Mistress Jaime, for certain there are better ways of sending this abroad than by my friends!"

"There is no other way but through you, Master Graves. I have to be certain that they will get it."

The man ran a hand over his balding head. "But you must have sent other letters to your kin, and you don't suspect that *they've* been lost, do you? What makes you think this one might not reach them?"

Jaime stopped her pacing and looked at the travel-weary man. His clothes still carried the reddish dust of the road between Cambridge and Kenninghall. Running to her chamber at first sight of the physician and his assistant, Jaime had waited impatiently for him to reach the house. Indeed, the healer had no sooner climbed down from his horse than Jaime had approached him for his help. After all she'd learned about the physician from Evan, the falconer, and others in the palace, she was nearly certain that Master Graves was her only hope. But now, standing alone with him in the music room, she could read the doubtful expression in his face, and she knew she had to explain—as much as she could.

She began slowly. "Even after being here as long as I have, I am always reminded that I am an outsider. Though I am more than a guest now, and the Howards call me cousin, the fact is they still think of me as half-Scottish. I believe they often keep an eye on me. I have wondered sometimes in the past if my letters are read before they are sent. There are times when I doubt that they trust me at all."

"Is there a reason why they shouldn't trust you, mistress?"

"Nay!" She flushed red at the question. "I would never do anything to hurt anyone here! There has never been anything . . . any news in my letters that might cause His Grace, the duke, to question my loyalties to him or to the family. Even now, I don't believe . . ." Jaime let out a sigh of frustration. " 'Tis never been a matter of *doing* something. 'Tis just that in the past I've never worried how all *this* might be perceived. Not until now!"

" 'All *this*'? All *what*, Mistress Jaime?" he asked, scratching his grizzled chin. "Let me tell you, mistress. His Grace is a cautious man. I've seen his fortunes rise and I've seen them fall. But he's kept his head when a great many others in his sphere have lost them. You don't accomplish that without knowing who stands with you . . . and who stands against you."

" 'Tis a letter, Master Graves. A letter to my kin. A letter that brings no ill wind upon Kenninghall."

"Some around here believe that any wind from the north is an ill wind."

"What of the winds from far to the west, Master Graves?" she asked quietly. "What of the winds from Wales?"

Graves pondered her words and stared at the letter in his hands. Then, with a quick glance at her, he stood and covered his eyes with one hand as he continued to consider the matter. After a few moments, he turned his attention back to Jaime.

"Years back, Mistress Jaime, I took an oath. I gave my word to serve His Grace loyally. Though I'm an outsider as much as you—if not more—His Grace thinks of me as a devoted servant, and of that I am proud." This time it was his turn to let out a long breath, but his tone remained gentle and kindly. "What made you think to ask *me* this favor? Of all people, why me, Mistress?"

"Because you are a good man, Master Graves. Because you were the only one who cared and worked hard to keep him alive." She knew there could be no doubt in his mind about the nature of her letter. "And because I know that, although you claim Welsh blood, you carry no grudge against him just because he is a Scot. You don't wish him dead just because of the place where he was born."

"How do you know I don't carry a grudge? I ply my meager skills where they are needed. That doesn't mean . . ."

Gently but firmly, Jaime cut in on his words. "And also because I know . . . because I know that your mother was a Scot."

"My mother died long ago," he argued after a moment. "I fought in the Scottish campaigns in my youth."

"And I left my family, having decided never to go back," Jaime told him.

Graves's eyes fixed on hers. "Who told you of my mother?"

"Does it matter, Master Graves?" she responded. "I only mention it to make you understand why I came to you."

The two faced each other for a long time. The physician finally broke the silence. "This letter carries news of the Highlander. It must. What makes you think that I won't take this directly to the duke and reveal your disloyalty?"

"I know that you won't do that," she answered. "But I promise you, I am committing no disloyalty to His Grace."

"You *are*, my dear," he argued softly. "The Highlander is the duke's prisoner."

"Not the duke's," she pressed. "The man is Lord Edward's prisoner. Edward's alone!" Jaime turned and walked to the window of the music room. She didn't want to say it openly, but she had also learned that as much as Master Graves respected the duke of Norfolk, he also despised the younger son and his barbaric way with prisoners.

"I've seen Norwich Castle, Master Graves. And I am certain that you have seen it, too."

As she gazed across the room at him, Jaime could see in his face that she had struck a chord in him. But the physician was not completely satisfied.

"What does this letter contain, mistress?" He waved the letter in the air. "How do I know that what you say in here will not bring the Scots wars back into England? How do I know that, in helping you, I will not be responsible for lives being lost?"

"The Highlander is no King James, Master Graves. As important as he is to his own clan, the Scots would never wage a war for him!"

"But you admit, then, that he is important enough to bring back a goodly prize."

"You know I was the one to tell Lord Edward that."

"Aye, a curious matter, in itself!" Graves stared at her for a moment. "But you are willing to risk *our* lives for his sake . . . with no more concern than the snap of your fingers."

She shook her head. "I don't believe for an instant that you think so poorly of me. I don't believe that you think I could ever endanger the life of as good and valuable a man as yourself."

The Welshman sat heavily on a chair by the worktable and laid the letter on the wooden surface. Beside him, a lute sat on a stand, and the physician idly ran his fingers over the strings a number of times before looking back at the young woman by the window.

"What you say is true, Mistress Jaime. And I'm not alone when I tell you how highly I do think of you. You are far different from most of the rest of them here. In the short time you've been with us, the common folk have come to trust you. They've seen the compassion in your manner, in the things you've done for their children. There is a goodness in you, my dear, that has won many a heart. But . . ." Here he faltered a moment, but soon continued. "But you have to understand my place. Before I do what you ask of me . . . I need to make sure that it won't hurt the folk I care most about. I want no part in any more bloodshed. I want no more killings!"

"You must take my word on this, Master Graves." She paused to dash away a tear. "In this letter, I am sending word through my folks to his kin that he is here and healing under our care. That's all I have said. Most likely, they are out of their minds with worry by now, not knowing whatever became of him on his journey."

"They'll hear from Lord Edward when he is ready to make his demands."

She shook her head. "I've heard that Lord Edward takes his time. He waits long enough for the kin to think all is lost, and then—when he feels inclined and can find no other use for the man—Edward makes his demand."

Graves said nothing in response, instead continuing to stare at the letter in his hand.

Jaime's voice wavered. "Too many times in the past, a prisoner's carcass has been all that the kinfolk get back in return. I know I cannot pick him up and carry him out of here, back to his people, Master Graves. I don't plan to. All I want to do right now is simply let them know that he is alive. It is their right to know."

"You know his kin, mistress, don't you?"

There was no point in denying the truth. She had been surprised that Edward himself had not pressed her on this question before he'd left. "Aye," she answered. "I do."

"Is that why you told Lord Edward about him at Norwich?"

She nodded again, blurting out her answer. "I simply couldn't leave him there. I couldn't let him die at the hands of those butchers."

"But he did die, mistress! Later, in the stables. I saw it," Graves whispered, standing and moving toward her. "And you somehow brought him back."

Jaime ran her hands up and down her arms to halt the chill that was suddenly invading her bones. "I didn't bring him back, Master Graves. I just called to him, and I prayed. It was God's will for him to live. It was God's will!"

"Perhaps, my dear, it is as you say. But, truthfully, what is the Highlander to you?"

Jaime looked up and stared back into his piercing eyes. "What makes you think he is anything to me?"

"I've laid to rest many dying souls. I have plied my skills, and prayed my heart out over many suffering men and women. In the stable cell, the Highlander heard *you*, mistress! His soul came back to *you*! What is he to you?"

She wrapped her arms tightly around her middle, conscious of the fear that, in revealing the truth, she could lose the magical feeling that she had so recently regained.

"Once, long ago," she whispered, "I thought of him as my intended!"

CHAPTER 19

A half-dozen children tumbled out as Jaime made her way into the cottage. The mother's scolding voice, followed as it was by shrieks of childish laughter, brought a smile to her lips. As the little group swarmed about her, Jaime gave little Kate's braids a playful tug to keep the young girl's face out of the basket she was carrying. She had to admit, though, the smell of fresh-baked bread was a temptation even for her. With a friendly pat on the back, Jaime watched the little girl run out the door and after her siblings.

"So, how are you feeling, Nell?" she asked, laying her basket on the rough wooden settle by the crackling little fire.

"Very well, mistress. I thankee."

The falconer's wife, Jaime thought, did indeed look well for having just had a child the day before. Nell was standing proudly over the babe's cradle, and Jaime crossed the stone floor of the little cottage to peek at the infant.

"Oh, my! Nell, he's a strapping lad, to be sure!"

"Aye, mistress. Like his father." Nell beamed, her green eyes sparkling happily at the compliment.

Glancing up at her, Jaime smiled. Nell's red braids, coiled neatly on her handsome head, were only slightly darker than the red hair of her daughter Kate. "And he has your red hair, it seems."

Nell nodded as she leaned down and ran a hand through the unruly wisps of soft hair. "Aye, he'll be an easy one to spot."

"A fine, handsome boy!"

"More likely a little devil, I'm thinking! Like his brothers and sisters."

They both smiled. Jaime ran her fingers along the smooth wood of the cradle, containing her urge to reach in and touch the child. "The children must be very excited to have this wee one to look after."

"He is still too little and too loud for them to find any joy in." Nell patted away at a bead of sweat on her brow. "But they are surely happy to have me back on my feet."

The new mother bent down and caught up the fussing child in her arms. As the woman settled heavily onto the bench Jaime could see—on closer inspection—the marked weariness of childbirth in her face.

"You are trying to do too much, too soon," Jaime whispered, her eyes fixed on the babe and his tightly closed fists—his beautiful, ruddy little face.

Perceiving the young woman's gaze, Nell leaned forward and held the baby out to her. "Would ye like to hold him?"

Jaime beamed as she nervously reached out to take the child. "May I?"

"He is my tenth, mistress. He is fortunate I don't give him to you for keeps."

Jaime's eyes shot up in surprise. Tired as she was, Nell's eyes were twinkling. The two women laughed.

Jaime settled down beside Nell on the bench, her arms gathering the infant tightly into her chest. Suddenly, she became aware of a burning knot in her throat. Of a tear trying to work its way down her cheek. Of the yearning deep within her to hold and care for a bairn of her own. She placed a gentle kiss on the babe's soft tendrils of hair and thought of Malcolm. Of how wonderful it would be to bear his child. Their child.

"After little Kate, Evan and I thought we were done with such things."

Nell's voice jerked Jaime out of her dreams. And she silently chided herself for having such idle and fanciful thoughts.

"Aye," she continued. "Two children ago, I thought myself too old to bear another." The mother's eyes grazed lovingly on the infant's features. "But then, Evan . . . well, he just has a way of . . . talking me into this."

Jaime smiled as the other woman's eyes flickered toward her face, before drifting down again to the baby's pink cheeks. It was amazing how different she felt now about such talk. Indeed, she was conscious of something changing within her. There was a sense of vague understanding that she had never had before. Certainly, she knew all about children and how they were conceived, how they were born, but she was beginning to see that there were mysteries hidden beneath the words. Mysteries perhaps only a mother could understand.

Even those days when she had thought of herself in love with Malcolm, she had lacked this knowledge of adult life, of adult passion. The desperate physical need that was so much a part of this thing called love. And motherhood seemed to offer something else, as well.

"I hear Master Graves's come back," Nell said softly.

"Aye," Jaime answered. "He told me that he will be stopping in to check on you and the wee one about midday."

"Ahhh. He is a good man, for one with so much learning. But he fusses over us, I don't know what for. I've done this now so many times that there is naught he can tell me about it, and the babe I've checked myself. I know Master Graves is a healer, but what do men know about birthing or babies, anyway?"

"Hearing your husband, Evan, one might think they knew a great deal."

Nell slapped her hand on her thigh. "Has he been talking, my Evan?"

"On the way here, I passed by the mews." Jaime lifted the babe and settled him on her shoulder. "Seeing the crowd of folk gathered about, I thought for sure the gypsies must have slipped in during the night."

"But it wasn't, was it?" Nell blushed. "It was my tomfool husband, carrying on about his new son."

"Aye. But that wasn't all. Evan is quite the storyteller, it struck me, listening to him."

"I'm thinking I don't like the sounds of this."

"To be sure, Nell. When he broke into the account of the birthing itself . . ."

"He wouldn't!" she gasped.

"And such an artist. Drawing in the dirt to explain to the young ones . . ."

"I'll be killing him for sure, I'm thinking."

Jaime laughed. "Nay, Nell. It wasn't your labor that was the topic, but his own pains and the waiting. Everyone on the manor had to know how he'd suffered, missing a good night's sleep!"

"The poor devil!" Nell scowled, her eyes flashing at the door.

"I'm making more of it than it was," Jaime said with a smile. "Evan was just so sweet—so excited about the babe. He's very, very proud."

"You've a bit of the devil in you, yourself, Jaime Macpherson," Nell said, breaking out into a wide grin. "But you're right about Evan. He has always been that way about the children. With each and every one of them. He is a man that truly loves having babies about."

"That's wonderful. Then you have plans for more."

"He might," Nell snorted. "But not while I still have my wits about me. If he said anything about it, 'tis pure wishing on his part, so far as I'm concerned. I'm not getting any younger, I'm thinking. In fact, now that you mention it, Evan's probably behind Master Graves coming by. That tomfool man of mine probably wants to make sure I could bear more children, blast him!"

"Look at you, Nell. You are still young enough for another half dozen, at least."

"Aye, a half dozen, at least, she says." Nell let out a long breath. "Oh, I love them, mistress. But after ten of them, a woman has to be wondering about her sanity, I'm thinking."

"I'm certain you know best, Nell," Jaime replied.

Nell shifted uncomfortably, and Jaime looked at her over the baby's head. She clearly had something more to say, but was struggling for a way to say it.

"I am here, Nell," Jaime whispered, her fingers gently stroking the baby's soft hair.

" 'Tis the birthing, mistress!"

Suddenly, she felt ashamed at not seeing it herself. It was not her sanity that concerned Nell, but the ability to bring so many children into the world, and still live to see them grow. Jaime waited until the woman looked up into her face. When she did, she could see worry etched in Nell's large, green eyes.

" 'Tis not an easy thing to be saying, mistress. But . . . well, I am afraid at the thought of having any more."

"But, Nell," Jaime replied, trying to ease her worries, "this delivery went so well."

"Aye. It went well enough. But there is a fear of dying that grows stronger with every babe I bear. Oh, the Lord has looked after me pretty well for ten times, I know. I've given Evan a healthy bunch of little tikes. But . . . but you hear stories more and more, I'm thinking. Women dying bringing their babes into the world. Not six months ago, little Annie, the wife of one of the stable hands died giving birth to her fifth. And then last month 'twas Ellen, the gardener's wife." Nell's eyes fixed with concern on her child's little face. "This tiny creature needs me. My children, they are all so young. They—all of them—need me. And as much as he is a grown man and all, Evan needs me, as well. I have too much here to want to let go of it."

Jaime looked gently into the flushed face of the mother. "Don't you think Evan would understand this?"

Nell shook her head. "I'm thinking I could never tell him . . . not the way I just told you. He is a proud man, Mistress Jaime. Proud of himself. Proud of the brood we've produced. I'm thinking, as fond as he is of me . . . and I know he is, surely . . . I'm thinking he'd find it hard to see it my way."

Jaime held the baby close as she considered the problem.

"But there is something, mistress."

"Aye, Nell?"

"Well, I don't truly feel comfortable asking, Mistress Jaime. It mightn't be right, you dirtying your hands in it."

"What is it, Nell?" she asked encouragingly. "You know I'll help, if I can."

"I'm thinking, mistress, suppose Master Graves were to hint to my man that with ten healthy children, 'tis time for quitting."

"The healer! Would he do that?"

"He knows you, mistress. If you were to ask him . . ."

"I?" Jaime asked, surprised at the request.

"Aye, mistress." Nell nodded shyly.

Jaime gave her friend a little smile. "I don't know that he'd do it, Nell. What's between you and Evan is between you and Evan."

"That's what the village priest told me a few years back. But I'm thinking we both are needing some new advice. Evan will listen to Master Graves."

"But for me to ask?"

"Aye, mistress. You are the only woman the healer will hear."

"If you think . . ."

The falconer's wife looked at her, hope and trust in her eyes. Jaime knew she could not refuse.

"I could go to him and say something. He's a trustworthy man—that I know."

Nell nodded—relief written on her features—and rubbed her callused hands against the rough wool of her skirts. "What you say is true, mistress."

Jaime stared as Nell lowered her head once again. "Is there something else, Nell?"

She nodded. "Aye, there is one fear—he's a man, and menfolk are bound together thick as flies. And being that they're both of Welsh blood makes it only worse, I'm thinking. If he don't agree, would he go to Evan and take his side?"

"It doesn't have to be a matter of sides, Nell. You are doing this not for yourself. This is for both of you. For all of you."

"You are right, mistress. And with you talking, I am sure he'll see it that way."

Jaime let out a nervous laugh. "You have great faith in me, Nell!"

"I do, Mistress Jaime." Nell's face cleared, and her hands reached out, touching her skirt. "You are a good friend to me, mistress. A good friend, indeed."

Both women fell silent, each touched deeply by the rush of emotion that suddenly permeated the room.

Nell broke the silence, clasping her hand over Jaime's. "I know I'm being bold, claiming you for a friend, Mistress Jaime. But I'm thinking the Lord is blessing us in a special way with you becoming Lord Edward's wife. We're all getting more than we deserve when it comes to you, mistress. For such a kind and gentle soul as you to accept His Grace's son."

"Don't!" Jaime blurted out. There was no point in going around and revealing her true feelings, even to Nell, but hearing the woman speak so openly of it sent a shiver down her spine. The best course, as Jaime saw it, was to deter such talk as being premature. "None of that has been settled, Nell. There is still so much that needs to be worked out between Edward and me . . . and between our families, for that matter."

With a slow nod of her head that betrayed her curiosity at the young woman's words, Nell acquiesced to Jaime's wishes. The infant quickly came to Jaime's rescue, squirming in her arms and moving his mouth in a persistent attempt against her breast. Jaime smiled down at him.

"Ahh, I'm afraid I cannot help you with that," she whispered, reluctantly handing the child back to the waiting mother.

While Nell eased gingerly back onto the settle to nurse her son, Jaime stood up and moved to the small table by the fire, and the two women continued their conversation—this time about the children and about Kate's musical progress. As they talked, Jaime realized that if she could remain anywhere—other than beside Malcolm—there was no place she preferred to be as much as in this cottage. Whenever she came to visit Nell, a comfortable sense of contentedness would creep into her. But now, the morning was wearing on, and Jaime knew Nell had little time this day for idle chat.

Walking across the cottage floor, Jaime emptied the basket of food and put out the small presents she had made for the mother and son, before heading outdoors and starting back for the house.

Her dealings with Nell and with the other folk working on the duke's land and in the palace always brought back memories for Jaime of her childhood in Scotland. There, in the Macpherson clan lands, the separation of the noble family from the people like Nell and her husband was unheard of. In many clans that Jaime knew of, the lairds and others of noble blood worked side by side with the common folk. The clan folk were loyal enough—they would die for the honor of their name without thinking twice—but the bonds that secured that loyalty were the thick cords of compassion and fair dealing. And this was the only way for Jaime.

Looking about and nodding to the passing workers, Jaime made her way through the grounds while her mind tried to think of ways to occupy the rest of her day. She had already held her music lessons with the children early this morning, so that was done. Breathing in the fresh spring air, she glanced over at the direction of the stables. But she shook her head. In spite of the fine weather, the idea of staying outdoors and going for a ride held no interest for her today. And she had every good reason for avoiding the falconer, so she steered away from the mews. But she also was in no mood to return to her room for an idle chat with Mary over the plans for the wedding that her cousin was busily fancying in her mind.

Jaime shook her head again. She had been intentionally ignoring all thoughts of Edward over the past few days. She had absolutely no desire to think of a wedding. Especially not one that tied her to him for life. She didn't want to spoil her day with such images, so she thought of Malcolm.

She hadn't seen him since the day before. Between Caddy caring for him, and the return of the physician, Jaime had decided that—since her own emotions were undoubtedly apparent—she should keep her distance. To be sure, she needed time to gather her wits about her and put a lid on the boiling pot of her passion. They had come far too close to being caught the day before. And they had gone way too far in giving in to their desires.

Even now, her heart pounded to think how forward she had been. How bold he must have thought her in presenting herself to him so openly. A mere kiss hadn't been enough. She had encouraged him to touch her in places she'd never been touched before. She had asked him to treat her as a woman.

For one with no intimate experience, she had almost fooled herself. Groaning inwardly as she thought of their encounter, Jaime now decided that killing herself for her boldness might not be out of the question. Now that he'd had time to think back over how wantonly she'd behaved, his earlier opinion had probably been confirmed. In Malcolm's eyes, she thought, Jaime Macpherson had become nothing more than an English harlot.

A discomforting, prickly heat swept through her, and Jaime decided that the music room could offer her the best refuge. As she strode up the path past the gardens, troubling thoughts continued to burden Jaime's mind; and a gnawing, empty feeling that accompanied those thoughts filled her with a rest-lessness and occupied her completely. Stepping across the threshold of an open door, Jaime looked up, suddenly con-scious that her legs, of their own accord, had carried her to a place other than her intended destination. Looking down the corridor that held the surgery, Jaime let out a long, slow breath.

Consciously, she had not wanted to be here, but here she stood, nonetheless. Against her better judgment, she had been drawn to his room. Something had taken control of her, led her to him, and—suddenly—Jaime felt somehow liberated by the moment. Moving down the corridor, she realized it didn't matter what he thought of her. It didn't matter if all the others—if everyone in England, for that matter—thought she spent too much time by his side. She would take the abuse. The only thing that mattered was that she wanted to see him. Nay! She needed to see him. She *would* see him.

Jaime glanced first inside the empty workroom of Master Graves, for the physician's door stood open. Bottles of ingre-dients and decocted brews cluttered the table that generally sat empty in the middle of the room. Steam rose ominously from a huge, half barrel in the corner, and the air smelled sharply of herbs.

Stepping past the room, she realized that there was some-thing amiss. None of the guards who had been posted in these corridors since Malcolm arrived were to be seen. They were all gone, and the corridor was eerily silent and empty. Jaime quickened her pace and advanced on Malcolm's closed door. Without pausing to knock or call, she lifted the latch and pushed the heavy oak door open wide.

CHAPTER 20

"**I** knew that I would find you here!"

Jaime swung around and stared blankly at the countess of Surrey.

"Come now, my dear. Come with me, at once." Frances reached out and grabbed Jaime by the hand. "Surrey has had servants out searching the entire palace. I believe they're preparing the grappling lines for a search of the trout pond. We mustn't make things worse by keeping him waiting, you know!"

Somewhat stunned, Jaime took a couple of steps, before recovering herself and planting her feet. "Wait!" she protested, turning and looking back into Malcolm's empty room. "I . . . I . . . Where is . . ."

Frances slipped her arm through Jaime's and propelled her with firmness down the hall. "Later, my dear. Later. We simply *must* hurry now. Surrey hasn't much patience, I'm afraid, when it comes to waiting."

As Jaime reluctantly allowed herself to be dragged away, her heart pounded fiercely and her mind worriedly searched for answers.

Something dreadful had happened to Malcolm, of that she was certain. But where was he? Had he been taken back to Norwich Castle? Someone must have decided he had recovered to the point of being . . . what, dangerous? Able to escape? But who, she thought. My God, she hadn't considered this before. What would become of him now that his wounds were healing? If he went back to Norwich he would certainly become fair game for the cruelty of the jailer, Reed. But who . . . ? Edward, she thought, her body suddenly filled with ice cold dread.

"Is Edward back?" she asked in a shaky whisper.

Frances never slowed her pace, but turned with a surprised look, before smiling and giving Jaime's hand an understanding pat.

Jaime cringed, certain that she would scream if one more person mistook her inquiries into Edward's whereabouts as stemming from affection.

"Nay, my dear, he hasn't returned as yet," Frances answered plainly. "We don't expect him back for another fortnight at least, unless you know more about it than Surrey does."

Jaime shook her head. Then why had Malcolm been sent back to Norwich? she wanted to ask. Certainly she would have heard if he had caused any trouble since she'd seen him last. Her heart sank in her chest. Could it have been that somehow the letter she had delivered to the physician had gotten into the wrong hands, and now Malcolm must suffer the added precaution of being put under tighter guard? Jaime knew that the physician's apprentice had traveled back to Cambridge the day after she'd spoken with Master Graves. Had the man been waylaid? Had he betrayed them all?

Reaching the double oak doors that led into the earl and countess's chambers, Frances paused and looked Jaime fully in the face.

"You seem pale, cousin. Are you unwell?"

"I'm feeling a bit winded," she whispered in answer.

Frances ran a gentle hand down Jaime's arm. "Be strong, my dear." And with no further words, she turned and nodded to the attendant to open the door.

Jaime felt the Surreys' large sitting room swallow her whole as she stepped into it. Her body vibrated like a hollow drum from the furious pounding of her heart against the walls of her chest, filling her head with such a noise that she wondered if it would render inaudible all other sounds. The room seemed unnaturally bright to her and, as she focused on the back of Frances's head as the woman moved quietly to her husband's side, Jaime thought for a moment that fainting was not out of the question. But the moment passed, and Jaime continued to stand by the door, awaiting the earl's first words.

"Cousin Jaime," he said, his voice warm and friendly. "You are more difficult to track down than a sparrow in the forest. I've had three pages and I don't know how many servants return empty-handed before Frances offered to look for you herself."

Straightening her back and lifting her chin, Jaime returned the earl's gaze. "I was at Evan the falconer's hut this morning, m'lord. His wife Nell has just delivered a healthy baby boy."

"God bless her! Let's see, how many children does that make it now? Five? Six?"

"This child is their tenth."

"By God, you know these folk better than I do. And how is the little fellow doing?"

"The mother and son are both in good health, m'lord."

The Earl of Surrey turned and took his wife by the hand. "Frances, you will be sure to send word to the kitchens about sending them a basket of some sort."

"I believe," Frances responded, nodding with a smile toward Jaime, "that someone has already seen to that."

"Ahh, very good," Surrey said, turning his attention back to Jaime. Waving a hand in her direction, the earl beckoned for Jaime to approach. "You don't have to stand by the door, Jaime. Come . . . come and join us. We've been waiting long enough for you to arrive."

As Jaime started in, the earl turned to his wife. "So, my love, where did you find her, at last? Did you have to go all the way back to the falconer's cottage?"

Frances shook her head. "Nay, I guessed that on the way back from the cottages, our good cousin would stop and check on you."

Jaime's eyes stared at Frances, realizing that her last words had been addressed to someone else in the room. Someone standing behind Jaime at the far end of the room.

Perhaps it was the quick turn of her head or perhaps it was her sudden relief, but whatever the cause, Jaime's light-headedness returned in an instant. Malcolm stood beside the fireplace, his arm folded over his chest. Staring at him, she realized that if her heart had been pounding before, it now threatened to burst within her.

"He is much improved, wouldn't you say, Jaime?"

He looked so different. So clean. Dressed in impeccably fitted doublet and hose, he was the picture of both nobility and manly perfection. Her eyes traveled the lines of his handsome face to his dark eyes.

"He is a quick healer," she said, hurriedly turning her gaze back to the earl and the countess.

"He owes his life to you," Surrey added.

She shook her head. "Master Graves was the one who saved him."

"But you were the one who talked that brother of mine into taking him out of Norwich. You were the one who sneaked into the stables and worked beside the physician until you knew he would live."

Jaime could feel the color rise into her cheeks. She had thought no one in the household other than Mary and Caddy had known of what she had done that day. She quickly glanced at Malcolm. He continued to stand as if he had not a care in the world—as if his name were not the subject of discussion here.

"Also, from what I hear," the earl continued while moving in and sitting himself in a chair, "when Graves left for Cambridge, you were the one who went to him and nursed him back to health."

"I wasn't the only one," Jaime put in. "My servant Caddy helped. Also Mary . . ."

The earl of Surrey waved her off with a smile. "Nothing against our cousin Mary," he said as he turned to Malcolm, "but you were far too dirty, too bloody, and too ugly for her to lay a finger on!" The earl turned his attention back to Jaime. "Unlike you, dear cousin, Mary has been brought up quite sheltered from the outside world and most unlikely to be of much help to you."

"She *did* offer," Jaime said weakly in her defense.

"No doubt." Surrey smiled. "None of us care to miss out on any excitement!"

Jaime opened her mouth to argue but then closed it at once. What was the point of all of this? Was he giving her credit for caring for Malcolm, or was he suggesting that some other motive had prompted her actions? Malcolm was still standing silently by the hearth. Though his face was still pale and bruised, he looked so strong that a casual observer might never guess that he had recently been so badly injured. He certainly was not being treated like a prisoner, standing in this chamber—unchained and unguarded—with the earl and the countess present.

Surrey's eyes traveled from Malcolm back to Jaime. "I assume you two have crossed paths in the past. In Scotland, perhaps?"

Jaime gave a quick glance in Malcolm's direction. The Highlander's gaze was stern and fixed on Surrey's face. How much had he already told Surrey about their pasts? Malcolm left his place at the hearth and seated himself in a chair directly across from Surrey.

"We have, m'lord," she answered as lightly as she could.

"Ahh, so that's how you recognized him at Norwich? Oh, Jaime, I haven't offered you a glass of wine." Surrey waved toward a crystal decanter on a side table and looked at his wife and at Malcolm.

Jaime declined and the earl proceeded to fill his own cup. His tone was light and conversational, but Jaime could see he was listening very closely to her responses.

"You two aren't by any chance related by blood?"

Jaime stared at Malcolm. They had spent many years under the same roof. They both were loved by the same family and raised as kin. But they were not kin.

"Nay, m'lord. We are not!" she replied, speaking truthfully.

"Friends? Acquaintances?"

"Surrey!" Frances interjected with a tone of mild admonition. "Why don't you ask her what you want to know? You're bullying the poor dear!"

"I?" the earl replied, his smiling face the very image of one unjustly accused.

But Jaime was not amused, and her eyes burned into Surrey's. If this was a test to compare whatever answers Malcolm had given him against hers, she felt certain that she was bound to fail. She certainly had no idea of how long they'd been talking. She had no idea, even, how well the two knew each other. Aside from both being former students of the great teacher, Erasmus, there was nothing that she could think of that would tie these two together. She weighed her words carefully, and her tone was resolute when she spoke.

"Lord Surrey, I have many friends. Here, in Scotland, in France. Among the common folks and nobles. I consider you and your wife friends. But your questions seem to insinuate something underhanded."

"It is true, Surrey," Frances agreed, moving beside Jaime. "You *do* seem to be implying something. Why don't you just say what you mean."

"My dear Frances, I'm merely interested in these two. My questions are certainly not meant to hint at *any* wrongdoing on *anyone's* part."

"You have had her on the rack with this inquisition of yours from the first moment she stepped in here, Surrey," Frances rebutted. "If I had known you wanted to bring her in here for this," the young woman dismissed him with a sweep of her hand, "I would never have found her for you."

With her arm around Jaime's shoulders and a threatening frown darkening her features, Surrey's wife forced a smile to his lips. He turned to the Highlander. "These women! I should have known that they would side together against us!"

Jaime's face flushed red as she tried to comprehend Surrey's words. She considered his use of the word "us" and wondered whether he meant more than appeared. After all, she welcomed Frances's support, but what was happening here seemed so vague and unreal to her, like a scene in a masque or a guild play. What was really behind the earl's questions? If this were indeed some kind of masque, Jaime wanted to know what role she was supposed to be playing. She decided on a direct assault.

"M'lord," she said. "In Scotland they say that opening a shutter brings more light than kindling a candle. If I knew what exactly it is that you are after, I am certain I could shed far more light on whatever you wish to know."

Surrey, obviously pondering her words, gazed at her as he sipped from his cup. With a parting squeeze on her arm, Frances moved away from Jaime's side and sat herself in a chair, picking up some needlework she had laid aside sometime earlier. The earl laid his cup down, and when he spoke, his voice carried in it a gentleness that had been absent before.

"I simply need to ease my mind on something, cousin," he said. "Tell me, Jaime, what is . . . I mean, what was between you and the MacLeod here? If you think about it, I believe you'll agree that it is my right to know."

This time Jaime caught Malcolm's eyes as they lifted to her face. As she searched their depths, she was shocked to find there no gentleness, no affection, no love for her in any form. The hard lines of his brow spoke of anger. She even thought she could sense a coldness, a hint of boredom in his face. As handsome as he now looked with his improving health and his clean clothes, she yearned for the old Malcolm.

She decided then to be done with it. She turned and looked directly at Surrey. "What I said before of us being no kin was the truth. But as you know, I am a Macpherson, and he—Malcolm MacLeod—was raised by my uncle and his wife. His father was Torquil MacLeod, a friend to the English, and Malcolm was orphaned at the young age of seven. For service to the Scottish king, my uncle was made laird of Malcolm's lands. He could have kept those lands for the Macpherson clan, but instead, my uncle and his wife chose to raise Malcolm as their own and have him take over the lairdship of his land once he came of age."

"So you were raised like brother and sister? Or rather like cousins? The way Mary and Catherine have been raised here?"

"Malcolm is older than I by a wide margin, m'lord. I was still just a child when he was sent abroad to study. And there were long periods when I traveled with my parents to the courts of Europe. Later, soon after Malcolm returned to Scotland, I was sent to France. It would be difficult for me to say that our paths have done much more than occasionally cross."

"But you still cared for him enough to try to save his life!"

"Aye, m'lord! I would have done the same for you. Or for any poor soul! I was taught that true compassion has no eyes, and yet sees all. I could not turn my back on him in his condition, or on the folk that I know rely on him in his own lands in Scotland. But it makes no difference, m'lord. He could have been the stable boy who had once cared for my horse, or the cook's girl who used to steal the ribbons from my sewing. I would have done the same for any of them!" Jaime paused and looked straight into Surrey's face. "And that day at Norwich Castle—after seeing the pain and suffering in that horrible place—I would have brought away every one of those prisoners, if I could!" She stopped as her voice faltered.

Surrey's face grew grim, and he and his wife exchanged a glance. "I don't know what my brother was thinking," he said quietly, "in taking you there."

Jaime shook her head. "As repulsive as that place is, I am not sorry that I went there. In fact, I am thankful that he took me."

"Aye," Frances put in. "You were given an opportunity to save a life!"

"And to add more gold to Edward's treasures. But all of these things, I'm sure," Surrey added, his face a mask, "must have only reinforced my brother's sense of your worth."

Jaime sickened at those words. She didn't care if Edward thought her worth a straw. That had not been the motivation for anything she did, but she scarcely dared to glance at Malcolm.

A knock at the door and the appearance of a page holding a large book drew everyone's attention.

"Ahh, finally," Surrey cried, moving across the room and taking the book. "And perfect timing, at that. Come to the table, Malcolm. You and I can peruse these letters from our old teacher and reminisce about old times. You see I've had them mounted in this volume . . ."

The two men moved away to a table at the far end of the room, and Frances motioned Jaime to the seat beside her. As she sat, Jaime felt that she could breathe once again, and worked at unclenching her fingers as she watched Surrey and

Malcolm conversing. Her gaze became a look of wonder as Malcolm, who towered over the earl, visibly relaxed to the point of joking with Surrey.

"You did well, Jaime," Frances whispered. "Much better than I would have done under the circumstances, I should say."

"What was . . . what was the meaning of all this, Frances?" Her voice was barely a croak as she continued to watch the men.

"Edward," the young woman answered with a meaningful nod. Frances cast a covert glance in the direction of her husband. "Surrey, I am fairly certain, believes that he may need to explain, when Edward returns, why he decided the Highlander deserves better treatment than he was getting."

"Then Malcolm is not going back to Norwich?"

"Nay," Frances said with surprise. "I hardly think Surrey would consider that very hospitable. The fact is, my dear husband and the Highlander have a great deal in common. I believe he has been enjoying his company immensely. Nay! I'm certain Surrey would find it difficult to part with him right now."

"I'm very . . . happy to hear that," Jaime said uncertainly.

"Aye? Well, I think Surrey asked you those questions because he knows Edward would be far less amenable to the Highlander's relative freedom if there were something between you and Malcolm MacLeod!"

Jaime entwined her fingers tightly in her lap. "Then it appears my answers satisfied Lord Surrey's concerns."

Frances nodded with a look at her husband. "That appears to be so, my dear!"

Jaime followed her friend's eyes to where the two men stood bending over the volume of letters.

"If he is not going back to Norwich, Frances, then where is he going to be kept?"

"Well," the countess replied, her eyes dancing with mirth as they looked back at Jaime, "at least until Edward returns, he'll be with us in the palace. In fact, Surrey has already given directions that one of the best rooms is to be prepared for his guest."

"His *guest*?" Jaime asked in shock.

"Aye," Frances nodded with a note of pride in her voice. "That's one difference between these two brothers. If Edward is going to treat this Scottish laird as a prisoner, then Surrey is sure to treat him as an honored guest."

"Frances, you make it sound as though your husband is doing all this simply out of spite for Edward!"

"I suppose there is some truth to that, Jaime," she said somewhat defiantly. "But more to the point, I believe there is a genuine fondness between Surrey and Malcolm MacLeod. Since last night, when Surrey went down to the surgery to pay a visit, my husband has been quite cheerful. Perhaps Erasmus is the bond that ties them, but I believe they delight in each other's company."

Jaime's eyes again returned to Malcolm. He looked to be relating to Surrey some old reminiscence. Since going to the table, he had never once glanced in her direction. It occurred to her that she had all but ceased to exist for Malcolm.

"I am glad you told Surrey the truth," Frances said, placing her warm fingers over Jaime's folded hands. "Surrey needed to hear it from you. Like everyone else, Jaime, he respects you and thinks very highly of you. It would have been painful for him to find that his trust had been misplaced."

"I assume he asked the same questions of me that he asked Malcolm."

"He did," Frances nodded with a smile. "And your responses matched."

Jaime stared at the needlework on Frances's lap, trying to think this through. There were birds in the pattern, perched effortlessly in twisted vines of ivy leaves. Jaime looked away. She knew she had every reason to be filled with joy since Malcolm would be well cared for, at least until such time as Edward returned. But she could not ignore the coldness she sensed in his manner—the lack of acknowledgment of her very presence—that made her heart shrivel with pain.

"Before I even came for you," Frances continued, "I knew that Surrey trusted all would be well."

"How so?"

"He told Malcolm of your upcoming wedding to Edward, and his reaction was . . . well . . ."

Jaime swallowed hard. "Aye? His reaction?"

"Well, he seemed to view the match favorably." The countess glanced at her only briefly out of the corner of her eye. "I believe he called it a union of two identical souls."

CHAPTER 21

Jaime tried not to think of the distance to the ground as she wrapped her fingers around the vine further up the wall. The leaves of the ivy covering the palace wall brushed against her face, smooth and cool. A stray tendril of new growth searching bravely in the night air for a place to catch hold, tangled in her hair and managed to pull back the hood of her cloak as she herself inched ever higher on the wall. She hadn't tried anything this foolhardy since she was twelve. In spite of herself, she smiled grimly at the irony of it. The last time she'd scaled a castle wall had been for the same reason. To see Malcolm.

She'd been restless for two days, unable to sleep and unable to eat. And it was her inability to have even a moment alone with him that had led to this reckless midnight climb.

It was obvious that he was angry at her. Nay, she corrected, Malcolm's few glances in her direction had told of a cold fury, intense and fierce.

But she had to see him. Having him now among the host of knights, ladies, friars, clerks, courtiers, lawyers, nuns, and travelers who shared every meal in the Great Hall brought her happiness and distress. Seeing his handsome face always turned to Surrey, so close to her and yet so distant, plundered her will to hold back, to wait, to be patient. Malcolm's public demeanor was dignified and manly, courteous to the point of being charming, but his attentions encompassed everyone around them except her. Jaime felt her composure slipping further with every encounter. She would go mad if she couldn't share in the warmth of his company.

But Jaime knew why he was so angry. Each time a conversation flagged, each time a new person joined the group eating at the head table, Jaime knew someone would launch into another detailed account of the upcoming nuptials between Edward and her. And each time, she saw Malcolm's face harden for a fleeting moment before he turned away with that bored, disinterested expression she was learning to know so well. Tonight, as the visiting archbishop from Norwich had jovially offered the ceremony here or at the Cathedral, Jaime had nearly broken down and told him exactly what she thought of his damned ceremony.

But she had restrained herself at the last moment. Such a spectacle would certainly be unwise—for a number of reasons. She must speak to Edward about the matter first—she felt she owed him that, at least. And Jaime certainly didn't care to bring any attention to herself at this point. She wouldn't hazard the chance of these people guessing at reasons for her "sudden" change of heart—for that was assuredly how they would see it. Nay, she wouldn't jeopardize Malcolm's newly attained position of safety.

Jaime looked up at the small ledge outside Malcolm's room. The edge was only a short distance above her outstretched fingers. And, of course, *this* behavior is perfectly safe, she thought with a grim smile. Digging the toe of her soft shoe between a vine and the wall, she pushed herself higher toward the ledge. The ivy up here must had obviously been cut away recently, for the vines were much thinner, and she could feel them pulling away from the wall.

Mary's chatter tonight had been the final straw for Jaime. Returning together to their room, Mary, dreamy-eyed and romantic, had spoken of nothing but Malcolm. She had gone on endlessly about his chivalrous manners, his manly looks, his talents, accomplishments, and charms. Jaime had found herself torn between thoughts of being ill and tearing her cousin's tongue out. But then it wasn't Mary's fault, Jaime knew, to be so taken with the rogue.

And that was exactly what he was. A scoundrel of the

lowest, most beastly type! A beautiful, battered, hatefully irresistible rogue!

She wondered, brushing an ivy leaf away from her face, if this was the way he intended to punish her.

As Jaime slipped the fingers of one hand over the top of the hard ledge, the vine at her feet gave way, and she dangled momentarily in the night air. Gingerly, she felt for a toehold, found one, and reached up with her other hand. In an instant, she had scrambled onto the narrow shelf and hidden herself in the shadows with her back to the wall. Far below, on the stone paving, she could just make out the forms of two guards conversing in the moonlight. They certainly exhibited no concerns about the Highlander. As she glanced back through the partially open panes of the long, leaded windows into the darkness inside, she hoped Mary would not decide to come down and visit her in the music room, two stories below.

Jaime shivered a bit with anticipation of what lay ahead, and at the rashness of the climb. Quietly pulling open one of the windows, she stepped over the low frame and through the heavy quilted curtains into the bedchamber.

The deadly silence that greeted her made the blood run cold in her veins. The last embers of the small fire in the hearth hardly illuminated the chamber at all. Moving cautiously across the freshly woven mat of rushes covering the floor of the room, Jaime almost cried out as her hip brushed roughly against a small table. Jaime spread her fingers carefully across the wooden surface and found a small wick lamp. As her eyes adjusted better, the huge black shape of a damask-curtained bed loomed in one corner. Fearful of calling his name in the dark, she took the wick lamp to the fireplace to light it. If by chance Malcolm had been moved out of this chamber . . . she shuddered to think of the consequences.

Jaime shook her head, keeping sight of the bed out of one corner of her eye. That he had been moved was highly unlikely, but still she knew she would feel more comfortable with even the smallest glimmer of light to assist her. She knelt before the embers of the dying fire.

As she was rising, the tiny flame of the wick lamp shielded

by her hand, his rough, masculine voice startled a strangled scream out of her.

"You are *late!*"

Jaime spun around, one hand raised in surprise, the light of the lamp falling fully upon the Highlander. As she stared at him, sitting in a chair beside the window's heavy curtains, her heart began to beat again with a vengeance, now pounding fiercely in her chest. She must have passed right by him as she entered the bedchamber.

Malcolm MacLeod was the image of elegance, his white linen shirt open at the throat, and his booted legs sprawled before him. But there was something about his expression that caught her eye. His face displayed more than just aloofness and indifference. Even in the lamplight, she could see fierceness, hostility there. But she had ached so long to be alone with him, that the thrill of this moment could not be subdued by the gleam of an eye or the curl of a lip. Jaime was so much in love with him that, for the moment, nothing else mattered.

"I expected you to come up here much sooner." His tone was no more than a low, sensual drawl, and Jaime's heart caught fire. "Though I hadn't expected you to come up the palace wall."

"I came out the music room window . . ."

Malcolm went on as if she hadn't spoken. "*Much* sooner, considering how short the time you have left before your entry into the blessed state of matrimony."

"That is all a mista . . ."

"Come, let's stop all this. You didn't risk your life for mere conversation," he interrupted again. "I believe the last time that we were alone we hadn't the opportunity to finish . . ." He paused, his eyes raking over her body in a way that took her breath away.

"Malcolm, I . . ." She took a step toward him.

"I've seen you watching. Every time I turned during this evening's meal, I found your eyes upon me. There was hunger in your eyes, but not for food. I knew you would come to me tonight . . . with something more than simple talk on your mind. Am I wrong, lass?"

"I . . ." Jaime wished desperately that she could lie. But she couldn't. Watching his sensual lips whispering into Mary's ear tonight had nearly driven Jaime mad. She ached to have those lips whispering in *her* ear, pressed to *her* mouth, to *her* skin. She gazed longingly at them now.

"Am I wrong?"

"Nay," she whispered.

Malcolm stared at her in a self-satisfied silence, forcing himself to look at her with the cold eye of the critic, and not with the eye of the fool he'd once been. He shook off the nagging thought that only a few days earlier, he'd really thought she loved him.

But she'd been lying. In the surgery she'd been ready to make love to him, all the while holding back the truth that she belonged to another. To that vile snake, Edward Howard! But he had learned the whole story. Though Surrey admitted that he himself was hardly privy to his brother's thoughts or plans, he'd told him it was common knowledge that Jaime had belonged to Edward for quite some time. Malcolm knew then that he'd been right from the first in thinking her so foully disgraced. She had freely given herself to one—to an Englishman—and yet still lusted after pleasure in the arms of others. Very well, he thought grimly, in this case, at least, he would satisfy the whims of his captors.

"Take off your cloak," he instructed curtly.

Visibly startled by the request and the sharp tone of his command, Jaime obeyed, folding it and turning to place the dark garment on the table. "Malcolm, I do need to explain." She gasped, turning her face back to him. "What are you doing?"

Malcolm was standing bare-chested by his chair, his shirt wadded into a ball in his hand. He was now all but completely healed, and he felt only the faintest twinges of pain in his shoulder and side at the abrupt movement. But there was a festering wound within that seemed to be growing worse every day.

Aye, he thought angrily. What *was* he doing? The sight of her beautiful face, gazing at him with that wide-eyed mixture of surprise and innocence, drove a shaft of molten steel into his heart. What *was* he doing? That innocence is nothing more than pretense, he reminded himself fiercely. Her body, so womanly and strong . . . her breasts, rising and falling with every rapid breath . . . her hands and fingers, thin and white and outstretched to him imploringly.

But what did *she* want? What was *she* doing?

Malcolm knew what she was doing. Suddenly furious with himself for thinking that he could somehow shame her by just taking her in his bed, he cast his shirt to the side and took her roughly by the arm.

"You are leaving here."

"Please don't." She tried to fight back, his grip hard on her arm.

"Aye, you're going out. I'll not have you here!"

"Hold, Malcolm! Please!"

"Nay," he seethed through clenched teeth. "You've become a seductress! A witch!"

" 'Tis untrue!"

"Aye, 'tis true! And I won't be added to your list of filthy lovers!" His face was a mask of cold fury.

Jaime's face went white with shock.

"You can go out this way for a change," he said, dragging her toward the door. "And you can explain anyway you like how you came to enter through the window."

She tried to drag her feet across the floor, but his strong hands lifted her, propelling her swiftly toward the heavy oak door.

"A fine thing. A pleasant surprise for your arriving husband. The entire serving staff—and the soldiers, too—talking of you, Jaime Macpherson, Edward Howard's own intended, tossed on her ear out of his prisoner's bedchamber. The rumors that would go about, of you climbing the walls to spend a night in the man's arms." Every muscle in his body flexed with anger, his raging eyes spewed flames as they gazed down at her. "But perhaps this is nothing new. Perhaps your beloved is used to sharing your body with others. Possibly I am expecting more of a reaction than I should!"

They reached the door.

"Well, perhaps these guards are accustomed to seeing you so late." With unexpected suddenness, Malcolm tore at the shoulder of her dress, exposing the ivory skin at the tops of her breasts. "Maybe this is more the way they know you!"

"Malcolm, don't!" she pleaded, clutching at his hand as he reached for the latch. "Please don't shame me before them!"

No longer able to hold back her tears, she threw her arms wildly around his neck and chest, and buried her face against him. "Please, Malcolm! Please don't."

Her sobs tore at him. His hand froze on the latch, and he closed his eyes, trying to shut out the sound of her pleading voice.

"Malcolm, you are the only man that I have ever loved. You are the only man I've ever cared for. Don't trample me under like this. Don't throw me away!"

His skin was wet with her tears. She raised her face, still clinging tightly to him, and pressed her lips against his chest. He felt the desire, strong and lusty, stirring forcefully in his loins.

"Edward is nothing to me," she whispered, the skin of her cheek hot against his flesh. "I've never . . ."

He grabbed a fistful of her hair and pulled her head back. She looked up and shuddered as she gazed into the depths of his eyes. He knew what she could see—passion, desire, and hunger—and he made no attempt to hide any of it.

"Never," he said, his words no more than a low rumble, an animal growl in his throat. "*Never* mention his name while I hold you in my arms."

Jaime stared at him a moment, and then, rising to her full height, moved to press her lips against his. But his movement was quicker, rougher, and his mouth closed over her lips like a vise, his tongue plunging into the soft recesses, conquering with a bruising passion. But it was a passion that Jaime accepted readily, a passion that filled her with a wild and stormy joy.

Malcolm's arms wound tightly about her, their bodies entwined, intimately pressed together to the point that it seemed to Jaime that the floor had fallen away beneath them, that they now floated in a place unbound by the laws of nature.

A place where lovers joined, and one knew not where her body ended and his began. All at once Jaime felt her body begin to quake, to shudder with that same delicious and terrifying joy.

And then the air, warm and sweet around her, began to stir and whirl, and she knew that they were moving. Vaguely, she felt herself being lifted in his arms, and she simply nestled her head into the crook of his neck, knowing that she was safe with him. She trusted Malcolm MacLeod, and she loved him, and she knew that he must love her. Once she could make him see the truth of what they were to each other, he would cherish their love as dearly as she did. And if making love to him was what would make him see, then so be it, she thought happily. She waited for no other. When or where she should surrender her innocence held no significance to her, so long as she surrendered it to him.

When he put her down on her feet beside the bed, she swayed a bit, focusing her eyes on his face as he stepped away. She shivered and stared at him, uncomprehending. The warmth and comfort that came with his strong embrace quieted her nerves, soothed her fears. But now, without his powerful arms about her, Jaime felt alone and strangely cold.

His eyes swept over her. "Undress!" he ordered, his voice husky and raw.

Malcolm stood before her. The look in her eyes cried out for words of love. He could see plainly that she yearned to reach for him, to make him take her into his arms again. But instead, he simply clenched his fists and watched as she reached behind her neck for the laces that held her dress in place. He could see plainly the trembling hands that struggled to undo the ties.

Malcolm avoided looking into her tear-rimmed eyes, but instead focused his gaze on her full lips, on the softness of her neck, on the soft ivory skin showing through the rend he'd made in the dress. When she'd unlaced the garment as far as she could, Jaime began to pull at the wide sleeves, and Malcolm's breath caught in his throat as the torn bodice of the dress slipped downward. Her breasts, high and round, pressed against the thin silk of her chemise. He could feel her eyes riveted to his face, but he forced himself to keep his own gaze averted, and as she pushed the skirts down and bent down to step out of them, the sight of her breasts swinging free of her undergarment jolted him with the power of a lightning bolt. His breathing stopped, and had still not resumed by the time she straightened, her hair cascading forward, the ebony locks concealing and accentuating the exquisite curves of her womanly form.

"Remove them," he growled softly, concentrating on her hands clasped before her. "The rest of your clothes—remove them."

When she hesitated, he glanced up at her, and the flash of her eyes toward the burning wick lamp. She wished to continue without the light.

"You will hide nothing more from me, lass." Malcolm's angry voice cut through the air like the blade of a dirk. "And you will look into my eyes when I make love to you. I want you to remember. I want you to see my eyes as clear as the winter peaks of the Black Cuillins, and I want you to think of my face . . . nay, I want you to *see* it looming above you the next time you're bedding that English lover of yours."

Slowly brushing away a runaway tear with the back of her hand, Jaime silently reached for the shoulder straps of her chemise and pulled them down, one at a time. The material tightened against her firm breasts and then released them. His throat went dry and he felt himself hardening at this sight of perfection, and as she slowly lowered the smooth fabric over the curves of her hips, Malcolm found he had to consciously force the air into his lungs. The chemise dropped to the floor, pooling at her feet.

The Highlander's eyes studied every bit of her stunningly beautiful body, trying to shut out the thought that this was Jaime. He looked at her—flawless in form—trying to think of her as if she were some wrought image—a painting, a statue. Feelings tore through him so completely contrary to what he wished to feel.

He wanted to feel—nothing.

Malcolm stared at her. She stood erect, hiding nothing. His eyes possessed her, but that was all. She wasn't his. His gaze traveled along the sensuous curves. The light of the lamp flickered on the soft planes of her belly, created shadows along her arms, the undersides of her breasts, the inside of her thigh.

He looked up into her face. Her cheeks and her eyes glistened with tears.

It had to be this way. He fought the weakness in his heart that screamed to show her affection. Longing . . . nay, lust was all that could bind them now. She had to be treated *this* way, he argued silently. She'd come to him with one thing in mind, and that was all he would allow himself to give. He took a step and reached the side of the bed, then threw back the bedcovers with a violence that made Jaime jump. But as she began to edge toward the bed, he grabbed her fiercely by the wrist.

"Nay, lass!" he growled. "Not so quick!"

There was surprise in her face as she stared up at him. Malcolm knew deep in his heart that this would be the last time he would ever have her. Her beauty represented in his mind a splendor unmatched this side of paradise. But he now knew all too well the workings of her fraudulent heart, and he also knew no other woman would ever hurt him as she had.

She wasn't his. She belonged to another.

Her touch—Malcolm wanted to feel the touch of her fingers on his skin. Then he would carry that memory for whatever time he had left in this life.

And he would force her if he needed to . . . because she would never belong to him.

"Come to me." His command, hoarse even to his own ear, echoed in the room. "Undress me."

Jaime hesitated for an instant. Then, slowly, she reached out her hand. With the speed of lightning, Malcolm clamped his hand on her wrist and jerked her toward him. Her body fell against his, her warm breasts pressing against him. She stared up at him, surprise and expectation mixed in her eyes. Deliberately, he took one of her small hands and drew it to his manhood. With an audible intake of breath, she turned her smooth, damp cheek to his chest, and Malcolm rested his mouth against her hair, breathing in her sweet scent. Her soft ivory body, close now, melded in the lamplight with his darker skin, creating havoc with his senses.

He was losing control, and he knew it. Of their own accord, his lips brushed against the satin softness of her hair. Without planning it, without considering it, he found his mouth moving downward to kiss and suckle the velvet skin of her earlobe. But when she tilted her head to the side to give him better access to the sweet-tasting skin of her neck, when she let out a low moan as he trailed his warm kisses over her flesh, Malcolm's brain cleared, telling him her actions were premeditated, the moment completely planned. He drew back sharply.

"Undress me, I said."

Her hands were clumsy and shaking as they drew down his breeches and his close hose. But before she could withdraw, he grasped her hand and pulled it to him. For a moment she resisted slightly. Such coyness, he thought. But then, as he held her wrist, her fingers slowly uncoiled and gently wrapped themselves around his hardened shaft. And then the Highlander ceased to breathe at all as he felt her thumb and fingers running over the skin, exploring the length and the thickness of him, feeling the texture, caressing him, teasing him.

Malcolm's control snapped.

One moment they were standing beside the bed, the next she was stretched across it with her legs spread apart by his body. Malcolm pinned Jaime's hands above her head with one hand as he suckled her breasts with a hunger that he had never known. Her body writhed against him, and her soft moans bespoke her own desires. Shifting his weight slightly, he used his fingers to stroke the folds of her womanhood, releasing in her the moist fluids that would open her to him.

Jaime's soft cries brought on a new, raw passion that filled Malcolm and threatened to push him over the edge. Every muscle in his frame taut as wire, he drew himself up and looked into her face. As he watched, he could see her expression change as the waves of desire poured through her. She kept her eyes pressed shut, but her hands reached up to pull him back down upon her.

This was more than Malcolm could take. Sliding his hands under Jaime's firm buttocks, he lifted her and found the place. With one mighty thrust he entered, burying himself deep within her.

And then came the awful revelation, as swift and as powerful as lightning. And Malcolm wished he were dead!

CHAPTER 22

Malcolm stood with his back to the hearth, his gaze transfixed on the open window. With the heavy curtains drawn back, the gentle predawn breeze blew freely through the room. The air was cool and damp, but the Highlander felt nothing. For over an hour he had been standing thus, and the lightening gray of the eastern sky meant nothing to him.

She had left him. Silently, her eyes averted, she had slipped into her clothes and started for the window. And he had watched her wordlessly. She had paused only once by the curtains, turning her head as if to speak. But no sound had emerged, and then, like a night bird taking flight, Jaime had gone, disappearing into the darkness and never looking back.

A deep sigh racked his powerful frame, and Malcolm turned his gaze toward the bed. The room was still very dark, but the whiteness of the bedclothes stood out in the emptiness. He could see in his mind's eye the space where she'd been. He could see the proof of her love, of her constancy, staining the whiteness of the sheet, burning into his soul a black and bloody guilt. A guilt that was his and his alone.

Malcolm looked away and squeezed his eyes shut. For a moment he thought of going back to his bed, but he never moved. After all, what relief could he find there? As if, he thought bitterly, by caressing the coarse sheets he could find some solace for his foul and tortured soul. As if he could return the warmth that she had taken with her when she had slipped out into the night. He covered his eyes with one hand and glared into the darkness of his mind. How wrong he'd been to treat her so unjustly, and how brave she'd been to endure what he'd done to her without a single word of complaint.

She had never belonged to another. He had been Jaime's first. And to take her as brutally as he had . . . By the Rood! To think that moments before she had told him how she loved him. But he, blinded by his own stupidity and anger, had not believed her. He, Malcolm MacLeod, the falsest of all men, had not believed *her*! He, the man who had tried to marry, not for love, but for the well-being of his bloody clan!

The Highlander raked his hand over his face, but he knew he could not wipe away his guilt. An ugly and terrible thought struck at him—he had become his father's son. Like Torquil MacLeod, his brutal and lust-driven father, Malcolm had become a vicious defiler of trusting women, a cruel and ruthless ravager of the defenseless.

With an anguished roar, Malcolm charged across the chamber and tore the bed apart. Wild with grief, he threw the bedclothes to the floor and struck the high mattress with the palms of his hands. To think that she'd trusted him and come here, so late in the night. She'd wanted to explain, she said. But she had never suspected him to be capable of such evil—and how could she suspect such foulness?

Dropping his head into his hands, Malcolm began to pray. For forgiveness. For *her* forgiveness!

The sun would be well above the mist-covered fields before he would raise his head, determined, defiant, his way finally clear.

Jaime coiled up beneath the bedclothes, her knees drawn tightly to her stomach. Lying still, she listened intently to the rhythmic sounds of her cousin's deep and peaceful sleep.

She had been so fortunate that Mary had not been awakened when she'd entered a few moments earlier. It would have been extremely difficult explaining the condition of her clothes. Moving quietly, almost mechanically, about the bedchamber they shared, Jaime had taken off her torn dress, folding the garment carefully and hiding it deep in the cavernous spaces of her great traveling chest.

As she had prepared herself for bed—washing herself, pulling the soft, cotton shift over her head, drawing back the bedclothes—Jaime had found herself performing each action as if in a dream. Unable to shake the feeling, she was glad that she'd had to answer none of Mary's usual questions. What had taken place tonight, Jaime had no desire to discuss with anyone.

Lying there in the secure confines of her bed, thinking of what she had done, Jaime suddenly found herself crying. The tears began without warning, trickling from the corners of her eyes, over the bridge of her nose, silently disappearing into the soft sheets. She only realized she'd been crying when her breaths began to shorten into sobs that wracked her body. The thought of awakening Mary, the thought of discovery jolted Jaime into awareness, and she buried her face into the billows of the mattress, only then allowing all of her raw emotions to spring forth and give muffled voice to her wretchedness.

Some time later, as her tears spent themselves, she thought back wearily over the events of this night. She had always considered herself a woman able to care for herself. In many ways independent, even. But since becoming an adult, she'd never acted with unrestrained freedom before—not before tonight. But it wasn't the price of this independence that hurt her so—the loss of her innocence, her maidenhead—it was Malcolm! She wrapped her arms even more tightly about her knees and pressed her forehead into them. Though making love to him had not been what she'd expected it to be, the truth was that she'd never really known what to expect.

What bothered her most was the confusion that she could see in his face, in his eyes—the fact that she'd not been able to reach him, to make him know the truth. The truth about her—the truth about the two of them. He had been so angry when she arrived, and she'd not known how to ease his hurt other than being amenable to his wishes. Though that had cut roughly against her nature, it hadn't been the worst. Nay, it was the determination that he could give her up that hurt her most. For she had seen the fire of desire in his eyes, felt the overwhelming power of his passion. With the exception of the instant when he'd driven his shaft into her—that devastating moment that had made her scream inwardly at the shock as much as the pain—she knew she'd been as crazed with desire as he.

But then, suddenly, everything had changed. She realized now that this change only added to her misery. The change in him had been as clear and distinct as the coming of night, as sudden as the passing of a summer storm in the Highlands. After his wild and powerful lunge, Malcolm had simply stopped as if struck dead.

Jaime had not moved. As she waited for him to stir, to continue, to do anything, the tearing pain had suddenly disappeared into the vagueness of a kind of stunned memory. The moment had hung in time like a dewdrop on a leaf. As if life itself were holding its breath, the air around them, the fire in the hearth, the lamplight, the very stars themselves, Jaime remembered thinking, had stopped, awaiting his next act. Then, with a low, anguished moan, Malcolm had withdrawn from her. Silently, with excruciating slowness—certainly with no hint of joy—he had lifted himself from her and moved carefully onto the bed beside her.

Manners, she remembered thinking. So it is manners that reward the act of loving. And extreme gentleness in manners, at that! Kindness, solace, and the utmost care in the handling of the woman. But no passion. Gone in a single thrust. Gone in a moment. Gone with a single low and anguished moan. Gone.

Malcolm had spoken no words to her, but he had gathered her into his arms like a bairn whom he'd just trampled. And she, confused with the suddenness of it all—the pain, the hurt of not knowing the reason for the change, for the obvious disappointment that she'd wrought in him—had simply waited for a few moments, and then had slipped quietly from his bed. Without a word from him, she had gone out the way she had come. He hadn't stopped her from going. He hadn't called after her. He hadn't even spoken her name.

The tears began to flow freely once again, and she lay back on the mattress, staring up into the black nothingness above her.

He didn't care for her. He didn't love her. How wrong she had been!

CHAPTER 23

The duke of Norfolk threw the partially completed letter facedown on the table as his page announced Edward into the chamber. Rapping his gnarled knuckles on the table, Norfolk motioned to his clerk to go out and wait, and then turned to acknowledge his second son. Something had to be done about the situation, he decided, but those very close to the king were being unusually tight-lipped, and it was difficult to make decisions without accurate information.

"Your Grace," Edward said as he stepped into the richly appointed chamber.

Beyond the open door, the duke caught sight of the two guards who had accompanied Edward to his chamber. He ordered his page to close the door and leave them be. As the door clicked quietly shut, Norfolk turned his scowling face on the young man.

"What have you done, Edward?" The duke's tone was harsh as he leaned forward on his arms and rapped the table again. "What?"

"By the devil, I've done nothing, Father."

"Nothing!" Norfolk spat disgustedly. "Save that for the king's torturers. Of course you've done something—many things! But what have you done that has reached the ears of the king?"

"Father, I . . ."

"Who are our enemies, Edward?" the duke rolled on. "What are they using against us?"

Getting nothing but silence for an answer, Norfolk banged the wood surface hard. He had been in this game too long to let down his guard, but none of the family's enemies were in any position at present to hurt him.

"It has to be something. Something strong enough to change the king's attitude toward you so drastically. Now think of whom you have wronged. Of whom you have angered to the point of risking their own position in besmirching you."

Edward looked back blankly at the older man.

"Edward, think!" he snapped. "What have you done?"

"Nothing, Father." he answered. "I've been accused wrongly and unjustly . . ."

"Oh, by the saints!"

". . . And if I could just find out the identity of the blackguard who has dared to muck about with my honor . . ."

"Honor!" The duke threw up his hands.

". . . In the king's company, I vow on my grandfather's sword I will tear the bastard's throat out with my teeth!"

Norfolk paused and studied his son's face. There was nothing there that told him whether Edward was keeping anything back. He hoped to God his son would not be so foolish.

"We are fortunate that mucking about is all that has been accomplished so far," the duke warned as he sank back in his chair. "But unless we do something to correct this situation now, an accusation is certain to follow. That's the way the court works . . . rumor becomes insinuation, and if insinuation appears to meet with a favorable response by His Majesty, then insinuation quickly becomes accusation!"

"I've already been accused! And convicted!" Edward, quite rattled by this new turn of events, banged his flat palms on the table. "I am followed wherever I go! There are guards posted at my own chamber door. I have no privacy. I am a caged animal, tormented with each breath I take."

"Don't complain, Edward. This could be much worse."

"I cannot see how! One moment I am called to court. I am welcomed in the king's company. I am heralded as a hero of the realm. Defender of His Majesty's seas. And now, in the next moment, I am guarded like a thief. Commissions that should have been given to me are being pissed away to white-livered wolves who have never stepped foot on the bloody deck of a surrendering gold ship."

"Edward, it's no use."

"I heard today that the Lord Great Chamberlain is sending for my crew . . . for questioning! About me!" Edward was now pacing the room, his hands balled into fists at his sides, his face crimson with rage. He stopped and looked directly at his father. "How could it be worse than this, Your Grace? How could they do more damage to me than they've already done?"

"Easily," the duke answered under his breath. "It is easily done! How do you think we arranged—just a few weeks ago—to have that bloody Cromwell arrested. We had him dragged out of a Council meeting. Accused of being a radical heretic and a traitor under the Act of Attainder, and easily enough accomplished." Norfolk snorted mirthlessly. "He has been a stick in my ass for a long time, but I'm a patient man. If Cromwell hadn't brought over that foul bitch, Anne of Cleves, for the king to wed, we might still be waiting. But as it is, his beheading will be a pleasure to watch."

Edward swallowed audibly as the blood drained from his face. "They could not do that to me, there is no proof!"

There was no evidence against Cromwell either, the duke thought silently. None that hadn't been invented. But he had become an increasing threat to the powers of the members of the Privy Council—to Norfolk's own power. And then fate had taken a decided hand in matters. After Cromwell had arranged the unsuccessful marriage of King Henry to Anne of Cleves—a simple accusation had been more than enough.

"Nay, Edward. You won't end up like Cromwell," Norfolk said, hoping his son would believe him. He didn't need Edward displaying anything but the utmost confidence. "But we'll have to make sure that there is nothing to be twisted into proof."

For a long moment Edward stood and watched his father's thoughtful expression. Gradually his color returned and he threw himself into a chair, his legs sprawled before him. "So what am I to do now?"

"Do? Nothing. You will simply go about your business as if nothing was wrong. You have been commanded to remain at court, so you will remain. I will see that your men say what needs to be said . . . and those whom we doubt will be taken care of at Norwich Castle." Norfolk turned a knowing look in his son's direction. He would cover whatever blunders Edward had made. "Some of them will disappear. The others will do what they're told."

"Aye, Father."

Norfolk continued to eye Edward. "And in the meantime, we will rely—to some extent—on the single bright star lighting our way."

A long moment passed before Edward's expressionless face suddenly lit up with understanding. "Catherine?"

The duke nodded slowly as he pondered his son's answer. "Aye, perhaps we might consider her . . . a star. But we must take care. The night sky is littered with stars of Catherine's type. And there is no way to catch a falling star."

"But, Father, her marriage to the king is certain to bring His Majesty's favor our way." Edward leaned forward in his chair and planted his hands on the desk. "Perhaps I should speak to her—have her go to the king on my behalf. Perhaps if she were to defend me . . ."

"I don't see much possibility of that," Norfolk answered shortly. "She left for Kenninghall this morning with her growing entourage."

A look of surprise came over Edward's face. "I had no idea she was planning to go back so soon. I thought she was planning to wait and accompany us."

"You mean . . . to have *us* accompany *her*!" The duke gazed at his knotted knuckles tapping lightly on the table. "I thought so, as well. But she was quite eager to go and ready herself for the wedding. When she came to me, she'd already gotten permission—reluctant though he was to give it—from the king."

His eyes followed his son as Edward stood and silently began pacing the room.

"So she left before I had the chance to seek her help."

"That would appear to be the case."

Edward's face darkened with anger, and he turned and

strode away from his father, pausing to run his hand over the new globe-shaped map of the world standing at the end of the room.

The duke of Norfolk leaned forward and picked up the unfinished letter. The clerk's quill pen, ink, and blotting sand still lay on the table before him. After a quick glance at the writing, he turned and eyed his son. "When I mentioned a star to light our way, I wasn't speaking of Catherine!"

Edward stopped—his finger resting on the globe and blotting out half of Scotland. His father's words finally sunk in.

"Jaime!" he said, whirling.

"Aye," the duke responded, nodding without looking up. "Jaime!"

As Edward crossed the room toward him, the old politician reached for his clerk's pen. "I am sending word for her to join us here at court."

"Then it's time!"

The duke cocked his head as he looked up at his son. "I believe the king will have a complete change of heart, my boy, when you tell him the truth."

CHAPTER 24

The mellifluous tones of her heavenly voice, combined with the pure notes of the children around her, was surely the most divine sound Malcolm had ever heard. Their faces glowing in the light of a thousand candles, the young singers and musicians sat in a small circle in the center of the Great Hall at Kenninghall. The occupants of the Hall, only moments ago boisterous in their merrymaking, now sat in silent awe. The sheer beauty of the performers, the clear accomplishment of their blessed talents and their training, but most of all the sweet sounds that now filled the air held all within hearing rapt and spellbound.

But Malcolm's attention never shifted from Jaime as his pained mind followed the tenor of her voice, and his eyes worshiped every line, every shadow of her face. She had coiled her hair high on top of her head—and he saw the loose tendrils seductively teasing the smooth planes of her neck. Her eyes told him—though perhaps only him—of their deep, shared secret; and her pale skin bespoke a woman who was no longer what she had been only a day earlier.

He so desperately hoped she would lift her eyes and at least acknowledge his existence in the Hall. He craved so desperately a moment alone with her. She could kill him if she desired—that would be an end Malcolm would readily accept. As long as she gave him a chance to say his peace, to seek her pardon, to allow him to pour out his heart, he would accept death at her hands in an instant.

As she tucked the small harp against her body and began to strum gently at the strings, he felt her fingers upon the strings of his heart.

". . . Don't you think so?" Surrey's loud whisper finally penetrated Malcolm's thoughts. "A most entertaining performance, wouldn't you say?"

The Highlander realized that the earl had been speaking to him, but, unable to tear his attention away from the vision of loveliness before him, Malcolm simply nodded in response. The words of Jaime's song were sad, plaintive, and her lilting voice went straight to the softest chambers of his soul. He listened, spellbound, aware of Surrey's eyes fixed upon him, but determined not to be distracted from her again.

Too soon for Malcolm and for everyone else in the room, Jaime finished the song, and began speaking quietly to the group of children scattered around at her feet. Malcolm watched in fascination as she extended her hand to a very young redheaded lass and, raising the child to her feet, brought her up beside the group of musicians.

"Most satisfying, having the children's talents developed with such care."

Surrey's words were quickly corrected by his wife, who sat beside him. "Aye, Jaime's care, my dear. All the talent lies with her. She is the one who is bringing these little ruffians around."

"Ahh, a nasty job!" Surrey put in jokingly.

"One might think so," Frances answered brightly. "But with Jaime in charge, they are like ducks in the water."

"These are definitely the most melodious ducks that I've ever heard, wife."

Malcolm strained his ears, trying to catch some scrap of the whispering going on between Jaime and the redheaded child. But his attempt was for naught with Surrey and Frances continuing to converse. She was so beautiful in the glow of the candles and the flames dancing in the great hearth.

"Was she always so inspired? Even as a child?"

Once again lost in his thoughts, a moment went by before Malcolm realized a question had been directed at him. The countess of Surrey was awaiting his answer, and Malcolm glanced at the faces of both her and the earl.

"She was," Malcolm answered, quickly turning his gaze back on Jaime. The little girl before her was pulling nervously at the pink ribbon in her hair and nodding to her instructor. The conference ended and the little singer took her place.

"Did she always have such a talent for music?" Frances asked.

"For as long as I've known her, she's been the most gifted of musicians," Malcolm answered.

"And has she always been so eager to teach? She really is a marvel."

"From the time she was little, she has been most eager to learn. It is completely in keeping for her to find a way to impart that knowledge to others." A small smile was tugging at Jaime's lips as she turned to acknowledge a word said by one of the older children. For the briefest of instants, her gaze lifted and she looked straight into Malcolm's eyes. His heart soared.

"Was she always so kindhearted?" Frances's voice was insistent. "Come, Malcolm, you must share what you know! She is so kind to everyone. Look how she treats that child."

"She has never been any other way," Malcolm replied, fixed on the memory of that brief glance.

"Has she always been so stunningly beautiful?"

Malcolm and Frances both turned their heads sharply, each of them sending withering looks at the earl.

"Has she?" Surrey asked seriously, not letting up on Malcolm.

"Nay," the Highlander answered shortly. "Jaime Macpherson was lanky and thin, and she was always sure to act far different from the other lasses."

Surrey nodded. "So she has changed greatly since you met her last!"

"Aye, that she has," Malcolm answered, his voice still retaining the surly, involuntary gruffness brought on by Surrey's notice of Jaime's beauty.

"I'm certainly glad of that!"

"May I inquire why you're glad, Surrey?" Frances asked, the slightest hint of suspicion and irritation in her question.

The earl turned to his wife. "If she hadn't changed, my dear, then I would have thought something quite amiss."

"Would you be kind enough to explain, husband?"

"It's quite simple, really. Besides you, my dear, our cousin Jaime is easily the most charming and accomplished young woman to step foot in Kenninghall in years." Surrey paused and gestured toward Malcolm. "To think that my friend here would allow such beauty and talent to escape his grasp—considering the open affection he exhibits now—well, I couldn't help but think that she must have been far different as a child. Either that or we must all be quite blind to her flaws."

"Jaime Macpherson has no flaws," Malcolm stated emphatically, setting his jaw.

"I believe we are all in agreement with that, Malcolm. And now your response—regarding how she has changed—has confirmed my own high opinion of her."

Frances cocked an eyebrow at her husband. "Surrey, what do you mean, 'open affection'?"

The earl looked straight at the Highlander. "I believe, my dear, our guest knows exactly what I mean. Am I wrong, Malcolm?"

"You are not wrong, Surrey."

"Well, I'm sorry for you, but it's too late, you see." Surrey turned and glanced over at Jaime. "She is spoken for. I told you so myself."

"Jaime has exchanged no vow. There has been no betrothal, yet."

"My friend, you've had your chance—a lifetime of chances—but you never claimed her as your own."

But I have, Malcolm thought silently, his inner pain blocking any sense of triumph.

"But my brother Edward," Surrey paused, looking about the room. "He has recognized her value."

"In gold perhaps," Malcolm added with disdain in his voice.

"Perhaps," Surrey conceded with a nod. "All the same, Malcolm, once Edward sets his mind on something that he desires—or on someone—there is no stopping him. And he wants Jaime."

The earl turned and exchanged a look with his wife before turning his attention on the Highlander once again. "And he doesn't mean to toy with her like some puppet, or play with her like some wench."

"Surrey!" Frances said, shocked dismay in her voice.

The earl did not look away from Malcolm. "Edward quite clearly intends to take Jaime for his wife. He means to have her."

Malcolm knew common sense dictated that he remain silent. That he withhold his rebuttal and not give voice to his opinion of this match, but they were talking about Jaime, and there was now nothing that would prevail over the feelings that he harbored for her.

"Nay." The Highlander waved him off. "You are speaking as the elder brother, Surrey, and not as a man of the world— educated by the great Humanist, himself. Nor are you speaking as the poet we all know you to be. These are not the utterances of a man dedicated to the search for truth. These are not your words, Surrey. Play the others for fools—your countess here and I don't believe you."

The earl smiled as his wife turned her head away, trying to hide her mirth. "Believe what you like, Malcolm MacLeod. And go to the devil while you're at it. I am giving you only the facts."

"You're giving us only what your brother wishes to have believed."

"I'm telling you what is sure to happen."

"Only if your brother is clever enough to match Jaime's wit. And, of course, assuming he is wise enough to value her learning. And then there is the question of whether he is broadminded enough to appreciate her goodness." Malcolm gazed steadily into Surrey's face. "I wonder if you truly believe Edward is deserving enough to win Jaime's hand. Though you were writing about your good and lovely wife, you could as easily have been writing about Jaime when you wrote,

> For what she saith, ye may it trust
> As it by writing sealed were.
> And virtues hath she many moe
> Than I with pen have skill to show."

His face suddenly pensive, Surrey reached over and wrapped a hand around his cup of wine. "Though I'll deny ever saying it, my friend, that *is* a tall order for Edward."

And how could you not think so, the Highlander thought silently, when he himself—Malcolm MacLeod—was not man enough to deserve her.

The music began again, and those in the Hall hushed immediately. Malcolm's eyes never left Jaime's face as the performers continued with their display of beauty and song.

Surrey's eyes were fixed on Malcolm's face when the music paused once again.

"Do you mean to press him with a challenge for her hand?" the earl asked, studying his face. When Malcolm glanced at his hosts, Frances was pretending not to hear the two men's talk.

"Now, that would be between your brother and myself, don't you think, m'lord?"

Surrey paused and raised his wine to his lips, speaking his words into his cup. "He plays quite dirty, Malcolm, and I should hate to see your head stuck on a pole at Norwich Castle, simply because you underestimated my brother."

This time it was the Highlander's turn to smile as he nodded silently in response to the earl's words. "I can assure you that I am already well attuned to his methods. And I agree completely with your concerns."

The sound of children's voices rising once again silenced the two men in the midst of their discussion. And Malcolm pushed aside all thoughts and turned body and soul to the woman before his eyes.

He knew that Edward would never accept a challenge from him for Jaime's hand. But one thing he hadn't mentioned to

Surrey was that getting his cowardly younger brother to agree to a challenge would be nothing compared to convincing Jaime that he truly loved her. Indeed, fighting Edward would be far simpler than getting Jaime Macpherson to trust, once again, in the power of his love.

CHAPTER 25

Quite remarkable how he'd mended, Master Graves had said, considering how battered and close to death Malcolm had been only a fortnight earlier. The Welsh physician had then nodded his head thoughtfully and given the Highlander an emollient to speed the healing of the jagged scars on his chest. Sending his apprentice out ahead of him, Graves had stopped to ask Malcolm if he needed any questions answered.

Malcolm had simply shaken his head. He did not think the physician knew how to ease wounds of the heart.

So, with a kindly nod of the head, the older man had left him. It was only a short time later that Malcolm had spotted the letter on the floor near the entrance of the bedchamber.

Pulling on his shirt, the Highlander crossed the room and picked up the letter.

". . . and various ladies and gentlewomen from the Pole family, as well! Servants and grooms? She must have *fifty* in her entourage now! Can you imagine? And in addition to all these people, she has brought in with her a dozen personal maids!" Mary wrapped her hands about her waist and twirled on her toes, watching the swirl of her skirts. "What I would do with so many people attending to *my* needs! But how can she keep them all busy?"

"Perhaps she'll ask you to join her circle, Mary. Conceivably, *you* could then have them to see to your needs. After all, there are plenty of them to go around!" Jaime's ironic tone was not noticed by her cousin, whose eyes were suddenly drawn to one of the windows and the stained-glass rendition of the Howard coat of arms that adorned the top of each of the music room windows. In spite of the darkness of the night beyond, the colors of the stained glass were vibrantly red and gold.

"Can you imagine what life would be like, progressing through the kingdom with the king and his devoted and beautiful queen?"

Jaime paused to consider the thought, then dismissed it with a crooked half smile and a shake of her head. But Mary was still gazing at the window, at the crown that sat above the shield and plumed helmet. Shrugging her shoulders, Jaime placed the stringless lute she was carrying against the wall by the door before moving back to her worktable to inspect one of the other instruments that had been piled on it.

"I would be a very useful member of her circle," Mary said dreamily. "I can easily imagine Catherine taking me back to court. I shall be one of her gentle ladies in waiting! Oh, the courtiers and knights I will meet then! They shall all be vying for my hand."

"Very useful," Jaime repeated, scowling at the breeze that had suddenly sprung up through the window beneath the colorful coat of arms, ruffling the music sheets stacked beside her worktable. Laying a small harp on top of the music, she quickly moved to the window and pulled it shut. The rain was coming down in torrents, and the wind pushed at the window in her hand. Like a summer storm in the Highlands, she thought with a smile. Jaime turned the latch before closing the window completely, causing it to stay slightly ajar. She had a wee bit more work to do, and she didn't need to suffocate doing it.

"But do you think he'll miss me?" Mary asked, plucking a harp string absently. "Do you think he will be upset by Catherine's decision to take me to court?"

Running her hand over her rain-spattered skirts, Jaime looked up quickly and stared into her cousin's face. For an instant she was afraid to ask the question, but then it was too awkward for her not to ask. She straightened up and pasted on her most indifferent expression. "Who, Mary? Who will miss you so dreadfully?"

Mary affected a nervous glance in the direction of the closed door before whispering her answer. "Malcolm, silly. Who else but my wild Highlander?"

"Of course," Jaime answered shortly before walking to the worktable. "How ridiculous of me to not realize you were referring to *your* Highlander!"

Mary giggled. "Then you think he would miss me!"

Jaime yanked the harp unceremoniously from beneath her cousin's fingers, not deigning to so much as lift an eye to the excited expression she knew must be on Mary's face.

"Please, Jaime, answer me! You *do* think so, don't you?"

"I hardly know what to answer, you foolish creature." Jaime turned the harp over in her hands and then stalked over to the door, leaving it on the floor with the others. "I hardly know him."

Mary cut Jaime off and grabbed her by the shoulders on her way back to the table. "But *I* know him. In fact, sometimes I lie awake in bed and think I've known him all my life. There has never been a man who has affected me as he does."

Trapped, Jaime looked into Mary's pretty face and drew on all the patience she had in her. In a moment, though, she thought, I'm going to knock her right on her affected arse.

"Jaime," Mary said with note of sisterly empathy in her voice, "now I know the torture you must be going through with Edward away at court. Oh, the loneliness you must feel when he is away!"

Jaime stood stock-still in Mary's grasp and felt a knot rising in her throat. She lowered her eyes, staring at her cousin's button of a chin. How wrong could one woman be? she thought, pressing her lips together.

"But, coz, did you see him tonight?" Mary asked, her voice rising excitedly as she abruptly turned the discussion back to *her* Highlander. "Did you see how devastatingly fierce he looked? In that long, black velvet tunic Lord Surrey had the tailors make for him, I could almost imagine him standing in his kilt on some windswept moor, his dark eyes flashing, his hair flying about his face."

Jaime drew in a deep breath. She had avoided looking at him all night. But in her mind's eye, she had no need to imagine him looking so gallant. Her memories were quite vivid.

Mary suddenly dropped her hands to her side. Then, with a quick glance at Jaime's face, she turned slightly, her bottom lip protruding and giving her face the pout of a spoiled child.

"But did you see Catherine?"

Jaime shook her head and silently moved past her cousin toward the table.

"Oh, it was disgraceful the way she pushed me out of the way to get the seat next to Malcolm. She certainly did not look like a woman on the verge of marrying the King of England! And to think that I had my eye on him long before anyone else around here, and Catherine . . . Catherine, just arriving tonight . . ."

Jaime had no interest in listening to things that made her heart wither in her chest. "Forgive me, Mary, but I still have a great deal to do," she said quietly, picking up the two remaining lutes from the table and turning back toward the doorway.

"Do you need help carrying these?" Mary asked breezily.

Jaime glanced over at the instruments already organized by the door and then back at her cousin.

"These are the last of them," she answered, moving away. "But you can put those loose sheets of music on the worktable."

"What are you doing with all these broken things, anyway?" Mary walked around the table, and picked up the harp that Jaime had placed atop the music. She held the instrument as if it were diseased. "They are good for little more than kindling, aren't they?"

"Nay!" Jaime corrected, turning sharply. "Most are only missing some strings. These others simply need a new finish."

"But what are you doing with them?"

"The instrument maker from Norwich is coming down in a few days," Jaime answered, taking the harp from Mary's hand. Bending quickly, she put the stack of music on the table, and put the harp in the appropriate stack. "We'll have them repaired."

"But why? We have so many fine, new instruments. The music teacher—the one whom Catherine, well, the one who left—he needed only half as many as . . ."

Jaime was in no mood to have an endless chat, so she just raised her hand, interrupting her cousin. "I am having these repaired for the children who are not living here in the house. I intend to have them take the instruments with them to their own cottages."

"You mean to borrow?" Mary asked in shock. "Do you trust them to . . ."

"Nay, cousin, I mean for them to keep the instruments!" Jaime answered.

"But, Jaime, these are valuable instruments. You just can't . . ."

"Hold for a moment, Mary," Jaime scolded, happy to find—finally—a way to vent her anger. "You just said they had no more value than kindling, not worth saving. But now, finding out they can be useful, perhaps even bring some happiness into the lives of some poor children—these pieces of wood have suddenly become precious in your mind. Which is it, dear cousin? Shall we discard them as worthless? Or shall we simply let them rot in that chest in the corner? Why don't you let me know what *you* would prefer, rather than what I was planning to do to them?"

"Jaime, I just . . . I just thought . . ." Mary spluttered to a halt and, blushing to the roots of her blond hair, waved a hand in the direction of the instruments, as if shooing them from her presence. "Do whatever you will with the things! I don't care anything about them. I was just trying to say that you have already given so much to these ungrateful brats. And . . ."

"Cousin, please don't make this worse. I only ask that you not meddle in my affairs."

"Meddle? I?" With a toss of her head, Mary marched toward the door. "I wouldn't dream of meddling."

Jaime watched, somewhat relieved that her cousin was leaving. But Mary never made it to the door. Her steps faltered halfway across the room, as if she'd just remembered something important. She stood still for a moment. Then, as Jaime busied herself at the worktable, her cousin went on a meandering tour of the music room. By the time she'd returned to Jaime's side, it seemed she had completely forgotten their disagreement.

"I believe I should talk to him," Mary announced with an air of decisiveness. "I shall take the first step. It simply wouldn't be right to let him hear from someone else that Catherine could be taking me back to court."

Jaime didn't answer, but instead looked around the room for a way to distract herself. The stack of loose sheet music definitely required resorting, and she turned her attention to the task.

"Surely, being a prisoner and a Scot, he would deem himself unworthy to approach me openly with signs of his affection."

The slam of Jaime's palm on the tabletop caused Mary to jump with alarm.

"Aye, Malcolm is a Scot! What of that? What is wrong in being a Scot?" Jaime snapped. Her eyes burned into Mary's flushed face. "Do save such idiotic snobbery for Catherine and those who relish such idle and pretentious chatter. I care nothing for it, Mary."

"Really, Jaime, you have no reason to become so upset. Just because . . ."

"I have every reason to be angry!" Jaime's voice shook as she spoke the words. "Malcolm MacLeod might be a prisoner of Edward's, but he is still an honorable man. The laird of his people. Surrey and Frances have seen fit to treat him as a guest and not as some barbarian; certainly, you might see fit—see it as your duty—to treat him in the same fashion."

"I have been treating him . . ."

"Mary!" Jaime interrupted her. "I just don't know what's gotten into you. One moment ago you called him a prisoner and a Scot as if he were a criminal or in some way disgraced. Apparently, you think him unworthy—simply because of your elevated—and imaginary—status. And that came immediately after telling me how you must fight for his attentions. And that, after praising him for his looks, his manners. Which is it, my dear? Is he false, or is he true? Is he the lowly cur, or is he the noble hound? Tell me how you will have it, Mary—will you hate him, or will you love him?"

Her eyes spilling over with tears, Mary stood gaping at her cousin.

"I love him," she whispered before turning and running from the room.

As the door slammed shut, Jaime sank to her knees beside the table. The noisy tears that Mary was shedding en route to their bedchamber bore little resemblance to the silent sobs that were wracking the frame of Jaime Macpherson. Burying her face in her hands, Jaime finally unleashed the pent-up power of her sorrow. Tears fell onto her dress as she huddled in that music room.

Jaime turned her eyes toward the windows. The rain continued to beat mercilessly against the glass, and her heart began to sink under a crushing weight of misery, the like of which she had never before known.

CHAPTER 26

As he pulled open the window, the wind and rain abated momentarily, and the Highlander stepped silently into the room.

She neither raised her head nor moved, but remained as she was—huddled on her knees with her back to him. Jaime continued to cry, he could see her shoulders hunched forward and quaking a bit. Without taking his eyes from her, Malcolm reached behind him and pulled the window shut. The wind and the rain picked up again, and the sound of the drops beating against the diamond-shaped panes, along with the dropping of the latch penetrated her solitude, and her head snapped around to face him.

Her look of surprise quickly gave way to relief and—dare he even think it!—happiness as recognition set in. But there was also something extremely vulnerable in her attitude, in her face. He took a step in her direction and then stopped as Jaime came quickly to her feet and glanced nervously at the music room door. Though he had certainly given her every reason to fear him, the last thing Malcolm wanted now was for Jaime to run away from him.

With a quick look over her shoulder, Jaime crossed the room to the door. Malcolm nearly called out to her, but hesitated, suddenly uncertain about what to say. He had been waiting outside the window, wishing Mary Howard out that very door, but he knew that if Jaime truly wanted to go, there was nothing he could say that could stop her.

She reached the door in a moment, and then paused. Jaime dropped the latchbar in place as Malcolm felt a sense of relief wash over him. She wasn't running from him. She wasn't going for aid. She wasn't afraid of being alone with him. He watched as she turned around and rested her back against the door.

"I had to see you, Jaime," he said finally.

Her voice was husky from crying. "You came down the wall—you could have continued on into the night. You could have escaped." She quickly wiped away the streaks of tears from her face.

Malcolm knew the truth would sound hollow and false after what he had done to her, so he held his tongue. How could he admit that for him, there was no leaving this place, unless she left with him. "How far would I get on a night such as this."

"True," she whispered. "And with no one to help you to get onto the north road."

The feel of the stiff parchment inside his boot reminded him of those who would help him, but this was not the time to bring that up. In truth, he'd only brought the letter in the event that she would reject his presence outright. He certainly didn't want her to think that the letter had anything to do with why he'd climbed down the wall to see her.

"Are you unwell?" he asked quietly, looking at the dark circles under her eyes.

She shook her head, clearly unenthusiastic about dwelling on herself. For the first time, she lifted her eyes to his wet hair and drenched clothes, and whispered her concern. "You are soaking wet."

Malcolm looked down at the pool of water around his boots and pulled the wet linen of his shirt away from his skin. "Aye." He grinned sheepishly. "There's a wee bit of fog out there. Made the climbing a bit of an adventure, as well."

"You've . . . you've been outside for a time, then," she said, looking down at her tightly clasped hands.

The Highlander could see in her face that she was trying to remember all that had occurred, all that he might have heard of the earlier conversation between her and Mary.

"Aye, a lovely night for a stroll . . . but for the howling of the wind and the rain, and the occasional clap of thunder to rattle about in a man's head. Though 'tis a poor excuse for the real storms we have in the isles, wouldn't you agree, Jaime?" His words were a lie, but he hoped they would ease her discomfort. "But I must admit, I was thankful when at last I saw that silly cousin of yours departing from the room."

The Highlander could feel her gaze upon him as he moved in toward the crackling fire in the hearth. He turned his head as she pushed away from the door and took a couple of steps toward him.

"I'm sorry," Jaime said, casting about the room for something to offer him. "I have neither wine . . . nor anything else to offer you."

The civility in her tone, Malcolm was quite certain, would tear his heart out. He wished she would be more angry—curse him and revile him. He would have felt better about treatment such as that.

"I need nothing more, lass, than what is in this room already. I only came down that wall with the hope of seeing you."

Jaime stiffened slightly as she moved toward the fireplace, but Malcolm could see no other response to his words. Wordlessly, she crouched before the fire and began to add pieces of wood to the warming blaze.

Malcolm admired the flickering glow of the rising flames on her pale profile. Standing only a couple of steps away, he fought the urge to reach down and pull her into his arms. To hold her until she granted the forgiveness he sought. In the light of the fire, Jaime appeared so beautiful, and yet so distant.

She held her hand out to feel the heat. Her eyes were focused on the crackling wood.

"I don't know what you want, but I am finished with what I was doing here." Jaime gestured vaguely toward the pile of instruments by the door as she straightened up. "So I should be leaving, as you should as well, before you're caught here. Of course, you are welcome to stay as long as you wish. Just unbar the door, if you please, before you take your leave."

Jaime found herself talking aimlessly, so she stopped and eyed the door.

Malcolm's hand on her elbow stopped her from moving away.

"Don't go, lass," he said gently. Her gaze was locked on his fingers where they rested on the sleeve of her dress. "I didn't risk breaking my neck, Jaime, to visit an empty music room."

The quick flash of her eyes, the sudden blush on her cheeks, reminded the Highlander that Jaime just might think he'd stolen away for another moment like the one they'd shared two nights earlier. He shook his head to the unasked question.

"Do you think, Jaime, that we might just stay here and talk?" Malcolm suggested, trying to ease her obvious concern. "It seems that we've not had a chance to spend even a moment together without . . . without something getting in the way."

Jaime hesitated—silent and unsure. There were so many things that she wished to say—a moment such as this was exactly what she had hoped for when she had scaled the walls to his room. But now . . . something in his soft words confused her. She wanted to trust this offer of peace. She wanted desperately to be near him.

"Stay, lass."

She saw the way his hand dropped from her arm, reluctantly, slowly. She knew he had the power to force her, the ability to charm her. She knew he could do whatever he wished with her. But instead, he was allowing her to decide.

His soft voice struck at the heart of her concerns. "About what happened between us that other night . . ."

"Don't!" Her gaze snapped up to his face. She couldn't do this. Her face burned with embarrassment at the mere mention of her foolishness. "I'll stay, but only so long as . . ."

Her words trailed off, but his slow and solemn nod told her that he understood—he would not broach that subject. At least, not now.

She watched him glance about the room and then stride over to two heavy carved chairs sitting against one wall. She watched his powerful shoulders, the confident steps as he carried the chairs back to her with incredible ease. He'd climbed down the palace wall in the pouring rain as if it required no more effort than walking in a garden. And his face showed no fear. She wondered at his lack of concern over the possibility of being discovered in this room. But then, perhaps she herself needed to be reminded that in climbing up to his chamber, she had acted as foolishly herself. In spite of herself, she smiled at the thought that perhaps there was something in their childhood so far to the north that had taught them to defy such dangers.

"I have an idea," he said with an easy smile. "Shall we pretend we are at Dunvegan Castle, m'lady?"

She glanced at Malcolm's handsome face as he held one of the chairs for her to sit in. He certainly had the ability to charm her, she thought as she began to sit.

"Nay!" she burst out, leaping out of the chair again. "What are we doing? Malcolm, you'll be put in chains if you're discovered here!"

"Don't even think it, lass!" he scoffed, patting the chair. "Not a soul is up and about but us. Who but two hardy Highlanders would be roaming about on such a night."

"Aye," Jaime answered uncertainly. "I know that Surrey and Lady Frances have retired."

"True enough." Malcolm smiled. "Sit down, Jaime, and let us imagine ourselves at Dunvegan, with the seabirds wheeling about in a sort of dance overhead, and the gray seals barking and courting in the loch. Aye, 'tis early summer there, too, my dove, and the season for wooing is hard upon the happy beasts. That's it, then! Here we sit in the Great Hall of Dunvegan."

"Perhaps it would be safer if we are at Benmore," she answered, keeping an eye on him and cautiously taking her seat. Dunvegan Castle, ancient fortress of the MacLeod clan, stood on a rock overlooking sparkling blue waters and guarding the western reaches of the Isle of Skye. But Dunvegan was Malcolm's castle—a place that Jaime would never go unless she were accompanied by her family. A place that now held memories for her of humiliation and sadness. On the other hand, Benmore Castle, sitting high above the River Spey, had been the Macpherson clan's stronghold for centuries. Jaime had been raised there. It was the place where she had first set eyes on Malcolm MacLeod.

"Nay, lass. Not Benmore," the Highlander replied, shaking his head as he sat down, drawing the other chair close. "I am afraid that cannot be so."

"And why not, I'd like to know?"

"The silence," he whispered, looking about the room. "Have you *ever* known Benmore Castle to be so silent and still?"

She cocked her head as a smile stole across her face. What Malcolm said was true. There wasn't a sound. "Never!" she answered. "Benmore is a far noisier place than Kenninghall."

"Have you ever come across a room at Benmore so empty?"

There always seemed to be—at any time, day or night—a dozen or so children running through the friendly interiors of Benmore Castle. Perhaps this had been the reason why she had originally opened the music room to the younger, lower-born students. She looked about the small chamber. Active or silent, the room was her favorite place of refuge in this palace.

But Malcolm was right. It was empty. And for the first time, she realized that it wasn't the charm of the room or its warmth that drew her here, but its solitude. It was a place where she could be alone—it was a workroom, a place of instruction. A place for her to practice her music and dream of happiness. Jaime loved Benmore Castle and its inhabitants, but this room offered something special, as well.

"Never," she whispered, her eyes drawn to his. "Nay, Malcolm. I cannot imagine Benmore like this."

"Then 'tis settled," he answered. "Close your eyes a moment, and . . . here we are in Dunvegan Castle."

Jaime closed her eyes and conjured a vision of the MacLeod stronghold. In her mind's eye, she could see clearly the thick stone walls, the towers and chambers added over the centuries. She thought of the last time she had sailed into Loch Dunvegan, but then she stopped, quickly pushing from her mind the recollections of that last visit. That day, as she'd gazed on the great structure looming over the water, she had thought that she was about to become the wife of the laird of the MacLeods. That day, he had wed another, and Jaime forced the thought from her consciousness.

"In some ways, though," Malcolm continued after a pause, "I think Dunvegan Castle may be a far more dreadful place than here, even. You're correct, Jaime. I don't think . . ."

"It isn't," she interrupted quietly, seeing the light gray walls rising above her. "The Isle of Skye is wild and beautiful—from the crags and peaks of the Cuillens to the breakers off Rubha Hunish. Truly, Malcolm, you must be a barbarian to think it dreadful."

"Ah, but it is, lass," he pressed, affably baiting her. "Dreadful, indeed. Why, don't you remember the way the heavy mists can settle in for days, only to break out in the end with a sky so blue it hurts your eyes?"

She could almost feel the gentle brush of the sea breeze against her face. "Aye, I can see your point."

"I knew you would agree." He shook his head. "And you certainly cannot have forgotten those contemptible knaves who inhabit the isles, with their rude tongues and unmannerly ways?"

"Aye, the whisper of their heavenly accent comes to me even as you speak," she answered, looking at him with an air of mild accusation. "And to walk down the paths of Skye only to have every crofter, fisherman, and herding lass smile with pleasure at the sight of you is a disconcerting thing, indeed. Aye, and to think—from the time of the Great Flood, these folk have survived in the face of it all—thrived, even, against the evils of both man and nature. There's something very wrong in their being so good-natured."

His eyes bore into hers, and Jaime could see his emotions lying so close to the surface.

"And that blackened pile of rock—Dunvegan, with its unholy dungeons."

She matched his gaze. "Aye, Dunvegan. The castle on the rock."

"A block of cold stone and wood," he whispered, "whipped by the sea's howling winds for as long as man has stood on Skye."

"Aye," she whispered in return. "A castle ringing with the echoes of God's own music and days gone by."

"Echoes," he said softly. "Aye, in empty halls and empty chambers, and an ill-tempered laird to haunt the place."

She smiled. "Feasting, good company, the lavish hospitality of a generous master who has brought nothing but honor to those halls."

"Och, 'tis a place without art—chambers without light."

She shook her head. "I can see it now—the Great Hall ablaze with the open hearth. The new drawing room and its broad, glazed windows."

"But sadly, no art."

"NO ART?" Jaime's whisper had the force of a shout, which in return made him laugh. From the way he leaned back in his chair—the way the lines of his face creased with amusement, it was obvious that he intended to rile her. And she was happy to respond in kind. "You are truly a barbarian, Malcolm MacLeod, if you fail to recognize the work of Philip Anjou, the greatest painter in Europe, as artwork of pure genius!"

"Very well, I will grant you that the works of Philip Anjou, or should we say Elizabeth Macpherson, your good mother, are indeed masterpieces without parallel. There is nothing in that castle that I value more."

She looked at him askance. "Nothing, m'lord? You wouldn't be exaggerating a wee bit just to find favor?" As she spoke, Jaime smoothed her skirts briskly with her hands, touching one of his knees unintentionally.

Malcolm gazed at her, clenching his fists in an effort to keep from reaching out and drawing her onto his lap. The fire that had been stirring in his loins now threatened to rage out of control. His gaze took in her shining, teasing eyes. The playful, seductive glances fanned the flames of his desire. He wanted her.

"Perhaps, if you gave it some thought," she added with a half smile. "Perhaps, if you stopped criticizing one of the most beautiful places in the Western Isles . . . in all Scotland, then perhaps you would recall other things, as well, to treasure in your home."

He frowned, his brow furrowed deeply as if he pretended to think. But he was not thinking of Dunvegan, or Skye, or Scotland. His thoughts dwelled solely on Jaime's beautiful face, on the curve of her cheek, on the waves of ebony hair cascading over slender, perfect shoulders. Malcolm turned abruptly in his chair, tearing his gaze from her. He needed to think of something else, but his need for her was ablaze in his brain, as well. He'd used this conversation as a way to bring her out of her shell. To give her the freedom to feel at ease with him . . . again.

"The beautiful landmarks . . . beautiful landmarks," he repeated, as calmly as he could. "But there are no views."

"The majestic view of the twin peaks of Healaval, MacLeod Tables, from the windows looking west," she corrected.

"Aye," he replied, by sheer force of will denying himself the pleasure of staring at her full, womanly breasts. "But within my castle walls, an empty enclosure. A barren courtyard." He was reaching deep.

"And have you forgotten the new water garden. Or at least, 'twas new when I saw it last." Jaime smiled brightly now, and her eyes looked off into the distance, seeing a scene of falling water appear before her. "And the path leading to it with the castle and Loch Dunvegan spread behind."

Malcolm's gaze followed the graceful line of her buttock and leg. Entranced by her loveliness, he could no longer tear his eyes away from her. The beauty, the excitement in her description of Dunvegan faded into the distance, replaced by a more vivid beauty, a more pressing excitement. He looked again into her face.

Her cheek flushed under the intensity of his open stare, but she did not look away. And as Malcolm continued to watch her, a shiver ran visibly through her frame. Finally, she tore her gaze away and stared into her lap, but too late. He had seen the reflection of his own desire.

Malcolm let a long breath escape, as the moment passed. The thought pushed into his brain that he couldn't rush her through this. He'd come down here hoping their talk would be a journey of learning and of remembrance. And that it had been—until this moment. But now he must cool his blood, he reminded himself. He couldn't rush her.

"No tradition!" he blurted out. Her eyes snapped up to his with the renewed challenge. "I know what is wrong with Dunvegan Castle—with either the MacDonalds *or* the MacLeods. Those islanders have no sense of tradition."

"And what of pipers of the MacDonald clan. And the Fairy Flag of the MacLeods," she suggested softly, rubbing her palm over her thigh. "And Rory Mor's Horn."

"Rory Mor's Horn?" He ran a hand over his jaw. He thought back over to the night he became laird of the MacLeods. It seemed so long ago. Malcolm squinted his eyes and stared at her challengingly. "You, lass, were far too young to recall anything of the last time the Horn was put to use."

She shook her head with a smile. "I was not too young!" Tilting her head to the side, she began to laugh at his obvious discomfort. "And I still remember."

"You were little more than a bairn, you villainous wench."

"My memories go back much, much further than that, I assure you," she drawled. "And besides, how could I forget such an exciting day. The crowded Great Hall at Dunvegan Castle. The ceremonial pouring out of the pitcher and half of claret into the Horn . . ."

"Nay, lass. Say no more!" Malcolm leaned forward, his elbows on his knees, his face buried dramatically in his hands. Through partially spread fingers, the Highlander peeked out at her.

"And you, such a handsome, strapping man, about to become laird of your people. I recall the hush of the crowd as you brought the ancient vessel to your lips. Tradition demanded a strong draught. You must drink it down, all at once. No setting the Horn aside until the wine was gone . . . and no falling down! Aye, this is tradition!" Jaime paused a moment, pursing her lips as if trying hard to remember the details. Malcolm cringed, awaiting her next words. "Ah, that's it. Now I remember. I can see it all clearly. I recall Aunt Fiona stepping over to the old priest. He had brought out an ancient box. She opened the lid, and carefully pulled out the Fairy

Flag and wrapped it around you. Aye, the flag that had been hidden away for so many years. Oh, Malcolm, how could I forget the cheers and the wild celebration that followed?"

He stared at her with a sudden look of relief. "That's what you remember?"

Malcolm sat back and placed his large hands on the carved arms of his chair. The lightning bolt feeling that had raced through him when Fiona had draped the Flag over his shoulders was a feeling Malcolm had never experienced at any time before or since. It was not so much a feeling of power, but a feeling of strength. Of magic. It was then that he had, for the first time, felt the touch of . . . of that other world.

"And I remember you getting ill." Jaime nodded, smiling mischievously. "Not long afterward, either."

The Highlander growled at her menacingly, but inwardly he smiled on the memory. At sixteen, it had been so important to Malcolm that no one know of his 'unmanly' aversion to wine and spirits. And he had, for days prior to the gathering, tried to shrug off the knowledge that even a mouthful of wine could bring on, in a very short time, a terrible tightening of the throat, an inability to breathe. And though he had hidden his secret, had downed the draught for the purpose of ceremony, he had also known full well the terrible sickness that would follow. But that was long ago, and the memory now held not a vestige of embarrassment for him.

"Why did you follow me out of the Great Hall?" His face formed a fierce scowl, but Jaime was not fooled. She could see the amused sparkle in his eyes. "I should have known that I couldn't escape you even then."

Though, indeed, Jaime thought, he had tried. Malcolm had escaped the Great Hall soon after quaffing the wine. Out the stout doors, across the crowded courtyard, through the low water gate and along the edge of a moonlit Loch Dunvegan to a place of solitude. There, in the shelter of a boulder, the young laird had crumpled to his knees, expelling what was to him poison until the waves of dreadful retching finally subsided.

And Jaime had followed, looking on, respecting his need to be alone, but watching over him all the same.

"I was worried about you, though I didn't know what wine could do to you."

"Aye, my dark and shameful secret. But after all these years, you are the only one who knows of it, lass." He reached over and roughly pulled her chair next to his, all the while maintaining his angry scowl. "But don't you know the magnitude of the danger you put yourself in that night? Of being the only witness to a laird's disgrace? Of admitting to it now? Don't you know what a desperate man such as I would do to preserve his honor? Och, such grave danger, Jaime Macpherson."

She shook her head, struggling to hold back her laughter. He yanked at her chair again, so that she now faced him directly.

"I hoped you wouldn't hurt me," she replied. "But I suppose I was safe enough, since—after emptying your belly—you were hardly able to sit up, Malcolm MacLeod."

The Highlander cringed, and then sat forward in his chair and took her hands in his.

"That was then," he growled, his hands sliding slowly up her arms. "But now, my dove, we must remedy that situation. For you do indeed still remember that night. You are still in a position of destroying my . . ." He paused, frowning as he tried to think of the right word.

"Your reputation?" she asked in a low and husky voice, shuddering as his hands caressed her shoulders.

"Aye, that's as good a reason as any." Malcolm wrapped his hands gently around her slender neck.

Her lips parted slightly. Suddenly this had become a moment of passion. The look in his eyes no longer spoke of amusement at a memory long past. His dark eyes sent a clear message of desire, while the set of his tightly clenched jaw spoke of self-restraint.

"Any last wish, m'lady?" His voice was raw with emotion. Malcolm's hands now cradled her face, and his thumb softly caressed her lip. "Speak, lass. Speak as if this were the last moment of life left to you. Say your peace, Jaime, and reveal your innermost wishes, before . . . before you pay for that horrible crime you committed as a wee lass."

Jaime came to her feet in a single bound, and Malcolm's hands dropped away from her face. Placing her palms on his shoulders, she pushed him back in his chair. His eyes searched hers, but she gave him little time to ponder the future.

Her mouth took possession of his, and Jaime Macpherson kissed him with all the passion she held within.

CHAPTER 27

At the soft tap on the door, Jaime leapt from Malcolm's lap, nearly stumbling and falling to the floor. But his hands lingering on her hips sustained her in the moment of panic.

"Who is it?" she called shakily.

"I bring a message from Lady Catherine, mistress." The woman's voice was a mere whisper.

Jaime looked warily at Malcolm. Though she tried to fight off his hands, he successfully gathered her into his lap. She gave a small cough, trying to gather her wits and find her voice. "What is it my cousin wants?"

"She requests your presence in her chambers, mistress."

"So late?"

"Aye, m'lady. She wishes to see you before she retires for the night."

"Very well. Tell her I'll be along."

As the sound of the servant's slippered feet moved away from the door, Jaime turned her gaze back to Malcolm and said a prayer of thanks for having barred the music room door.

"Let Catherine go to hell," Malcolm whispered against Jaime's lips as he gathered her more tightly in his lap. His mouth closed on hers quickly, before she could voice her next concern. A moment passed, or an eternity—she didn't know which—as they both breathlessly savored the kiss. Finally, Jaime tore herself away.

"I do have to go," she whispered against his ear as Malcolm ran his tongue along the sensitive skin of her neck. Jaime cherished the way his arms held her so tightly to his chest—the way his hands roamed across the smooth linen of her dress—making her skin burn at his touch even through the layers of clothing she wore.

"She will surely send back someone else," Jaime continued, leaning into his touch as his fingers moved up from her waist and spread caressingly over her breast. "Knowing Catherine, I'm certain she'll be impatient, and . . ." The words dried up in her throat as Malcolm pulled at the low neckline of her dress, exposing one breast. Her body arched as his mouth latched onto the erect nipple. "Oh, Malcolm," she gasped, bolts of lightning shooting from her chest into the very core of her belly.

Jaime stiffened in his arms as the sound of another set of footsteps could be heard approaching in the hallway. Malcolm reluctantly pulled his mouth away from her breast and drew her dress up into place. The footsteps continued on past her door.

"What is it about these damned English?" Malcolm complained, pushing a loose strand of hair off her brow and tucking it gently behind her ear. "Suddenly, they don't have anything else to do except bother us! Don't they know we want to be left alone?"

She laughed softly and leaned her head against his shoulder. "I hope not!"

He glowered at her, then smiled before leaning down and kissing her chastely on the lips. "But, lass," he growled. "Are we not sitting in Dunvegan Castle?"

"I do wish we were," she whispered. Putting a hand on his shoulder, she pushed herself off his lap and began to shake out her skirts.

He stood up as well and, casting a critical eye over her rumpled condition, gave out a low chuckle. "I trust you're not planning on going directly to your cousin Catherine's chambers."

"Am I a mess?" She looked up at him with smiling eyes.

"At least, I don't look like I've been climbing the palace walls in the pouring rain!"

"Nay, Jaime, you don't." Malcolm reached out and caressed the smooth, creamy skin of her cheeks, then touched her hair, running his fingers through the satin softness of the ebony waves, so beautiful in their disarray. Lightly skimming the tips of his fingers down her neck, he touched the spots where his mouth had aroused such pleasure. "The only problem for me is that, in seeing your tousled condition, she might draw the conclusion that we've . . ."

As his words trailed off, her cheeks took on a deeper shade of red—a crimson that reminded him once again of his transgressions against her—and reprimanded him.

But she gazed into his face, and her eyes held no reproof. "You are a rogue, Malcolm MacLeod," she said, planting her hands on his chest and turning him toward the window. The Highlander allowed her to push him across the chamber, but planted his feet a few steps from the way he'd come in. He turned to her and took her hands in his.

"Am I forgiven, then, lass?" he asked, his voice low and gentle.

There was no reason for him to explain what he meant, and there was no reason for her to ask. They both knew what he was referring to.

Jaime nodded in response. "I blame you for nothing, Malcolm."

As he opened his mouth to pursue the matter, she pressed her fingers firmly against his lips. "No more," she whispered, raising herself on her toes and replacing her hand with her lips.

She felt his arms encircle her, and then she found his mouth possessing hers—and her body yielding to his.

Inside Jaime, molten flames erupted, consuming her, torching all reason, engulfing all thought. His body pressed intimately against her, and she could feel his manhood hardening against her thigh. Jaime found herself instinctively arching against him as his hands clutched at her back, his tongue darting across her lips.

Jaime angled her head, allowing him to delve deeply into

the recesses of her mouth, and then turned slightly in his arms, her body responding to his growing need. Raw desire was running through her veins, a growing, raging force that was building with unchecked momentum. She wanted him.

With that realization, Jaime awoke to the consciousness of an entirely new woman, and her senses flooded her spirit with a fierce hunger that matched Malcolm MacLeod's—and it was a hunger that would not be denied.

Suddenly, she pulled away. Nay, this has to stop, she thought with a start. His face was only a breath away, the glazed mark of desire in his eyes. Nay, Catherine was waiting, and Jaime could not risk Malcolm being caught here. She took a deep breath, shook her head, and turned him once again toward the window.

His voice was hoarse as he looked back at her. "Perhaps you'd prefer that I come back?" he asked, a smile tugging at his lips as he pushed at the window frame.

"I will certainly go mad if you don't."

"Then in the interest of your sanity, perhaps I should stay right here until you get back."

She smiled, her heart pounding with excitement of this prospect, but common sense prevailed, and, after a slight pause, she shook her head.

"Nay, Malcolm. Not tonight. 'Tis far too late, and I don't know what my cousin wants me for." His look of enticement made her want to explain more—not so much for his sake, but rather to convince herself. "I don't know how long I will be detained there. And besides, I . . . well, there is the risk of you being found out of your bedchamber. Think what would happen if they found you missing?"

"Coward!" he whispered, leaning over and stealing a last, quick kiss.

"Villain!"

He laughed and swung his legs out onto the stone terrace. The hard rain had stopped, and the air was clearing. Looking up, he could see patches of sky and stars had broken through the thick banks of clouds, and an ivory moon now flirted with the dark puffs scudding past. His sharp eyes scanned the fields that led away from this gilded prison ... to freedom ... to Scotland.

"Jaime?" he called at the last instant.

She peered out at him from the window, her form silhouetted by the light of the candles in the music room beyond. His breath caught in his chest at the beauty of the tableau.

He had intended to tell her of the message he'd received, the letter dropped inside his door, but now that seemed so unimportant to all that had transpired.

"They might see you, Malcolm," she warned softly. "Please go!"

"Aye, lass," he said, yielding to her wish. With a nod, he found his way along the shadows of the wall to the thick vines leading to his bedchamber.

Each stroke of the brush through her hair only served to feed her fury. Sitting before a looking glass and watching the dark strands of her hair come alive beneath the hands of her serving women, Catherine cursed the wretched Jaime.

"Didn't you tell her to come at once?"

The young servant's nervous hands, in the act of turning down the bedclothes, came to an abrupt stop. "Aye, m' lady."

"Didn't you tell her that I am retiring for the night, and that it is of the utmost importance for me to see her right away?"

"I did, m'lady. I swear!"

"Then why is she not here?" Catherine complained, tugging irritably at the rings on her fingers and throwing them onto the table before her. "Is she *trying* to rile my temper?"

There was no answer by any of her four serving women who focused busily on seeing to their mistress's needs. In fact, other than the young servant girl who had taken the message to Jaime, the others were clearly pretending not to hear any of what it was being said. And that was exactly the way Catherine preferred her servants. Tongue-tied!

Looking back at the glass, Catherine reached behind her neck and removed the ornate, jeweled necklace that Henry had given her before she'd departed from Nonsuch Palace. Carelessly regarding it, she tossed the gift onto the table beside the rings. She sat forward as the women continued to stroke her golden brown hair. For the first time in a week, she was feeling free of the stifling prospect of her upcoming marriage. Her eyes wandered lovingly over the face that gazed back at her. She admired the creamy complexion; the long, slender neck; the flawless skin exposed above her silk night shift. Letting her gaze continue to drift downward, she silently amused herself with thoughts of how easy it was to draw men to her— a tilt of the head was all it generally took, or at most a glimpse of those alluring curves and shadows between her breasts. Catherine sighed and, as she watched her full, orblike breasts rise and fall, she could feel a growing tightness at the juncture of her legs.

Leaning her head languorously to the side and letting the strokes of brush follow the movement of her head, Catherine imagined Edward in the room. She felt herself grow moist at the thought of having him in here now, of his face buried in the valley between her breasts, his mouth suckling her and drawing out the essence of her pleasure. She imagined herself atop him, guiding him into her, taking him deep and feeling herself close around him like a sheath. Catherine ran a hand caressingly down the front of her shift and took between her fingers the hard, erect nipple protruding through thin cloth.

"Bastard," she swore suddenly under her breath, conscious once again of the memory of his greedy lack of regard for her.

"Harder. Brush harder," she practically shouted at the women stroking her hair. Then, slapping their hands away from her, Catherine pulled a silk shawl about her shoulders and twisted in her chair, turning her full wrath on her cowering messenger. "I don't care if you have to drag her by the hair, you bring that foul wench back to me at once!"

The young serving woman couldn't move her feet quickly enough as she dashed for the door.

As she wandered, wick lamp in hand, through the long corridors of Kenninghall, en route to Catherine's chambers, Jaime was soon lost in a contented dream over this latest visit from Malcolm. Hardly even aware of her surroundings, Jaime was practically trampled by the girl hurrying out Catherine's door. The look of relief on the young woman's face as she raised her sputtering candle spoke volumes to Jaime.

"Oh, Mistress Jaime," the young woman cried. "Thankee. Thankee so very much!"

Glancing from the serving girl's face, to the closed chamber door, and back again, Jaime gave a low chuckle. "That bad, is it?"

The servant just nodded, gnawing nervously at one of her fingers.

"Well then, perhaps I should wait and not bother Her Majesty tonight ... or rather Her Soon-to-Be Majesty!" Jaime's words were made in jest, but they only served to bring a terrified expression to the younger woman's face. "You don't think I should wait until tomorrow, when she might be in a better mood?"

"Nay, m'lady!" the girl replied quickly, shaking her head emphatically. "She'll have me skinned alive if I don't return with your ladyship, at once."

"Skinned?" Jaime repeated. "I cannot believe that dear Catherine does such things. And to an innocent young woman such as yourself!"

"Aye!" The serving girl bobbed her head, her voice barely a whisper. "Though I have only just joined Her Maj ... Her Ladyship's staff, I believe that the others, well, I think they must have had something horrible done to them. They never speak, mistress. You'd think she's had their tongues cut out!"

Jaime held back her smile as she nodded toward the door. "Well, my friend, let's not tarry here in that case. Lead on. I don't think I could forgive myself if I were the cause of you losing either your skin ... or your tongue!"

"Don't you find this larger bedchamber less cozy than our old one, Catherine?" Jaime stood in the doorway and looked around her. This room was far different from the one she had shared with Catherine and Mary, the one Jaime still shared with Mary. But Catherine, now destined for the throne of England, had to be accommodated in a style suitable to her station. This was, by far, the finest of the guest chambers in the palace. But for all her teasing, Jaime envied nothing about her cousin's situation.

Jaime took in the splendor of the royal suite, dutifully impressed by the carved oak panels and mantelpiece, the sumptuous red velvet of the drapes, and the fine quality of the down-cushioned furniture. Though she had been brought in through the "lady's bedchamber," she was quite certain that the sitting room, and the bedchambers beyond would be equally well appointed. She glanced at the huge, canopied bed that filled one side of the room, with its cloth of gold curtains and the insignia of King Henry in evidence on the embroidered bedcovering folded on the chest at the foot of the bed. The material sparkled in the light of a score of candles, and there appeared to be at least a dozen fine dresses lying about. She had the feeling that she had walked in on someone preparing for a feast. But then it occurred to her, Catherine *was* preparing for a feast. Her own triumphant wedding feast.

"I'm so happy you, at last, could find time for me." Catherine's voice dripped with sarcasm, but Jaime ignored it, turning to find her sitting before a table with two servants, armed with the finest boar-bristled brushes, hovering over her.

"I did try to procrastinate, but there was nothing left to do in my room," Jaime responded brightly, turning again to marvel at the finery lying about. It was no surprise to her, now, how Mary could have grown so quickly enamored of all this. "So I decided I would come by and see whether you . . . needed anything."

"How very thoughtful of you to come," Catherine returned, waving off her servants, "considering I had to send for you twice."

Moving confidently about the room, Jaime glanced over her shoulder. "So why did you want to see me, Catherine?"

"Always the impatient creature! But can't you think of any pleasantries that you wish to convey to me before we begin? Are they *that* unschooled in Scotland?"

Jaime turned her gaze on Catherine, who now began to look at herself in the looking glass. The serving women moved silently about the room, busying themselves with imaginary tasks. Not one lifted her eyes. In fact, it occurred to her that not one had acknowledged her arrival in the room. And not one had spoken a word. Suddenly, she thought with amusement that perhaps the serving girl, who had judiciously remained outside in the hall, had actually been telling the truth! Jaime fought down an urge to laugh.

"Oh! How could I forget?" she burst out, her voice ringing with mirth. "Congratulations on your upcoming wedding. A more suitable match, I could not imagine!"

Catherine stared at her in the mirror, and Jaime looked innocently back at her. For a moment the king's intended struggled visibly to restrain her temper and then, with a sharp motion, waved the rest of her serving women out of the room. One by one they curtsied to their mistress and then filed out, again without so much as a second glance at Jaime. And once the door had been closed shut behind the last departing soul, Jaime watched Catherine come to her feet.

There was an appraising, predatory look in Catherine's face. She was a hunter, and she moved like a cat across the chamber. Instinct told Jaime to back away from her cousin, to raise some barrier against the expected blow, but she stood her ground. She had known Catherine long enough—and she had no fear of her.

Catherine's voice was low and insinuating. "I hear you yourself are to be congratulated. I heard news of your own upcoming wedding."

As Jaime just stared at her cousin, every last vestige of the joy that had filled her soul while she'd been with Malcolm, drained out of her. What was she to do? How could she argue and set the record straight with these Howards? How could she speak her peace to this woman, when she still had not had a chance to talk to Edward, himself?

"A most fortunate match for you, from what I can see," Catherine continued. "When I first heard news of it—at court—all I could think of was what a clever, young girl you turned out to be, after all. You don't show that you are carrying his child. How did you convince him? Or his father, the duke, for that matter?"

"That is a vile thing to say, Catherine," Jaime responded in a whisper. If this was the tack her cousin chose to take, Jaime decided that—no matter what Catherine said—she would let nothing provoke her into revealing the truth.

"Oh, spare me that!" Catherine sneered, walking around the motionless Jaime. "We both know this marriage will give you every right to remain in England. How suitable for one who despises her own native land!"

"Despises?" Jaime said quietly. "I've never despised Scotland."

"Nay? But here you are, isn't that so? For over a year, now, and apparently staying!" Catherine's slow smile made Jaime curse her own judgment in remaining at Kenninghall so long. "And tell me, how many times have you been back to your beloved Scotland during this time? Or visited any of your kin? But nay, that would be difficult, would it not?"

Jaime stared at her cousin's golden brown hair, at the haughty look on her face. There was no point in explaining. Not to Catherine, anyway.

"A most interesting match," the king's intended pressed. "A new life. And then, not to mention the name and title you'll gain by marrying Edward."

Jaime folded her arms across her chest, digging her fingers into the flesh of her arms, restraining herself to remain silent.

"And with one blow," Catherine continued, "ridding yourself of an accursed Scottish name and replacing it with the noble . . . Howard!"

"You've said enough, Catherine!" Jaime said shortly. "I will not stand here, only to listen as you attempt to belittle me, and my home, and my family. Is this why you sent for me? To use me as a target for your warped arrows of vanity and pride? Whatever have I ever done to you, Catherine, to deserve this treatment?"

Catherine never so much as acknowledged her questions. The two women glared at each other, and though Jaime's first thought was to turn and leave the chamber, something inside balked at the thought of letting Catherine drive her from the field. So she stood her ground and weathered the withering gaze that her cousin was directing toward her.

"When did he come to you first?"

Catherine's question plummeted like a fireball from the sky, and Jaime started, her heart pounding with fear. How could she know about Malcolm? Jaime's voice wavered slightly as she answered. "I . . . I don't know what you mean!"

"Spare me the innocent drivel, cousin. You forget I am an expert in the art of appearing blameless!"

"I have no idea . . ." Jaime frowned. "Who . . . who do you mean?"

"You're wasting my time. When?"

"And I might say the same of you, Catherine" Jaime shot back, her temper again beginning to flare up. "I have no time, either, for standing here and listening to your vicious riddles. I'll not be trifled with, cousin! I'll take my leave." But she hadn't taken a step toward the door, when her cousin's voice spun her around.

"Halt, headstrong slut! You know I mean Edward. Now tell me *when* he first came to you."

It took great restraint, but Jaime succeeded in hiding her shock. "You are asking if Edward . . ." She shook her head. "When he came to me *first*? To my *bed*?"

Catherine nodded, an unpleasant smile plastered on her face. "He generally likes them younger. I think he likes children, really. So I was wondering if you—being past the age that he likes . . ." She waved a hand nonchalantly in the air, but Jaime was not taken in by the charade. There was a look of desperation in her eyes as her questions became more pointed. "I want to know if he took you when you first arrived here a year ago. I want to know if he's been having you all this time. I want to know . . ."

"You want to know what doesn't concern you," Jaime snapped. "I assure you that Edward's foul interests are of no interest to me, whatsoever. And as far as whether he and I," she felt herself blushing deep, "have ever shared . . . have ever been intimate . . ."

Jaime cut her words short. Why was she letting this woman

fluster her? There was no reason to explain anything to her. Catherine had no right to know.

"This discussion is finished, Catherine," Jaime announced, moving quickly toward the door. Pulling the door open, she stood and gazed back at the young woman. "And, in future chats, be so kind as to spare me such 'pleasantries'!"

"You are no virgin!" Catherine muttered under her breath as the door slammed shut behind Jaime. "That bastard has already taken you to his bed. Aye, poured his seed into you, he said. And you couldn't even deny it!" It has to be so, she thought. If Jaime were innocent, she would have denied the accusation. She would have shed tears over the questioning of her virtue. That was the way women are, Catherine thought, nodding. So many fools . . . thinking of their virtue like it is some pot of gold, the jewels of Suleiman. As if—untouched— it were something to brag about! And to weep over, when lost! But Jaime hadn't done that. Nay, the slut hadn't done that!

Pushing the silk shawl off her shoulders and letting it fall to the floor, she walked to her bed, a smile working its way onto her face. This was going to be easier than she'd thought. Jaime had become rattled with so little probing, Catherine was certain that with just a bit more effort, she could drive the foolish girl away in shame. And then there would be only Edward remaining. Arrogant, insufferable Edward!

CHAPTER 28

"Fly, beauty," Surrey called as he released the black falcon, and the three mounted hunters watched the bird soar higher and higher in the brilliant azure sky. When the bird was circling far above the open meadow, the earl turned to his falconer. Evan stood a dozen yards or so from the mounted party, and Jaime could see the group of men and boys beyond him. On the horse beside her, Malcolm sat watching the preparations of the hunt. It did her heart good to see him out in the air, though a pang of sadness struck her with the falseness of the scene. He was less free than the falcon that circled above. But like that noble bird, when the day had worn into evening, Malcolm would be returned to his cage. Her eyes met his, and her heart leaped at the exchange that told her his approval of her decision to join them at the last moment.

"Very well, Evan," Surrey called. "Have the lads drive out some game."

The riders urged their horses on and the men and boys spread out, moving slowly across the field, and down a small incline to the edge of a small brook, all the while beating the long grass and the brush with their thick sticks. A clump of willows and birch that overhung the bank of the bubbling water looked to be an ideal hiding place for the pheasants they were after, and Jaime kept her eyes trained on the spot.

The stag, strong and swift, bolted from the grove with a suddenness that took away Jaime's breath.

As a cry went up among the men, Surrey took a lance from one of them.

"Bring down the falcon," he shouted to Evan, spurring his horse after the running deer. In an instant, the men—and the falconer, as well—were running across the field in pursuit of the earl and his prey.

The rush of men, the shouting, the confusion that surrounded them, inspired Jaime with the thought that this was the moment to act. Now, quickly, in the light of this blessing that fortune had bestowed upon them. Digging her feet into the side of her horse, she urged him forward, galloping quickly to Malcolm's side.

"You must go now, Malcolm! You can escape."

Seeing the look of disbelief on his face, she leaned over in his direction and practically shouted her plea. "Go, Malcolm! We must seize Opportunity by the forelock! They won't even know you're missing till it is too late. And even then, when they do, I'll tell them that I sent you back to the palace . . . for some . . . for something. I'll think up a lie to tell them."

Malcolm still sat on his horse, as if rooted to the spot, and Jaime looked anxiously across the field at the men straggling along in Surrey's wake.

"They could come back at any moment. For heaven's sake, Malcolm, there may never be a better time than this! Just ride north. Go, Malcolm!"

Malcolm shook his head.

"But why?" she pleaded. "Don't you see? Surrey *wants* you to escape!"

The Highlander shook his head again, and as she stared with amazement into his face, she knew that he would take no action in response to her plea.

"Are you so eager to be rid of me, lass?"

"By His wounds, Malcolm, this is no time to be questioning my motives!" Jaime's temper flared. "What I am telling you to do is for your own good! You must go! There is no way to know when Edward will return. I fear if he finds you so . . ." her words trailed off in a feeling of helplessness. Frustrated by his unwillingness to seize the moment, she turned her face into the westerly breeze and dashed away an angry tear as she tried to subdue the turmoil within her.

Malcolm turned his horse around, and Jaime watched as he urged the mount forward until the Highlander was nearly face to face with her. When he reached for her hand, she thought he was reaching for the reins, and her eyes flashed at him. His hand was warm and strong as he took hold of hers.

"What is it you fear, Jaime?"

His eyes seemed to claim her with a power she could not withstand. It took her a long moment before she could gather her thoughts to answer. "I cannot see you hurt again," she whispered softly. "And I fear you will feel the weight of Edward's wrath when I tell him that I have no intention of accepting his offer . . . of marriage."

"Don't you, lass?"

"Nay Malcolm. I'll not be his intended. I'll never be his wife."

The increased pressure of his hand and the flash of excitement that lit his eyes made Jaime's face burn with pleasure. Malcolm obviously did not share her fear. But he was clearly pleased with her response. She watched almost shyly as he drew her fingers to his lips.

"Jaime, there is something I need to speak with you about." Malcolm turned his gaze across the field. "I don't suppose, though, that this is the appropriate time."

Her heart pounded as he turned back to face her. His face was clouded with uncertainty, but as he looked into her eyes, she saw his face clear.

"Well, lass," he continued with a smile, "as you say, Opportunity is bald behind, so we'd best take hold of him before he passes!"

Without another word Malcolm swung his leg across his horse's neck and dropped lithely to the ground. Reaching up, he helped her down, as well. Jaime went willingly into his arms.

There might have been only the two of them in the meadow, since most of the men were long gone in pursuit of the fleeing stag, and the few who remained were so distant, skirting the far edge of the field, that they presented no threat to the two lovers.

Shielded by the two horses' great bodies, Jaime was slow to remove her hands from his shoulders after being lowered from her steed. And Malcolm never eased his grip on her waist as he held her to him.

"I love you, Jaime," he whispered as his mouth tasted her sweet lips. "I know I am a base and undeserving scoundrel, and hardly worthy of your love or your hand. I admit that I have done you wrong and caused you pain . . . on the Isle of Skye and here in this godforsaken place. I readily accept your condemnation if you think me a rogue and a villain. A good-for-nothing Highland beast of a man who has done nothing else but bring ruin into your life."

Jaime smiled brilliantly and shook her head, the tears that now ran freely down her cheeks glistening in the sunlight before soaking into the black velvet of his tunic. Resting her cheek against his heart, she slipped her arms around him and hugged him tightly to her.

"Will you marry me, Jaime?" His voice was hoarse. "Will you be my wife?"

Jaime looked up into his handsome face, the difficulties of their position swept away by the joy of his question.

"Malcolm, I have waited my entire life to hear you say these words."

He smiled mischievously and cocked his head to the side. "Do you mean, that I am a villain, a rogue, and a beast of a man?"

She laughed as she planted her fists on his chest. "Aye! Though I believe I'll cherish the 'base and undeserving' part most of all."

"Oh, you will?" he said with a half smile. Then he drew her tighter to him, all humor suddenly gone from his face. "So will you marry me?"

"Aye, Malcolm. That I will," she whispered, raising herself on her toes and bringing her mouth closer to his lips. "I'll love you and I'll marry you and I'll cherish you for the rest of my life."

Her words wrapped themselves caressingly around his

heart—they warmed his life's blood. As they stood together, Jaime felt her soul pour out of her body, only to meet with his somewhere between them, and she felt their spirits entwine.

No longer able to hold back, Malcolm's mouth seized hers, stealing her breath as his hard body backed her into the horse's side. With a moan deep in her throat, she slid her arms around his neck and kissed him back, welcoming the thrusting rasp of his tongue, glorying in the crush of his lips as he kissed her harder, yielding with pleasure to the loving press of his hips.

Nothing can stop us now, she thought.

No one will ever come between us again, he vowed.

And in the sky far above them, once again the falcon circled, searching patiently for her prey.

CHAPTER 29

"Catherine!" The suddenness of the earl of Surrey's voice startled the young woman, and she whirled to face her elder cousin. "Have *you* any idea why my father would make such a request? Why, in God's name, should His Grace want Jaime sent to court on such short notice? After all, he and Edward are planning to return soon enough to Kenninghall. Why now, Catherine? And why in such haste?"

Catherine shook her head as she pondered her response, for she, too, wished to know the answer. She had been quite careful in her private talk with the king. She had needed to make certain that Edward and the duke would never guess the identity of Edward's accuser. But now, hearing this news of Jaime's summons, Catherine wondered if the two had somehow found her out. For a long moment she stared at the duke's letter as it dangled from Surrey's hand. But how could they have learned anything? She was certain that Henry would not betray her and ruin her relationship with her own family. Or would he? she wondered. Nay, she decided quickly. The king was still quite enamored of her, and she planned to keep it that way.

But what purpose, Catherine mused, turning her thoughts back to the letter, could be served in bringing her Scottish cousin to Henry's attention.

"Perhaps Edward is pining over his separation from Jaime," Mary suggested, drawing all eyes to where she sat with a piece of needlework across her lap.

Catherine stifled her laughter with a cough.

Mary nodded with conviction. "Perhaps His Grace believes this is the best way to soothe Edward and Jaime's aching hearts. If you ask my opinion . . ."

"Which no one did ask," Catherine put in shortly.

Mary glanced in her direction, disconcerted and blushing. But upon seeing the sudden awkwardness of her position, Surrey stepped over to her, encouraging her to continue as Catherine turned away. "You were saying, Mary?"

With a quick glance in Catherine's direction, the younger woman started again. "Well, it seems to me that having Jaime summoned to court is, in many ways, a blessing for her. And she has been so forbidding in her attitude since Edward left. I for one have been praying for his speedy return and an end to her misery."

From her chair by a window, Frances looked up from her own needlework and entered the discussion for the first time, coming to Jaime's defense. "I don't think Jaime has been visibly upset nor miserable. She has certainly been busier than any one of us in seeing to what goes on in the palace. So if she seems a bit distant, I should think she's entitled. I am quite certain she has a great deal on her mind."

Mary shook her head and turned her gaze downward. "I am not being critical, Lady Frances. I've just never seen her so irritable before now, and I think it must be . . ." Mary chanced a peek at the earl who was once again perusing the contents of the duke's letter. She continued, but this time in confidential tones directed toward Frances. "Well, lovesick or just busy, I don't care for the way she is treating us."

"Treating *us*?" Frances returned with a kindly laugh. "Are you certain you are not imagining all this, Mary?"

"I am not," she returned petulantly. "Why, just this morning—knowing that I would be greatly interested in joining the men on their hunt—Jaime left our bedchamber without awakening me or even leaving a message for me." She stared round-eyed at Frances. "She never so much as gave a thought to extending Lord Surrey's invitation to ride to any of the other ladies."

"There was no invitation for her to extend," Surrey put in bluntly, looking up from the letter.

Mary's startled face blushed scarlet and then subsided into a pout as she turned to Frances in embarrassment and a touch of temper. "Is he saying that *you* were not invited, either? That Jaime Macpherson is the only woman in Kenninghall worthy of joining the men in their sport?"

Frances turned away from Mary, only to find her husband's smiling eyes looking directly into her own.

"Oh, my love!" Surrey interjected with a look of feigned surprise. "I had little thought that you were interested in riding . . . well, I just thought that after last ni . . ."

"That will do, Surrey!" Frances ordered, fighting down the rising blush in her cheeks.

The earl tore his eyes away from his wife's glowing face and looked at Mary.

"Cousin," he said seriously. "Malcolm and I, by chance, came across Jaime on our way to the stables. The offer of her accompanying us was not one that we had arranged earlier."

"But still, my lord . . ."

"That is all there is to tell, Mary!"

Frances's attention snapped to her husband's face. Surrey was not one to indulge in shows of temper—unlike Edward, whose open displays of rage were second to none. But the earl did have the uncanny ability—particularly when annoyed—to stop a talker cold with just the slightest inclination of his head and an even slighter change in his tone. Frances recognized the change and looked steadily at him. Mary, on the receiving end of the earl's annoyance, sat a moment—her mouth opening and closing once or twice—before quietly turning her attention back to the needlework in her lap.

Catherine's movement toward the windows drew Frances's gaze. The young woman was smiling, and seemed to be enjoying the efficiency with which Surrey stopped Mary's talk. Frances watched the king's intended as she moved away, now clearly preoccupied with her own thoughts. Frances looked around and found Surrey's eyes once again upon her. At his silent command, she stood up, and together they moved to the far end of the chamber.

"Jaime has to go," he whispered. "I have no choice but to send her at once."

"Have you spoken with her about this, yet?"

He shook his head. "The letter only arrived since we've come back from riding. I've had no chance."

Frances stared at the fine weave on her husband's doublet. "So you haven't spoken to Malcolm yet, either."

"It is not his concern."

"Is it not?" Frances asked softly, raising her eyes to her husband's penetrating gaze.

Surrey did not answer.

"Can I talk to Jaime first?" She threw a covert glance in the direction of the two other women in the room. "Before she hears of it from them."

Gently, Surrey placed a hand on Frances's cheek. "You are trying to buy her time, my love. But she must go when she is summoned."

His wife leaned her face against the palm of his hand. "You won't force her to act against her will. This must be her decision."

"She is in England, my sweet. And she has placed herself under my father's care. It is a bit late for her to have a change of heart, considering the reasons behind the duke's summons." The look of doubt in Frances's face told him that she wasn't convinced. "Just think back to when we first met. You must have had as many reservations about marrying me as Jaime has regarding Edward."

"More! Without question!" Frances teased.

"I knew it!" He laughed. "But you see? The human heart can *learn* to love. Now honestly, don't you agree?"

"Let me talk to her first." Frances turned her face and softly placed a kiss on his palm.

"As you wish, my love."

"But, Surrey," she said, smiling as she looked into his face, "Edward is *nothing* like you."

His eyes shone with his love for her, and their gazes held for a long moment. Then, as Surrey smiled, he remembered the letter in his hand.

"Frances, one thing more," he said, holding it out to her.

"I'd like you to look at this. There is something more in it that should help convince Jaime to go. Perhaps 'tis the reason for the summons, though I don't . . ."

As Surrey's words trailed off, Frances reached out and took the parchment from his hands. Moving toward a window, she quickly perused the duke's letter. But before she had gone halfway across the chamber, she turned and raised her eyes to his.

Jaime started at his approach, questioning him with a clear note of anxiety. "How did you get in?" Malcolm backed her against the wall and stopped her question with a kiss.

"Through the door," he replied, drawing back only a breath. Without hesitating, his lips descended upon the soft curve of her cheek, the velvet skin of her neck.

Jaime placed her hands against his chest and tried to push him away.

"Malcolm, you just go out the way you came! Lady Frances is . . ." Her words were silenced once again by his mouth closing over hers. It took a long moment before she was able to free her lips and catch her breath. Jaime looked anxiously at the direction of the door and, seeing it was now barred, turned and unsuccessfully tried to push him toward the window. "I received a message that Frances wishes to meet with me in here, and she is bound to come in soon. You'll have to go out by way of the terrace."

"In broad daylight, lass?" he crooned. "The duke's soldiers will surely cut me down . . ."

"We cannot allow her to find us here together!" she interrupted, again trying to move his giant body across the music room. But her effort was futile.

He wrapped an arm more tightly around her waist and hugged her as he stole another kiss. "I've missed you, Jaime."

"We saw each other only an hour or so ago!" She tried to step away, but his arms were like steel around her.

"I couldn't stay away."

"You are a scoundrel, Malcolm MacLeod, but you must give in to my wishes this time," she whispered softly against his face, and as she turned in his arms, the Highlander now reluctantly gave in, releasing her and allowing her to lead him across the chamber. "It would be a terrible end for you if Frances found us together here. I know she must already be on her way. You must go now, Malcolm!"

Jaime pushed open the diamond-paned window. "Now go!" she commanded.

Malcolm leaned his head out and looked up and down the stone terrace, golden in the afternoon sunlight. "Are you certain I must go this way?" he asked, looking back at her.

She nodded. "Aye, and be quick about it!"

"But, Jaime. Someone is sure to see me climbing the palace wall."

"You should have thought of that when you made your way down here, you great fool!" she scolded lightly. The knock on the door, though, made her stiffen where she stood. She hurriedly pushed him into the window frame. "Do whatever you need to do, Malcolm, but don't let Frances find you here."

He placed a gentle hand against her face. "Very well, my love. Just go and unbar the door—don't worry about me."

Jaime placed a quick kiss on his outstretched fingers as he slipped out the long window. Heading for the door, she straightened her skirts and ran a quick hand through her hair. Jaime lifted the bar and greeted the waiting woman standing in the wide corridor.

"Ah, Jaime. I was unsure . . . well, I wasn't even sure if you had come back from the gardens yet."

"I arrived back only a moment ago," Jaime responded, pulling the door open wide and encouraging Frances to step into the room. "The servant whom you sent spoke of a matter of some urgency for this meeting. Is there something wrong, Frances?"

Frances walked straight to the middle of the room. "I'll tell you what I know, once . . . oh, I am so glad you are already here."

Jaime turned sharply in the direction of the countess's gaze. Seeing Malcolm seated at her music table brought on a moment of confusion. His expression was blank, and he certainly looked as if it were perfectly natural for him to be here. He smiled at her innocently.

"Well, I can think of no reason to wait," Frances began. "Jaime, if you don't mind . . ."

Jaime was staring dumbly, still not fully recovered from her shock at finding him in the chamber. Suddenly aware of the countess's eyes upon her, she shook herself out of her daze and pushed the heavy door shut. An unexpected dizziness swept over her, and she leaned her back against the door. She put a clammy hand to her forehead, and, as abruptly as it came, the unsteadiness went. He knew Frances was expecting him to be here! Her anger growing within her, Jaime gave him as withering a look as she could muster. The rogue could have told her the truth and saved her from all this unnecessary panic.

Frances was clearly in the mood to waste no words. "Jaime, a messenger has arrived from court with a letter from the duke. His Grace requires your presence at Nonsuch Palace, at once."

Jaime paled once again as she looked in confusion at Frances. The other woman's face betrayed no joy in conveying this news.

"There is no reason given for this summons," Frances continued. "Other than the fact that it is extremely urgent for you to leave immediately for court."

"But why? What does this mean? It cannot be, Lady Frances!" Jaime shook her head. She wouldn't go, she thought miserably. Feeling as though a steel rod had been plunged into her heart, Jaime sought out Malcolm's face. The sudden anger in his expression had furrowed his brow into a mass of dark creases. She saw him stand from his chair and turn to the countess.

"It is so, my sweet," Frances went on. "And there are a thousand preparations that need to be attended to. We must think of the . . ."

Malcolm's voice interrupted her. "Hold, Lady Frances. She is no Ward of Henry's court, nor is she the dependent of the duke of Norfolk," Malcolm put in coldly. "She is a guest in this house. And what right does His Grace have to summon her against her will?"

"But he does! As her true uncle . . ." Frances paused and

looked at Malcolm's stern expression for a moment before continuing. "Surrey is certain that you know what I must say, though we are unsure of whether Jaime is aware . . . well, that is why we had you sent for. She must know the truth."

"What truth?" Jaime cried, looking anxiously from Frances's face to Malcolm's. She called softly, "Malcolm!"

Frances continued to address the Highlander. "His Grace . . . in his letter . . ."

"Please, Frances!" Jaime demanded, slapping the palm of her hand against the door. "What truth? What is in the letter?"

The countess turned and looked into Jaime's eyes. "Come," she said quietly, "come and join us." Frances pleaded, stretching a hand toward Jaime. "I know that, between the two of us . . ." She glanced over at Malcolm. "Perhaps we can all understand . . ."

"I'll have no part of this, Lady Frances," the Highlander said darkly. "No part."

Jaime's knees were wobbling as she stared at the two of them, and yet she still somehow managed to take the few short steps to a chair. She had to sit, since somehow she knew that whatever it was she was about to hear, her life would never be quite the same.

Frances took a deep breath as she again glanced over at Malcolm. "Knowing how short Surrey can sometimes be, I insisted that he allow me to do this, myself. But now I find myself searching desperately for the right words."

"Why don't you just get on with it," Malcolm practically barked as he planted his hands on the table. "Speak plainly, Lady Frances, what you must, and then let her be."

Frances turned to Jaime. "Perhaps . . . perhaps this information should have come from those you know to be your parents."

"There was no reason for any of this to be revealed," Malcolm interrupted again, banging his fist on the table before straightening to his full height. "Where is Surrey? No good will come out of this, I tell you. Tell me what vile purpose lies behind all this? Who chooses this path, Lady Frances? Where will it all lead?"

Frances sank into the closest chair. "In truth, Malcolm, I cannot say what lies at the end of this."

"Please! The two of you!" Jaime pleaded. "You are discussing me as if I am not even here. And yet 'tis clear that this information—this truth—may be of the utmost importance to me and my kin. Of all people, Malcolm, you of my native land . . ."

Frances's head snapped around as she stared at Jaime. The look in her face still spoke of her discomfort. But Jaime could see the resolve in her eyes.

"Your native land is England, Jaime," she corrected. "For you are the king's daughter."

CHAPTER 30

Anger tore through her like the jagged ice of the winter flood.

"Nay!" Jaime whispered icily.

"Your mother, Mary Boleyn, was the true niece of His Grace, the duke of Norfolk. She was also, for a short time, mistress to King Henry. Your mother stole away to a foreign land, and you were born in secrecy. Later after your mother's death, you were raised by your aunt, Elizabeth Boleyn, and her husband Ambrose Macpherson, to the world's eyes as their own. Tell her this is true, Malcolm."

"I admit to naught," the Highlander replied, his face a steely mask. "The story I have heard is that Mary's *son* died in childbirth."

Jaime's mind raced as Frances stared at Malcolm. As Jaime looked at her intended, she knew that what Frances said was, of course, true—about being Mary's daughter—and that Malcolm was simply trying to protect her.

"Tell me what you know, Frances," she said quietly, turning to the woman.

"I can tell you very little more. I simply cannot understand why Elizabeth Boleyn chose to hide you . . ."

Jaime watched as Malcolm's anger suddenly boiled to the surface.

"And this is the truth?" Malcolm cut in, looking accusingly at Frances. "Even if we allow that there is the slightest chance that what you have heard is correct, have you considered that perhaps this is not the whole truth? You talk as if Elizabeth Macpherson committed a crime in trying to keep Jaime away and safe from the English butchers. Have you considered what you would do yourself if your sisters were killed one by one at their hands?"

Frances flushed as she searched for an answer. "Killed? But Queen Anne . . . well, she was guilty of . . . well . . . Anne . . ."

"Aye, what of Anne?" Malcolm argued. "You see no butchery in that? What guilt lies in bearing a stillborn child? And this after giving birth to a healthy daughter! How is it that the guilt must lie with her when your king had already turned his lecherous eyes on Jane Seymour? Witchcraft? Nay . . . lust is what lies at the bottom of this!"

"Nay . . ." Frances gasped, lifting a hand to her mouth. "You cannot say such things."

"You think not?" Malcolm waved aside her words. "And Anne's sister? Why don't you ask how Mary was killed by the blade of an English knight—before Elizabeth's very eyes?"

"Malcolm," Jaime pleaded, raising a hand to him as she came to her feet. Taking a step toward him, she looked steadily into the fury ablaze in his eyes. "We have much to talk about. And you know that Lady Frances means me no harm."

The Highlander paused a moment as his anger subsided. He ran a hand down his face and then turned once again to the sitting woman. "Aye, as you say. But, Countess, your husband and I learned from the same teacher that there is perhaps only a hair that separates Truth and Falsehood. Over the past weeks, I've come to know you are a woman of wisdom and fairness . . . as is your husband, as well. So I only ask you to consider more carefully before you so freely place blame. Whether Jaime is the daughter of Elizabeth and Ambrose Macpherson or the daughter of Suleiyman himself, I can tell you everything they've done for her has been done out of love for the lass."

"I believe you, Malcolm," Frances said quietly.

"Then I must apologize to you, m'lady, for speaking so strongly. I just cannot stand back and listen while folk I care about are dishonored."

Frances stared down in her lap for a moment before nodding in response, then came to her feet. "Jaime, I believe you and Malcolm have matters to discuss. I meant no dishonor to anyone you hold dear. As to your heritage . . ." A sad smile crept across the countess's face. "True or false, His Grace believes it. And so, it seems, does Edward."

Jaime looked into the gray eyes of the countess as the woman reached out and touched her affectionately on the arm. The gaze was steady and true.

"And now I'll leave you two." Frances turned toward the door but, remembering something, stopped. "Oh, I've asked Surrey to give you an extra day to prepare, so you and your escort won't be leaving until the day after tomorrow."

"M'lady!" Malcolm's sharp call brought Frances to a halt by the door. She turned and peered in his direction. His voice took on a much gentler tone. "What you say of Jaime's birth . . . where did you and others hear of this?"

Jaime knew that Frances didn't have to answer Malcolm's question. So she was surprised when the other woman decided to do so.

"I was unaware that you were truly kin of the Howards—until today," Frances replied, turning to Jaime. "But from what my husband told me—his father the duke has been aware of it since—" She paused and stared uncomfortably at the floor.

"Since when, Frances?" Jaime asked.

The countess's face could not hide her distress at what she was about to say. "Your aunt, Anne Boleyn, revealed what I've told you to the duke of Norfolk on the eve of her beheading. I believe she did so with the hope of having her uncle somehow use it with the king . . . to spare her life."

"But His Grace never did as she hoped, did he?" Jaime asked.

Frances shook her head. "I don't know. Though His Grace served as the king's representative in her trial, he lost a great deal in the fall of Anne Boleyn. Whether the duke ever went to Henry, I cannot say. But 'tis possible that her information was simply . . ."

The countess shrugged and looked resignedly at Jaime. No

words were needed. They all knew that if Henry had learned of this, Jaime would have been summoned to court long ago.

"Anne lost her head on the block," Frances continued. "That's all I know!"

Without another word, Frances left the chamber and the door closed behind her.

Jaime stared in the direction of the departing woman. Suddenly, she found herself surrounded by images and voices from long ago.

A barge rocked gently in the river current. Outside a tiny window, the green fields of France drifted lazily by. A pretty ebony-haired woman, opening her arms with an effort, welcoming Jaime inside of the dark cabin. Her poor, sick mother, hardly ever out of the narrow bunk.

Jaime remembered Mary, her mother, very clearly. She remembered the affection that she had bestowed on her only child in those last painful days. Jaime had been that child.

Now, standing beside Malcolm, she wrapped her arms around herself to block the coldness that was penetrating her bones.

A freshly dug grave in a town half destroyed by fire. She, a small and lonely lass, standing beside it. She didn't know whom they were burying in it, for her mother had gone to heaven—that was what she'd been told. The warm embrace of her uncle, Philip. The little secret that the two of them shared—that Philip was really her loving aunt Elizabeth, disguised as a man for years. Working as an artist to provide for them. To protect them.

Jaime remembered the long journey after her mother's death—the guilt—the unanswered prayers for forgiveness. She had been certain then that it had been her fault that her mother had gone away. She had even wondered whether God had decided to punish her for loving Elizabeth better than her mother.

The large hands and strong arms embracing her there in the damp of the churchyard. The deep voice of a scar-faced man promising to take care of them and never let Elizabeth leave for heaven. She could still see his deep blue eyes—the color of the sea on a sunny day. Eyes shining with goodness

*and friendship. Ambrose Macpherson. The man she would
learn to love as her father.*

Jaime was suddenly aware of her body beginning to shiver.
Nay, Henry of England had never been her father—Ambrose
was. And Elizabeth had always been there. As far back as
memory traveled, Elizabeth had been there.

Malcolm's arms encircled her, and Jaime leaned back into
the hands that drew her to him. Wordlessly, she turned and hid
her face against his solid chest, finding comfort in the strength
and the feeling that emanated from his presence.

He held her tight, his hands gently stroking her back.

"I am sorry, Jaime," he whispered softly into her ear. "I am
sorry that the truth had to come out this way." His hands found
her shoulders, and she raised her eyes to his face. "What the
duke knows *is* the truth, and 'tis a secret that has been well
guarded. I've known the folk you've called kin for most of my
life—and I want you to believe me when I tell you that
they've always loved you as their own daughter. And the only
reason for them to hold back any of this has been for no other
purpose than protecting you from . . ."

When Malcolm's words faltered, Jaime finished them for
him. ". . . From the wickedness that I now must face. From the
dangers I have willingly exposed myself to!"

He pushed a strand of her hair behind an ear as he looked
deeply into her eyes. "Are you angry with them? At Elizabeth
and Ambrose for what they have done?"

"Nay!" she cried, surprised at his question. "How could I?
How could I be angry at those two for loving me, for protecting me, and for caring for me as their own child." Jaime
rested the side of her face against his chest and listened for a
moment to his strong heart beating. "They never treated me
any differently from my brothers, Michael and Thomas, and I
have always loved them for it. Malcolm, I have always known
I was not their true child."

He paused, then took a hold of her chin, raising it so he
could look into her eyes. "You knew the truth?"

"That part of it," she answered. "I always knew my true
mother was Mary, and I remember the journey on which she
died. But I never knew how she died."

"Aye," Malcolm said. "What I said was also the truth."

Jaime turned her eyes away as they misted slightly, but then she looked back into his face. "And about my father. As a child, I never thought to ask who he was. And later, though I knew Ambrose was not my true father, I learned to know him and love him for his tender care of all of us. He and Elizabeth were the only ones that mattered."

"And you always called them your parents."

"Because I wanted them to be. Because they are! And I prayed to God that they would think of me as their own!" Suddenly, Jaime felt her throat close, choking her. With an effort, she swallowed her emotion.

"You know that they do, lass."

"Aye, but there is more. To this day, 'tis difficult for me to admit that just days before Mary lost her life, I secretly wished for Elizabeth to be my true mother." She dashed away a glistening tear. "You see, the bare memories of Mary that I have are always tainted by the images of us in Florence, and of her . . . rejection of me. But Elizabeth . . . Elizabeth always showed her love. Whatever my mother failed to be, my aunt *was*."

A few more tears rolled down her cheeks. Suddenly embarrassed, she lowered her head. "How foolish of me to say all this. To blame her after all these years—after all that she must have suffered—to die so young, in such a horrible way!"

Malcolm raised her chin and looked into her glistening eyes. "It is only foolish to blame yourself for how you feel!"

"She did change so much before she died," Jaime whispered. "I think she even tried to make peace with me—as few as the days were that she had left, she did her best to show me that she loved me. I know that's what I should remember her by and not what went before."

"We don't choose what we remember and what we forget, lass. But I believe that, in time, once you've learned to forgive, those last days with her may be all you remember her by."

She nodded in response and once again melted into the warmth of his embrace.

"You never knew about Henry of England, did you?"

Jaime shook her head. "And I don't care to know anything

more about him. To me he is nothing more than a lecherous man who has brought only misery to so many women in his wretched life."

"But you *are* his daughter."

"And that means nothing to me, Malcolm. Mary could have slept with the lowliest of peasants, it makes no difference to me." Jaime realized that her two closed fists were planted firmly on his chest. "With regard to my life, 'tis not the one who planted the seed that matters, but rather those who raised me. Those are the ones that I cherish."

Malcolm gathered her tightly to his chest. "I wish Elizabeth and Ambrose could have been here to hear these words. Your mother was heartsick with worry before I left Scotland, fretting over how you would feel when you finally knew the truth."

Jaime pulled back and looked questioningly into Malcolm's eyes. "You spoke to my parents about this before you left Scotland?"

"Well, aye, Jaime." The Highlander cast around for the right words. "Elizabeth thought ... well, that if I were to come across you in my travels ..."

"You said you were going to Rotterdam, not to England. How could you come across me ... ?" Jaime stared at the suddenly sheepish expression on his face. "Malcolm! What are you holding back?"

"What makes you think ..."

She thumped her fists once solidly on his chest, her eyes blazing. "I've had quite enough of playing the half-wit for one day. Don't treat me like one any longer."

He gathered her hands into his and brought them to his lips. "Never, Jaime. I shall never again treat you ill nor think you any less than the marvel that you truly are."

"Don't try flattering me with your Highland charms, Malcolm MacLeod. Speak the truth. For what reason did my mother take you into their confidence? I know Elizabeth, and she would not have spoken of this to anyone unless there were a good reason for it. So tell me what reason you had for knowing, Malcolm."

The Highlander placed both hands on her shoulders.

"Ambrose and Elizabeth told me everything just before I left Scotland on this trip . . . well, because . . ." He paused and looked deep into her eyes. "Because they knew I was to be a son to them."

"A son?"

"Aye, Well, a son-in-law!" he clarified. "Husband to their daughter! They thought 'twas important for me to know the truth, and also they felt that it imperative that I tell you everything . . . before I spirited you out of England."

Her heart soared at his words, but she shook her head, perplexed by them, as well. "Elizabeth and Ambrose knew of our intended marriage before I knew of it? You asked their permission first—and they accepted—without knowing if I would even have you?"

The Highlander took both her hands in his. "I don't think such things as logic or propriety apply to us, my love. After all, you yourself announced our marriage to the world without ever consulting me on the subject. You did all of that before the age of five."

"Not *before,* you bold-faced liar . . . I *was* five!"

"Very well!" he responded, conceding with a shrug of his shoulders and a crooked smile. "Have it your way. But even so, after what you've done, I cannot see any wrong on my part in speaking with them!"

She placed her hands around his neck and glared into his eyes. "Whatever I did, m'lord, I did before your wedding. Things changed after that day. Or have you forgotten that I was hurt, wounded, humiliated!"

"Nay, lass," Malcolm replied, his face growing serious. "How could I forget such a thing?"

"How indeed?" Jaime looked into his solid, handsome face. How long had she loved this face, the look of tenderness in these dark eyes. A feeling of warmth, of happiness flowed through her. "But, Malcolm, you were not headed for England. As far as you were concerned I was staying in this land for good. As far as anyone could know, I had no intention of ever returning to Scotland!"

" 'Tis true. And I knew that you hated me, as well! I remember very well, my love."

"Then what, in the Holy Mother's name, gave you the idea . . . the idea . . ."

He placed his hands lightly around her waist. "The idea of seeking your hand in marriage by talking to your parents first? Of traveling to Rotterdam with plans already in place to come and get *you*? Of having thought so far ahead as to have a ship meet us on the coast of England at the right time?"

She couldn't find words for the uneasiness that was beginning to settle in. This was madness—he couldn't possibly have known.

"I had a dream," he whispered as he nestled her closer to his body.

She stared at him in awe.

"Aye." He nodded. "You forget that I am the laird of a people who believe in fairies and spirits."

"And the dream told you what was to come?"

"Only partly, lass. James, the seer, came to me in this dream."

"Who is this James, Malcolm?" she asked softly.

His hand caressed her back. "An old man, ancient when I was no more than a bairn. To everyone's thinking, he died long before you ever set foot on the Isle of Skye. When I was a lad, I used to see him sitting by the gate of the old Priory and talking to all who passed. Many islanders said that he had the second sight. Others said, when the old prioress wasn't in earshot, that he was a spirit—passing through the old man's ailing frame for the time being. There were even stories of him appearing to the king before Flodden Field and warning him of his coming death. And there were many other tales of James giving warning of what was to come. He always scared me as a lad—until one day when his words actually saved my life."

"He foretold some danger?" she asked.

"That he did!" Malcolm added. "Danger to me and to Fiona. But being eager, I ignored his warning. And when it all came true, he appeared to Alec Macpherson and sent him to save us."

Jaime ran a light finger over his knotted brow. "You believe in his magic."

"I believe in his sight," Malcolm corrected. "He disappeared after that, and everyone figured he was dead. But I saw him again—the day of the gathering when I became a laird. He was there. Many whispered 'twas James who had hidden the Fairy Flag for so long, waiting for a just man to become laird of the MacLeods. Others must have seen him, as well, for word of his presence there spread like a moorfire through the Great Hall at Dunvegan. I think it convinced many that I was indeed their rightful leader."

"His spirit may have helped, Malcolm," Jaime argued. "But you *are* the true heir."

He shook his head. "I was Torquil's only son, but illegitimate, being born out of wedlock. My father had been laird, that was true. But he was a man who had sold his soul to the devil in his youth and had never cared spit for his people during his treacherous and miserable life!" Malcolm let out a deep breath. "And my mother was a simple crofter's lass seduced or forced—it does not matter which—by Torquil's wickedness. They told me she didn't even live long enough to look into my face after I was born."

Jaime didn't try to hold back her emotions as she embraced him tightly in her arms. "Oh, Malcolm! We were both such lost souls. Born of fathers who cared nothing for us, and mothers who died too young."

The Highlander gazed lovingly into her eyes. "And we were both fortunate enough to be found and cared for by folk who loved us as their own. To think that your path and mine would never have crossed at all if it weren't for these Macphersons."

Jaime drew back and smiled tenderly as she ran her fingers over the chiseled edges of his broad face. "You said he came to you in your dream? This James, the seer!"

Malcolm nodded. "Aye. After Flora died, my life became as dark and bare as the dungeons at Dunvegan. Empty, but for the ghosts that were haunting me day and night. And believe me when I tell you, 'twas not love for her nor even grief that created that terrible . . . void. It was just that I knew I'd done a great wrong somehow. That by marrying her I had betrayed some trust. That I had perhaps even caused her death—and robbed myself of . . ." He took her chin between his fingers and raised it, until he could gaze into her eyes. "And you had disappeared, you minx. I could find you nowhere."

"You wouldn't have wanted to see me just then, I think."

"But I did," he answered. "That last look you gave me—while you stood in that stunning white dress, by the chapel door. I couldn't forget that look. You were haunting me, Jaime, even from far away."

She blushed under his burning gaze. "You said the seer came to you in your dream!"

"He did," Malcolm's fingers caressed her face, tracing the outline of her dark hair. "He told me that 'twas time I came after you."

"After *me*?"

He nodded. "He asked me to go to the far land, England, and bring back my true intended to Skye. The one with good blood, he called you. The woman who still suffered by my past wrongdoing. For she'd done nothing to deserve such unhappiness, he said. Then he said 'twas time—that my soul would never be truly at ease until 'twas matched with its fitting mate."

She melted at his words. "How did you know *I* was the one of whom he spoke?"

"Because I saw you." Malcolm's large hands framed her face. His eyes were as dark as the night sky and yet trusting. "As James spoke, there were no other visions before my eyes than you. Your face was all I could see. Your beautiful body wrapped in that white dress, haunting me, punishing me for being such a great fool."

"Malcolm," she whispered his name while brushing a kiss across his lips. "I never intended to bring you pain."

He held back his desire of crushing her mouth to his. "Leave with me next week—go back with me to Scotland."

Remembering the horrible news that Frances had brought, Jaime jerked back in his arms in a sudden panic. Her eyes filled quickly with tears. "But they are sending me to court before then. I cannot go to Nonsuch Palace, Malcolm. I cannot. But how can I stop them?"

Malcolm's voice was reassuring. "Your father, Henry of England, cannot know of the truth of your identity. If he did—

if he had recently learned of it—there would be an entourage of knights and ladies ready and waiting to escort you back to court. I assume that in summoning you to come in such haste, the duke of Norfolk—or Edward—must have some under-handed plan for gaining power or favor with the king."

"But how will that bring them anything? Surely, now that he has an heir, Prince Edward, the king will care nothing . . ."

"Nay, lass. I don't think it is succession that the duke is thinking of." Malcolm released her and turned toward the window. "There is something else . . ."

"Whatever it is, Malcolm, I must find a way to convince Surrey not to send me there!" Jaime could hear her voice quiv-ering. "I've made a mistake of placing myself under the Howards' care—and now I am as much a prisoner as you are."

Malcolm, his face animated and alert as he thought the problem through, turned at her words and again caught her up in his arms.

"Perhaps if I tried to run," Jaime cried in despair. "Perhaps if I disguised myself and disappeared into the dark of the night."

"You will do no such thing, Jaime." Malcolm scolded. "Where would you go in this countryside? Who do you know outside of this palace?"

"But my own mother did it. And Elizabeth . . . years ago . . . while my mother was still carrying me."

Malcolm placed his hands firmly around her waist and glowered at her. "Think no more on that, Jaime. Those were different times, and Elizabeth had help. We, however, have other possibilities that we haven't pursued."

"Aye?" she asked, staring up at him. "What possibilities, Malcolm?"

"I told you before about arranging for a ship to meet us. Well, 'twill be arriving by the full moon at Midsummer's Eve, at a small fishing village north of Harwich."

"A ship! So it is real," she whispered.

"Aye, as real and sure as you and I standing here!"

Jaime's eyes narrowed as a thought struck her. "But Mid-summer's Eve is more than a week hence! I could be sent off to Nonsuch Palace long before that."

"You will not," he promised. "I give you my word . . . that will not happen."

Threading his fingers into her hair, Malcolm pulled her forward and kissed her. A moment later, still dazed from the suddenness, from the thoroughness of the kiss, Jaime opened her eyes as he drew away.

"But promise me that you will not do anything foolish, Jaime."

"Foolish?"

"Aye. You must trust me when I tell you that we have friends." He placed a finger on her full, soft lips, and then moved as if to back away. "You cannot be running away—or going into hiding—or putting yourself in danger. Promise me?"

"Where are you going?" she asked, instead of making the pact.

"To pursue an idea, lass. If I am successful, we might have our way out of this."

She held on to his hand. "But when will you know?"

"I do not know . . . perhaps tonight."

Jaime stared at him intently as the glimmer of a plan began to emerge in her mind.

"You'll come to me later, then."

"Aye." She nodded.

After I have pursued a design of my own, she finished silently.

CHAPTER 31

"**A**nd you expect me to poison her?" The Welsh physician cut in on Malcolm with a tone that was more a growl than a response. The man was too thickheaded even to hear the Highlander out.

"Have you lost your mind?" Malcolm asked angrily. "If she gets even a wee bit ill from this, if she has even the slightest discomfort, I'll wring your scrawny neck with my own hands."

Graves shot to his feet, rising onto his toes like some outraged bantam cock. "*You'll* wring *my* neck! Why, you arrogant, bull-necked savage! One moment, you're asking me to find a way to sicken her so she can avoid going off to court—the next, you are threatening my life if I do just that! Which is it, man?"

Malcolm forced down his anger. "I . . . I only asked you to help her feign an illness. It must all be pretense!"

"And why would I do such a thing? You want me to risk hanging for disobedience of the duke's wishes!"

Frustrated, Malcolm fought the strong inclination to strangle the man. As good as it might make him feel right now, though, he also knew that such happy violence would do nothing to help Jaime. He let out a long, slow breath and tried to check his temper. "I appreciate your family loyalty, Master Graves. And after all you've done to help me these past days, after the messages you've had sent back and forth between me and my people, I don't want you to think I'm slighting the trust between us."

The physician lifted a bony finger and pointed it at the Highlander's chest. "I did all of that because Mistress Jaime asked it of me, you baboon. In truth, I've been wanting to get rid of you from the first moment they dragged your carcass in here. But what you are asking me to do now is to interfere with that lass's marriage to my master's son."

"She will not marry Edward Howard. You can take my word on it."

"Aye, so long as you are around, she won't. But were I to get rid of you—if I helped you to go back to your people— then I believe she would."

"Nay, Master Graves. 'Tis not so simple, as you well know." Malcolm shook his head. "You know better than I that Edward is not deserving of her hand."

"And *you* are, I suppose?"

"Perhaps not," Malcolm answered seriously. "But I don't intend to force her to go anywhere against her wishes. And I am not dragging her to court for some vile use designed to further my own interests."

"You're saying that is what is being done to her?"

"How do you explain this summons from the duke and his son?" Malcolm pressed. "If Edward's intentions in wanting Jaime at court were honest, then why such a rush? What reason is there for all the secrecy? She has been told nothing but to prepare herself and leave on a day's notice. So far as she knows, her life could be in jeopardy there!"

" 'Tis not for me to question the duke's plans for the woman."

"By the Rood, man!" Malcolm threw up his hands.

"Aye, and though you're allowed to walk about and ride with Lord Surrey, you're still a prisoner here, and hardly in any position to be questioning anything, either!"

"What I ask is for Jaime, you old fool!"

The physician remained silent for a moment, running a hand over his bald head and studying the Highlander's face as he pondered Malcolm's words. "And you are asking me this on her behalf? You have no interests of your own at stake here?"

Malcolm stared down at the little man. "Don't twist my words, Master Graves. And don't force me to lie. My motives I've voiced to Jaime already, since she is the only one concerned. But as far as what I am asking you to do, you can believe that I have her welfare and happiness in mind. You have to accept my word on that. But if she leaves for Nonsuch Palace as the duke has ordered—there will be no turning back. She will be lost . . ."

A light knock on the door stopped his words, and the physician, ignoring the interruption, scowled at the Highlander. "Is this her wish, man? You must tell me that."

Malcolm nodded. "Aye."

"Then I will get word to you."

"When?" Malcolm pressed, ignoring a second knock at the door.

The physician took a step toward the closed door. "What are you planning to do, Highlander? Burn down the palace if I don't agree?"

"I'll do whatever needs to be done, Master Graves. She doesn't wish to go, and I will do whatever I can to make that wish come to pass."

The physician walked stiffly toward the door. "You'll hear from me before nightfall."

Catherine wished she could make out the muffled words coming through the door. The voice of the Highlander was consistently the most distinct, though every now and then the pitch of the other's voice reached her more clearly through the thick oak door. They were clearly arguing over something, and Catherine's curiosity was aroused. Fanning her golden brown tresses over her shoulders, she waited, straining to hear what Malcolm was saying. Interestingly enough, the High-lander aroused more than just curiosity in her, and she had missed seeing his ruggedly handsome face.

Aye, she thought, the man definitely interested her. Last night, lying alone in the huge bed of her cold chamber, she had found herself considering the fact that she had never had a Scot. There was no reason why she should let her plans to punish Edward interfere with her sport. Indeed, this man, Malcolm MacLeod, had much more presence than Edward. Taller, he was, and far more handsome with his tumbling brown hair and dark, brooding looks. His broad, powerful build; the way he'd looked last night at dinner with his massive arms crossed over the black velvet of his tunic; the way the sinewy muscles of his thighs and calves showed through his hose. Catherine's lips parted at the memory as she felt the start of that familiar stirring at the juncture of her thighs. He would be an excellent lover, she was certain of that. And that silly Mary—with her infantile crush on the man! Catherine smiled and drew in a deep breath. What would a dim-witted virgin like Mary know about satisfying a man like Malcolm?

With a glance up and down the corridor, Catherine ran her hands over the bodice of her dress, smoothing the quilted velvet. Seeing no one, she let her fingers linger on her breasts. She could feel the aroused nipples through the fabric. She would have him in her bed, and she would have him soon. Her body cried out for a man's touch, and the Highlander would do quite nicely.

The voices on the other side of the door were no longer audible at all. Impatiently, Catherine raised her hand and knocked at the door. She had to settle this business first. She was too smart to allow Edward to ruin her plans. He had yet to suffer for his sins against her.

Catherine's bright eyes never left Malcolm's face as she called over her shoulder. "I'll speak with you in a moment, Master Graves."

Malcolm let his eyes travel from the woman's face to the small, white hand resting on the crook of his elbow. He tried to hide the annoyance he felt at having Catherine accost him so openly in the corridor.

"I would like to see you in my chamber tonight, sir," she whispered in a tone meant, no doubt, to be inviting.

Malcolm continued to stare at the thin, jeweled fingers and

thought himself extremely lucky that the physician had moved away into the murky interior of his surgery. He was glad the old man hadn't heard this woman's invitation. Aye, he thought, that was *all* he needed—to have Graves think he was having an affair with every female in Kenninghall. That would certainly help to advance his character in the man's mind, Malcolm thought wryly.

" 'Tis something specific, m'lady, that you would care to see me about?" He tried to think of a way of not directly offending her, for there was something about Catherine that made him believe she would be extremely dangerous when crossed.

"Must I really tell you in detail what I have in mind?" she cooed, her voice still soft and seductive.

"Perhaps not," he replied quickly. "But I'm afraid, m'lady, that I do have other commitments for the evening."

"Are you to be put back in chains?" she asked.

Malcolm looked steadily into her face, uncertain if her words were a suggestion or a threat.

"The earl has asked to see me," he said, moving enough to cause her hand to drop away from his arm. "I believe he wishes to spend some time going over some manuscripts he's just received from the library of our late master, Erasmus."

"Well, that should take no time."

Malcolm took another step back. "Ah, one never knows with Lord Surrey." He bowed chivalrously in her direction. "But I mustn't detain you, m'lady."

"Perhaps another time?" she called after him.

But Malcolm said nothing as he disappeared down the corridor.

Catherine straightened her skirts around her feet, folded her hands in her lap, and looked coyly at the aging physician. "Oh, Master Graves, I think I have never yet known a man to age as handsomely as you. I was just telling Lady Frances last night that at court we are not blessed the way she is, having such a fine-looking man to look after her health." Her ample bosom rose and fell as she sighed, and looked at him from beneath her fluttering lashes.

The man's skin reddened, the blush spread from his cowled neck to the top of his balding head, and he busied his hands straightening rows of herbs laid out on his worktable. "What might I do for you today, Mistress Catherine?"

"I have this pain." She reached a hand behind her head and rubbed gently at the base of her neck. "Here, Master Graves. It began last night and kept me up half the night. There is a knot—I feel it right now . . . ouch!" She frowned, feigning a sudden discomfort.

The physician walked around the table and moved to her side. Gently pushing her hand away, he placed his callused fingers against the skin of her neck.

Catherine tilted her head and moaned seductively in response to his touch. "Oh, Master Graves, you certainly have the touch." The man's hand continued to search for the non-existent knot. "Aye, that is feeling so much better already," she whispered.

The physician pulled back sharply, but she turned quickly and took a hold of one hand. "Oh, don't let me continue to suffer, Master Graves."

"I can find no lump . . . no knot indicating a spasm. I . . . I cannot find anything wrong with you," the man stuttered.

Without releasing his hand, Catherine came slowly to her feet and stepped closer to him. "Oh, but just now, when you were touching my neck . . . I felt a sharp pain go right to my heart . . . here!" she whispered, lifting his large hand and placing it firmly against her left breast, just above the low, square neckline of her dress. He tried to pull back again, but she held him there. Stepping even closer, she pressed his fingers into the firm flesh. "What do you think this could be from, Master Graves?"

The man's eyes were riveted to her chest and his mouth hung open.

"Oh, perhaps you need to take a better look," she cooed. Slowly reaching up with her free hand, Catherine pulled down the bodice of the dress, exposing the rosy tips of her full breasts. With a jerk of his hand, the panicked physician withdrew and practically ran to the other side of the room. She watched his back with a smile and then pulled her dress back up in place. "Do you have any idea what my ailment might be, Master Graves?"

With his back still to her, the man shook his head and mumbled something inaudible in response. Greatly satisfied with herself and the success of her teasing, Catherine moved softly across the room in pursuit. She couldn't let her prey off so easily.

"Oh my," she said with surprise, coming to a stop behind him. "Look at the marks your fingers have left on my skin."

Graves whirled and stared with dismay at the red imprints on her milky-white bosom.

"Master Graves, certainly you—an esteemed scholar and physician, a man of science, a healer of renown—certainly you must be able to do something for me. You won't just let me suffer now, will you?"

The physician backed away as the young woman stepped closer. Scurrying around the worktable, he held up a hand to ward her off. She stopped, smiling innocently.

"Aye, mistress. I'll make up something for you. A potion to drink. I'll send it up to your chambers. It will relax the knot in your neck . . . help you to sleep."

"Ah, a potion to help me rest!" Catherine smiled as she picked up a bundle of rosemary from the table. She held it to her face and inhaled the distinctive scent. She pursed her lips and looked at the physician. "But how will I know how much to take? If I take too much, won't I get ill?"

"Of course you will, mistress!" the physician growled, running his hand over his glistening pate. "But I'll . . ."

"Perhaps you should come up and administer it yourself, Master Graves . . . as I prepare for bed, you could . . ."

"Nay, nay, enough of that, Mistress Catherine! I'll send up clear directions with the potion."

Catherine pouted at the man, and then held the bundle of herbs up again, seemingly studying them. "Whatever you send up, Master Graves, would you send enough that I might share some with my cousin, Jaime!"

"The man's eyes snapped up to hers. "You let that lass be. She has no sickness that I know of that requires the medicine I'm sending up to you."

Catherine drew her face together in a tight frown and laid the rosemary on the table. "Oh, you haven't seen her since she got the news today, have you?"

"What news might that be, mistress?" Graves said evasively, turning and looking at the jars of ingredients that lined the shelves of the surgery.

She stepped around the table and shook her head in exaggerated distress. "The poor creature. She is being dragged to Nonsuch Palace to be with Lord Edward at a time when he is . . . well, let us just say this is not the best time for her to go." Catherine picked up a bundle of nightshade and another of wolfbane and gazed at them. "Perhaps whatever you're planning to send me might not be strong enough for all she must bear."

The old man's frown told her that she had his attention.

"Few people here at Kenninghall know what is happening to Lord Edward at court." Her voice carried a confidential tone as it lowered to a whisper. "He is in a great deal of trouble, Master Graves. He had fallen from favor with the king." She lowered her voice even more and placed the herbs back on the table. "I know the truth only because I just left him there. He is guarded by the king's men at all times, and he isn't permitted to leave the palace grounds. I fear for him. And the duke, he is trying as best as he can to keep it all hushed."

"What kind of trouble is he in, Mistress Catherine? And what purpose is served in bringing that poor lass into the middle of it?"

Catherine shrugged her shoulders in ignorance. "I wish I knew more. Perhaps they are thinking Jaime might charm the king with her looks and her music. But I cannot see anything she might do that would soften His Majesty. After all, I did all that I could, and to no avail, I fear. And she is half-Scot, besides." She looked knowingly at the physician. "You know what it feels like to be an outsider, Master Graves. Jaime will be miserable. She is already quite, quite distressed." Catherine shook her head. "And she has every right to be. My future husband's wrath is nothing to trifle with; Jaime knows full well the sad end that came to our cousin, Anne Boleyn. And now, here is our Jaime, a Boleyn and a Scot, besides. I worry about her safety, for who knows that Henry's ire will not extend the Jaime. Who knows if she may not turn out to be the one who really suffers in the end."

Catherine turned her back on the physician, patting tears away from dry eyes and giving him a chance to ponder her words. Short of assigning someone to hurt Jaime, which she wasn't ready to do, yet, this old man offered her the best way of stopping that wench from going to Edward. She thought her words had been effective, quite convincing. That might be all it would take—a medicine of some sort—a potion that would make her ill to travel. Catherine wanted Jaime here, alive, within her grasp. This was where she could turn the wench's mind from thoughts of Edward. One more twist of the knife to make him suffer all the more.

Catherine swung around and faced the physician. "There must be something that we can do. We must! Don't you agree, Master Graves, that it is our duty to help her through this—before she does something rash on her own?"

"You think she might?"

Catherine nodded. "She is so proud and yet so timid in seeking other people's help. I fear she very well could. Who knows what trouble she might get herself into!"

The physician's bushy brows bunched up in a frown. "I'll see what I can do, Mistress Catherine."

She successfully fought back a smile of triumph. "Should I remain here? Perhaps I might be of some help!"

"Nay, I thank you!" The physician quickly walked to the door, pulling it open wide. "Be on your way, Mistress Catherine. I can manage quite well!"

As she strolled toward the door, she considered whether she should do any more prodding. But the physician's grim expression told her that he was convinced and that he was already designing a plan.

"You will not forget me?"

"Nay, mistress. I'll not be forgetting you."

"Very well," Catherine said, smiling to herself as she left the physician's chamber.

CHAPTER 32

"**B**ut why must I wait? I want to go to court now!"

Jaime ignored Mary, but Frances, obviously far more annoyed by the young woman's whining complaints, snapped at her.

"This is hardly the time to discuss *your* wishes, Mary! Things are difficult enough trying to get Jaime ready."

With a sigh loud enough for everyone in the room to hear, Mary sat down on the edge of her bed and sulked.

"When the time comes, Mary, you will be leaving with Catherine, if she'll have you. Don't forget, though her entourage is large now, after she is wedded to the king she will have countless more attendants. Just think, aside from the six 'great ladies,' there will certainly be at least four or five ladies of the privy chamber, and a dozen attendants of exalted rank, besides the maids of honor." The countess motioned to the servants to bring out an empty trunk and leave it open before them. "Surely, there will be a place for you, as well, but right now we are here to help Jaime prepare. Have you already forgotten that you volunteered to be of some use?"

Frances's question was never answered and Mary continued to groan and complain about the unfairness of it all. But as the two women continued with their argument, Jaime turned a deaf ear to them. She didn't want to do this—nay, the pressure of being forced to go to Nonsuch Palace at the duke's summons rankled her greatly. Looking about the room, she shuddered at the mess surrounding her. Like snares of twisting rope, everything seemed to catch at her—to trap her at every turn.

Jaime stepped back as a serving girl opened another trunk before them. She was supposed to be choosing her wardrobe for court. Glancing in the direction of Frances and Mary, who continued to bicker by the bed, Jaime could not help but smile wryly. With a wave of her hand, she motioned the serving girl away and gestured for her own servant, Caddy, to help her. She didn't need all this attention; she didn't need all these servants. She wished all of them would simply go away and let her be. Jaime reached blindly into the depths of the trunk and pulled out some rolled-up material and handed it to Caddy.

It wasn't until she was handing Caddy the next item, a carefully folded dress, that Jaime realized her serving woman had not moved and stood still, holding the unraveled material out in front of her. With a frown, Jaime snatched the dress back and stared at the torn shoulder. Suddenly feeling extremely embarrassed, she balled the garment in her hands. This was the dress she had worn that night—the night she'd crept up to Malcolm's room and to his bed. Holding the bundle to her chest, Jaime quickly looked around. Caddy was already occupying herself pulling other garments from the trunk and laying them out for Jaime's choosing, as Mary and Frances continued to argue.

Holding the soft wool against her breast, Jaime thought of Malcolm. He had told her that he would come up with a plan—one that would keep her from being sent to Edward. Now, though, feeling more and more desperate as the moment of departure crept ever nearer, she worried about how much danger he might bring upon himself. He had no connections— no trusted friends—no kin or fellow warriors in this palace. How could he save her from her uncle and her cousin without exposing himself to terrible, perhaps insurmountable risk?

Trying to distance herself from all the commotion around her, Jaime moved to a small worktable by the window. Glancing over her shoulder, she found, interestingly enough, that her retreat was viewed with very little concern by anyone in the room. Turning her back on them all, she stared out into the gardens, spreading out beneath the window and bursting with color.

Malcolm had mentioned there was a vessel coming in to a nearby fishing village within a week. All she had to do was to somehow drag her feet for that time—until they could escape to Scotland. With that simple thought, a warmth spread through her, and Jaime felt her heart bloom with joy. It would be so different this time, she thought. She would go back to Skye knowing that he wanted her for his wife. Closing her eyes, she tried to imagine her family—their loving faces. By the Holy Virgin, how much she missed them now. What a fool she had been to think that she could distance herself from them and still be happy. In truth, she could see now that she'd been miserable—until Malcolm had come.

The sun, golden in its descent, radiated warmth through the diamond-shaped panes of glass. On impulse, Jaime pushed open the window and breathed in the sweet smells of summer. But soon the joys of nature dropped away into oblivion as she considered, once again, the pressing matters still before her. For how could she remain where she was . . . and still keep Malcolm from laying siege to Kenninghall.

Jaime stared in confusion as the physician scowled at her and blocked her entry into the surgery.

"I said you don't waste much time, do you, young woman?"

Jaime glanced behind her into the empty corridor, searching for the person who Master Graves's words were intended for. "I don't?" she said at last, raising her eyebrows questioningly.

"Nay, not you, mistress. The pixies and fairies dancing in the corridor there behind you." The man shook his head and swung the door open, heading back inside the chamber. Totally perplexed, Jaime silently stepped in and closed the door.

"Of course, you!" the physician continued irritably, slapping his linen coif on his head and tugging it roughly into position. "Your last messenger left only a moment ago. And the one before that . . ."

"My messengers?" Jaime interrupted, following closely behind the physician.

The Welshman never answered her question nor did he

acknowledge her interruption. Coming to a stop by his work-table—which was strewn with different herbs, a mortar and pestle, and some bowls of various sizes—he appeared to spoon something into a small leather pouch. Jaime looked with curiosity over his shoulder, but she couldn't make out exactly what he was doing. However, she could see that his motions were quick, angry. She watched with a frown as he turned his back and blocked her view. His sour mood made no sense, but he was obviously angry with her for something she'd done. Well, for the life of her, she didn't know what it was she *could* have done, but if he wanted to have it out with her, then he'd have to be the one to pursue it. She had more important matters to attend to, and if the old man was going to be disagreeable, then she would need time to figure out something else.

"Master Graves," she said, clearing her throat. "I came down here to ask a favor of you reg . . ."

"So you don't have any intention of marrying my master's son!"

Jaime opened her mouth and then closed it again as the elder physician turned and faced her. The man's direct question and chilly gaze left no choice for her but to speak the truth. "Nay, sir. That I don't," she acknowledged firmly, shaking her head.

"Too good for him, I suppose."

" 'Tis really not a matter . . ."

"And does he know of this, mistress? Does Lord Edward know?"

Jaime again shook her head in answer.

"And His Grace, the duke?" The physician's face was accusing.

She let out a long breath, temper unexpectedly bubbling up within her. "Nay, Master Graves. None of the Howard family has been told of my decision regarding this marriage. And I'd like to know how you . . ."

"Then don't you think it's time you told them of the truth—of your wishes?" The man waited for her answer, holding the small bag in one hand, and then in the other.

"Aye, 'tis true," she replied after a moment. Jaime searched for words to explain, but then smashed her fist into the palm of her other hand in frustration. "But I will be damned if I'll do it at the king's court. If I go there now—as I've been summoned to do—then I am declaring publicly that I am agreeable to this match. What voice would I have when I get there? I, a Scot and a woman. None!"

The man peered into her face, and Jaime found herself glaring back at him. Judging from the man's attitude and look, she knew she had probably said too much. But at the same time she felt her own cheeks burning with the desire to defend her decision.

" 'Twas my doing, was it not?" he asked at last. "You would have stayed here in England and married Lord Edward if it hadn't been for me meddling with the Highlander's life, helping you to keep him alive, passing on your letter to those who could send it north!"

Shocked by the turn in the conversation, Jaime gazed back at his darkly frowning face. There was a gentle heart beyond that rough exterior, and evidence of it was peeking through.

"Nay, Master Graves. None of this was your doing. It was fate—a turn of Fortune's wheel. 'Twas meant to be this way." She looked beyond him at the fresh and dried herbs on the table. "Malcolm and I were destined to be together and nothing he nor I did—no matter how great the distance we put between us—nothing could keep us apart. I believe that regardless of whether you helped us or not, we would still somehow end up together."

"Aye, you'll end up in some dungeon, and I'll be keeping you both company, I fear."

"And whose company do you think I'd prefer being in?"

The man's bushy eyebrows seemed to relax a bit. "You are trying to make me feel better, lass."

Jaime couldn't hold back the smile that was breaking through. "Did you say 'lass,' Master Graves? I'm beginning to think you have more Scot in you than you'll admit to!"

He waved a hand in the air denying the accusation. "I just want to make sure that I won't be held responsible for you leaving us for good. And 'tis not for the fear of any men that I say this," he was quick to add. " 'Tis just . . . well, I think the folks that really matter around here . . . well, with you leaving us . . ." He pulled his coif from his head and tossed it onto the table, running his hand over his balding skull. "Look at the children—the joy they get out of spending time in that music room of yours. Just think of the women—how they think of ways to draw you to their cottages just to chat, so as how they can brag to the rest of their cronies how you'd been spending all day with them, how you shared a meal with them. And have you seen the men? 'Tis a wonder the women are not tearing you limb from limb with how well the men think of you. If it weren't for the fact that you are as good as you are beautiful, I don't know what their feelings would be regarding you. One passing smile from you and the young lads, at least, are dreamy-eyed for a fortnight." The physician paused and frowned. "You leave, Mistress Jaime, and I think it'll not go easy with any of them."

Jaime paused and stared at the man. She'd never heard him say so much, so eloquently. She swallowed the lump that was rising in her throat.

"Nor with me, either," she said gently, placing a hand on the physician's arm. She had to say her peace, though she feared that—once she started—she might find it extremely difficult to keep her emotions in check. "I've grown fond of the folk here at Kenninghall. But I have to go back to where I belong, Master Graves. I have to wed the one I love. Fate has given us a second chance by crossing our paths here. I cannot turn my back on Malcolm. I cannot simply forget the love I have for him."

She looked down at her hands, fighting the surging emotions that threatened to bring forth tears. She didn't want to weep here before this man, when she still had yet to ask his help. The thought that he might consider her tears a cunning, feminine way to convince him to help her was not a particularly attractive one to Jaime. Especially after all he'd said of how upsetting her departure would be to the people he cared for the most.

Blinking the tears from her eyes, she looked up into his face. "The reason why I came here, Master Graves . . ."

"Aye, mistress. 'Tis ready," he said, holding out the pouch to her.

She stared at the gray bag that the physician held in his burly fist. "What is ready?" she asked quietly.

"They won't question my judgment, mistress. No one will be taking you away to court—not unless that is where *you* want to go."

She reached out, and he placed the pouch in her hand. "But I don't . . ."

"You take this tonight before you go to bed, and tomorrow morning at first light I'll find an excuse to send a servant for you. And when they cannot get you to wake up, then I will come in myself to check on you."

Jaime opened the tie of the pouch and peered inside. "What is this that I will be taking?"

"A compound of gilded lettuce seed, white poppy, and mandragora seed. Mix no more than this much in a drink." He showed her, demonstrating the measurement with the end of his little finger. " 'Tis sure to give you a good night's sleep. I often give it to folk who cannot sleep."

She looked up at the physician. "And what will happen when I do finally wake up?"

"By then, Lord willing, someone will be frightened enough to send for me." He reached up and massaged his sore shoulder. "After checking on you, I'll tell them you could have green sickness and a touch of spleen. They'll take my word for it when I tell them you must remain in bed."

Jaime glanced hesitantly from the bag back up to the physician's face. "Do I have to pretend to be sick? I am afraid they'll see through such a ruse."

"I don't see how they could," Graves answered confidently. "Tomorrow, when I come in to you, I will put a cloth treated with a strong medicine on your forehead. That should make you sleep the day away. Trust me, the earl will not send you on the road when he sees your pale face in the bed tomorrow."

"What will be in that medicine?" Jaime asked curiously.

"Oil of violets, a bit of opium, and milk. I mix them and wrap them in a linen cloth, and lay the poultice against your temple for a few moments at a time."

"And that will make me sick?"

"Nay, mistress, only if you use too much of it. The way we

will do it, you will just sleep and sleep. And the beauty of it is that we can do this for as long as you want to remain an invalid. Just take the compound I've given you each night, and I'll have the poultice prepared beside your bed, so we can place it on your temple as required."

Jaime clutched the pouch tightly in her hand and gathered it to her chest. "Will I be able to snap out of this when the time comes to . . ." Her words trailed off, though she continued to gaze at the Welshman steadily.

"Aye, mistress," he answered. "Just stop taking the compound, and don't use the poultice for a day before . . . before your time comes, and you'll be fine."

She placed the leather pouch in the pocket of her skirt and then reached out and hugged the man. "Thank you, Master Graves!"

"Just go before I change my mind, mistress," he replied gruffly as he patted her gently on the back. "Just go, lass."

CHAPTER 33

M alcolm stretched his long arm out of the window and
drew her into the chamber. She was as light as a bird.

"You must promise me not to make this climb again, lass,"
he said, pulling her into his arms without even giving her a
chance to remove her cloak. "You'll be sure to break your
neck if you so much as miss a foothold."

She tilted her head back and smiled into his handsome face.
"Well, there was little chance of me falling. I think the angels
held me up."

His hand reached up and pushed back the hood of her cloak.
His fingers gently traced the softness of the skin at her temple,
her cheek, her parted lips. The cloak was cool and damp from
the night air, but her skin was warm, and her eyes sparkled
like stars in a moonless sky. "Were you so eager to come
to me?"

She nodded, turning her face slightly and placing a kiss on
the tips of his fingers.

"Oh, Jaime," he groaned, unable to hold back. He crushed
her body to his chest as his lips devoured her sweet mouth. "It
has been hell, my sweet, waiting up here for you. I cannot tell
you how many times I thought to come down that wall after
you."

Teasingly, she placed light kisses along the lines of his
chin. "I am glad you didn't come after me. The room I share
with Mary is a battlefield of unwanted people and trunks.
Lady Frances! Caddy! Every servant in Kenninghall! It took

me quite a while to push them all out. And then I went to see Master Graves."

Malcolm reached under her chin and undid the tie of her cloak. "So he thought of a way to keep you from being sent to Nonsuch Palace."

She pulled back and looked him in the eye. "You know?"

"I knew he would."

She placed her hands against his chest and smiled into his face. "So you went to him, as well?"

"What do you mean, as well?"

"I went, too," she answered. "But by then he was already determined to help us through this." She hugged him tightly and then looked into his face again. "We thought the same."

"Aye, lass," he said hoarsely, suddenly entranced with her shining eyes and beautiful face. His hands moved of their own accord and pushed the cloak from her shoulders and onto the floor. He gathered her roughly to his heart.

Jaime wrapped her hands tightly around his neck and raised herself on her toes. "I love you, Malcolm. And I know everything will be fine. We'll be leaving this place within a week, and we will sail to Scotland."

"And we will be married at Skye, if that suits you," he whispered in her ear.

Malcolm closed his eyes for a moment and silently vowed once again to keep her safe until the time came for them to leave. The last message Graves had delivered said that the ship was still due to arrive as originally planned during the Midsummer's Eve celebration. Malcolm knew that if he were not in a longboat at the meeting point, they would sail away and return at the next full moon. But he would be there . . . with Jaime. And for now, the two of them would just have to sit back and bide their time. It was simple enough to say, he thought. Actually doing so was another matter entirely.

"Malcolm!" she whispered, snuggling closer against his chest. "When I went to Master Graves at first, he said something . . . he implied that there was more than one person who had visited him today, before I arrived, asking the same thing of him on my account."

"You think there was someone other than I?"

She nodded. "Aye, he was irritated to see me, at first. He said something about me sending messengers!" She pulled back and looked into his eyes. "Other than you, I just cannot think of anyone who would want to side with us on this. I believe everyone at Kenninghall wants to send me packing for Nonsuch Palace."

Malcolm ran a hand through her silky hair. "When I was leaving the physician's chamber, I did see Catherine go in. Do you think she might do something on your behalf?"

Jaime rolled her eyes. "I would be afraid to hazard a guess why my cousin might have a need to see the physician, but I doubt very much she would do so for *my* benefit. I have had the honor of spending a few moments in her company since she returned, and I can assure you that she has no interest whatsoever in helping me." She caressed his chest with her palms. "Catherine doesn't like me much, Malcolm."

"Not a very good judge of character, I'd say," he growled teasingly, lowering his mouth to her neck.

"In fact, I think she hates me."

The Highlander's kisses were hot on her skin. "Then we'll just have to hate her back."

Jaime, trying to focus on their words, found herself increasingly caught up in the sheer pleasure she felt of his lips against her sensitive skin, and she tilted her head, giving his mouth better access to her throat. "I still wish I knew who it was that went . . . to Master Graves . . . on my beh . . ."

Like a flower dropped into the sliding current of a mountain brook, her own interest in the topic was quickly slipping away. She felt her breathing quicken as her body molded to the hard muscular lines of his frame. The tightness in her breasts, the fluttering ache deep in her belly—these feelings were all so wondrous, so far beyond anything she'd ever felt before. Suddenly, all that mattered was having his hands on her—on her face, in her hair, on her skin. She thought now, longingly, of the wonder of feeling his fingers searching out the secret folds of her womanhood. The tightness of her dress was suffocating her as she recalled the feel of his mouth suckling her breasts.

His voice barely broke her reverie as his hands casually skimmed the sides of her breasts. "If it wasn't Catherine, lass, then who could it be?"

She couldn't find her words. All she wanted him to do was to cup her swollen breasts with his strong hands.

He did. Her breath stopped as he ran his hand along the soft velvet of her bodice to the curve of her breast. "What of Mary? Might she be one to do something like that on your behalf?"

She shook her head. Her voice was hoarse to her own ear. "She has learned to dislike me, as well." Jaime wasn't quite sure how she'd managed to get those words out. Her tongue was dry and her body on fire. If he would only touch her there, where she burned the hottest, she thought feverishly.

Jaime closed her eyes as he gently pulled her against his hardening desire. His hands traced the curves of her buttocks, and as her middle slid against his protruding manhood, a moan escaped her lips. She knew that he was feeling it, too, for he drew a sharp breath and tipped her head back with a kiss that was wild, all-consuming. And when he pulled back, he was breathless. She gazed up into eyes clouded with passion, and saw he was struggling to control something within him . . . something raw.

"Jaime," he said, his voice ragged. "Who else . . . who do you . . ."

"I . . . I don't give a damn who hates me!" she managed to get out. "Malcolm . . . I want . . . I want you to take me!"

A look of relief lit his features, as if a great weight had been lifted from his shoulders, and he laid his forehead against her hair. Seeing his response, her shyness dissipated into thin air, and Jaime tugged open the front of his shirt.

"Are you sure, lass?" he rasped as her lips kissed and tasted the skin of his chest. "Perhaps if we were to wait, you'd feel more . . ."

"Show me things, Malcolm." Hesitantly, she slid one of her hands lower over the rough scars of his chest, over the hard lines of his stomach.

"But would it not be easier for you, Jaime, to be in our

own . . ." He could not finish. Her hand was stroking his hard member through his close hose.

"Teach me how to make love to you, Malcolm," she whispered between soft kisses as her lips moved over the sinews of his chest.

"I? Teach you? Lass, you steal away my control. My sense of reason." As she gazed into his face, Jaime saw the light in his eyes change, and Malcolm's will joined hers. "Aye, my love, my Jaime. Our time is now."

She had yearned. She had wished. She was his.

How he swept her up and carried her to the giant, curtained bed, neither would ever recall. But there on the high mattress, by the light of a single candle, the clothing that encumbered them was torn away with a vengeance and cast to the floor. But as skin touched skin, Jaime felt Malcolm set his muscles and slow the passion that surely raged within him.

There would be no rushing him. And as she looked into his face, she knew that he was determined to honor her request.

"Aye, lass," he said. "This night I mean to give you pleasure. I mean to show you love as it should have been the first time."

The first time they'd made love, she'd been far too nervous, too confused, to even consider what she should do. But it was all different now. Lying there naked beneath the Highlander, Jaime gave herself up totally to the feelings he was stirring within her as his mouth and lips paid homage to every inch of her body. As her body heated, as he suckled first one breast and then the other, she had a vague sense that he might drive her to sheer madness. She reached for him, trying to take him into her hands. Her mouth was desperate to taste him—to do to him what his torturing mouth was doing to her. This was nothing like what they had shared before, so she followed his lead, taking pleasure as he directed.

Malcolm raised his lips to hers, his fingers combing through the black silken waves of her hair, while his tongue sought to discover every soft recess of her mouth. Jaime writhed beneath him, her hands restless, insistent, succeeding finally in wrapping her fingers around his throbbing member. His breath caught in his chest as she lifted her hips to guide him in.

He tore his mouth away. "Nay, my love. Not yet!"

She watched him through half-lidded eyes, her breaths short and quick as he scorched a trail of kisses down her body. She arched her back, knowing now the sweet torture of his lips closing around her nipple, of his tongue stroking the stretched skin as he sucked. She didn't have long to wait, and his mouth closed around her flesh, eliciting a moan from deep in her throat. But he wasn't done with her. When his lips left her breasts and moved down over the sensitive skin of her belly, she grasped his hair with both hands. And at the next moment, when his hands moved beneath her buttocks, raising her up, when his tongue found the soft folds of her womanhood, Jaime was certain she was about to die.

Catherine glanced stealthily around the corner at the young serving girl toying enticingly with the broad-shouldered guard outside of the Highlander's chamber door. She couldn't help but smile as the young woman turned coyly, giving him the chance to draw her to him and squeeze her breasts in the act. The servant, in turn, responded by reaching back and running a teasing hand over the ties of his codpiece. Even from where she stood, Catherine could tell that the guard was ready to pin the young woman to the wall and take her right there. But she had paid the girl too well for her to mess up the future queen's plans. Moving back into the shadows of the wall, Catherine watched as the young wench whispered something in the man's ear before breaking away from him with a laugh.

"Though his guard duty goes until dawn, he'll follow in five minutes, m'lady," the girl whispered as she broke around the corner. "And the Highlander is alone."

Catherine tried to hide her shiver of excitement as she glanced down the hall. Her whole body ached for a man's touch—for this man's touch. Pulling the cloak tighter around her, she tried to contain her lustful anticipation. She'd be writhing beneath him soon enough—she just had to be patient and let her serving girl do her job.

"You must keep the soldier busy," Catherine said, with a jerk of her head in the guard's direction. "For the night!"

The young woman curtsied with a wry smile. " 'Twill be my pleasure, m'lady."

Jaime cried out in joy when he entered her at last. Answering his thrusts with her own synchronous movements, together they climbed to heights of pleasure that transcended all thought, all emotion, all consciousness.

Moments later, she languorously threaded her fingers into his tousled hair and smiled at the satisfied expression on his face. Malcolm lay sprawled over her with his face resting comfortably on her breasts. The rush of feeling—the ecstasy she had felt in the splendor of their lovemaking—had been like nothing she could ever have imagined. Jaime blinked back a tear. She couldn't allow the grandeur of the magical moment they'd just shared to be spoiled by silly weeping. Over and over again Malcolm MacLeod had taken her to the stars, letting her revel in the heat of their radiant light, and then brought her back to earth to share in her pleasure. And the last time—she arched her back as he rubbed his rough cheek against her sensitive breasts—the last time had certainly been a glimpse of paradise.

"Am I crushing you?" he asked, turning his head and taking her nipple into his mouth.

"Aye, crushed, broken, splintered with bliss," she answered huskily, sinking her fingers deeper into his hair.

His lips released her breast, and he moved up to her neck, all the while teasing and tasting her skin.

"I just cannot get enough of you, lass," he growled. His hand skimmed over her ribs and came to rest on her hip. Instinctively, she wrapped her leg around his waist. "But I should let you rest awhile." He took her soft earlobe into his mouth.

"Do you remember when you asked me to have your bairn?" She raised her hips slowly, feeling his heavy manhood hardening as she moved. He lay his head on the pillow next to her. She reached her hand between them and took hold of his now-erect shaft. "Do you think we've already planted the seed? Do you think I am already with child?"

He raised his head and stared deeply into her eyes. She saw

love, passion and happiness there. "How would I know, my love?" he replied with a tender smile. "But perhaps we should try once more—in case."

"Aye, just in case," she repeated breathlessly, guiding the tip of his shaft into her opening.

Catherine watched the guard disappear down the hall. From behind, she thought she saw the young man already undoing his codpiece before he even disappeared into the darkness. Pulling the hood of her cloak forward to cover her face, Catherine leaned down and picked up the trencher of the food that the serving girl had left behind for her. Though it was unlikely that she would see anyone at this hour, she couldn't allow herself to be caught by any meddling passerby. Stepping into the light of the torch, she moved past it toward the chamber's entryway. The girl had passed on to her that there was no latch on the Highlander's door, that the bar inside had been removed. But, for a moment, Catherine paused, contemplating whether she should knock on his door and wait for an invitation or just go in and surprise the handsome Highlander.

A thrill raced through her as she decided that she liked the latter choice the best and put her hand upon the heavy iron door handle.

Malcolm wrapped his arms around her, trying not to break the connection of their bodies as he rolled them both in the bed . . . and successfully brought her sprawling on top of him. She was giggling as he pulled at her knees until she knelt up straight, straddling him.

"I didn't know we could do it this way," she whispered before gasping as she took him deeper into her.

He reached up and pushed her hair off over her shoulders, cupping her breasts in his hands. "And many other ways," he managed to get out. She looked so stunningly beautiful, her ebony hair long and wild, her eyes clouded with passion. Her full, round breasts, high and proud with their nipples fully aroused, beckoning to his touch.

Malcolm watched her move up and down on his engorged manhood, her rhythm quickening as she rocked with deepening moans into his carefully timed thrusts. Once again, he was ready to pour his seed into her. Once again, he was desperate for release.

So he closed his eyes to the beauty before him and tried to buy some time.

The sudden sound of steps and serving women's voices down the corridor caused Catherine to turn in panic and brush lightly against the thick oak door. Turning her face in sudden panic, she considered moving off down the hall and disappearing into the shadowy corners beyond. But she was so close to her aim that she could not tear herself away. Reaching for the handle, she quietly tested the door. The girl had been right—there was no bar securing it. She quickly placed the tray on the ground and disappeared into the room.

CHAPTER 34

Appraising his son's haggard state, the duke of Norfolk shook his head disapprovingly.

"Just because you were advised to remain in these chambers, Edward, you needn't look as though you've been sentenced to death." He stalked angrily into the middle of the room and kicked a chair out of his way. "How do you expect anyone to think you innocent, when you yourself look as if you've been three days on the rack."

Edward ignored his father's disdainful attitude and got up from his chair to fill his cup. "I heard that the king has rejected our written plea."

The duke's eyes locked on Edward's profile. "Who has been in here?"

Edward picked up the wine pitcher from the table and filled his cup to the top. "The honorable Robert Radcliffe, earl of Essex, your ever good friend, the Lord Great Chamberlain."

The duke's scowling face darkened further with displeasure. "When was he here?"

"Just this morning."

"What did he want?"

"He was kind enough to tell me what my own father does not have the courage to tell me."

"EDWARD!"

The duke's shout brought the younger man up abruptly. Quickly recovering, though, he cast a sneering look at his father and drained the wine cup. "Bah!"

"What did the Lord Chamberlain say to you?"

Edward's lip curled as he noticed the hint of restraint that now marked his father's question. "He said that any pleading that is to be done must come from me. And I have three days to defend myself against the 'rumors' that circulate about me. If these serpents' tongues cannot be answered, I will be presented with a formal indictment, and they will convene the Court of the High Steward." Edward refilled his cup and lifted it in his father's direction. "And, Father, here's to the good fortune that you will not be a member of that court!"

The deepening color in the aging man's face, the clenching of his jaw, the flashing anger in his eyes—in the past—would have been enough to stop Edward cold. But now, raising his cup again to his lips, he gave a short, unpleasant laugh.

"You are a fool, a drunken fool!"

"Am I, Your Grace? Am I a fool to think that you are—above everything—the king's man? Were you not the judge in the trial of your own niece, Anne Boleyn? Were you not the one who so bravely told her that she was an adulteress and so therefore must lose her head?"

"Enough, Edward!"

"But, Father, you forget yourself. Anne was *no* adulteress. She was truly innocent, and yet you did nothing to save her life. In fact, you did your best to assure a guilty sentence."

"She had to die. The king wanted her removed."

"And you obeyed." Edward again laughed bitterly. "In fact you went as far as to invent . . ."

"The fortunes of the family were at stake," the duke growled.

"And so she dies." Edward shook his head. "So, Your Grace, does the king wish to have me removed, as well? Does your loyalty to the king surmount all paternal bonds? Do the 'fortunes of the family' come before the life of your own son? Were you, Father, the one who told the king of the treasures I've not surrendered?"

"You are drunk, Edward! And you begin to disgust me." The duke looked disdainfully in his direction before turning toward the door. "I tell you your future bride will arrive by the week's end. Once she is here and has been presented to

His Majesty as your wife *and* as his daughter, all will be resolved—unless you are so determined to ruin everything!"

Edward gave a shrug of disbelief before filling his cup once again.

"Get a hold of yourself, boy. She will save your neck from the executioner's blade. And I tell you she may be your only chance. But you must try to act a bit more noble. By the devil, you are a Howard, Edward!" The duke punctuated his admonishment with a hard rap of his knuckles on the table.

"Aye, by the devil," Edward repeated with a bitter laugh.

The duke shook his head and stared into the glazed eyes of his son. "And though we will use her to our profit, remember this, Edward. Jaime is a good woman. You might pretend, at least, to deserve her."

CHAPTER 35

The wretched beasts, she thought.

Staring past the draped opening of the heavy bed curtains, Catherine cursed in silence the woman's bare back, her heart-shaped buttocks lifting and descending on the Highlander's shining manhood. She watched his hands grasp her hips as their tempo increased, and she longed for them to hold her that way. Catherine couldn't see the wench's face, but the waves of black hair spread over the flawless back suddenly infuriated her.

She wanted to tear the woman from his embrace and throw her into the corridor, but she held her anger in check. She could not expose herself. Catherine withdrew into the black corner by the foot of the bed and waited—and watched. Letting her eyes travel up the Highlander's muscular legs to his straining thighs, to the fully extended shaft at their juncture—driving again and again into the woman. Catherine found herself quivering with excitement, becoming moist with anticipation. Her hand slipped inside of her cloak. She was wearing nothing beneath it, and her fingers caressed the voluptuous curves of her breasts, circled the hardened tip of her nipple.

She cursed the slut. She herself should be the one riding him now. And she was ready, she thought, her fingers sliding down over her belly and into her moist folds. She had come here willingly to share with the Highlander a night of passion that would pleasure them both. And here, she must wait. Oh, and he, too, was ready—that she could see. Driving harder, again and again, and then lifting himself off the bed and suckling the hussy's breasts.

Catherine fought down the moan that she heard begin in her own throat. But there was no point in stopping them now. As the glow of heat spread through her, she pressed her back against the wall. But they'd better finish soon, she thought threateningly.

The young woman's panting cries were becoming sharper, and Catherine's attention was drawn, momentarily, to her. Tomorrow, she'd have the wench whipped. Perhaps she herself would do it. The whore's perfect back and buttocks would carry her mark from tomorrow onward, of that she was certain. And then she'd be shipped to Norwich Castle—to please that vile jailer Reed and his men. Aye, by the time they were done with her, she would be sorry she ever looked at this man, at any man.

And him? Catherine's eyes narrowed on his powerful body. She'd use him. Whenever she liked. She'd demand that he please her—again and again. And she would enjoy that. Punish him if he failed her. She would punish him, anyway. She could already feel his long, thick shaft inside her. How much better he would be, after all, than Edward.

Hurry, damn you both, she cursed silently, her body screaming for satisfaction. *Finish your business, for I am next. And I don't care to wait for anyone!*

Her body arched at the moment of her release, and Malcolm felt her tighten like a sheath around him. As she cried out in ecstasy, the last vestige of his control exploded in a fireball of passion. There was no holding back—there was only the need to pour his seed into her.

"Jaime!" he called aloud, rolling her onto the bed beneath him. As they clung to each other, a few fierce strokes were all that were needed to leave them both panting and spent.

Malcolm's mind cleared in a few moments, and though he still had not recovered enough to roll to his side, he realized that through the haze of their climax, he had heard a noise from over by the door. Raising himself and gazing down into her smiling face, he realized that if there had been something, Jaime had not heard it.

Malcolm peered across the room at the dark oak door. Had a door opened and closed somewhere nearby? he thought. Carefully, he lifted himself off of Jaime, covering her with the bedclothes, and reached for the flickering candlestick.

He listened as he crossed the chamber toward the door. There was nothing but silence. The Highlander put his ear against the wood, but still heard nothing. Pulling it open a crack, he peered into the dim light of the corridor. Surprised at seeing no one standing guard at the customary spot, he pulled the door open further and stepped out of the room. No one in either direction. Not a soul. Malcolm scratched his chin and went back into his bedchamber, shutting the heavy door behind him.

"Was someone there?" Jaime asked quietly, sitting up in bed, the covers tucked demurely around her.

"Nay ... well, perhaps some passing wench," Malcolm answered, picking up a pitcher of wine from the table before starting back toward the bed. "For my ever vigilant guard has managed to disappear. She must have been quite a lass to entice him from his post."

Jaime threw off the covers and jumped from the bed. "If he is no longer there, then perhaps I should leave now ... by way of the door."

Malcolm filled his lung deeply as he gazed at the perfection of her naked body. She smiled and picked up her dress. With a sigh, he peered down at the jug in his hand and then glanced over his shoulder at the door.

"Aye, Jaime. We'll just have to keep this thing for another time. I do very much prefer to have you get back to your room safely ... and not go climbing down that wall again."

Jaime walked slowly toward him, her eyes sparkling. As she neared him, Malcolm felt his composure beginning to slip. He couldn't ignore her womanly curves, her long legs, the black hair tumbling over her high, firm breasts.

"What were you planning to do with this drink?" she asked, dropping her dress to the floor as she came to a stop before him and placing her hands against his chest.

"Well, lass," he began hoarsely. "Since I only have one cup, which you must use, being the guest, I was thinking of laying you down here and pouring *my* portion of this wine all over you. I believe I could drink the whole pitcherful that way."

"But, Malcolm, we both know wine acts like poison in your body."

"Ah, but having the pleasure of sipping from your curves, lass, I welcome the pain."

Even in the dim light, he saw her blush. But then she reached out and took the pitcher from his hand, replacing it with another pitcher from the side table.

"Water?" she asked, touching him on the arm.

"Aye, Jaime. Why?"

"I find myself dying of thirst, my love. And I think your idea for drinking is one that needs to be tried out."

"And the guard?" he replied with a smile.

She cocked her head prettily. "Let's hope the wench is his own true love."

"And keeps him busy till dawn!"

She smiled and tugged at his arm. "Somehow, I think she will. Aye, Malcolm, I'm certain of it."

CHAPTER 36

J aime tried to roll over and let her mind drift back to sleep, but the rough callused hand on her temple kept her in place. She tried to open her eyes and look into Master Graves's face, but her eyelids, heavy with drowsiness, would not move at her silent command. There were people about the room, she could hear their voices discussing her condition. But the man—the physician's voice—was the one that carried a note of alarm.

". . . there have been many who've died of spleen . . ."

"But how could it come so sudden? She had no symptoms of any ailment last evening!"

Jaime recognized the ring of disbelief in Frances's voice, so she prayed for a convincing answer from the physician.

"I've seen many cases of it in my years, m'lady, and it often comes on suddenly. An ailment 'taken in a thought,' as the tutors say in Cambridge."

Jaime felt a wetness against her temple—the stretching of a cloth over her forehead. This must be the potion the physician had talked about, she thought. The one that would make her sleep.

"The term really refers to severe depression, Lady Frances," Master Graves continued. "What the Galenists still call an imbalance of the humors. Any kind of anxiety or concern could bring on the ailment. But what we must be careful to avoid is a brain fever."

"Oh, Master Graves." Jaime noted the alarm in Frances's voice now.

"Now, m'lady, if you wish to know what causes the attack, we need to think back. Was it possible that she has received some distressing news? Was she upset by anything in the past week or so?"

All was going well, Jaime thought through a growing haze. The physician had quite cleverly turned the questions back on Frances. Jaime tried to gather all her wits about her so that she could hear what was being said. She waited for Frances's explanations. But the countess seemed unwilling to reveal what she knew to the Welshman.

"Lady Frances," Mary's pretty voice cut through the short-lived silence hanging about the room. "What of her leaving for court tomorrow? His Grace is expecting her to arrive this week. Poor Lord Edward—we can't keep him waiting!"

"That is the least of our concerns right now, Mary," Frances answered. "Master Graves talks of young women losing their life to this wretched sickness all the time. As far as I am concerned, Lord Edward can wait."

"But still . . ."

"Mary, I think you need to find something else to do." The countess's voice betrayed an edge to her temper. "You surely haven't forgotten that my husband happens to be Lord Edward's brother. Surrey will make all necessary explanations to Lord Edward. Jaime, on the other hand, needs to be cared for, and it is our job, my job, to help her through this. *Her* well-being is the primary concern now. Do you understand?"

Even with her eyes closed and her mind drifting, Jaime could hear Mary grumbling audibly as she left the chamber angrily.

After a slight pause—or was it an hour?—the countess spoke again, but her tone was now entirely different.

"What can we do for the poor dear, Master Graves? How can we help her through this?"

The poultice on her temple was warming her skin. As a sensation of pins and needles spread from her forehead, a light-headedness was beginning to make her head spin. But still Jaime's heart warmed to Frances's genuine concern. She truly seemed to care for her.

"You have to let her rest, m'lady. The sleep shouldn't do

her harm. Did I mention that she also has been fighting a touch of the green disease for a while?"

"Aye, you did say so."

"Ah. Well, I fear that has weakened her."

The physician lifted the linen cloth off her forehead and spread a bit more of the wet potion against her skin. Jaime had a sudden sensation of falling—slowly, like a leaf or a feather. But she also had a growing sense of fear . . . that an abyss spread out beneath her, and she could find no handhold to stop her slow, irrevocable descent.

"If we were to try and force her into some semblance of consciousness right now, 'twould be the end of her, I am certain. Brain fever would set in, and that would kill her for sure, m'lady."

"Will she recover?" Frances asked, the alarm in her voice reaching a new pitch.

"Aye, she might very well. With no disturbances and plenty of rest, her body might just decide to cast off this unholy misery. She might just wake up from this . . ."

Jaime tried to strain to hear more, but the voices now became blurred and muffled.

Surrey . . . a message . . . potion . . . Malcolm . . .

In the depths of her mind, Jaime opened her eyes in search of him—but the blanketing darkness and her continuous fall were all that she comprehended.

Malcolm ignored Catherine's whispered question, turning in Surrey's direction and focusing on the earl's discussion with Lady Frances. They were talking about Jaime and the messenger who had been sent earlier with the news for the duke. When they had broached the subject of Jaime's condition, Malcolm had acted his part well, showing great surprise and sadness. He simply could not allow these good people to suspect that it was all a ruse.

Catherine's hand on his knee jerked Malcolm's head about.

"Oh, as I asked before—there must be something you can think of that would be responsible for this horrible illness that has taken our cousin!"

Malcolm casually brushed her hand off his knee and looked

questioningly into her face. "What makes you think I would know anything more than you, mistress?"

"Well!" Catherine cooed tracing patterns with her fingers on the linen cloth of the table. "You two *are* from the same land, and I hear you were raised practically in the same household. I just thought you would . . . well, in Scotland, don't the men and women share any of the same interests? Perhaps some of the same passions?"

"I do not know what you are . . ." he began irritably. "People are the same, mistress. It doesn't matter whether you come from England, India, or the New World—we're all the same. But still I cannot see what this has to do with Jaime's illness!"

Catherine paused and licked her lips, all the while studying his face from beneath long, golden lashes. But the woman's full lips and creamy complexion did nothing to attract him. In fact, Malcolm found himself repelled rather than aroused at her candid appraisal and open invitation. Tiring of her shamelessness, he turned his attention back to Surrey, but Catherine's hand quickly took hold of his arm. Reluctantly, he looked back at her.

"It is difficult," she said, leaning forward and speaking in a low voice. "So difficult to speak plainly in this crowded hall! Perhaps, if we were to . . ."

"Nay, mistress," Malcolm responded, all too sharply, moving his arm so her fingers dropped from their resting place on his elbow. "We must remember who you are."

"Aye." She sighed. "So we must." She shrugged her shoulders, her mouth turning downward in a pout. Her fingers fluttered as she moved them to the low, square neckline of her dress. Pretending to smooth the material over them, she glanced with a knowing smile into his face.

Malcolm, angry with himself for being lured into looking at the tops of the voluptuous breasts spilling out of the tight bodice, tore his eyes away.

"I thought as much," she teased in a low voice. "Your chamber, perhaps? Or would you prefer to come to mine?"

"Neither, mistress."

She again placed a hand on his knee. "Well, what if we

meet in Jaime's bedchamber. She will be unconscious. We could be alone there."

This time Malcolm roughly pushed her hand off of his knee. He looked straight at her, searching for a way to make the woman understand. But she continued without a pause.

"I do like to be on top," she whispered, totally ignoring his rejection. "And from what I've . . ." She stopped and gave him a half smile. "Well, that *is* acceptable to you, is it not?"

Malcolm pushed his chair back abruptly and, with a short excuse to Surrey and his wife, strode angrily from the hall.

Catherine glanced casually in the direction of the unconscious Jaime as she made her way toward the table beside the bed. Feeling the pair of eyes staring at her uncomfortably from the chamber door, she turned shortly to the serving girl. "What are you waiting for? Go and do as you were told."

The nervous girl clasped her hands tightly in front of her. "But, m'lady, I was told by Master Graves not to leave her bedside for any reason until Cad . . . Mistress Jaime's servant returns."

"You are not deserting her, you silly creature! I am here with her. And you," Catherine snapped, "are going to my room for my russet cloak—the one with gold flowers embroidered on the borders. You don't think I'd go anywhere until you return, do you?"

The girl shook her head. "Nay, m'lady. 'Tis just that . . ."

"Be off with you, and no more talk! You could be there and back already, you brazen thing! Away!"

Catherine watched the young woman disappear quickly through the door. Then, glancing again at the motionless Jaime, she moved closer to the table, studying the various pitchers and bowls. The foolish servant—happy to answer her questions when Catherine had first arrived in the room—had volunteered everything she needed to know about the bowls and the folded vellum packets of medication that lay scattered on the table. This was much better than she had hoped, Catherine thought, smiling as she picked up one of the powdered mixtures.

Turning to Jaime, Catherine leaned over the bed and looked into the young woman's face. Jaime looked quite unwell.

Master Graves, Catherine thought with a wry smile, would be quite useful in the future, for he certainly had demonstrated his resourcefulness here. The wench would not be soon going to Edward.

A linen poultice lay across a bowl on a small stool beside the bed. Sniffing at the cloth and then at the packet of medicine in her hand, Catherine decided that they were the same. She looked hard at Jaime. She knew that the medicines Graves administered could be poison. She recalled the unkind gossip that had circulated when the duchess of Buckingham, being treated for a headache, had lost the use of both legs after taking too much of the medicine a court physician had given her.

Catherine had little time before the servant would return. Dampening the linen poultice in the bowl again, she poured the powdered mixture over the cloth.

What a wench! she thought, laying the poultice across Jaime's forehead. This might be better than whipping. But the Scottish witch was good, getting Edward so crazed that he would actually seek her hand in marriage. Catherine was not about to forgive her. Aye, seeing her sleeping with the handsome Highlander had been too much for the future queen to bear. Jaime would pay dearly for trying to steal Catherine's men from her!

Jaime whispered something in her sleep and moved her arms restlessly, pushing back the covers to her waist. These had to be potions to make her sleep, Catherine was certain of it. Glancing back at the table, she looked at the pitcher with the cup beside it. Whatever Master Graves had in mind for Jaime was not strong enough, as far as Catherine was concerned. She would give her more—a great deal more. Reaching for the cup half filled with water, Catherine poured in more of the powdery contents from the packet.

Jaime moaned. It was a long, plaintive moan, and Catherine looked back at her. Turning, she sat on the bed beside the sleeping woman, and, lifting her head, placed the cup to her lips. Jaime seemed to struggle at first, but then relinquished the fight and sipped the drink.

Catherine watched the pale face of the woman lying in her arms convulse slightly before slipping into total oblivion.

"Slut," she whispered.

Pulling away, she stood up and placed the drink beside the pitcher. This would be much easier than she'd thought. If this didn't do the trick, Catherine decided, she would simply come back tomorrow . . . everyday, in fact . . . and supplement the dear physician's ministrations with her own.

She would enjoy these visits immensely. She would, indeed.

CHAPTER 37

The sound of the horses' hooves clattering on the stone paving combined with the barking of the dogs and the shouts of handlers, muffling the two men's voices. But Malcolm and the physician paused in their conversation as several servants hustled past carrying crossbows, longbows, and lances. The Highlander's eyes were drawn to the great north entrance of the palace from which Surrey would emerge momentarily. Four young maids holding baskets of food stood by, chatting amiably away with a pair of burly guards.

Malcolm discreetly tucked the folded message inside his belted tunic as he patted the flank of the excited hunter he'd been given to ride.

"You do not care to ride with us, Master Graves?" he asked loudly as a page passed leading a fine black steed toward the entryway.

"Bah!" the physician returned. "I've more important things to . . ."

The man stopped short as the smiling earl of Surrey strode out into the yard and, yanking his gloves on, headed directly for the black hunter.

Master Graves watched the earl thoughtfully. "If only he cared for these people with the same passion that he cares for his hunting and his books!"

Malcolm followed the man's gaze. "When the time comes, he will. He knows that he has a great deal to learn, but his father, the duke, is still quite healthy. And his brother Edward, though ignorant of anyone's needs but his own, commands the father's favor. Nay, Master Graves, 'tis not a matter of passion. Surrey sees it as a matter of patience."

The physician gave the Highlander a thoughtful look but said nothing, turning his attention in the direction of the English nobleman.

"How is Jaime faring, Master Graves?" Malcolm asked in a low voice.

"Resting. As she should!"

"Is she getting enough to eat and drink?" Malcolm probed, working hard to keep the worry out of his voice. "I heard from Lady Frances at dinner last night that Jaime has not been even slightly awake now for two days. This is all part of the ruse, is it not?"

The physician placed a hand on a sore shoulder and began to massage it gently. "She could be an actor in the saint's plays, I should think. I reduced the amount we've been giving her yesterday, so my medicines should only be making her a bit dozy. With that, she should have only drowsiness and short stretches of sleep, not the stupor she appears to be in. But again, I haven't seen her alone since then. Since there have always been others around, she may be acting even with me."

"I want you to stop giving her whatever it is you have been," Malcolm stated firmly. "Surrey has already sent a message to his father that she has taken ill. I think he is resigned not to send her to court for a while."

Graves nodded. "I was thinking myself that it is the thing to do. I think Mistress Jaime's serving woman Caddy is becoming quite concerned about her mistress. She is devoted to Jaime."

Malcolm swung easily into his saddle as the hunting party prepared to move off.

"When do you plan to take her?" the physician asked quietly.

Malcolm leaned over, pretending to fix a strap on his stirrup. "Midsummer's Eve. Perhaps the day before."

"That is less than a week! Highlander, she might not have her legs under her by then."

"We must do what is necessary." Malcolm looked determinedly at the physician and then patted the folded letter tucked inside his belt. "But who knows what news you brought me today. It may just be that . . . everything has been delayed. We might, Master Graves, have more time than we think."

Edward slipped the unopened letter from Catherine into his belt as his father entered the chamber.

The duke of Norfolk didn't accept his son's offer for wine nor his motion to take a seat. In fact, Edward now noticed that his father had advanced no further than three steps into the room. So, he thought, the duke was rejecting him, disassociating himself with his own kin and with whatever wrongdoing Edward was being accused of. This was suddenly quite apparent in the old man's behavior and quite, quite clear to Edward.

But he already knew the reason for this visit. The same messenger who had brought him Catherine's letter only moments ago had also brought Surrey's message to the duke. The man had relayed to him the news of Jaime, though he had known very little of the details other than a sudden illness had struck down the mistress. But before leaving, the man had suggested that Lady Catherine's message might provide more answers. Edward patted his belt—where her letter lay.

"So, Father, I hear my dearly beloved has decided to play the unwilling bride!"

"She is sick, Edward. But she will mend," the duke added. "Surrey has assured me in this letter that as soon as she takes a turn for the better, she'll be sent here to Nonsuch Palace."

"But by then my head may be on a pike and halfway to London Bridge!" Edward said with a false smile as he reached over and filled up the cup in his hand. Pausing, he pushed the drink away and stared at it. "Do you think I can use my dear brother's letter in my defense, Father? Do you believe the great lords of the High Steward's Court will pardon me based on my own words?" He laughed bitterly. "Could you just see me making my plea? *My lords, you have to spare my head on the block. After all, I am the future husband of Jaime Tudor.*

Aye, my lords. Tudor! She is the bastard daughter of the king. It is because of me, my lords, that her true identity has come forth. Reuniting a father and daughter—what generous heart I carry! I . . ."

"I will write His Majesty a letter and ask for a delay in your hearings," the duke said shortly, interrupting the younger man's talk.

"But don't you think I'd be better off if you didn't?" Edward asked with a smirk. "Knowing you and your reputation, Father, I'd be afraid that your letter might do me more damage than good." He grabbed at his cup. "Am I not a terrible liability to you now? Before these ridiculous rumors ever started to surface, you were again favored in the king's eye, thanks to his lust for Catherine. But now—an accused son! What a disgrace you must think me." Edward raised his cup in salute to the older man before draining every drop of it.

The duke of Norfolk growled at him from where he stood—so far away. "It's not your alleged villainy that disgraces me, Edward, but your cowardly behavior now. All because you have been detained . . ."

"Imprisoned," Edward corrected.

"Imprisoned? Have you forgotten what that really means? You, the man who have made Norwich Castle a terror for all who had ever been put in chains. You consider *this* a prison?" The duke's eyes glanced at the direction of the pitchers of wine and the rumpled bed at the far side of the room. "We don't allow whoring and drinking in our prisons, Edward."

Edward laughed. "Whoring?"

The duke waved a hand in the air. "I don't care how much gold you throw away on these wenches—all I care about is for you to once again *look* respectable."

"I don't believe the vultures who pick at the dead bodies after the executions are very discriminating when it comes to looks."

"Edward, continue to act like this and you are doomed."

"Am I not already?" He reached over and picked up the pitcher of wine again.

"I have spoken to His Majesty."

Edward paused, the pitcher in hand. "You told him about Jaime?"

"I've only hinted," the duke said encouragingly. "I didn't mention her name nor her whereabouts. But I did speak as if I had heard rumors of a royal love child."

"And?" Edward asked, suddenly more revived than he had been in days.

"His Majesty was quite interested in finding out more. Edward, it doesn't matter what the verdict of High Steward's Court might be—the king has the power to pardon."

Edward placed the pitcher and cup back on the table and looked up into his father's face. "And you think he would pardon a son-in-law?"

"He seemed pleased—curious and yet pleased to hear what I had to say." The duke's face reflected the confidence in his words. "So stop playing the doomed martyr. Prepare yourself. Surrey will send her here as soon as she is well, and then you'll have the chance to present her—your wedded wife—to His Majesty."

Edward leaned back in his chair and thought over everything he just had heard his father say. "But what if the fact that I have married her angers him more? My head will still adorn a pike atop London Bridge."

"I've already thought that through."

"You have?"

The duke ran a hand down the front of his velvet robe. "Aye. We'll twist the truth a bit and tell him how shocked we are in learning it ourselves. And then we'll offer to have the marriage annulled ... as a token of your loyalty and goodwill."

"Annulled?" Edward stood up quickly.

"Aye." The duke raised his hand to silence his son. "But there will be no annulment. I am having documents drawn up as we speak, dated two months ago, attesting to the betrothal. The banns have been waved by the Archbishop of Norwich and all that is left is a simple ceremony and the consummation." Norfolk cast an eye toward the unmade bed. "And you should be able to handle that, I should think."

"You make it sound all so simple."

"It is," the duke stressed. "The king will be satisfied that his daughter—even without the condition of legitimacy—has found a suitable marriage with a great family that is loyal to him. All you need do, my boy, is sit back and wait for her arrival—perhaps in a few days."

Edward took a walk around his chair and placed a hand on his belt where Catherine's letter nestled.

"Clean yourself up and be ready. Things are certain to improve."

Edward acknowledged the older man's words with a nod. But a moment later, as the heavy oaken door swung shut behind his father the duke, he pulled Catherine's letter from its hiding place and broke open the seal.

CHAPTER 38

After letting the Highlander in, the small woman looked hesitantly up and down the hall before backing into the room and closing the door firmly behind her. An instant later Caddy followed Malcolm MacLeod to the side of Jaime's bed. As he leaned over the sleeping frame of the young woman and touched her gently on the cheek, the older woman looked on, her anxious expression matching the grim one on the man's face.

"I am so glad you've come. She hasn't been well, and I didn't know who to go to, m'lord," the woman's voice carried on over Malcolm's shoulder. "I mean Master Graves is the one supposed to look after her, but whatever it is he is giving her has been making my mistress terribly sick. She hasn't even opened her eyes in two days. The first day that she took to this bed she slept most of the day away, but still she woke up every now and then. She knew where she was, but this time . . ." The woman nervously wrung her hands. "I just can't help thinking that there is something wrong."

Malcolm's fingers traced Jaime's dry lips and caressed the soft skin of her face. "The physician said he was stopping all his potions yesterday." He removed a soaked linen cloth from her brow. "What is this doing here?" he asked shortly, bringing the cloth to his nose and shaking his head. The sweet cloying smell of opium.

"I don't know, m'lord," the woman whispered worriedly. "Just thought that it had been left by Master Graves. I didn't know there was anything on it. But I haven't put it on her brow, anyway. Since yesterday, when the physician said he was cutting back on the medicines, I haven't given her anything. But then I . . ."

Malcolm touched Jaime's hands. They were cold and clammy. "Who has been looking after her when you are not here?"

"One of Lady Frances's servants has been sitting with Mistress Jaime whenever I go to the kitchens for food." The woman leaned over and took the soaked linen cloth out of Malcolm's outstretched hand and gave him a dry one in its stead.

"Who else?" Malcolm questioned as he gently wiped Jaime's wet brow. "Who else has been left alone with your mistress?"

The woman followed Malcolm's gaze as he nodded toward the table. Understanding his silent request, she quickly poured some water from a pitcher into a wooden bowl.

"No one else," she said, handing him the bowl.

As he began to dip the cloth in it, Malcolm stared down at the liquid, then lifted it to his face and sniffed at it.

"Something has been added to this. Has she been drinking water from this pitcher today?"

"Not today, m'lord." The woman leaned over and stared in disbelief at the cloudy liquid. She shook her head firmly. "On my mother's soul, she hasn't! I tried to have her sip some broth I brought back from the kitchen earlier, but she was too sleepy to have anything to do about it. But then . . . I know I washed out this pitcher and put fresh water in it this morning. But here . . . these things on the table. Perhaps someone mixed in something."

Malcolm glanced in the direction that the older woman pointed. There were still remnants of what the physician must have used earlier laying about. "Who else, other than the servants you spoke of, has been here? Who from the house?"

As she talked, the older woman began to quickly gather

what remained of the medicines onto a small tray. "Lady Frances comes in every few hours to check on the mistress, but whenever she's come—I've been here. And Mistress Mary was here the first day that this poor child took sick, but she hasn't been back since. In fact, she has already had all of her things taken out of this chamber." The old woman paused a moment, and then brightened as a thought struck her. "Wait! The serving girl that was here when I got back with the broth told me that Mistress Catherine had stopped here before her ride."

Malcolm looked over his shoulder and glared at Caddy. "Was Jaime left alone with Catherine?"

The woman reddened in the face before nodding in assent. "She did tell me . . . she said something about Mistress Catherine sending her up to her chamber for a cloak. Oh my, she did also mention that this was the second day in a row that Mistress Catherine was forgetting something in her room and sending her after it. And yesterday, too, the girl told me that her ladyship waited here with poor Jaime until she returned." Caddy held a small sack of herbs to her chest. "You don't think that *she* would want to hurt . . ."

The look of anger in the Highlander's face silenced her.

Malcolm turned his gaze back to Jaime as he threw the linen cloth to the side and framed Jaime's cold face in between his hands. She looked pale and lifeless, her breathing heavy. He stared at the dark circles under her eyes. Damn Catherine, Malcolm swore under his breath. This was her doing. It was all clear, now. She had been poisoning Jaime, giving her more than she needed . . . or giving her something else.

"But why, m'lord?" Caddy croaked. "Everyone loves . . ."

The older woman continued to talk but Malcolm was too angry to listen. He should have guessed that Catherine was up to no good two nights ago when she had invited him to meet her in Jaime's chamber—as she lay unconscious. Malcolm swore under his breath, the filthy wench! He would kill her right now if she were near!

"Go after the physician," he barked to the older woman. "Go after him and bring him here at once."

Caddy, moving like a woman half her age, scurried out of the chamber and down the corridor.

The long stone corridor wound downward into the dark, ever downward into the void. Hands caught at her as she ran, holding her back, pushing her on. Her heart pounded so hard she thought it ready to burst; her lungs were at the point of collapse. Jaime twisted and turned, tearing away the hands, trying desperately to push ahead.

And the sound of Edward's steps—sharp, terrifying as thunder—grew ever nearer.

"Whore! Slut! WHORE!" His shouts continued, wavering in their clarity, as if his words were being plunged—over and over—in some thick cloud, in a swirling muddied pool, in a shroud.

And on she ran. Jaime glanced over her shoulder at the masculine shape lurching after her. She fell against the wall. The grasping hands were gone, replaced now by wet, slick stones that stung her skin like poison. Needles of pain shot through her flesh, etching her bones in a thousand places.

Her legs were failing now. Her shoulders and face ached with fatigue. Further, she thought. A bit further. She could see the abyss. Blackness gaped ahead. The stones moved beneath her feet, and still he came nearer.

Sound of men. Other men. Their muffled voices nearer. Above.

Jaime tried to scream, to ask for help. But there was no voice. No sound.

Edward's breathing was right behind. She must cry out! Jaime's hands clutched desperately at her throat, her mouth. Her fingers clawed in panic at skin and bone, until a horror swept through her with the cold dampness of death.

She had no mouth.

"You can't get away, whore. Your end is here."

Malcolm pinned Jaime's arms to the bed as the physician barked orders at Caddy, who hustled about the chamber.

As the young woman thrashed about in the bed, her head twisted from side to side and her legs kicked viciously at the bedclothes.

"Jaime." The Highlander shook her softly. " 'Tis a dream, my love. A dream."

She opened her mouth in her sleep, but there was no cry. In a few moments the agitation began to subside, and she grew somewhat calmer, though her hands continued to pry at his grip on her.

"Wake up, Jaime!" Malcolm said, releasing her and pulling the covers over her shivering frame.

The Highlander had to fight back his emotions when he saw the stream of tears roll down her eyes and disappear into her dark hairline. Malcolm wrapped the blanket tightly about her and lifted her onto his lap, holding her tightly against his chest. His eyes carried more than a hint of accusation when turned on the physician.

"How is it that she sleeps so quietly for three days and then suddenly comes down with this attack?"

The older man never took his eyes off the mixture that he was preparing at the table.

"Catherine must have given Jaime something more than what was here. 'Tis a risk to give her anything more, but if we can neutralize the . . ."

Suddenly, before her loomed a man, blocking her way with his broad, powerful bulk. Her eyes were drawn to his eyes, glinting in a fleshy face that looked shockingly soft, even in the darkness. His hands reached out, and Jaime felt herself being lifted into the air. Far into the space above, and then falling, falling. Down past the portly giant, down into the darkness, falling and then landing. A stairwell and the damp, heavy smell of death.

She could feel Edward coming. There was nowhere but down. Around and around the dark steps she flew, more like falling than running. But downward, ever downward.

His curses swirled about her head like burning wind. Edward was still right behind her.

But there! Again she could hear them. The sound of voices. So close!

Graves stood at the end of the bed with the empty cup in his hand.

"There is nothing more we can do now but wait."

Malcolm looked down at Jaime, huddled in his arms. Droplets of the liquid still glistened on her lips. She hadn't opened her eyes. She hadn't spoken a word. But she had allowed him to give her the drink.

He cursed Catherine again. How easy it must have been for the devil-woman to prey on Jaime while she was so vulnerable, while she was so incapable of fighting back. But why this way? Did the woman really intend, after toying with her, to murder Jaime? What motive could she have for such evil?

He clenched his teeth in silent fury. How could he have been such a fool as to let this happen?

"How long before she awakens?" Malcolm asked, holding her closer to his chest.

The physician looked wearily into the fierce face of the Highlander. "I wish I knew. The body has it own ways. And what we have always believed about it is changing."

"How long, Welshman!"

The physician pulled off his coif and ran his hand over his bald head. "These medicines have been making her sleep for days now. It might take her at least that long to come out of it. But then again . . . she may never awaken."

Malcolm looked away for a moment. When he looked back, his face was a mask. He glanced over at Caddy, who was now busily working on the other side of the room, too far to hear their words. "I am taking her with me."

The physician looked down at the empty cup in his hands. "Mistress Jaime told me as much herself. But I have to warn you that 'tis best for you to wait until she has her legs back under her, before you drag her overland to some ship . . ."

"You know better than I that we have no time left." Malcolm's eyes were piercing. In three nights he would meet the ship. This meant Jaime had to be well enough to travel in two days. "If she is still unwell when the time comes, I will need your help again."

The physician turned and placed the cup on the table. "Even if she has awakened, 'tis doubtful she will be ready to travel. And you must consider the great danger you are putting her in. Traveling with a sick, or weakened woman ... with the duke's men sent after you. How far do you think you will be able to get before they overtake you? What do you think will happen when they drag you back? What do you think will happen to Jaime when they do?"

"Don't waste your words, Master Graves. I am taking her with me." Malcolm's tone carried the power of his conviction. "You have already helped us a great deal, but let me assure you there are others who will help us find our way to the coast."

"Then what more do you need of me?"

"If she remains ill," Malcolm replied, "I will be needing you."

The older man stared at the Highlander and then placed his coif back on his head. "Ah! Well, a fool's life is a merry one."

The torture of each step threatened now to kill her. Jaime had been running for her whole life. Down the steps, forever downward.

And Edward was not giving up on her. She heard the sound of steel as she reached another landing. As she glanced over her shoulder, she could see the long, broad sword in his hand. Plunging headlong into the darkness, she pushed on against her pain.

"You will never escape me, whore!" His voice pounded in her brain. "You are mine. Mine! And you'll pay with your blood."

When Jaime moaned and stirred, Malcolm—holding her securely in his arms—shook her slightly, but to no avail. The young woman fell silent and still once again.

The Highlander glanced up at Caddy, who had been hovering nearby, and who again took her seat by the end of the bed. He cleared his throat and looked for the right words.

When she glanced up at him from her sewing, he nodded to her. "I haven't been very kind to you in the past. And yet you've treated me very decently. Better than I've deserved, I would say."

"Aye, m'lord."

Malcolm nodded again with a gentle smile. "You have been with Jaime since she left Scotland for England?"

"Nay, much longer, m'lord," the woman answered. "I first came to my mistress when she was being sent to France. She was just a lass, though a bonnie one . . . as you know."

"I do not think I knew . . ." Malcolm's eyes rounded in surprise. "So you were with her when she came to Dunvegan Castle?"

She nodded. "Aye."

Malcolm shook his head in disbelief. "Then it truly amazes me that you just didn't kill me instead of taking care of me when I was wounded."

"I could never do that," the woman said simply. "My mistress has always cared for you far too much."

"Aye," Malcolm whispered softly, looking at the sleeping woman in his arms. Since he had lifted her in his lap hours earlier, she seemed to be fretting less.

"I am staying here with her if you want to go after your supper." Malcolm looked up encouragingly at the older woman.

"Perhaps I might bring you something, m'lord?"

He shook his head. "Just go, Caddy. I'll look after her."

The older woman nodded in response as she lay aside her sewing, and rose from her chair. Pausing by the door, she turned and looked at the Highlander and her mistress.

"I know you will, m'lord," she said. "Look after her, I mean." With a curtsy she scurried out of the room.

"Jaime! Can you hear me, lass?"

"Help me, Malcolm." She ran toward the sound, suddenly aware that she was calling out. She felt for her mouth, lips, teeth. She cried out again, stumbling over her torn skirts as she moved on toward his voice. "Where are you, Malcolm?"

Edward answered from behind her. "You will never get away from me, wench. Never!" She heard the whistling sound, felt the cold wind of his sword cutting through the air. The blade tore through her hair, nicking the skin at the base of her neck.

"Here, Jaime. I am here. Just reach out, lass. Take my hand."

"I cannot, Malcolm!" she screamed in fear. The feel of blood trickled down her back. "MALCOLM!"

"You must be punished, adulteress. Whore!"

"MALCOLM!"

She saw the pane of glass straight ahead, and through it, the outline of a man beyond. It was his shadow. Malcolm's shadow waiting, his hand outstretched.

The image changed. All she could see was her torn dress, a weary face framed by wild and ragged hair, a bleeding body staggering forward, carried on by exhausted legs that dragged onward toward the looking glass.

"Where are you, Malcolm?" In the reflection, she saw the sword lift behind her, above her. The sharpness of its edge gleamed like amber in the darkness. Like a weapon forged in the fires of hell.

"You'll be used, wench. By me. By my men. And then you'll die!"

She reached the glass. Spreading her fingers, pinning her body against it. Pressing her face against the warmth of the pane, she cried out his name once more. "MALCOLM!"

Her heart ceased to beat in her chest. Right over her shoulder, out of the darkness of her terror, Jaime watched in the mirror as Edward advanced in the murky gloom. With nowhere to go, no way to fight, she watched him draw the dagger from its sheath as his other hand reached for her hair.

She half turned. She would not die. She would not yield.

"It is finished," Edward said, his eyes glowing like coals.

The hand came through as if the glass were water. Jaime looked at it a moment, then at Edward. His mouth hung open, his dagger dangling limp at his side.

Jaime reached out, grasped Malcolm's hand, and melted into the surface. She moved through a mist, borne on a cloud, the sound of Edward's frustrated threats growing ever fainter as she moved through the silver and into the light.

CHAPTER 39

"Have you seen the king?"

"Nay, lass. Nor do I care to."

The early-afternoon sun was shining down on the gardens and the meadows beyond, and Malcolm sat in the window seat trying hard to concentrate on the view. It was quite difficult feigning indifference to the sound of the splashing water behind him. At the far end of the chamber, discreetly hidden by a massive screen, and with Caddy standing guard looking as ferocious as a she-lion, Jaime bathed happily in the wooden tub that had been brought up for her use.

Never mind the king, he thought. Fancies of throwing Caddy bodily from the chamber and seeing to Jaime's bath himself were wreaking havoc with his imagination.

"But they are not even watching you?" Jaime's voice, still sounding weak from her ordeal, conveyed her excitement, nonetheless. "No guards? No one at all?"

"Nay. And Surrey tells me that as long as I stay out of sight—preferably in my own chamber—he will not put me in chains, either." Malcolm glanced out the window as a large party of courtiers, Surrey and Lady Frances among them, came out from the palace. The king did not appear to be with them. Nor did Catherine. As they moved out across a strip of greensward, the Highlander decided the party was heading down to the meandering river at the far end of the flower-studded meadow. "With King Henry arriving at Kenninghall as unexpectedly as he did this morning, Surrey thought the best thing was not to draw attention to the fact that the Howards are holding a Scot for ransom. Especially when it appears Edward never declared he had such a prize in his possession."

Caddy came out from behind the divider, shot a look of suspicion at Malcolm, and then carried a stack of towels back to her mistress.

"Frances came in for a short visit this morning, while you were with Lord Surrey," Jaime called, though Malcolm found his attention distracted by the sound of her standing and stepping out of the tub. "And after giving me news of the king's arrival, she told me you were brawling with Surrey."

" 'Twas hardly a brawl, lass," Malcolm challenged. "I simply needed to remind him of his responsibilities as earl."

"Which, Frances said, included looking after my welfare."

"Aye. 'Tis only right!" Malcolm sat back in the window seat and spread his legs before him, his eyes locked on the carved wooden screen, imagining what exactly she was doing on the other side. "My precise words to him were that he had proven himself a worthless host, and had failed miserably in looking after you. Considering what Catherine almost got away with . . . well, in so many words I made him understand that from now on I would be looking after you, myself."

"And he agreed to that, Malcolm?"

"Aye. After our wee bit of brawling, he did!" Malcolm, finding himself no longer able to remain seated, got up from his seat and began pacing the room. There was something that he hadn't told Jaime, though, for fear of sounding too hopeful. In the course of their argument, Surrey had given him a brief summary of what was happening to his brother at Nonsuch Palace, hinting at the charges that could be leveled at Edward. And, to Malcolm's surprise, the earl had admitted to him that he was happy that Jaime had not been well enough to make the journey. Something unspoken had then passed between the two men, giving the Highlander heart.

"Do you think he'll ever do anything about Catherine?"

Jaime's question stopped Malcolm cold. He looked up and watched as Caddy retrieved a dress from the bed. "Nay, she is beyond the judgment of mere mortals, now. And with the king here, I'm quite certain nothing will even be said . . . by them. Any public reprimand would only bring more disgrace on the Howard family. And *that* they will never risk. Surrey's feelings were that we should try to guard you and keep you safely . . ."

". . . away from Catherine." Jaime finished his sentence from the other side of the wall.

"Which shouldn't be too difficult, with Henry here." Malcolm stopped once again before the window. The company of men and women were just dropping out of sight across the meadow.

He considered telling her his plan, but he didn't want her to be overly burdened while she was still so weak. Seeing her awaken last night, courageously fighting off the effects of the drugs, the Highlander had rejoiced, although he knew that she needed time to recover. But time she didn't have, for they would be leaving here tomorrow night.

For days now, Malcolm had sensed Surrey would not be sorry to see him escape, and their conversation this morning had confirmed that. Whether it was in defiance of his father and brother, or as a token of the friendship that they shared, Malcolm could not tell. Perhaps it was a combination of the two, but it didn't really matter. What did matter was the added complication of the king and his entourage roaming about Kenninghall. These were problems that he needed to consider.

"You don't think the king is here because he has learned something about me, do you?" Jaime stepped from behind the wooden screen.

The words he had formed in answer melted away, forgotten on his tongue as he gawked helplessly at the vision before him. His eyes drank her in as if desperate to quench some inexorable thirst.

"Have I changed?" she asked, looking down nervously at the creamy linen of her dress. "I am much thinner, am I not?"

"Nay, Jaime. You are perfect."

"But you look at me . . ."

He nodded as he walked toward her. Lost for words he pulled her into his arms and held her tight. The rush of emotions that crowded his heart, the sense of relief he felt at seeing her beautiful face, awake again and bright, all made him foolish with the desire simply to hold her.

"I think *I* have changed," he whispered into her ear at last. "I would never have thought it possible, but my love for you has managed to grow even more . . . far more than I had ever thought possible. I ache at the thought of you." He threaded his fingers into her still wet hair and tilted her head back until their gazes locked. "I am a madman without you, Jaime. A howling, crazed fool. Seeing you now, finally knowing that you are well again, makes me want to fall to my knees and . . ."

She raised herself on her toes and silenced his words with her lips.

They drew apart as Caddy coughed politely, each shaken with the power of their love. But Malcolm would not let go of her hand as he walked her to a chair beside the window.

"So do you think, Malcolm, that Henry's visit here might have something to do with me?"

"Surrey didn't think so, and I asked the same question of him." Malcolm's eyes watched Caddy as she worked diligently on the other side of the room, obviously trying to give them their privacy. "He thought that the king's visit was purely a whim on his part to see Catherine. Apparently, Henry was hunting and never even took the time to tell the duke he was coming here."

The look of relief on Jaime's face was all too apparent, but her face quickly clouded over with concern. "What of our plans?"

"Actually," he said, stroking the smooth skin of her hand, "having had a wee bit of time to think this through, I believe his visit here might prove to be a blessing to us."

"Is it?"

"Aye." He smiled. "At least now we know where Catherine will be as we prepare for flight."

"Our flight," Jaime repeated, her face glowing once again. "Tell me what I should do."

Henry VIII, King of England, ignoring the tumblers entertaining in the center of the hall, turned the huge emerald ring over in his meaty palm as Catherine looked on impatiently. A moment later, after the king had studied the ornate setting of the large jewel carefully, he took hold of the chain that passed through the ring and let it dangle before his eyes.

"Well, my great bear?" Catherine asked, petting the king's knee and trying not to sound overly eager. "Is it yours?"

Henry ignored her question as he continued to study the swinging chain, a frown furrowing his brow. "You say this was in the possession of a cousin, Cat?"

Catherine glanced in Mary's direction. The blondhaired woman sat across the Hall, her face flushed with anger. Her gaze had not lifted once toward the king—or toward Catherine—since she'd entered.

Sick of Mary's whining ways, Catherine had already taken care of her. This afternoon, Henry had agreed to send Mary Howard north, to join the entourage of his sister Margaret, the ailing Queen Mother of Scotland. This was sure to be the end of all of Mary's dreams of grandeur, Catherine thought. But let it be a lesson to her. To think, the little fool wanted to attend *her*!

"In truth, sire, my cousin Mary, whom you know, tells me she came upon this by chance. So she brought it to my attention. I recognized it, of course, as a ring almost identical to the one that already adorns . . ."

"By chance?" Henry asked shortly. "The woman came upon an emerald as precious as this by chance?"

Catherine felt herself becoming flustered under the piercing glare of Henry's eyes. "Well, Mary was being removed from a chamber which she has been sharing with a distant cousin, a Mistress Jaime. And this ring . . . well, it has somehow been in the possession of this distant cousin. And I suppose it was misplaced . . . these things happen, sire . . . and by mistake the ring fell in with Mary's things."

Henry's cold eyes moved slowly from the swinging chain, softening only slightly as they came to rest on Catherine. "Who is this Mistress Jaime?"

"As I said, my love. A distant cousin!"

"And she lives at Kenninghall?"

"She has for the past year," Catherine answered quickly.

Henry looked about the crowded tables. "She hasn't been presented to me."

"She has been sick in bed for a few days, but I just heard she is mending, at last."

Henry's eyes again returned to the dangling ring.

Catherine did her best to hold back her satisfied smile as the king's brow knotted. At last, it seemed as though he was taking the bait. Though she didn't know what would come out of Henry knowing that Jaime was Thomas Boleyn's granddaughter and a half-Scot at that, Catherine's instincts told her it would be worth the trouble. And the fact that Jaime had been clearly hiding one of Henry's rings seemed to hint at something underhanded. At least, so Catherine hoped. She had tried to pay the wench another visit today, but that ill-mannered servant of hers had blocked her entrance.

"Whose daughter is she?"

Catherine smiled demurely at her intended. "She is a granddaughter to Thomas Boleyn." She didn't miss the rounding of Henry's eyes as they flashed back to her in surprise. "Her mother. . . ."

"Bring her to me," Henry ordered, cutting her off.

"But she, being ill . . ."

Henry stood at once and turned to bark at the earl, who was watching from a short distance away. "Send this Mistress Jaime to my chamber, Surrey, at once."

"Sire," Thomas Culpepper, a gentleman of the King's Privy Chamber approached. "Those three you wished to see have arrived from Norwich, and the jailer Reed is on his way."

The king grunted and turned away as the gentleman bowed and smiled handsomely at his future queen.

Catherine watched, smug and satisfied, as Henry, with his entourage in tow, marched from the hall with the chain and the ring clasped tightly in his fist.

Jaime looked with unseeing eyes into the looking glass, feeling anxiety and anger struggle for dominance. She drew in a long breath, and then stared at her hands' reflection. They were trembling. Jaime tucked them deeply into the pockets of her dress and watched Caddy tuck the last unruly wave into the thick blanket of hair trailing down her back.

"Let me go after Lord Malcolm," the older woman said gently, pinning the starched linen cap into her mistress's hair. "He might be able to help."

"I can't have him show his face before the king, Caddy," Jaime answered. "He'd be in great danger. He mustn't know."

"But what of you?"

"I'll be fine," Jaime argued. "Lady Frances only said that the king wishes to have me presented. That's all. There is nothing more to it." If she could only make herself believe her own words, Jaime thought.

Finishing her hair, the old woman started straightening the puffs of Jaime's sleeves. "He'll be so angry when he finds out that you left your chambers—while still being so weak. Are you sure you don't want me to go after him? He returned to his chamber not an hour ago. He won't be sleeping before his supper is brought up to him."

"Nay, though I thank you," Jaime said softly, smiling inwardly at this newly developed affection that Caddy felt for Malcolm. "So long as the king and his men are roaming about, Malcolm puts his life in the gravest danger each time he steps into the corridors."

"But he didn't want you to be left alone. I gave him my word, mistress. Let me go and at least tell him."

Jaime shook her head. "I forbid you to go to him, Caddy. There is nothing he can do for me that I cannot do myself." The young woman stood up from the chair and gently laid her hand on her servant's arm. "All will be well."

"But you are so pale."

The woman's loving concern brought a faint smile to Jaime's lips. "Please go and tell Lady Frances that I am ready."

CHAPTER 40

With a heat only men accustomed to great power can generate, the King of England continued to relentlessly blast the three men standing before him, and Jaime stood motionless by the great bedchamber's closed door. The room, lit by a dozen candles and lamps, seemed to resonate with the energy of the monarch's fury. She and Lady Frances exchanged a furtive glance, both of them happy that Henry Tudor had chosen to ignore the fact that they had even entered.

Jaime glanced again in the direction of her friend, gratefully acknowledging with a nod the small smile that she knew Frances meant to instill confidence in her. How would she ever thank the woman for not leaving her at the door to face this man alone.

This man! Jaime glanced in the direction of the raging king. Her father! As her eyes studied his portly features, livid with anger, his eyes snapped away from the men and focused on her face. Matching his gaze, a sudden and uncontrollable anger of her own flared. The king paused only fleetingly in his tirade before turning his attention once more to the men. She suddenly wondered at the furious battle of words raging in her head, and how she could restrain her tongue from uttering them.

Even with his age showing in his ponderous bulk and the sagging flesh of his face, Henry Tudor was still a formidable man. And watching these men openly flinch at his sharp dismissal from the room, Jaime couldn't help but wonder whether her mother had been thrown out so brutally. Seething with more hate than she thought herself capable of, Jaime glared at the king. This man had been responsible for the deaths of her mother and her aunt, Anne Boleyn. And now she, too, stood so vulnerable before him. She knew that as far as he was concerned, she would be nothing more than yet another undesirable Boleyn.

With fittingly careful deference, the disfavored ones humbly bowed out of the room.

"Countess." Henry glared at Jaime as he addressed Lady Frances, his voice conveying a note of impatience. "There is no longer any need for you to remain."

Frances curtsied and glanced doubtfully at Jaime. "Sire, if it pleases you, I would be happy to stay in case Mistress Jaime's illness returns."

Henry stared at the two women.

"Your Majesty," Jaime added, with a curtsy. "I have only left my sickbed today. If Your Majesty might indulge us?" Anger and disappointment stung her inwardly, for her excuse sounded cowardly even to her own ear. But despite the hostility she felt toward this man, she knew that Frances's presence offered the protection of civility, and she didn't want to throw away Malcolm's and her chances when they were only a day from realization.

Glancing back at the king, she searched for a sign in his expression. A long moment passed before he nodded his assent.

Turning to Lady Frances, Henry's words were gentle as he invited her to approach and take a seat. But Jaime, still standing by the door, found herself the target of two piercing eyes. She wondered if there was a resemblance that he was searching for. She knew her mother was much shorter in height than she herself was. From the paintings her aunt had done, Jaime also knew Mary had been more voluptuous in bosom and hip than she. Jaime looked more like Elizabeth than she did her own mother. Perhaps that was one reason it had been so much easier over the years to pretend to be her daughter. But that could all be for naught, now.

For though she hated to admit it, as she studied the king's

features, she saw something in his countenance, in the curve of his cheek, that she knew could be found, even by the light of these candles, in her own face.

The edge in Henry Tudor's voice cut through the air when he finally spoke again. "I hear that you are a granddaughter of Thomas Boleyn."

"That I am, Your Majesty," Jaime answered quietly.

"It is peculiar that we never heard of you while your grandfather was at our court."

"I was brought up elsewhere," Jaime answered. "It wasn't until much later in his life that I had a chance to spend some time in his company."

The king's eyes again dwelled on Jaime's features. Then, abruptly, he reached over and picked up a chain from the corner of the table. The bright green emerald flashed in the light of the room. "What is your age, mistress?"

"Nineteen," she answered feeling the hackles rise on her neck at the sight of her ring in the king's possession. As much as her curiosity—and her rising temper—stabbed at her to inquire how he'd come by her ring, she fought back the question.

Henry's eyes seem to notice Jaime's gaze on the ring in his hand. "Is this . . . this bauble yours?"

She paused, her eyes studying another ring—one encircling the king's finger. One identical to the ring dangling at the end of the chain. "Aye, Your Majesty."

"And how is it you came to possess it?"

Henry began to swing the chain back and forth, allowing it to wind around his fingers and then back. Jaime's eyes, drawn to the action, riveted on the ring that adorned his finger.

"The ring was a token, given to me by my parents," she whispered at last.

Dropping the ring carelessly on the table, the king moved across the room to where she stood.

Jaime glanced uncomfortably in the direction of Frances, who sat quietly with her hands in her lap, her eyes on the king.

"We haven't asked you about your parents. Your mother would be daughter to Thomas Boleyn." Jaime felt her palms begin to sweat as Henry approached her.

"She *was,* Your Majesty."

Henry came to a halt only a step away. As he loomed over her, Jaime suddenly felt all the courage of a few moments ago drain out of her soul, and she lowered her gaze from his face to the large medallion hanging about the king's neck. A long silence followed as she felt his eyes studying her face.

"You have her dark hair, her fair complexion."

The way he spoke the words left no doubt in Jaime's mind that he was speaking of Mary Boleyn. And when his fleshy hand reached out, she had to fight hard not to flinch as he took a loose tendril of her hair between thick fingers. She stood, motionless, holding her breath until, after a moment, his hand dropped to his side. She was certain now. The faraway look in his eyes had told her so much—he knew the truth. He knew she was Mary's daughter.

"And Jaime has also been blessed with some of her artistic nature, as well." Frances's voice swung the king's head around. Stunned, Jaime looked on her friend, realizing what Frances was trying to do. "Being the great connoisseur of music that you are, sire, you would be charmed, I am quite certain, if you were to hear Jaime play and sing her music."

Gathering her wits about her, Jaime quickly wiped her wet palms on the smooth linen of her dress. "If a person's friends will not overstate her talents, Your Majesty, who would?" She smiled serenely as the king turned back to her. "But in all humility, being raised in a house finely attuned to the arts, having the finest scholars and artists of Europe as regular guests, a young woman could hardly avoid developing her talents to the best of her ability."

Henry's eyes were probing when they glanced from Frances back to Jaime. "We don't recall your mother having any great talent."

Bastard! she cursed inwardly, thinking of her poor mother lying dead in the ground. She struggled to retain her composure.

"But, sire," Frances put in. "You yourself are the possessor of several products of those talents."

"Eh? What's that?"

"Paintings of Queen Margaret and her family, I believe."

"What, my sister?"

"Aye, Your Majesty," Jaime added, noticing that his eyes had rounded in surprise. "But Elizabeth Boleyn's talents were of the kind that she couldn't and wouldn't practice in the open. At least, not until your sister, the Queen Mother, invited her to join her court at Linlithgow. Why, the portraits of the royal family adorn every royal castle in Scotland. If I might say so, Your Majesty, their exquisite use of color and texture are now rivaled only by your own Holbein's best work."

It seemed to Jaime that Henry had hardly listened to anything she had just said. But she was certain that he did not suspect her knowing of his infatuation with Elizabeth so many years ago, during the tournament at the Field of Cloth of Gold. It had been her aunt's rejection of his lecherous advances that had forced the young woman to run away and live her life as a painter.

Finally, he addressed her. "You are daughter to Elizabeth?" he asked, incredulity in his voice.

There was no pause in her response, nor any doubt in her mind when Jaime opened her mouth in reply. "I am, Your Majesty."

The King of England ran his fat fingers through his beard as he considered her statement. Jaime pondered the lie she had spoken to her own father. But somehow she knew that this was the way her mother intended it to be.

"Elizabeth, I always wondered what happened to her." Henry turned and wandered pensively across the chamber.

"She went to Florence, Your Majesty, mastered her art in the studio of Michelangelo himself, before going to Scotland and settling there."

The king reached down and picked up the chain and the ring again. "And your father?" he asked, turning toward her.

"Ambrose Macpherson."

"Aye, the Scottish diplomat," Henry put in. "Of course."

Jaime's knees suddenly wobbled beneath her, and the king and Frances were beside her in an instant. The relief of having him accept her story delighted her and yet made her lightheaded. They sat her in a chair beside Frances, and her head cleared immediately, though the king insisted on pouring out a cup of wine for her.

She watched him as he settled his great weight into a chair facing her, and again picked up the ring.

"Did you know that this bauble once belonged to us?"

She shook her head. "Nay, Your Majesty."

Henry's eyes glinted as they stared at the dark green of the stone. "Then we assume you do not know how your parents came to have it."

She shook her head again.

"Your father won this ring in the tournament we held at the Field of Cloth of Gold. He downed the best of our English knights in a joust to win this token."

Jaime stared at the ring. She knew it had been there that Ambrose and Elizabeth had first met.

"But now, meeting you and . . . knowing your age . . ." A smile was breaking out on the king's portly face. "We would say the prize he earned was worth far more than this bauble."

She looked at him with raised eyebrows.

"Your father is too fearless, too blunt to be a very good diplomat. No really good diplomat can be respected . . . or even trusted, you see. But where were we?"

"The tournament, sire," Frances suggested.

"Ah, indeed. We recall that after the Scot collected this prize, he approached none other than the daughter of our French ambassador, Sir Thomas." He turned to Frances with a rumbling laugh. "He gave her the ring."

"A generous gift!" Frances added.

"Wouldn't you say that the return exceeded his investment, Lady Frances?" Henry placed a hand on Jaime's shoulder as he smiled at the countess. "You see it now? This young woman is, we believe, the finest thing produced by that Field of Cloth of Gold."

As Frances rose from her chair, Jaime stood, as well, unsure of how to respond.

"Lady Frances, we thank you for this visit," the king said, leading them toward the door. He detained Jaime with a light touch of his hand. "And the next time you visit your father, send my regards to him. Even though twenty years ago I was ready to draw and quarter him for foiling my plans regarding France, over the years I have learned to value such talent."

Jaime dropped a small curtsy and turned toward Frances waiting by the door.

"And your mother," Henry added.

Jaime swung around to face the king.

"She was the smartest of the three. Send her my best."

She paused for an instant. Elizabeth was the only survivor of the three, and Jaime wondered if that was what he meant. But she didn't dare stay and ask.

"Oh, you've forgotten something."

Jaime opened her hand as the king dropped the ring in her palm. As he turned and made his way back across the room, she stared for a moment at the emerald and then at the man who would never know the truth.

CHAPTER 41

"I will be grateful to you for as long as I live," Jaime whispered, gently squeezing the firm hand that took hold of her arm at the great oaken door of the king's chamber.

Relying on Frances's physical support now, Jaime felt as if each step she took was made with the weight of a hundred tons dragging at her feet. She realized now that it had taken all her strength to face the king. But she didn't think she would ever have been able to go through with it without Frances's help.

"Let's just hope that it is a long life that awaits you . . . and me . . . considering what we've just done to ruin the duke of Norfolk's plans."

Jaime turned her head and looked at the other woman's resigned expression.

"Oh, as well you should know." Frances shrugged her shoulders. "Edward is being held prisoner at Nonsuch Palace awaiting the High Steward's Court to convene."

Jaime looked steadily at her friend. "What does that mean, Frances?"

"The accusation may be one of treason." Frances said simply. "From what Surrey has heard, someone has come forward with the rumor that Edward has held back booty he captured in the king's name at sea."

Jaime kept silent. She knew this to be the truth. Many times since arriving here, she had heard Edward boast of his cleverness in this matter. "So what does this news have to do with us? What plans have we ruined?"

Frances looked into Jaime's eyes. "Your sudden summons to appear at court . . ."

"Aye?" Jaime whispered.

"Surrey and I discussed this, and we decided that the king must have had no knowledge of . . . another daughter, which now we know to be the truth."

"I think the king was relieved to think that I was not Mary Boleyn's daughter."

"True. The Crown Prince is a sickly little fellow. If, God forbid, he should die before the king, another daughter would only complicate the succession."

"But what of the duke's plans?"

"The duke and Edward summoned you to marry Edward in haste—before presenting you to His Majesty. Once he was married to the king's daughter, a royal pardon for Edward would be assured."

"And we have prevented that by going to the king."

"Of course, we had no choice when he sent for you."

Jaime's heart pounded joyfully at her good fortune in not going to Nonsuch Palace when she had been summoned. Then a thought occurred to her. "But if the earl knew so much from that letter . . ."

Frances patted Jaime on the hand. "Surrey deserves your trust, my dear. He did not learn everything until you were bedridden. The Archbishop of Norwich sent a messenger to Surrey—naturally assuming my husband was in on his father's scheme—seeking some information in order to draw up the papers on your betrothal with Edward."

"Drawing papers without ever having my consent." Jaime stopped and looked worriedly into her friend's eyes.

Frances nodded. "Aye, they are dated two months back."

"But how could they?" Jaime brought a hand to her brow and leaned heavily against a carved wooden panel.

Frances led her to one of the window seats. Looking up and down the empty corridor, the countess waved a hand dismissing Jaime's fears. "I don't think you need worry about what has been done. Leaving His Majesty's chambers, I have no doubt that he was convinced that you are Elizabeth's rather than Mary's daughter. So the duke can say all he wants. You have already given the king enough reason to disbelieve the claims. Norfolk will not be happy, though."

Jaime touched Frances gently on the arm. "You knew all of this and still helped me. I should have thought, being married to a Howard, your first loyalty would be to them."

Frances smiled. "It is, Jaime. But I am devoted only to Surrey, for he is a man of honor, and truly the most worthy of them all."

"I see that." Jaime smiled, but then her face clouded over. "He is a far cry from his brother."

"True," Frances replied. "Not since Cain and Abel have two brothers been so different."

The candles spread about on various tables only managed to deepen the shadows lurking in the chamber.

Catherine pulled aside the covers as the tall, portly man approached the massive bed. Lying back and curling up coyly, she watched him with slow, lingering eyes as he opened the front of his robe. Though it was difficult, she managed her usual look of awe at what she saw beneath.

Coming to her knees as he beckoned to her, she scooted to the edge of the bed. Raising her hands straight up in the air, she smiled as the king pulled her silk chemise over her head. With great satisfaction, she saw his eyes focus on her breasts. She didn't wait for him to lick his lips; she reached up and drew his mouth to one nipple.

It was always like this. Always the same, she thought. He pushed her back onto the bed—his mouth still latched to her nipple. She used her knee to rub against his manhood. If only she could find some pleasure in what he did to her. He was hard now, but for how long? Spread beneath him—with her hands, legs, and hips going through the motions of what she knew he liked—she stared at the canopy covering the bed and recalled the scene she had walked in on between that wretched Jaime and the Highlander.

She could almost feel the Scot upon her. She could imagine his passion. Malcolm was now suckling her breasts with a firm mouth, a tantalizing play of tongue and teeth. She let her hands travel the back of her lover's back. She encircled his waist with her legs.

Henry lifted his great bulk and moved from her breast to her neck, nestling his mouth in the soft place beneath her ear. Catherine knew what would come next, and she was prepared when he entered her, sudden and quick. She moaned her customary response and continued to stare at the canopy above.

She could envision Malcolm's long, muscular legs, his broad, scarred chest, his hands shaping and squeezing her breasts. She could feel his long, thick shaft driving into her. Again and again, driving so deeply into her.

Catherine imagined her hand to be the Highlander's as she reached between their bodies. She could feel his strong fingers slide between their bodies, and found herself growing more excited with each thrust. She could feel his fingers stroking the source of all pleasure. He was now breathing heavily in her ear, and his relentless pace was pushing her ever higher. With a bearlike growl, he spilled his seed into her, and her own lusty release was only a moment behind.

But seconds later, the scrape of his boarlike whiskers brought back the truth of it all. It was no Highlander nestled between her legs. Henry Tudor sprawled atop her. Catherine turned her face in disgust.

The great bed creaked as the king rolled off of her and onto his back. His hands crossed comfortably on his heaving chest. "If we thought you missed us this much, Cat, that little visit this evening with your cousin would have been postponed."

"And how did it go, your little chat?"

"Nothing for you to concern yourself with," he answered shortly. But then rolling himself with some effort, he laid one beefy hand on her breast. Henry squeezed her erect nipple between his thumb and forefinger. "What a tigress you were a moment ago. I've never heard you cry out before."

Hiding her disappointment about his refusal to discuss Jaime, Catherine plastered a smile on her face. Feeling his thumb rub over her nipple, she turned and gazed into his eyes.

"You are just so magnificent," she replied, letting her fingers graze the skin of his chest and move down over his distended belly. "Such an exciting lover. You know that the mere thought of you drives me wild. I cannot wait to be married, my lusty bear."

Henry's laugh rumbled deep in his chest. "Just remember, Cat, after we are wed, I still can't spend all of my time between your legs."

"And why not?" she asked, putting a pout on her face in retort. Raising her knee and laying it over his groin, she rested her head in the palm of her hand. "I know many men who would give their lives to take your place."

The flash of anger in the king's face shut Catherine's mouth in an instant.

"Beware, woman, of such talk," he snapped, turning and shoving her back onto the pillow. "Don't forget your place."

Catherine stared as Henry's face loomed above her.

"Disgrace yourself, and your head will adorn my chamber wall. Do you understand me, Cat?"

Catherine Howard nodded. There was little room to disagree.

CHAPTER 42

The soft knock at the chamber door drew both women's eyes to the oaken entry. With a nod in Caddy's direction, Jaime swung her legs wearily over the edge of the bed and reached for her robe. She had retired but a moment earlier, and she was desperate for rest in both body and mind.

Glancing back again at the door, she saw Caddy arguing softly with whoever stood beyond. A moment passed while Jaime tried to decide whether it would be quicker going and handling this late visitor herself or letting her serving woman do it. Casting a wistful look at her pillow, she knew what she really wanted was simply to get back into bed and fall asleep. But clearly, whoever was calling on them was not taking rejection easily. With a sigh of resignation, Jaime stood up and started for the door.

Before she had crossed half the distance, she saw the door swing open and Malcolm step in. Behind him, Caddy went out of the chamber, closing the door after her.

Her weariness evaporated into the night air as she dashed into his arms. Malcolm held her tight against him, kissing her face, grazing her lips with his own before lifting her into his arms and taking her back to her bed. Without a word, he deposited her gently into the middle and began to pull the bed-clothes over her. She fought off the covers.

"You should not have left your bed," he scolded. "Now stay put and stop fighting me."

"Nay, bully. You will need to get in here with me and hold me in place," Jaime whispered with a smile.

"I cannot, lass. I came in here to talk . . ."

The words were lost on his lips as she slowly undid the belt that held her robe in place. Tossing the outer garment to the side, she smiled at the flash of desire glinting in his eyes. Though her shift was cotton and certainly modest, his eyes surveyed her as if she wore nothing at all. She lay back on the bed and opened her arms.

"You are a witch," he whispered hoarsely, shaking his head and reaching once again to pull the covers over her. Once the thick blanket separated her body from his, he leaned into her embrace and kissed her with a thoroughness that left her breathless.

When he pulled away, Jaime sighed happily.

"Jaime, my love, we've had a sudden change of plans," Malcolm said seriously, holding her face in his hands.

"You are not going without me!" she said, panicky and unable to keep the note of fear out of her voice. "You *have* to take me with you, Malcolm. You *have* to. I *am* well enough to travel."

"I will never take a step without you, lass." Malcolm leaned down and kissed her lips again. This time, as he tried to pull away, she held him tightly and thoroughly kissed him back.

This time *he* sighed as she broke off the kiss.

"Tell me about this change of plan," she whispered.

It took Malcolm a moment to gather his thoughts. But then his eyes once again focused on her face. "We had originally planned to leave on Midsummer's Eve."

"Aye, Caddy tells me that even though the celebration is three days' off, the folks are already gathering from miles around. It may offer a good diversion for our escape."

"True, but we won't be waiting till then."

"Oh?" she said, her voice rising with excitement.

Malcolm smiled as he let his fingers linger caressingly over the soft skin of her face. "Aye. Evan sent word to me tonight."

"Evan?" she asked in amazement. "That good man is helping us with our escape?"

"He is." Malcolm nodded. "Well, our ship came in two

nights ago, and they're coming back in tomorrow night, so we are leaving earlier than planned."

Jaime thrilled at the thought of leaving. "So it is real. We are going home."

"Aye, lass, we are. Tomorrow morning at first light," Malcolm answered. "Surrey told me today that the king is planning to ride back to Nonsuch Palace after breakfast. So if we leave at dawn, it could be hours before anyone even notices—with all the commotion surrounding the king's departure."

Jaime couldn't hold back her excitement as she threw her arms about his neck and held him tight. "I'll put on my clothes and be ready in an instant."

"Nay, my love." He placed a kiss on her lips before pushing her back on the pillow. "I want you to get as much rest as you can in the next few hours. I'll come after you before dawn."

Jaime paused, a troubled look creeping into her eyes. "Malcolm, I'd like to bring . . ."

"I am sorry, my sweet. But I'm afraid you will have to leave all your things behind."

"Nay!" She shook her head with a slight smile. "I meant Caddy. I don't know how I could leave her."

Malcolm's brow knotted for a moment as he gave the matter some thought. "Does she know anything about it?"

Jaime shook her head. "Nay, Malcolm. I haven't told her."

"We'll take her," Malcolm said matter-of-factly. "We'll just have to steal an extra horse."

Jaime brightened again as she ran her fingers through his hair. "There is no need. I could ride on your lap. Remember how you used to take me for rides when I was but a wee thing?"

"You were a child, then, Jaime, but you are a woman, now," he whispered, resting his brow against hers, smiling into her eyes. "With you sitting on my lap, I fear we'd lose Caddy in no time. In fact, I do not know that we'd ever reach Harwich in a day."

She coiled her arms tighter about his neck and drew him down onto her. "If you were to get in this bed with me now, perhaps tomorrow you'd have an easier time with me riding in your lap."

"You think so?" he teased, using his tongue to trace the line of her lips.

Jaime nodded as the soft knock came at the door. They both stiffened.

" 'Tis only Caddy." He said it like a curse. "On second thought, I think we'll not be taking her with us."

Jaime smiled. "Has she been standing guard outside the door?"

"She wanted to stand guard inside, to keep . . ."

"You from kissing me?" she finished, lifting her face and grazing his lips with her own. "Or perhaps touching me?" She let her hands move over the sinewy musculature of his back. "Or was she afraid of you making love to me?" She lay back and looked at him suggestively.

The Highlander swallowed once. "I believe she was more worried about me than you. I mean, she knows how vulnerable I am, and how demanding you can be."

She hit him squarely on the chest. "You are a rogue, Malcolm MacLeod."

"Aye, but I am your rogue, my love. Yours alone."

The second knock at the door separated the two. After giving her a lingering kiss on the lips, Malcolm stood to leave.

"Until dawn?" she asked.

"Until then, my love."

Damn Henry, she cursed. No man would tell her what to do. Catherine repeated his words in her mind as she made her way up the stairs. Well, say what he will, she would do as she pleased, and she would accept no master.

And damn Edward, as well, she muttered as she reached the top floor of the palace. If he hadn't been so cruel, she thought, if he had treated her better, then it would be *his* bed she'd be going to. Damn him.

Damn them all.

Malcolm sensed her presence as soon as he closed his chamber door.

As he stepped into the room, he felt the anger rise in his

chest. The cast-off cloak, thrown carelessly to the floor, told him that his instincts were correct. Catherine was here.

Glancing in the direction of his curtained bed, he saw a candle flickering dimly on a side table, but the woman wasn't there. Turning his head, though, he quickly found Catherine, sitting quietly in a chair by the window. Her golden brown tresses cascaded over her shoulders ... and whatever it was she had wrapped herself in.

"I was beginning to wonder if you were ever going to return," she cooed. As she spoke, Catherine stood up slowly, allowing the blanket that she was holding to drop in a pool at her feet. The skin of her naked body glowed in the candlelight. "But then, I knew it would only be a matter of time before you got tired of that silly wench."

Malcolm remained where he stood, though every impulse in his being cried out to cross the room and break her neck.

"You can't resist me, Highlander, and you know it." She smiled, raising her hands to her breasts, lifting them enticingly. "I have watched you, taking these in with your eyes. Now they are yours ... as is the rest." Catherine swept her hand invitingly downward, caressing her own skin as she did.

Malcolm was not even close to falling prey to Catherine's charms. He continued to struggle against the violence he felt toward the woman, his hands curling into fists at his sides.

"Come to me, Highlander," she purred, walking slowly toward him. "I was here, you know. I watched you with her. I know what you are capable of. Aye, I saw the way you drove into her, again and again. But she can't satisfy a man like you, can she? That's why you've come back from her chamber now. You need more of a woman than Jaime is, to see to your pleasure. You need me."

Catherine's hand came up and touched his shirt, sliding lower over his hard belly. He caught her wrist with a force that made her cry out in pain.

"You animal," she laughed, twisting her wrist free. "I am only *glad* to help you get ready."

"Leave, woman." Malcolm's eyes blazed as they looked piercingly into Catherine's. "Leave now."

She laughed heartily as she shook her head. Placing both

her hands on his chest, she gazed up to his face. "I won't, you see. Not until you've repaid the debt you owe me."

"What debt? I owe you nothing."

"But you do," she whispered, once again tracing with her fingers the lines of his stomach. He caught her wrists again, with even more force than before, and pushed her away. She laughed once more. "That night when I found you fucking that wretched Jaime, while I, Catherine Howard, stood there in the corner—naked and ready to come to you, myself—that was the moment when you both incurred your debts to me."

"You are sick, woman," Malcolm answered through clenched teeth.

"Nay, foolish man. I made *her* sick," she answered. "That was how she has begun to pay. By making her sick, by giving her more than she needed—more, anyway, than that doting old physician intended—I began to collect on her debt. But only began, for I am not yet done with her. She has more to pay yet, much more. But from you, I need . . ."

With a movement like lightning, Malcolm grasped her hair with one hand and jerked Catherine's head back. Her eyes flashing with anticipation, she looked up at him, and her lips parted with a knowing smirk.

"Listen carefully," he growled into her face. "You can take your whore's tricks elsewhere. They will get you naught, here. And I will tell you something else. You speak of paying debts? This dangerous game you are playing has a price, as well. That price is your life! And I am not speaking of your future husband's fondness for replacing wives." Malcolm jerked her head back again, this time making Catherine cry out in pain. "If you even try to get close to Jaime, if you harm her in any way, I will strangle you with my bare hands."

"You wouldn't dare to hurt me," she scoffed haughtily.

Malcolm stared at her for a moment. Then, with a growl, he dragged her to the window with such violence that she lost her footing. Shoving the windows open wide, he pushed her naked body half out of the opening, holding her only by one arm and her hair. Her white skin looked almost blue in the light of the moon, and her other arm flailed about in the empty air.

"I am a Highlander, remember?" he rasped. "No more than a filthy barbarian."

The woman's eyes widened in fear as she gaped at the paving stones far below.

"Use your imagination, wench." Malcolm shoved her out a bit further. "Your twisted body mashed on the stones there. Can you not see them, the guards all passing by and smirking at your naked limbs? Can you not hear them, telling stories about who'd slept with you the most. And all of them claiming they'd only done it out of pity." He shook her, loosening his hold on her arm.

"Don't drop me!" she cried aloud, waving her hands desperately in the air. "PLEASE!"

"Why not? Why should I let you live?" He pushed her out still further. She hung now with her feet barely touching the edge of the window casing. "After all you've done, 'tis you who must pay the debt, Catherine."

"I swear. I swear," she wept. "I'll never have anything to do with you, nor with Jaime. Don't let me fall."

Malcolm again shook her, eliciting sobs from her, as it appeared he clearly meant to let her drop.

"Please!" she choked. "I'll do anything you want."

His movement was abrupt as he pulled her with one swift motion back through the window. But her feet hardly had a chance to touch the floor, for Malcolm dragged her quickly across the chamber.

"Aye," he spat. "You will." Jerking open the chamber door, the Highlander threw her, naked and weeping, into the corridor.

Catherine crouched, stunned at the rapid turn of events, and gaped at him.

"You will stay out of my life," Malcolm ordered, shutting the door and leaving her in the darkness of the deserted hallway.

Catherine grimaced as the heavy door closed tightly in her face. Looking up and down the hall, she quickly rose to her feet and ran to the deeper shadows of a nearby alcove.

"Pig! Animal!" She cursed Malcolm under her breath as she ran a hand through her wild tresses, causing her golden hair to fan out over her bare breasts. He wasn't worth her spit. And that slut Jaime. Let him have her for all she cared. After all, it was Edward whom she wanted to keep from marrying the bitch. She was finished with them both.

Furtively, she made her way down the stairway back toward her room, pausing in every shadowy corner, alcove, and window seat. As she padded along with stealthy steps, dead Howards leered down at her from the paintings that hung on the walls. The long corridor stretched out before her, lit only by the moon that shone softly through windows lining one side. Anyone could walk these halls at this time of night, Catherine thought. But then, suddenly, the whole idea amused her, thrilled her even.

Catherine stepped up into a window seat, and pressed her warm flesh against the cool panes of the window. Perhaps she needed to expand her circle of . . . friends. She was already attracting better-looking men than she had in the past, Catherine reminded herself. In her position, she deserved men who would respect her, men she could teach to satisfy her every need. Men that she could control.

Catherine brightened at the thought, recalling the handsome face of Sir Thomas Culpepper and that other one, Sir Francis something. They were both gentlemen of Henry's Privy Chamber, and neither had taken his eyes off of her—even once—during dinner.

Aye, that was what she needed, Catherine decided, chills racing through her. Stealing back the way she had come, she turned down the corridor to where she knew the two men shared a bedchamber. It was always worth knowing where the young gentlemen resided.

Reaching their door, Catherine once again ran her fingers through her hair, arranging it carefully to display just the right amount of her ample breasts.

Her soft knock on the door was answered by the shuffle of sleepy steps, and then the shocked gaze of a man, standing in his shirt at the open door and staring with his mouth agape at her naked body.

"Sir Thomas," she whispered sweetly, sounding almost surprised that he had found her standing naked in the hallway at this time of night. "I don't know how ... I wonder if you might help me with something."

The man glanced anxiously over his shoulder as another man approached.

"Ah, Sir Francis," she drawled. "I was just telling Sir Thomas that I was hoping you two gentlemen might not be too tired to help a poor maiden in distress."

Both men shook their heads as if dreaming.

"I am so glad," she said happily, taking the two men by the elbows and leading them toward the bed.

CHAPTER 43

She could not breathe.

Edward's fingers were wrapped around her throat, pressing hard. She pried at his hands, trying to fight him off, loosen his grip on her. But he was too strong. Feeling the last of her breath burning in her chest, Jaime fought him with all her might. Her hands scratched at his face as her feet tried to kick free of his weight.

But she could not breathe.

Gasping for air, Jaime Macpherson sat bolt upright in her bed, her sweat-soaked shift sticking to her body. Filling her lungs with great gulps of air, she nearly wept at the wonderful sensation of breathing again.

She shuddered at the vividness of the dream, at the horror of coming face to face with Edward. At the hate that oozed from him as he strangled the life out of her. It was so much like those other dreams, the ones she had experienced as she lay in that terrifying slumber, drugged and dead to the waking world. She felt the tremors run involuntarily through her frame.

These were only dreams, she reminded herself, glancing at the open window. The moon, bathing the chamber with a pale glow, was sinking in the western sky, and darkness still reigned over the earth. Soon, though, she thought. Soon enough, she would be leaving here and put her fears behind her. Put behind her any chance of facing Edward. Soon enough.

Feeling cold from the breeze coming in the window, Jaime shivered again and reached down to pull up the bedclothes that she had kicked off during the restless night.

And then she saw him.

Out of the darkness, like a slow-moving fiend coming to possess her soul, his dark form approached with evil intent. She stared at him in disbelief, thinking that he was just a specter, a shade, created in her dream-clouded mind, but when he drew his dagger from its sheath, she knew he was no shadow.

"Edward," she managed to utter, staring at him in terror.

"That is all you have to say?" he asked, coming ever closer. "After all the time I've been away, that is all the greeting I get from my bride?"

She scurried back toward the head of the bed. His eyes swept over her hungrily, fixing on her breasts through the clinging shift, and Jaime snatched a pillow from the bed, shielding herself from his malicious scrutiny.

"What are you doing here, Edward?" she asked, her voice quaking slightly. "No one expected you . . ."

Reaching the side of the bed, he snatched the pillow away and threw it across the room. Like a wounded bird, she scuttled further from him.

"No one expected me to escape what? My prison?" He snarled. "My fate? But you were all wrong, my raven." With a quick grab, he took hold of her wrist and dragged her across the bed. "I am a pirate far more than I am a courtier. Escaping those fools was no more than a mere nuisance for one with my . . . desires."

She fought him, twisting away, but stopped as her eyes riveted on the dagger that now pointed at her face. She had no doubt he would use the weapon on her. She looked up into his face and saw the evil curl of his lips.

"Why are you here?" she whispered.

"Much better," he hissed. Dropping the dagger on the table beside the bed, Edward grabbed her other wrist and dragged

Jaime up against his chest until her eyes were at the same level as his.

"She asks me why I am here." He smiled malevolently, bringing his mouth down, giving her a bruising kiss on her lips.

Jaime felt the bile rushing to her throat as she twisted her head to the side.

"I am here, my intended, to escort you to a priest." He shook her hard, forcing her to look again into his face. "I am here to make you go through with our betrothal—to make you live up to your promise of becoming my wife."

"I *never* made that promise!" She shook her head. "We never . . ."

Edward released one of her wrists, and in a single motion, took hold of the front of her shift and tore the front of it away, exposing her flesh to his lascivious gaze.

"And I am here to consummate our marriage," he sneered, grasping her breast brutally as he shoved her down onto the sheets. "In fact, I like this order of things better. A marriage will follow. After I am done with you. Stay where you are."

Straightening up, he unbuckled his sword belt and dropped the weapon onto the end of the bed. Seeing her chance, Jaime tried to twist away, but Edward grasped her ankle and dragged her roughly to the edge. She opened her mouth to scream but his hand clamped down hard on her lips. She felt his leg shove between her legs. With his weight on her, he fumbled with the ties of his codpiece.

She bit on his palm with all of her might. She tasted blood.

"Slut," he shouted, drawing his hand back to his mouth.

She opened her mouth again to scream, but this time his hand closed around her windpipe, strangling her cry in her throat. Jaime found herself gasping for air.

"So I am not as good as your filthy Highlander, is that it?" His blazing eyes bore into hers. "Aye, I have heard."

She shook her head, lights beginning to flash before her eyes.

"After I am done with you, you'll think different." As he again yanked at his codpiece, his grip on her throat eased a bit, allowing some air into her burning lungs. "And if you don't please me, wench, we'll take a little trip to Norwich Castle. There, I'll have you whipped by my man Reed. Do you know what he does to women while they are being beaten?"

Jaime started thrashing in terror as she felt his member swing free, scraping hard against the inside of her thigh.

Edward reached down to guide himself into her. "He has one of his men drive into the slut while . . ."

Jaime saw the flash of the dagger above his shoulder, and before he could finish his words, she saw it sink into his back.

Edward contorted in pain, lifting himself and trying to turn to face his attacker. It was all the chance Jaime needed, breaking herself free from beneath him and rolling to the side. A look of horror was etched on Caddy's face as she stepped back, and Edward staggered to his feet, the hilt of the dagger protruding from his back. As he lurched toward the older woman, Jaime sprang into action.

She jumped from the bed, reaching for the closest thing she could find. His unbuckled sword lay beside her. Jaime grasped the sheathed blade and, with all her force, swung the hilt at the attacker's head. Edward's knees buckled under him, and he dropped like a stone to the floor.

Staring down at the motionless form at her feet, the sword hanging in her hand, Jaime pulled together the front of her torn shift. Dropping the weapon, she stepped back and wiped away a tear that was running down her face.

"He is dead!" Caddy announced, pushing at him with her foot.

Jaime looked up and, unable to hold back any longer, rushed into the older woman's arms. "You saved my life!" she cried. "And I would have preferred death to what he was about to do."

"I'm so sorry, mistress. He must have come right by me. Lord Malcolm asked me to stay close to you tonight. I was sleeping in the alcove just outside of your room when I heard your cry. I know I should have called for help, but I . . ."

Jaime shook her head. "There wasn't time, Caddy. If you hadn't come when you did . . ." She couldn't continue.

As the tears began to flow freely now, the older woman held

her tight in her arms and stared down at the demon sprawled at their feet.

"Who should I go to first?" Caddy asked finally. "The earl himself, or . . ."

"No one." Jaime pulled back, shaking her head adamantly. "Edward is dead. There is no reason for us to call upon them now. They'll find him soon enough, and by then we'll be gone."

"Gone?"

"Aye, Caddy, we are leaving here tonight. We are going to Scotland." Suddenly chilled to the bone, she gave the woman's hands a squeeze and stepped around Edward. Pulling a blanket from the bed, she wrapped it around herself, but it did little to stop the quaking that had settled into her body. "Malcolm intended to come after us at first light, but I want you to go to his chamber and tell him that he is to meet us outside the south entrance right away. Then you must go and ready yourself for the trip."

"You are taking me with you, mistress?" the older woman asked with a tremulous voice.

"How could I go without you?" Jaime choked on her tears again. "But please go. We don't know if anyone saw . . . him . . . arrive at Kenninghall."

With a quick nod of her head, Caddy wiped her hands at her skirts and rushed from the room.

Left alone with Edward, Jaime continued to shake as fear and shock battled for control of her body. She never took her eyes off of him as she hurriedly dressed in her traveling clothes and slipped out of the chamber.

Nell, Evan's wife, held the sleeping infant in the crook of her arm as she handed Caddy the basket of food. Malcolm stood by the horses beneath the trees and talked privately with the falconer and Master Graves.

Jaime, crouching before the young Kate, tried desperately to hold back her tears as the little girl tied her pink ribbon around Jaime's thick ebony hair. " 'Tis for good luck, mistress, and also for you to remember me by."

"But when I gave this to you—it was for keeps," Jaime whispered.

"And I kept it, mistress, and it brought me luck," Kate answered, coming around Jaime and hugging her lovingly. "Now I want you to have it . . . to bring you luck, and keep you safe."

Jaime placed a gentle kiss on the young girl's soft cheek and reached inside her cloak. From around her neck she removed the long chain. Opening Kate's little hand, Jaime placed the emerald ring and the chain in her palm. "You give this to your mother to hide and to keep safe for you. And someday, when you are older, it may bring you *more* luck."

Kate's large eyes stared in awe at the ring as Jaime, placing another kiss on the young girl's fiery hair, pushed herself to her feet.

Nell's eyes were teary when they met Jaime's. When Jaime opened her arms to embrace her, the woman nodded and hugged her fiercely. Words were meaningless in expressing the abundance of emotions that they both felt. Pulling away, Jaime caught Malcolm's gaze.

In his face she could still see the remnants of rage that had nearly swept him over into the grip of savagery. Only by begging had she kept him from going back to her chamber and hacking Edward's dead body into a hundred pieces. Caddy had told him the truth of what occurred, and Malcolm, wild with fear and worry, had rushed to Jaime, only to find her gliding silently toward the stairway. As Malcolm had drawn her into his arms, she had made him promise to take her out of the palace without a moment's delay.

And now they stood, gazing lovingly at each other beneath the trees at the edge of the meadow, freedom in their grasp.

CHAPTER 44

Jaime had thrilled at the very sight of her cousin.

Alexander Macpherson, the eldest son of Alec and Fiona, sat in the best cabin of the armed merchantman, master of the ship that was carrying them northward. His presence had been a surprise even to Malcolm, who had expected a Flemish ship to rendezvous with them.

"You don't expect me to sit aside and let someone else take care of family, now, do you?" Alexander, following in the steps of his seagoing forefathers, had already established himself, at twenty-three, as a force to reckon with in the German Sea.

As Jaime watched Malcolm's handsome face relax in the presence of Alexander, a man he had grown up loving as a younger brother, her mind wandered back over the flight that had brought them to safety.

Their daylong ride along the winding roads to the fishing village north of Harwich had been hard, but mercifully uneventful. And once there, Malcolm had been able to hire a longboat and the men to row it, in no time. So they had sat at the stern of the boat, Malcolm with a sword on his lap, eyeing with suspicion the swarthy rowers, and they had met Alexander's ship under the light of the full moon. But it was not until they'd boarded the sleek *Elizabeth,* and the wind had filled her sails, that Jaime had felt the tension begin to melt out of her body.

"We'll have to move off the coast and tack northward," Alexander said, leaning back, a cup in his hand and his long legs stretched out before him. "The wind is coming from the north, so be prepared for a slow journey home."

"Thanks, lad," Malcolm said. "We're planning to make good with any idle time on our hands."

Jaime felt herself blushing crimson at Malcolm's suggestive words and mischievous glance. Hiding a smile, she tore her gaze away from her intended—the rogue—and looked innocently at Alexander. But her cousin's raised eyebrows made her blush even more.

"So when is the wedding?" the handsome young Highlander asked with a grin.

"As soon as we arrive," Malcolm answered.

"Will it be at Benmore Castle?" Alexander probed. "We haven't put on a good wedding there since . . ."

"Nay, Alexander. On the Isle of Skye," she corrected quietly. Jaime looked steadily at Malcolm. She had to slay the demons of her past. She would stand at that Priory altar as Malcolm's bride.

"Well, then, we'll just have a nice summer voyage around the Orkney's and drop anchor in Loch Dunvegan, if that suits you."

Alexander's blue eyes twinkled with mirth as they traveled from Malcolm's loving expression to Jaime's matching looks. Putting his cup down on the table and folding his hands over his flat belly, he jutted out his lower lip and took on a fatherly pose, frowning at the two sitting across from him.

"Now, mind me, you two," he said sternly. "You mustn't forget that you are under my safekeeping. So as master of the *Elizabeth* and all who sail on her, I am telling you now that I'll be glad to help you two keep your distance from each other. I've already given my dearest cousin Jaime the use of my chamber, and you, Malcolm—foul beast—will sleep with the rest of my scurvy, pox-infected sailors in the forecastle."

In response to Malcolm's growl, Alexander raised a hand.

"I know. You appreciate my looking out for you. But that is not all that I will do for you. When you two meet while aboard this ship, I'll make certain that a chaperon, preferably myself, will oversee your visit."

Seeing Malcolm come to his feet, Jaime fought back a giggle.

"Of course, you'll want to stay away from any kisses—any fondling—any act that . . ."

Alexander's chair splintered beneath him as Malcolm kicked out one of the legs, and an instant later the Highlander stood with a boot on the younger man's chest.

"If you're thinking that because you have grown to be as tall as me, I'll be treating you any different from before, then you are in for a great surprise," Malcolm snarled. "You might be master of this ship, and feared from the Shetlands to Calais, but I can still handle you with the same ease that I have since you were a wee bairn."

"Jaime." Alexander turned his blond head to face her. "How could you marry a man this old?"

But before she could answer, the young mariner grasped Malcolm's ankle firmly with one hand and upended the MacLeod laird with the other. In another moment the two warriors were locked in combat on the floor.

"Some things never change," Jaime said in disgust, coming to her feet and backing away to a safe distance. "You two remain the ruffians and rogues you were when we were young."

As the two turned their heads to look at her, she extended a hand toward Malcolm. "A person would think one of you, at least, would grow up."

Alexander bounced to his feet first and extended a hand to help Malcolm up. But the Highlander instead accepted Jaime's outstretched hand. The ship's master turned to her, as well.

"Jaime Macpherson, do not think that anyone here is about to accept this motherly admonishment. Do not forget that you are much younger than me and . . ."

"Four years, my piratical cousin," she corrected, jabbing

Alexander in the chest. "But knowing your dull-witted lack of good sense, I figure though you are four years my senior, I am still twelve years your superior in wit *and* in wisdom."

"Are you saying that I have only a fraction of your reasoning abilities?" he asked, towering over her.

She nodded sweetly as she moved snugly into Malcolm's protective embrace. "But I will admit that your skull is four times thicker than mine."

Alexander feigned a menacing look at the young woman. "You can't hide by the Giant's side forever, lass."

Jaime laughed. Giant . . . that was what the children used to call Malcolm when they played so many years earlier. Wrapping her arm tightly about his waist, she looked up into her intended's loving gaze.

"But that is exactly what I plan to do."

Malcolm followed the direction of Alexander's gaze to the galleon that had appeared in the distance.

"The men spotted him on the horizon about three hours ago." Alexander's expression told of his concern. "Now here is sunset, and the blackguard is ready to bugger us."

"So you think he is following us?" the Highlander asked.

"With the wind blowing steady from the north, it just might be that he is tacking the coast, the same as we are." Alexander beckoned to his ship's mate. "But then again, it could be that, whoever it is, he's decided to take us."

"Can we stay ahead of him, Alexander?"

"Well, our wee barque hasn't the sails that the galleon has, but into the wind we'll give him a run for his money . . . and we are not about to lie down if he catches us." Alexander gave him a wink, and Malcolm knew that he was talking about the cannons that all the new Macpherson ships had been fitted with.

Malcolm watched the young mariner begin to give orders for changing course and knew he was not needed on deck. Remembering the promise he had given Jaime of checking on her, though, he turned and started for the cabins belowdecks.

"Let me know if I can be of help," he called over his shoulder.

"Aye," Alexander replied. "But they will not try to get any closer till dawn. That you can be certain of."

When Malcolm had last gone below, Caddy had been a pale shade of green from the turbulent motions of the sea, and Jaime had been seeing to the older woman with all the care of a loving daughter. But now, the Highlander knew that he had to convince Jaime to leave Caddy in his care and take a rest herself. With all that had occurred in the past few days, he knew that the young woman had not so much as closed her eyes since they'd left Kenninghall.

He caught up to her right outside Alexander's cabin. One look at her weary expression and he knew, whatever argument she might put up, he would force her, if need be, to take a rest.

"She is sleeping peacefully in the mate's cabin," Jaime said.

Malcolm pulled her into his embrace and warmed with satisfaction at the way she buried her face against his chest.

"When Alexander came down to check on you both," he asked wryly, "he didn't poison the poor woman?"

Jaime giggled softly but didn't release him. "Why, did you ask him to?"

"Now, why would I do such a thing?"

"To be able to have some time alone with me," she teased, squeezing him tighter.

His hands caressed her hair. His mouth placed a gentle kiss against her soft, black tresses. "You are falling asleep, standing here in my arms. Why not go to your room, lass, and rest a little . . . while you can. I'll keep an eye on Caddy for you."

She slowly pulled away and took hold of his hands. "She should sleep the night away. The poor thing gets sick the first day of every voyage, but she mends after that. She was exhausted, but feeling better when she dropped off tonight. Come with me, Malcolm," she said softly, opening the door of the cabin.

He lifted her chin and looked gently into her face. "You need to rest."

"Aye, so come and help me get ready." Jaime smiled over her shoulder as she drew him into the room. "Unless you want me to ask Alexander to find someone else to come and help me undress. For with Caddy sleeping . . ."

Malcolm growled at her teasingly as he closed the cabin door behind them. A small wick lamp swayed and flickered from the bulkhead by the bunk. "No one but I will help you with that task. Do you hear me?"

The smile that brightened her face was brilliant. "I was hoping you would say that." She reached behind him and latched the door and, drawing him to the middle of the cabin, she half turned. "Will you help me undress?"

Malcolm stared at her beautiful profile. At the straight, perfect nose, at the tantalizing smile that was daring him to resist. "You *will* rest . . . first," he said as she unhooked the cloak that covered her. But as the cloak came away in his hands, he stared at the solid back of the dress. "But there are no buttons to undo."

She turned around slowly and gave him a view of the laces that held together the front of her dress.

"But you don't need my help with . . ." His words trailed off as she lifted his hand and placed it on the knot at the top of the laces.

"I believe I do."

The muscles in Malcolm's jaws clenched as he struggled to control his desire. She was tired. And, well, the knot did look somewhat difficult. And, after all, it is only a wee thing she was asking.

His fingers pulled slowly at the lace of her dress as his eyes gazed deeply into hers. He could see the vulnerability in their depths and he thought of what she'd gone through only two nights earlier.

"Are you afraid, Jaime?" he asked gently.

"I am afraid of being left alone," she whispered. "I am afraid of falling asleep and having the nightmare of him coming after me again."

His hands slid the dress off her shoulders to her waist. She herself pushed it down over her hips and stepped out of it. Malcolm took her hand and brought her palm to his lips. Once again, their eyes locked.

"We are going home, my love," he said huskily. "To where you will be safe. And I swear to you, I'll give my life before . . ."

"I know," she whispered against his mouth, brushing her lips softly against his.

No longer could he hold back his fiery desire, his blazing love. He gathered her into his arms and kissed her with all the passion that burned within him.

A moment later, as he ended the kiss, she sank against him. "Stay with me, Malcolm," she asked. "Hold me and keep me safe."

He lifted her in his arms and carried her to the small bunk. Pulling back the blanket, he placed her in the middle, his eyes never leaving her. He stared at her ebony hair, spread across the ivory skin of her shoulders. At her face, glowing like the light of the moon. At the curves of her flawless body, firm and womanly beneath the thin chemise.

She watched him with a loving eye as he straightened up with a deep breath and moved busily about the room. Seeing him now, dressed in a kilt, a borrowed Macpherson tartan about his shoulder, she was reminded of all the longing, all the anguish she'd suffered for him through the years of growing up. But all that pain was nothing compared to the yearning she felt for him now.

Her eyes drew his gaze to her. Slowly, she raised herself up and reached out a hand to him. He sat beside her, his lips grazing against hers as she pulled at the brooch holding his tartan.

A moment later, as the two of them—relieved of their

clothes—lay down on the bunk, it was their love and a desperate need for healing that set their pace. She caressed his powerful body—her hands learning, her heart soaring—as she grew in the knowledge of his love. His mouth played on her skin, drawing out her essence—giving her pleasure—making her see the beauty, the sureness of their love, as he hoped all the while that he might somehow blot out the brutality of the past.

When she guided him into her, it was the joining of their bodies—and two hearts beat in flawless symmetry. But when they climaxed together, it was the union of their souls—and two spirits sang in everlasting harmony.

Malcolm's hand caressed her silky hair as he continued to gaze at his angelic, yet sleeping lover. He couldn't remember how long he'd been watching her this way. As tired as she had been before their lovemaking, there had been so much they had wanted to say to each other, and they had lay awake for quite a while. He had told her about Catherine and her presence in his chamber when he'd returned that night. And Jaime had told him of her visit with Henry Tudor, her father, the same night. Only two nights had passed since then, but it all seemed so long ago to them. They'd already set their minds on the future and the happiness that surely lay in store for them.

The future was all that mattered now.

Jaime opened her eyes and looked around sleepily as the sound of the men shouting above made Malcolm sit up in bed. He touched her cheek and pushed aside the covers.

"Wait for me," he said. Donning his kilt and his shirt, the Highlander yanked on his boots, grabbed his sword, and reached the door just as Jaime pulled her chemise quickly over her head.

She knew it was only a short time that he was gone from the cabin, for she had barely gotten herself dressed, but to her it seemed like an eternity.

"What is wrong?" she asked, as he knocked and pushed open the cabin door.

"They have a small fire on deck. Some cannon powder had sparked." He picked up his tartan and draped it from one shoulder across his chest, and buckled on his sword. "I am going on deck."

"Is the ship in danger of burning?" Jaime reached for her cloak. "I have to go to Caddy!"

Malcolm put his hands on her shoulder and held her in place. "The fire was nearly under control and may, in fact, be out by now."

"But still I have to check on Caddy."

"I've seen Caddy," Malcolm replied. "And she is bringing down some breakfast for the two of you. Jaime, I want you to stay here and latch the door."

"What is wrong?" she interrupted. "There is something . . ."

" 'Tis nothing, lass. 'Tis just that there's a ship that has been following us, and with this fire, now . . ."

"A ship?"

"Aye, Jaime, a galleon. 'Tis probably nothing. A merchant ship, in all probability. But if there's trouble, I'll come and take you forward."

She opened her mouth to argue.

"Don't, Jaime," he said, cutting her short. "Please do this for me."

He took hold of her chin and raised it until their eyes met. "Please, my love."

She nodded and stretched up to give him a quick kiss, but he took her in his arms until they were both flushed with the embrace.

"Soon, my love," he whispered, making his way out of the cabin.

Jaime pushed open the broad shutters at one end of the cabin. A small launch was secured just beneath the portal, but when she leaned out, Jaime could see the larger ship sailing not a league behind them.

Turning back to the cabin, she spotted Malcolm's dirk on the table, and frowned. Donning her cloak, she slipped it into the inside pocket as a knock sounded at the door. Either he remembered the dagger, she decided, and was returning for it, or her dear Caddy had made her way below.

But as she swung open the door, the person await-ing her in the narrow gangway was neither Caddy nor Malcolm.

The Highlander ran the back of his hand over his face, wiping the soot and sweat out of his eyes. "You do not like the looks of it, do you?" he asked.

"Nay, Malcolm," Alexander responded, looking about at his sailors, who were securing the barrels and buckets they'd been using to quell the fire. "I don't."

"You think someone started it?"

"It is possible," he replied.

Malcolm shook his head and glanced at an aging sailor working by the railing. But as he did, the sailor turned his gaze to him, and something in the old man's look sent cold waves of fear deep into his soul. Stepping back, he suddenly felt as if the ground had opened beneath him. Within the depths of those blue eyes, he felt the power, he saw the reflection of the seer James. The ancient one who had come to him in his dream.

"JAIME!" Malcolm turned and shouted, running like a madman toward the door leading below.

But he never reached the door, for Caddy burst through onto the deck, her eyes wild with worry.

"My mistress is gone!" she cried, her arms flailing.

Malcolm grabbed her by the hand.

"Longboat away!" came a shout from high in the rigging.

Every eye on deck turned upward toward the lookout's perch.

"Away to the stern!"

The Highlander bounded onto the stern deck of the ship with Alexander at his heels. There in the wake of the *Eliza-beth*, with the galleon bearing down quickly, the launch that had hung from the stern rode up and down amid the rolling seas. From this distance, Malcolm could see the form of a man.

And as the launch pitched slightly, he could see in the stern, the bound and gagged figure of Jaime.

CHAPTER 45

The barque *Elizabeth* came about in a matter of moments, and as sailors swarmed over the rigging, setting sails for a run before the wind, Malcolm watched in agony as the galleon's master pointed her directly into the wind. The great ship slowed to pick up Jaime and her kidnapper.

The Highlander felt the barque surge ahead as the billowing white sails snapped taut above him.

"They'll not turn to in time," Alexander said with certainty, squeezing Malcolm's shoulder with a callused hand.

The Highlander nodded at the young Macpherson and glanced about him. As the ship cut through the water, sailors scurried about, clearing the decks for battle. All along the sides of the barque, portals opened and the mouths of cannons slid into view.

"We can't fire on them, Alexander," Malcolm said. "We can't take a chance of hitting Jaime."

"We must!" the young mariner argued. "If we don't cripple the galleon in the first pass, she'll set her sails and be away like a bird before the wind. We'll never catch her."

"Do what you must, but I am going aboard that ship."

Alexander turned and barked at his ship's mate. "Prepare the grappling lines, and tell the gunners to fire into the rigging."

"How close are we going in, m'lord?" the mate responded.

The young mariner whirled and faced the crew. "All hands arm yourselves. Prepare to board the galleon. We take her now, lads!"

As the shout went up among the crew, Malcolm watched as Alexander ran aft to direct the helmsman. Then, without another word, he turned and searched for Jaime as the galleon's sailors began to hoist their sails.

Jaime twisted and kicked like a she-devil against the grip of the men dragging her over the railing of the ship. But the sailors used the rope that bound her hands behind her to control her, and without ceremony threw her facedown on the deck beside a door leading below.

She grunted, trying to regain her breath, the scrape of the wood decking against her cheek stinging her skin. As she rolled to her side her eyes glimpsed the thick-soled boots coming out of the dark opening of the door.

A rough hand yanked her up by the hair, the other grabbing her cloak between the shoulders and twisting the material for a grip. As she felt herself being dragged to her feet, a burly, foul-smelling man in the boots stood right before her. Reed, the jailer from Norwich Castle.

The ship lurched as cannons in the ship's stern boomed out. Not far away, the *Elizabeth*'s guns answered, and Jaime felt the man's grip on her ease as all eyes jerked upward. The mainmast—demolished by the ripping force of the first Scottish cannon shots—came crashing down in a thousand pieces, lines and sails with it.

Seizing the moment, Jaime kicked with all her strength at the groin of the foul one.

Reed doubled over in pain, gasping for breath and cursing as he grabbed his crotch with two hands, and Jaime broke loose, dashing away in the only direction that lay open to her—through the open door.

"Leave 'er to me." The sound of the jailer's rasping shout chilled Jaime to the bone as she stepped into the gloom of her nightmare.

* * *

The cannonball skipped along the water and glanced off the *Elizabeth*'s hull in an explosion of splintering wood and a jolt that nearly knocked Malcolm to the sand-covered deck.

The enemy vessel's two stern guns continued to fire away at them, but the Scottish bow gunners were clearly doing the greater damage. The rigging of the larger ship was in tatters—the mainmast cut in two and the galleon's lines and sails a tangled web of rope and rag. Relentlessly, the *Elizabeth* continued to close with the galleon, and the two ships were so near now that Malcolm could see his foes' faces clearly.

Rage burned within him. If even a hair on her head had been disturbed, he swore . . .

They were so close now that the Scottish sailors stood ready with their grappling lines. There would be no chance for a cannonball to skip by now, but the opposing stern gunners had no time to fire another round as Alexander brought his ship alongside the enemy vessel with a scraping, shuddering crash.

Hell's gates opened as the shouts of warriors combined with the clash of steel, and Malcolm leaped across the divide onto the galleon's deck.

Jaime moved further back into the murky shadows of smoke and darkness, twisting her arms around her and struggling to pull Malcolm's dirk from the inside pocket of the cloak. Finally, pinning the weapon between her hip and the bulkhead, she managed to pull the dagger from its hiding place. The confused shouts of men outside, the sudden, jarring blasts of cannon fire, and the lurching movements of the ship all served to steel her nerve—her survival depended on this, she knew. With fierce, awkward jerks, she cut away at the rope binding her hands.

"The bitch 'as nowheres to go! Get on wi' ye."

Reed's rough voice by the door filled her with cold dread. With one more desperate yank, the ropes gave way, and Jaime pulled her hands free. Rubbing her wrists in pain, she looked wildly about her in the dark, the smoke stinging her eyes, the dirk held ready in her fist. A stack of barrels lashed to the bulkhead offered her the only place to hide, but it would not be enough.

There was no place for her to go but down the steep steps. Perhaps, once below, she could find a portal to slip out of. But with the brutal jailer coming in, any movement toward the steps was sure to get his attention. Her only hope was for Reed to walk past her and go below. Perhaps then, she thought with stubborn hope, she could make a break out the door and across the deck. With the battle raging, perhaps she could get over the side. Unbuttoning her cloak, she dropped it beside her in the passageway.

She saw his shadow block the light. Pressing her back against the wall, Jaime waited and held her breath. Go down, she chanted silently. Go down the steps.

But as if the monster could hear her silent plea, his eyes turned and stared at where she stood in the darkness. She pressed her back tighter against the wall, but he started toward her.

"I knew ye wouldn't go far," he jeered. "Ye wouldn't miss the jolly time we'll be 'avin' at Norwich, now, would ye? Well, may just be we won't wait so long!"

"Get away from me," she said from between clenched teeth, all the horrors of what Edward had told her about this man coming alive in her mind.

He was now only two steps away. "Stabbin' the master . . ." He shook his head in disapproval. "And then runnin' away."

Even in the dark, she could see his rat's eyes traveling the length of her.

"We'll 'ave a fine time whippin' ye into 'arness." Reed licked his lips and stepped even closer. "And for myself . . ."

She drove the dirk upward under his ribs and straight toward his shrunken heart.

The burly man stepped back in shock, his hands wrapped around the hilt of the weapon. He stepped back again, banging into the bulkhead, his eyes wide open in surprise, and she could see in his face that he knew his end was near.

The crunching impact of the two ships colliding pitched both Jaime and Reed to the deck. Leaping to her feet, Jaime stared at his body twitching in the final agony. She turned and started for the door, but then stopped at the sound of shouting right outside.

She didn't pause. Turning, she dashed down the steps.

In spite of the sand spread around, the galleon's deck was slick with blood. Bodies, lines, and splintered wood littered the deck, but Malcolm—cold needles of despair beginning to creep into his soul—continued to slash his way through the throngs of fierce fighters.

Nowhere above decks, she had to be below, he decided, driving his sword into the chest of a foe. There, beyond the riotous combat of a dozen men, a door stood open, and Malcolm lurched toward it, shoving aside those in his path.

He had to find her.

Blindly, she dashed down the steps. Downward she flew through wisps of rising smoke, falling more than running. But downward, ever downward.

She knew they would be coming after her. There was nowhere for her but down. And all the while the acrid, burning smell of death warned her of what lay below.

She slipped once, going down, clinging to the treads until she regained her footing. And then downward she went again. The sound of voices at the first landing forced her to continue, the shouts so close in the smoky air. She didn't know what would be waiting for her at the bottom, but she knew a hellish wind was swirling about her here.

At the next landing she stopped. Flattening her body into the shadows, she listened. There were voices again. Men cursing in anger. Then she heard the voices coming toward her. Pushing away from the wall, she moved blindly along the passageway, glancing over her shoulder as she ran.

As she banged solidly into him, Jaime felt a viselike hand lock on her wrist, and she turned.

Edward.

As Malcolm ripped his dirk from the jailer's dead body, the first of the gunnery crews attacked him. Cutting the three men down with sword and dagger, the Highlander leapt past them toward the steps.

"Jaime!" he shouted into the smoking darkness below.

When Malcolm dropped down to the next deck, the second group of gunners was waiting for him. They came at him from three sides at once, the bloodlust in their eyes.

Grasping the wrist of the first knife-wielding attacker, Malcolm drove the weapon into the throat of the man behind him, and then—without pausing—the Highlander threw his attacker into the body of the third. As the two warriors scurried to their feet, Malcolm ran them both through, pinning them together against the bulkhead.

"Jaime!" he shouted again.

Hearing nothing but the sounds of battle above, the Highlander drew his dirk and turned once again to the steps leading below.

"You look as if you've seen the dead rise, my raven." Edward's one hand held tightly to Jaime's wrist. "But I suppose you are not accustomed to having someone come back and haunt you."

She felt the shiver race through her, and Jaime clenched her teeth to keep them from chattering. But her eyes, riveted to his face, convinced her that Edward Howard was alive . . . and then a different kind of fear took hold of her. A patch of matted and bloody hair at the side of his head told of her failed effort to kill him before.

Edward's hand grabbed Jaime roughly by the hair, and with unleashed ferocity, he slammed her hard against the wall. She gasped for breath, sure that her teeth had come loose with the blow. He pressed his forearm against her chest, leaning all of his weight on her.

"Aren't you wondering how I come to be alive?"

She stared him in the eye, all her hate and anger welling up within her, waiting to boil over.

"My man Reed was waiting for us that night. It was he that came looking for me in your room. It was he that found me unconscious. You see, my raven, if your foul serving woman hadn't scratched me in the back with my own dagger, then the good jailer could have come and joined in our little party." Edward's eyes bore into hers as he released her hair and groped malevolently at her. "And where was it that we left off?"

Jaime spit in his face. "Bastard," she swore.

He drew back and laughed, wiping the spittle from his cheek. "You see, I was very disappointed with the way things worked out. So to remedy the past, I thought of this little game."

"Only a madman like you would think of the killing going on above as a game."

"Ah, the ever considerate Jaime." He jammed his forearm higher, against her throat, pushing her still harder against the wall. "But why is it, you are never considerate of me? You see, little raven, you are the reason for my ruin. Because of you, I am an outlaw to my king and a disgrace to my family."

"I had nothing to do with your ruin."

"But you did," he insisted. "If you had not lain with the Scot like some whore—if you had come to Nonsuch Palace and wed me as we planned . . ."

"You only wanted me for the power I would give you with the king."

Edward laughed. "So she knows!"

Jaime felt her whole body swell with anger. "You bastard. You stupid, half-witted brute. Did you think that you could fool me forever? Did you think I would go through a marriage with you by force? How could I, when I am in love with . . ."

"Your pathetic Highland dolt?" he finished. "Aye, you heard me! Who else but a dolt would pay Reed's own spies to take you to your ship. They were waiting for you. Didn't you wonder how you were brought back to me? It was one of them who, after dropping you off, boarded the vessel secretly. The others carried back the news to us. All we had to do was catch you. The dolt. Of course, he'll be dead after I'm finished with him."

Malcolm's voice, calling her name, cut through the darkness.

"Say all you will," Jaime responded. "But it is your ship that is now under attack. And it will be your carcass floating in the sea."

"But at least we will be floating together, you and me." Jaime saw the flash of his dagger. She drew in a sharp breath as he brought the blade to her throat.

"Perhaps in the next life, my raven, we will pick up where we left off."

At the sound of Malcolm's boots hitting the decking behind them, Edward whirled and backed away, dragging Jaime with him as a shield, his dagger still at her throat.

The Highlander's face was a steely mask of fury and hate, and he advanced on the pair, his dirk held high.

"Hold, Scot," Edward hissed.

"Let her go," Malcolm growled ominously.

The Englishman sneered. "Lay down your dagger."

Jaime watched as the thought flickered across Malcolm's face. And then his face hardened.

"Kill him, Malcolm," she cried. "He'll cut my throat, no matter what you do."

The warrior stared at her a moment, and then turned his gaze back to Edward.

"There is no way out, fiend," Malcolm growled. " 'Tis just you and me now, and there will be no stabbing me in the back."

"Aye, so it is. But if you intend to send me to hell, Highlander, at least I won't be going alone."

With an evil smile, Edward Howard pressed the blade to Jaime's throat. But the slashing motion he had planned withered in an instant as Malcolm's dirk whistled through the smoky air, piercing Edward's eye and coming to rest deep in the demon's brain.

Jaime and Malcolm clung together in the darkness at the base of the steps, their hearts pounding as one. Far above them, the sound of fighting suddenly ceased, and as they looked at each other, a rousing cheer could be heard.

"Do you think that was a Scottish cheer?" Jaime asked, gazing into her intended's eyes.

"Aye, lass. I've no doubt of it."

"Then we're truly going home?"

"Aye, Jaime," Malcolm answered as Alexander's voice called down from above. "We're going home."

EPILOGUE

The Isle of Skye, Scotland

Blades of golden light from the small slits of windows cut brightly through swirling clouds of incense. At the altar of the Priory chapel, in the sight of a congregation filled with islanders and family, the bride and groom exchanged loving glances, and listened to the ancient priest who stood at the altar with his back to them.

They made an impressive pair. She, beautiful and radiant with the happy knowledge that she already carried their child. And he, magnificent and glowing with the emotions that surged in his heart.

For they had both received the blessing of the seer. He had come to them, stepping out of the crowds that had gathered outside the chapel door. There, after Ambrose and Elizabeth had placed the hand of their daughter into Malcolm's loving care, the ancient seer had appeared. He had held in his hand a golden branch of rosemary, as a symbol of their love and fidelity.

The silence that fell over the throng had been stunning. James had come to them and gathered their hands in his own. A thousand ears had strained to hear when the old man looked into Jaime's eyes and told her of the child she carried. The one who would be heir, and the cupbearer of peace, and the protector of all the clans of Skye and the Hebrides.

Now, as sunlight played over Jaime's ebony hair, Malcolm

smiled into the face of his bride. Seeing her blush at his open display of affection, he reached out and entwined his fingers in hers. She smiled back at him and turned her eyes to the priest.

Behind them, the congregation stirred restlessly in the little chapel, waiting in anticipation for the exchange of vows. The people of Skye—the MacLeods and MacDonalds—thrilled with all they had seen and heard outside, were more than eager to begin celebrating this cornerstone to future peace between the clans.

Alec Macpherson, former laird of these lands, guardian of Malcolm's youth, stood straight and tall, holding onto his wife Fiona's hand. And next to them, Ambrose Macpherson gathered his own tearful Elizabeth to his side. Behind them stood John Macpherson with Maria, Regent of the Netherlands, while a legion of Macpherson children crowded around them in various stages of disarray.

The priest's voice rose and fell in the measured cadences of the mixed Latin and Gaelic. From behind the grate of iron bands to the right of the altar, the sound of women's voices— the nuns of the Priory—could be heard responding to the prayers.

The priest raised up his hands in offering, and then turned and preceded his acolytes down from the altar. Malcolm turned and faced his beautiful bride, as she gazed back at him.

The priest paused for a moment, and the congregation seemed to hold its breath. The chapel's silence was profound, so silent in fact that Malcolm's eye was drawn upward at the crackling hiss of a candle on the far wall. The incense was curling upward in a lazy spiral, and the young laird's eyes settled once again on the face of his beloved bride. There was nothing that would ever tear them apart again, he vowed silently.

The candle on the far wall flickered again, and Malcolm became aware of a sound at the entrance to the chapel. Turning his head, he could see the great oak door had swung open, but he could not see who was entering, only that the folk by the door were backing away with looks of surprise.

When the young man stepped quietly into the chapel, his swaggering expression only hinted at his embarrassment.

Alexander Macpherson had almost slept through his step-brother's wedding.

"When is that lad going to grow up?" his father rumbled under his breath to his wife.

"Not until he finds his match, I should think," Fiona whispered, hugging Alec's arm. "It took *you* at least that long."

Alec turned his attention back to the altar and to the magnificent couple standing hand in hand, exchanging their vows.

"I love you, Malcolm MacLeod," Jaime whispered as he brought her snugly to his heart. "To the day I die, I will."

Author's Note

When we set out to write this book, we already knew so much about Malcolm and Jaime, having introduced them to our readers as mere children in *Angel of Skye* and *Heart of Gold*. So the challenge in this book lay in the portrayal of the real sixteenth-century Howard family, and their historical and fictional presence in the lives of our hero and heroine.

For the many purists and history buffs among our readers, our use of the Howard family is fairly accurate—with the exception of Edward, our villain, and Mary, the cousin. In fact, even the H-shaped palace of the Howard family (with its ivy-covered red brick and its Gothic windows) existed at Kenninghall in East Anglia until 1650. And although we may have stretched Catherine Howard's fondness for companionship, she was indeed beheaded on charges of adultery. Thomas Culpepper and Francis Dorand, two of her lovers named in the novel, were also executed for their indiscretions. Our sincere thanks to Mark E. Turner of Norfolk, England, for his help with our research regarding Kenninghall.

And for those of you who have not yet read *Heart of Gold*, our representation of Jaime as Henry VIII's illegitimate daughter originated entirely "from whole cloth," a happy product of our mischievous minds.

We love to hear from our readers. You can contact us at:

May McGoldrick
P.O. Box 511
Sellersville, PA 18960
e-mail: mcgoldmay@aol.com

Please turn the page

for an exciting sneak peek at

The Jeweled Cup

the next Topaz historical by

May McGoldrick

on sale in the fall of 1998

The charred shutter, high in the ruined tower, suddenly banged open as the afternoon breeze moved around to the west, and the golden rays of sunlight tumbled into the scorched chamber.

Huddled in the corner on a pile of straw, a startled figure pulled her ragged cloak more tightly around her. Even though it was summer, she found it more and more difficult to shake off the chill that had crept into her bones. Perhaps it was because she so rarely saw the sun, she thought. For she was now a creature of the night, a mere shadow.

She shivered slightly, acknowledging the gnawing pangs of hunger in her belly. She shook her head, trying to dispel the feeling. There would be no food until tonight, when the steward and the servants that remained all slept. Then she would partake of her nightly haunt. Then she would search the kitchens for some scrap that might sustain her.

Those remaining in the castle thought her a ghost. What fools they would think themselves if they only knew how human her needs were.

The wood plank continued to bang against the blackened sill, and she glared at it. This was her rest time, she silently scolded the troublesome shutter. Like the bats and the owls, Joanna now lived in the night. For it was only under cover of darkness that she could move about freely in this burned-out prison she had once called home.

Pulling herself to her feet, the ragged creature moved silently across the floor. As she neared the offending shutter, she was suddenly aware of the sound of horses in the distance. Shouts came from the courtyard below, and as she listened, the yard below seemed to explode in a frenzy of activity.

Taking hold of the shutter with her swathed hands, Joanna eased it shut without peering below.

The doomed man, she thought. The cursed laird had arrived.

The pawing hooves of the tired horses against the soft ground raised a gray cloud that swirled about the riders' heads. Gavin Kerr lifted his eyes from the approaching grooms and stared at the huge iron cross fastened to the rough stone wall above the archway of the great oak entry doors. From the blood-red rust stains on the stone beneath the cross, the new laird judged that it must have hung there for ages. Tearing his eyes away, Gavin glanced around at the buildings facing the open courtyard.

The castle itself was far larger than he'd expected. Stretching out in angles of sharp stone, the series of huge structures wrapped around the courtyard like a hand ready to close. Far above, small slits of windows pierced the walls of the main building as well as the north wing. The south wing's upper windows were larger. A newer addition, he thought. Gavin let his eyes travel slowly over what he could see. There was no sign of the fire that had claimed the life of the previous laird, his family, and their servants. The winter sleet and rains had scoured the stone of any trace of smoke, no doubt.

He caught the movement from the corner of his eye—the slow closing of a shutter in the tower at the top of the south wing.

However, the men approaching drew Gavin's attention earthward again. The tall one scolding the running grooms had to be Allan, steward to the last four MacInnes lairds. The man's graying hair and beard bespoke his advanced years, while his powerful frame—slightly bent though it was—told of a strength necessary for the position he had held for so long.

He hadn't thought much about these people before now, about the small group of servants and retainers who had remained here, loyal to the place. With the exception of a few of their names from Lady MacInnes, he knew little about them. Mostly clansmen and women who had lived on these lands for all of their lives. How strange they must feel, Gavin thought. To live in a place where their masters all die young.

Dismounting from his horse, Gavin nodded to a groom and handed off his reins as he exchanged greetings with the bowing steward.

"You did indeed arrive just as we had expected, m'lord. Not a day too soon nor a day too late." The old man's hands spread in invitation toward the entrance of the castle. "I took the liberty a day or so ago to have Gibby, the cook, begin preparing a feast for your arrival."

He paused as a dozen household servants, along with a dwarfish, sickly looking priest, came out to welcome the new laird.

"Your neighbor, the earl of Athol," Allan continued, "has been quite anxious for you to arrive, m'lord. If you wish, I can send a man over now and invite . . ."

"Nay, Allan. That can wait for a day or two." Gavin's gaze took in once again the towers at either end of the courtyard. "While my men settle themselves in, I want you to take me through this keep."

The older man nodded his compliance as he fell in step with the new laird, who was striding toward the south tower. "You might, m'lord, wish to start in the main part of the house—what we call the Old Keep—and work toward the kitchens and the stables in the north wing. There is very little to see in the south wing."

Gavin halted abruptly, glanced up at the south tower, and then looked directly at the steward.

"Much of this wing was ruined by the fire, m'lord," Allan explained quickly. "From the courtyard, it looks sound, but inside, especially where the wing joins the Old Keep, the damage was extensive. The roof is gone in some places, and I've had the outside entrances to the building barred to keep . . ."

"Barred?" Gavin interrupted, staring at the tower.

"Aye. The worst of the damage is on the far side, though, where the tower looks over the loch. That's where they were all sleeping when the fire started, God rest their souls. By the time the rest of us in the Old Keep and the north wing smelled the smoke, the whole south wing was ablaze."

Gavin strode to the stone wall and peered through the slits of the lower windows. He could see shafts of light coming through the rafters of the floors above.

"A terrible business, m'lord," the steward continued, shaking his head sadly. "There was no sign of life from their quarters that we . . ."

"Why do you allow servants into this wing?" Gavin asked shortly, making the old man's face suddenly flush red. "Those upper floors look dangerous, even from here."

"No living person, m'lord, has stepped foot in this wing since the fire," the steward responded with conviction. "As I said, I myself had all the doors barred and the inside corridors walled up. With the exception of some badger . . . or a fox, perhaps . . ." His voice trailed off.

Gavin stepped back from the building and looked upward at the windows in the tower, his eyes finally coming to rest on the last one in the top floor. "I saw the shutter in that chamber move."

The steward stared briefly at the tower windows, then looked at his new master.

"Aye, m'lord. We see the same thing from time to time, but 'tis just the wind." As the new laird moved along the front of the edifice, Allan followed along. "The smoke was everywhere, and the stairwells leading up to it are ruined. Of that I'm certain. The roof there may be sound, though, and a bird or two may have taken up lodging there.

And wings are what you'd be needing to make your way up there."

Gavin peered up again at the looming tower. A number of shutters were banging against stone in the rising breeze. Nature, it appeared had the upper hand in every window . . . but one. The window that he had seen open before, now stood closed against the north wind.

So the birds of the Highlands can latch a shutter, Gavin thought to himself. Turning without another word, he started for the main entrance of the Old Keep, his steward in tow.

No one ever dared step into her domain.

The crumbling, fire-damaged roofs; the gaping holes in the walls overlooking the sheer cliffs of Loch Moray; and the scorched, unsteady floors all combined to make the south wing of Ironcross Castle a forbidding place to enter. But as Joanna made her way quietly through a blasted room toward the wooden panel and the secret passageway that would take her down to the subterranean tunnels and caverns, she suddenly sensed that someone had been through there, and quite recently.

She paused and looked about her in the encroaching dusk. There was little to be seen. Dropping softly to her hands and knees on a plank by the doorway, she peered closely at the ash-covered floor of the passage beyond the door. She herself always avoided those corridors for fear of being discovered by some intrepid soul snooping in this wing.

Squinting in the growing gloom, she saw them clearly—the faint imprints left behind by someone coming from the Old Keep. There were no returning footprints, that she could make out. Whoever it was had gone in the direction of her father's study . . . or what was left of it. Quietly, Joanna rose and, hugging the wall, followed the passage toward the study.

Standing rigidly beside the door, she peeked inside the charred study. The room was empty. She peered into the murky light of the corridor again. Since she had just come from the top floor, whoever had come in here must have continued on and descended the nearly impassable stairwell to the main floor.

Relieved, she wrapped her cloak tightly about her and glanced inside the study again. Her chest tightened with that familiar sorrow as she stepped inside the fire-ravaged chamber. Nothing had changed here since that terrible night. All lay in ruin. Hanging from one wall were the scraps of burned rag that had once been a tapestry. Elsewhere the scorched table and the broken sticks of a chair. Everything ruined.

Everything but the foolish portrait hanging over the mantel of the fireplace. She stared loathingly at the face that smiled faintly back at her. Her throat knotted at the sight of herself, of the picture of perfection she had once been. What vanity, she thought angrily.

She wanted to cross the room and take hold of the fire-blackened frame. She wanted to pull it down, smash it, destroy it as it should have been destroyed long ago. But the unsteady floor stopped her approach. From experience, she knew every loose board, every dangerous plank. Nay, she hadn't survived this ordeal so long just to break her neck falling through the floor. But those eyes dared her. Challenged her to come ahead. She hated that painting. Why should this blasted thing survive when no one else had? No one, including herself.

As a tear welled up, Joanna dashed at a glistening bead. Turning away from that vain and beautiful face, she pulled her hood forward and headed for the darkness of the passages that would take her deep into the earth, where no one would see what she had become . . . a ghostly shadow of the past, a creature of the night, burned and ugly, miserable. Dead.

Disappearing into the dark, Joanna MacInnes thought once again of her poor mother and father, of all the innocent ones who had perished in the blaze with them.

It was her destiny, now, to hide and await her chance for justice.

As the fire's embers burned out beneath, a huge log crashed down, sending crackling flames and sparks flying in the Great Hall's huge fireplace.

The new laird's face was in shadow as he looked around at the young features of the three men sitting with him. Scattered about the Great Hall, servants and warriors slept on benches and tables, and a number of dogs lay curled up amid the rushes covering the stone floor. Most of the household was already asleep, either here or in the stables and outbuildings, but Gavin had kept these three trusted warriors with him. In the short time since they had all arrived, these men had been tasked with determining what needed to be done to secure the castle. Each man had gone about his business, and now the Lowlander leaned forward to hear them.

Edmund combed his fingers through his flaming red hair and then crossed his arms over his chest. He nodded when Gavin turned his eyes to him.

"I heard with my own ears the steward passing on your wish to have the south wing opened for you to view in the morning."

"Aye," Peter broke in, gruff and impatient. "And a couple of the grooms and the old smith hopped to the task of pulling down one of the blocking walls."

"The steward has fine control of the castle folk," Edmund added admiringly.

"Aye, that he does," Peter agreed. "Though a body would think barring a door might have been plenty good enough. Building a wall to stop trespassing . . ." The thickset warrior spat critically into the rushes on the floor. "Why, most of the servants are too old even to lift a latch unaided!"

Gavin interrupted the two men. "I can see Allan's concern. He told me that, after the fire, he wanted to be sure that no one would go in that wing, not until such time as Lady MacInnes or the next laird came along to go through what was left." The Lowlander sat back and lifted a cup as he looked about the silent hall. "With so many accidents plaguing the lairds over the years, I am certain it shows good judgment to leave everything untouched. What did you find, Andrew?"

Andrew, the largest man of the group after Gavin, stroked

his chin thoughtfully before answering. Finally, he cleared his throat and spoke. "In my ride over to the abbey, m'lord, I ran into some of the earl of Athol's men heading north. I chatted with them for a few moments."

"Chatted! I would have loved to see that, I would!" Peter laughed, drawing a glare from Andrew.

"Aye. We chatted. They all spoke of how strange it was here after the fire. None of the last laird's warriors stayed behind, they said. It seems that they all fled into the mountains as if they had the devil himself on their tails."

"Dirty Highland cowards," Peter scowled.

"Watch what you say," Edmund warned. "We don't need the axes of clan rivalry testing our necks. So far these people seem unmindful of us being Lowlanders."

Gavin drained his cup and put it back on the table as he turned to Andrew. "What can you tell us of the abbey?"

The giant warrior ran a hand down his face as he looked up with keen eyes. " 'Tis an odd place, that abbey. Nary a league from here, following the shore of the loch, but 'tis nothing but a heap of stones and ruined wall in the shelter of the high hills. The place is surrounded by pasture and farm land and some crofters' cottages, though there is an odd lack of farm folk about the place."

"But they are religious there, we were told."

"I do not know, m'lord," Andrew replied. "Those who remain live in the center of the ruined cloister, in stone cottages they've patched together from the old buildings."

"Is there an abbot, or someone in charge?" Gavin pressed.

"Aye, a woman they call Mater."

"A woman?" Peter blurted out.

"Aye," Andrew responded slowly. "They are all women there. All that I saw before they disappeared, at any rate." He paused. "And that abbey, m'lord, seems quite unprotected sitting there in the open as 'tis!"

"And is that not like these Highlanders," Peter huffed, "leaving a pack of women . . ."

Gavin felt the hackles on his neck rise as his attention was drawn to the far end of the Great Hall. In a dark corner by the

passage into the kitchens and the north wing, something had
moved. A shadow ... something ... he was certain of it.
Peering into the darkness, the firelight at his back, Gavin
studied the sleeping figures on the benches as he continued to
listen to his men. The servants had been dismissed hours ago.
Other than the three men sitting with him, it was unlikely that
anyone else in the keep would be roaming about.

"I took it upon myself, m'lord, to tell Mater that you would
be stopping by yourself in a day or two. To pay them a visit."

"That's fine," Gavin answered. He shook his head slightly
at his fanciful imaginings and filled his cup with more ale. He
was tired, he decided, dismissing the notion with a last glance
at the far end of the Hall. His first night in Ironcross Castle,
and already he was falling prey to the strangeness of the place.
Suddenly, he realized one of the dogs had come slowly to his
feet. The gray cur trotted toward the kitchens. Pushing the
mug away, the laird came to his feet as well.

"Also, the earl of Athol's men mentioned that he'd be
giving you a visit before the week's end." Andrew's eyes followed his leader as Gavin rounded the table where they sat.
" 'Tis only a day's ride, they said, and if that's unsuitable ..."

"That's fine," Gavin answered absently without turning
around. "All three of you, get your rest. There is a great deal
to be done tomorrow."

The three men watched in silence as their master walked
quietly toward the darkened kitchens.

These newcomers were going to be more than a nuisance, she
thought. They were going to be downright dangerous. And
there were so many of them.

Coming out of the passages after the sounds of feasting had
died away, Joanna had been surprised by the number of people
remaining in the Great Hall. From past experience she knew
that she would have more chance of finding food there than in
the kitchens, but clearly that plan would no longer work. She
only hoped the usually tightfisted Gibby had not locked everything away, as was her custom.

Entering the kitchens, Joanna peered into the corners for

stray sleepers, but with the warmer weather, not a body was in evidence. The embers in the huge fireplace flickered, and she could see the rows of bread dough rising into loaves on a long table. Well, she thought, with the added men in the castle, perhaps she might eat a wee bit better.

Moving to a sideboard, she found a large bowl with broken scraps of hard bread. Scooping out a handful, Joanna placed the bread carefully in the deep pocket of her cloak, then cocked her head to listen. With more people around, she would have to be far more careful than she had been in the past. Being discovered would mean the end of her plans. It would be the death of her only wish—the one that had been driving her to hang on to her threadbare existence. If she were discovered, there would surely be no meting out justice to those who had murdered her parents. That she was certain of.

Joanna glided silently down through the kitchen, and then paused with a sigh by a locked larder. The gentle nudge of the dog's nose against her hip made the young woman's heart leap in her chest. Shaking her head as the corners of her mouth lifted in a wry smile, she crouched down to pet the gentle beast. All the dogs in the castle were quite accustomed to her, but shaggy Max was the only one that ever came to her. Accepting a wet kiss on the chin, Joanna gave the dog's head a gentle pat. Wordlessly, she straightened and continued her search for more food.

The heavenly smells of bannocks and roasted mutton still hung in the air, making her mouth water, but to her dismay there was nothing else left over that she could find. High in the rafters, she could see the dark shapes of smoked meat, but she didn't dare be so bold as to steal anything that would raise a hue and cry. Hearing Max sniffing in a dark corner, Joanna spotted two balls of cheese hanging from strings on a high pegboard, just out of the dog's reach. Gratified at the chance to add something different to her spare diet, she reached for them.

"I am certainly sorry you'll have to shoulder the blame for both of these," she whispered with a smile to the happy dog. "But you can only have one." Rolling his share playfully along the stone floor, Joanna placed the other in the pocket of her cloak.

The dog leapt across the kitchen after it, but suddenly stopped short, and the deep growl emanating from his throat sent Joanna scurrying for cover. Quietly, she moved into the deep shadows behind the giant fireplace, to the narrow door that led down into the root cellars. From there she could get into the labyrinth of passages, but she paused for a moment, her hand on the panel, ready to run if the need arose. Her other hand rested on the dirk in her belt.

"What are you hiding there, you mangy cur?" The man's voice was deep and strangely gentle. "Just you and the hearth fairy, eh?"

Joanna pressed her face against the warm stone of the chimney as she listened. From the dog's friendly panting and the man's deep-throated chuckle, she could tell the newcomer had already won over the animal's affection.

"Och, I can see already you are in for trouble. A thief you are, is that it? A piece of cheese. A capital crime, if that cooks finds out, lad. Hmm. I'll not throw it for you, you slobbering beast. You'd do best to finish it and destroy the evidence."

Joanna knew she should go, but she couldn't. Curiosity was pulling at her, driving her with a desire to put a face to that voice.

"So, you want to play! You want me to chase you, is that it?"

He had to be one of the new laird's men. She could imagine him leaning against the edge of the long heavy table in the center of the kitchen.

" 'Tis too late in the night, you beast. Very well. Bring it here and I'll throw it for you. But once only, do you hear me?"

The dog's low-pitched growl was now playful, and again the man's deep chuckle brought a smile to her face.

"Smart too. For a Highland cur!"

So they are Lowlanders, she thought. Scowling now, Joanna edged forward slightly and peeked at the man in the dim light of the dying fire. Just as she had imagined it, he was sitting on the edge of the table with his back to her. At the moment, he was preoccupied with wrenching the ball of cheese out of Max's mouth.

"Now, don't force me to get rough with you!"

She studied his broad shoulders. The warrior was larger, by far, than any of the men her father had kept in his service. The red of his tartan was muted and dark. As he stood up for a moment, she drew back, but he only crouched over the dog again. He was certainly a giant, and not just for a Lowlander. His long dark hair was tied with a thong at the nape of a strong neck. In wrestling with the dog, he turned his face, and she got a quick glimpse of his handsome profile. Suddenly, she was aware of a strange tightening in her chest. Drawing back further, she felt her face flush with heat. What was wrong with her? she thought, fighting for a breath.

What did it matter that the man was handsome, she thought with annoyance. What difference did that make to her, a ghost! In the dark of the kitchens, it was easy to let imagination control reality. In the light of day, he might be the ugliest man in Scotland, though she would never see it. Darkness. Perhaps it was the place for both of them, she thought angrily. Who knows, in the gloom of this chamber, he might not even see her deformities. Bringing a shaking hand up before her eyes, she gazed at it momentarily, and then pulled her hood forward over her face.

Nay, no one was that blind.

"As your laird, I order you to share that cheese. Och, you are a pig. You've eaten it all."

Laird! Quickly, Joanna drew back behind the hearth. Her face grim, she slipped through the panel and into the blackness of the passageway. Feeling her way down the stone steps, she continued past the wooden door that led into the root cellars. Silently, she made her way through the winding, narrow passages, down more carved stone steps, and through wide, cavernous openings until she was far from the kitchens. Climbing to the top of another set of steps, Joanna stopped, trying to catch her breath, and leaned back heavily against a rough-hewn wall.

Laird! She wished she had never laid eyes on him. It would

be ever so much easier to mourn his death if she had never seen him. The poor soul, she thought, starting to move quickly along the tunnel again. He wouldn't have a chance against the evil that surrounded him.